WINNER OF THE 2018 CW/

Doc Slidesmith & Yakk adventure. Dago, presic *Motorcycle Club*, and one of apparent accident. Before wife makes an unusual request, one which Yakky fulfils with characteristic stoicism.

The funeral is a particularly tense affair and it becomes clear to Doc that there's more going on than initially meets the eye. All is clearly not well within the ranks of *The Handsome London Boys* and when Doc starts asking questions about the circumstances of Dago's accident and the disappearance of a young pledger, he and Yakky find themselves being dragged into the secretive and potentially dangerous world of the 'one-percenters'.

Doc & Yakky need to tread very carefully if they're going to ensure the truth is revealed, justice is served - and they both get out of this alive.

Praise for Russell Day

"Russell Day is an artist - one who paints pictures with his words..."

"A brilliant book, one that has cemented Russell Day straight into my must read authors list."

"Russell Day has established himself as one of the best new crime writers of recent years. I cannot wait for his next novel."

Ink To Ashes

This edition first published 2019 by Fahrenheit Press.

ISBN: 978-1-912526-51-2

10 9 8 7 6 5 4 3 2 1

www.Fahrenheit-Press.com

F 4 E

Ink To Ashes

By

Russell Day

Fahrenheit Press

For Brother Pat

1.
Burying Ink and Burning the Evidence

Wednesday 13 September

The house, once Dago and Sue's and now just Sue's, was in an upmarket cul-de-sac. As close to a suburb as you get in north London. An area where people parked at least one of their cars on the driveway and still had room to maintain a lawn. What estate agents called a professional location.

Sue was on the doorstep as me and Yakky pulled up. Lips pursed around a cigarette, she inclined her head with a sharp snap by way of greeting. I'd known her almost as long as I'd known Dago, but I didn't hug her, she wasn't the touchy-feely type. We left our bike gear to drip in the porch and followed her into the house, Yakky with his rucksack.

She led us down the hall. I wanted ominous sounds for what we were doing, but the hardwood floors made our footsteps sound busy and clinical.

The room we were taken to was 'for best'. A place to receive visitors, it felt unrelated to either Dago or Sue. There were no books or CDs there, no clutter, nothing personal. Family portraits on the coffee table were studio shots with the hard reality of their subjects soft-focused away. Skilfully executed.

The coffin rested on trestles tactfully hidden behind frills of taffeta. Dago had been disguised in a suit and tie. Outside of work it wasn't how he'd have dressed, but I was glad of it. It camouflaged him in some way, putting his death at a comfortable remove.

Yakky, poker-faced as always, emptied the rucksack and set up his tattooing gear. Sue and I both watched him. I wanted to see if his demeanour would crack and wasn't surprised when it didn't. Before he touched the body, he turned to Sue.

"You sure you want me to do this?"

Sue said, "That's what you're here for," and left the room.

The busy heels clattered down the hall again and a door slammed. Yak looked at me for confirmation. I shrugged. He moved the tie aside and unbuttoned the shirt.

I was glad it was Yakky's commission.

I had volunteered to take the job over, but watching him work, I doubted I could have made good on the offer. The idea of leaning over my friend and breathing the smell of the coffin didn't appeal.

I'd known Dago when he'd still been Colin. I'd been with him in eighty-nine, when his duffle bag – with C O JONES stencilled along the side – had delighted a custom's guard in Bilbao. 'Cojones', it transpired, was the Spanish for testicles. It said a lot about him that he'd been nicknamed Dago and not Gonads.

I found Sue on the patio, staring into space and blowing smoke rings. The cigarette was held in a fist, pinched between index and middle finger. On the garden table an ashtray had filled with rain and dogends. A score of them dissolved slowly. The filters survived longest, waterproofed with lipstick.

When I asked her if I could put the kettle on, she drowned another cigarette and said she'd do it. I told her she didn't have to, but she shook her head. Earrings rattled.

"I'd sooner be doing something."

The house evidenced her need to keep busy. Everything gleamed with that finish you only get with grief or OCD. The kitchen, huge and stone-floored, echoed with the buzz of Yakky's needle from the adjacent room. Sue put the radio on, loud enough to drown it out.

"It's good of him to do this," she said, keeping her back to me. Being delicate about the noise embarrassed her. "Dago hated that tattoo."

"Why did he wait so long to get a cover-up?" I asked.

Sue let out a breath and tobacco jostled with the smell of cleaning sprays. Only briefly, the odds were against it.

"Because he was a typical male, he'd never admit he was wrong, not even about joining the army. Macho thing."

"Men, eh?" I said; it felt like I was trying to avoid an argument.

"Yeah, men."

She didn't temper the statement with any humour and, as she filled the kettle, her movements were fast and jumpy. Behind the layer of makeup her face was set. I didn't bother saying anything. For the time being anger was getting her through and until she started grieving, that was enough.

"Big man decision of course, running off and joining the army. Only it was me living with the bloody fallout all the time." She slammed the kettle down on the granite worktop and made herself jump. She was still angry but her shoulders sagged when she added, "I found him out on the patio about a month ago with a packet of my cigarettes –" she turned and mimed stubbing one out on her chest. "That was the last straw. I told him straight: either get it sorted out or –" she shook her head. "I'll never forget that smell."

"It's getting covered now." I told her.

"Good. Does…" Yakky's name escaped her and she jerked her head in the direction of the buzzing noise "…take sugar?"

"Just milk. Where's Mary today?"

Sue, fussing with the tea, flicked a look to the child's swing in the back garden.

"College."

"College?"

I bumped into Dago on a regular basis but the last time I'd seen his step-daughter, she'd been barely into her teens.

"Twenty-one now," Sue told me. "The time soon goes."

She puffed out a mouthful of air again and I could see what the time had done. More than just forty a day had cast its shadow on her. The lipstick, always put on too thick, was seeping into lines around her mouth.

There was an obvious question in the air.

"How's she coping?"

Sue flicked another look at the child's swing. She'd soon be out on the patio again with her lighter.

"She isn't."

I nodded, it was the answer I'd expected.

"Lot of anger?"

"Angry, stroppy, you name it. I tell you, Doc, the teenage years are going on forever."

She stopped the rant before it got started and I respected her for it. To move onto easier ground, I asked what Mary was studying at college.

"Beauty therapy." I looked blank and she laughed, which was good even if it was forced. "What used to be hair-dos and nails. And you're right, it won't do her a scrap of good."

A lot of people would have cried then, but Sue spun on her four-inch heel and headed to the patio and another smoke.

"There's a tea here."

I put Yakky's mug on a glass table that had been pushed aside to accommodate the coffin. He told me thanks and straightened up slowly with one hand bunched into the small of his back. The trestles were the wrong height for him to work at. Getting Dago into a better position wasn't an option.

The undertakers had done a good job and, business suit aside, Dago looked like he usually did. Even closed, his eyes showed his good humour. The pain was there too, the set of the jaw, the scars.

Yakky sipped his tea and gave the work he'd done a once over.

"You think anyone's ever done this before?" he asked. I shrugged, I doubted he was the first to tattoo a corpse. If you can imagine it, then someone's doing it and probably putting it on Facebook. "Reckon it's legal?"

It was blunt curiosity. Like most bikers, Yakky's primary worry on matters legal was *can I get away with it*, not *am I allowed*. And lo, for on the eighth day God created motorcycles and bestowed the eleventh commandant: don't get caught. Forever and ever. Roads without end. Amen.

"I'm sure there's a law being broken somewhere," I told

him. "Want to get some legal advice?"

Yakky looked over his work again before replying, "By the time I've done that the evidence will be gone."

It was a good point. Dago had an appointment at the crematorium that weekend. I leaned closer to the coffin, looking at his new tattoo. Yakky had done good work. The regimental insignia, endured so long, was now submerged in ink that said what really mattered: Sue and Mary.

Yakky asked me where the toilet was. I told him top of the stairs and right.

I listen carefully and when I heard the bathroom door shut, I took a cigar and a miniature bottle of spiced rum from the side of my boot, I slipped them under Dago's pillow, out of sight. A metal charm, the size of a key fob, went into one of his pockets. Then I said a prayer in Creole.

When Yakky came back, I noticed I'd left the pillow askew. He caught my glance towards it and held his hands up.

"Spare me the details, Doc, alright? I don't want to know."

I nodded and left him to tidy his gear away.

Voodoo. Not everyone's cup of tea.

Saturday 16 September

The service had little to recommend it other than brevity. A man in a dog collar talked about an atheist he'd never met while we fidgeted on blonde-wood pews and waited for it to be over. Then he asked us to say a prayer, and pressed a button while our heads were bowed. The coffin glided discreetly away.

For some of the mourners, that was it. The contingent of suits that had known Dago as a businessman delivered the required platitudes and melted away across the gravelled car park. I'd have happily joined them, but Sue had made a point of inviting me, and Yakky, to the wake. We were welded to the funeral by the business with the tattoo.

The phalanx of vehicles from the crematorium divided at the North Circular. The cars merged with the treacle-slow files of traffic and the bikes disappeared into gaps between lanes. I hung back, riding behind one of the cars and marking time, until the last half mile when the rain came in and I made a dash for it.

I gave a nod to Black Micky as I went into The Jericho's function room. He probably wasn't on the door officially, but that's where he stood, slightly inside, in the dry for the sake of his suit. I guessed it was tailor-made and wondered how he kept it crease free under his riding gear. We smiled sad smiles and agreed it was terrible about Dago.

I'd started tattooing at sixteen. Worked out of my bedroom, graduated to my parents' garage, used homemade needles and cast-off gear to puncture less-discerning friends. Dago had been the first of them to pay me. It marked my transition from amateur scratcher to professional tattooist. At least in my mind. The last time I'd seen him alive, he was in my shop discussing a cover-up piece.

A beginning and an end both cast in ink. There was a certain symmetry to that, not that it brought any comfort.

Since the days when I'd evict the family car before starting work, my premises had moved on. And now the business boasted a second tattooist. I'd steered Dago away from my list and onto Yakky's. I avoided tattooing friends. They always wanted your best work and lowest price.

Dago's regimental insignia was inscribed on his chest, dead centre. Even if I'd known something about military markings, I'd have been hard-pressed to identify it. The tattoo and the skin that held it were disfigured with several scars. Fingernails, cigarette ends and at least one blade had left their mark. The army had been a bad time for Dago.

Yakky had looked over the collection of ink and damage with neither comment nor expression. He assured Dago that a cover-up wouldn't be a problem and didn't ask about the DIY removal attempts. The new design, a heart, wrapped in a banner with Sue and Mary's names in it, was estimated at four hours' work. Price was agreed, and a deposit paid. Dago was booked to come back in two weeks for a morning slot.

Sue appeared in the shop two days before the appointment. Face slack with widowhood, she asked if we'd tattoo a corpse.

The Jericho was an old pub between Wembley and Harlesden, and a bikers' haunt for as long I could remember. Attempts had been made to rebrand it, but the changes never stuck. The regular clientele put off whatever new demographic the brewery hoped to attract.

The function room was divided fifty-fifty between dance floor and drinking space. The change from green industrial carpet to woodblock marked the border. Apart from a few dedicated drinkers, anyone under forty was on the parquet. The volume was set to ear-splitting and the tracks were all anthems. An attempt to convince everyone they were celebrating a life. Bikers' funerals are like that. One last scramble to pull something back from death.

Girlfriends and old ladies danced while the men lined the walls and looked serious. For the wallflowers, dress code was outlaw chic with black hooded sweatshirts and heavy leather cut-offs. Most of the sweatshirts bore the legend HLB along the sleeves.

On the same Madrid run where Colin Jones had become Dago, a loose group of friends had become the HLB: The Handsome London Boys.

The name was ironic or delusional depending on how drunk you were. It started with the single guys on the run putting the moves on the local senoritas and scoring a perfect zero. The jokey name stuck. The HLB developed a collective identity and became a club. Dago had, ipso facto, been its president. I'd stayed in touch but never been a member.

Yakky was already at the bar when I got there, talking tattoos, buying drinks and handing out cards. I didn't begrudge him a bit of networking. He wanted to be there less than I did and he'd only known Dago as an occasional face at the shop. Business is business. We both had a living to make.

I bought myself a drink and stayed at the bar with the older contingent. There was more sad smiling and agreeing that it was terrible.

The cars from the crematorium finally escaped the North Circ and a second wave of mourners began to filter in. Wanting to make my excuses early I kept an eye on the door, looking for Sue. She was one of the last to come through.

Black Micky was still at the door. Smudge, another Handsome London Boy, had taken a position opposite him. Indifferent to the rain, Smudge leaned against the doorframe and scanned the car park. He was wearing one of the Handsome Boy sweatshirts, the sleeves pushed up to his elbows. The outlaw aesthetic was at odds with his soft-blonde baby face. Until you reached the eyes. Then everything married up.

He was talking to Sue as I made my way across from the bar. I didn't hear what they said – the music was blasting at my back – but it was clear Sue was asking him something. Smudge shook his head and held up his hands: *haven't a clue.* The gesture looked aggressive but afterward he pulled Sue into a hug. They separated and Sue turned to Micky. Micky, possibly fearing for the line of his suit, restricted himself to squeezing her shoulder.

I made my excuses but didn't manage an escape. Sue had something she wanted talk to me about. *Would I wait a few minutes*? She began a circuit of the room and I headed outside, away from the music.

As I stepped into the rain I heard Smudge tell Micky, "If Johnny don't turn up soon, he's going to get his fucking arse kicked."

The rain eased off to a dull drizzle and more people drifted from the function room. Most of them were topping up the nicotine levels but some were escaping the music. We gathered around a concrete planter that stank of wet tobacco.

Johnny's name came up again. One of the young guns, all bristle-cut hair and sour expression, flicked a dogend into the planter and glanced towards the door.

"Anyone seen Johnny?" Bristle-cut asked. No one had.

"Well that'll ruin Smudge's day, won't it?"

One of the older hands gave a short laugh.

"You might want to keep that thought to yourself, Vic. Don't look like Smudge is in the mood."

Smudge was still propped against the doorframe. Now he was talking to Frenchy. I couldn't hear what was being said but Frenchy was saying most of it. Even without hearing the dialogue, Smudge's resentment was clear. Equally clear was his deference to the older man.

The exchange ended when Smudge nodded, turned away and vanished into the function room.

Frenchy looked older than fifty-four, though hardened rather than worn. Top and bottom lips highlighted with scar tissue where they'd been split. Similar markers of his history bisected both eyebrows.

The patch on the front of his cut-off read: V.P. Vice President. Now Dago was gone, Frenchy'd be likely to step up.

"Trouble?" I asked, when he joined us at the planter. He replied with a carefully blank look and I nodded in the direction of the door. "Smudge looked pissed off."

"It's a funeral," he said. "People get emotional."

Then he pulled off a Gallic shrug like a native.

Tied to the wake by Sue, I ended up staying far longer than I wanted. The DJ kept the volume cranked up beyond my pain threshold and the choice of tracks shifted from anthems to battle chants. Some of the wallflowers peeled away from the edge of the dance floor and formed a knot at its centre. They roared along to any chorus they deemed inspiring enough.

It was hard to judge whether the music was reflecting the mood or leading it. Either way the atmosphere was poisonous.

Maybe she didn't pick up on the tension, or perhaps it suited how she felt, but Sue stayed the better part of three hours. I spent the time watching the clock over the bar and only went back to the car park when I saw her begin the rounds, saying her good nights and accepting more condolences.

Sue had parked her BMW next to my Sportster and I sat side-saddle, waiting for her. Black Micky had risked taking his suit outside and was chatting to a pair of underdressed women in their twenties. They obviously weren't part of the crowd from the function room. His patter was going full tilt and I was glad to hear them laughing and playing along. That was the playlist Dago would have chosen for his final party. Not the wolfpack howls of the function room. The sky was properly dark now, with evening rather than rain, and the wake was showing no signs of winding down.

When Sue finally came out, she was caught in another round of condolences with the older hands and smokers around the planter. Yakky appeared more or less on her heels and made his way over. He was holding his crash helmet.

"You off too?" I asked.

"Yeah." He jerked his head in the direction he'd come from. "The smell of testosterone's getting a bit much in there."

"Something happened?"

He began fishing through his pockets for his bike keys. He didn't look particularly concerned, though his face seldom gave much away.

"Word got around that I'd done a cover-up on Dago. Rubbing out the regimental colours didn't go down so well in some quarters." When he didn't elaborate, I made a twirling motion with my finger. "It didn't come to anything," he said, "but I thought it was time to stop handing out business cards."

I hoped it hadn't gone public that the cover-up was applied post-mortem. A reputation for tattooing the dead I could do without.

When she got to us, Sue used her first breath to make the end of her cigarette glow bright. The second she turned into a deep sigh. She'd had enough for one day and whatever she wanted from me it was obviously another burden. Which meant I was there to share it.

"Thanks for waiting." The gratitude seemed to include Yakky and so tied him to the deal. Whatever it was. "Dago told me you helped him find some people, one time. People who owed him money."

She sounded doubtful. I could understand that. My business was tattooing, my shop offered high-quality ink. Finding missing persons wasn't an obvious sideline.

"I do the odd skip-trace now and then," I told her. I tried to sound noncommittal. Sue gave me what I'd call a knowing look.

The first half of her life, the time before Dago, was rocky with the milestones of hard-graft and disappointment. Life with Dago might have been more stable, but stable isn't the same as smooth. She knew the noise people make when they don't want to talk out in the open.

"There's a guy from the club, he hasn't been seen for a while," she said. She'd come a step closer and dropped her voice. "I want him found."

The wording of that statement brought several questions to mind. Top of the list being, why?

Standing so close, I got a blast of second-hand smoke when she answered.

"Because I think the little bastard's about to have a little bastard of his own."

"Mary?"

Sue nodded. "I'm going be a grandmother."

"So, who's the guy?"

"Johnny Simms."

2.
WWMMD?

Details of Johnny were at Sue's home so I said I'd follow her back. Yakky came along too, probably for want of a better offer.

I didn't mention my sideline in skip-tracing to everyone. Not that it was any big secret, it just didn't make for a great story. Tell people you trace missing persons and they start to imagine glamorous scenarios. Then they ask for details and you disappoint them. The banality of the whole process is a lousy punchline.

The clouds had moved on for the night and the temperature had dropped. As we'd crossed Hanger Lane gyratory, I the saw the driver's window of Sue's BMW seal shut against the cold. She burned a chain of cigarettes on the way back to Kew and as she stepped from the car, a cloud of smoke exited with her. The smell followed us into the house.

A black parka with a dozen badges on it had been left over the newel post at the bottom of the stairs and a matching fabric shoulder bag was on the floor. Sue hung the coat on a rack and picked the bag up without a word, but she let out a thin-lipped sigh. From a room, off to the left of the hall, came the sound of an American teenager hitting the obligatory high C.

"Mary?"

"Yeah," shouted back over the teeny-bopper sound track.

"Will you please not leave your stuff all over the floor?"

"Okay," in petulant fifteen-year-old manner.

"I'll make some tea," Sue told us and moved in the direction of the kitchen. "Have you eaten, Mary?" she called over her shoulder.

"I had dinner with aunty Tanya."

Yakky was pulling off his boots, almost on his arse as he hopped about on one leg. I didn't say anything but pointed at the doorway where the noise was coming from before putting my head around it. Yakky followed.

"Hello Mary," I said.

Mary had dyed her hair black since I'd last seen her and developed a taste for silver jewellery. She was curled up into a corner of a huge cream-coloured sofa, legs tucked under her, cuddling an oversized toy guinea pig. I noticed her thumb was wet. Like the PG-rated high school kids on the screen, the guinea pig was at odds with the wannabe goth look she was parading.

"Hi," she told me and I doubt she remembered who I was.

She wanted to look away quickly, so I wouldn't see she'd been crying, but the tattooed jawbone and teeth snagged her eye.

The ink on my right cheek was Yakky's work. I'd had him apply it a couple of years before. Someone had said my smile was disturbing. Now I could disturb people without smiling.

"This is Yakky," I said, and she looked around again trying not to show her face. "Yakky, Mary."

They exchanged greetings and Yakky even attempted a smile. I could see he'd got the point when we came back into the hallway. Mary was twenty-one, almost twenty-two.

"Very mild learning difficulties," I said. He nodded and I didn't explain further.

"Hard time for her," he said.

In blunt terms, Mary wasn't overly bright but not many people are. Her real problems were emotional, not intellectual. The teenage years had come late and with twice the trauma. The hard-won ground towards adulthood was currently strewn with the challenges of losing her step-father.

"Tea or coffee?" Sue asked us in the kitchen. I saw Yakky scan for a coffee machine and not finding one, ask for a tea. I knew the first thing he'd do when he got home.

Sue began leading us towards the room where the coffin had been that morning but changed her mind and took us to the backroom instead. That suited me. The backroom, like the rest of the house, smelt of polish and grief but it was still where the family had lived and laughed and argued and been who they were.

There were photographs everywhere, the walls barely visible between the gaps. Sue and Mary and Dago, sometimes alone, at others lost in a sea of faces. Some of the pictures I knew and at least one I'd taken: Dago with one arm around Frenchy and the other around Sue, Mary, about five, perched on his shoulders with a handful of hair to rein him in. In the background, a city of tents and bikes and a stage with a band cranking out covers. Everyone in the picture was laughing. The good humour had lasted the weekend, even after Frenchy, blind drunk, tripped and broke his ankle. It was his left one, the prosthetic, and we'd lashed it up with duct tape.

Now Dago was dead, the laughing five-year-old was in her twenties, and still a troubled teen, and Sue was holding it together with nicotine and furniture polish. I took a deep breath and told myself all things change.

"Did you ever meet Johnny?" Sue asked once we'd all sat down.

I told her I didn't think I had, but Yakky nodded.

"Bodybuilder type, rides an old GSX," he said. When I still couldn't place the name, he added, "He wanted those knuckle tattoos."

And the face came to me.

Johnny had been coming to the shop every few months or so for about a year. He was a six-footer with muscles he'd sculpted in a gym and decorated with aggressive, old-school ink, panthers clawing blood, skulls pierced by daggers. I referred to him as Knuckles. Not an entirely kind nickname.

Sue took a sip at her tea which was too hot and put it down on a low table in the centre of the room. Then she picked it up again and stirred it. I knew she didn't take sugar, but denied cigarettes, her fingers were getting restless.

"I know him from the shop," I said. And I barely knew him there, Yakky did most of his ink. "He was fairly new to the club, wasn't he?"

Sue nodded. A lot of the photos were taken at bike rallies or bikers' parties. Several photos from different weddings too. Handsome London Boys starred in most of them.

"Yeah, he came in about a year ago. No one's seen hide nor hair of him since Dago died."

"And Mary's put Johnny in the frame?"

"She hasn't said anything about it yet. She doesn't know that I know."

"Are you sure?"

"That it's Johnny's?"

"That she's pregnant."

Sue had a shoulder bag; she'd taken it off when we'd come into the house but kept it close. She leant sideways to retrieve it from the floor. The box she threw to me was slightly bigger than a packet of cigarettes.

"Did a big shop, day before yesterday, trying to take my mind off things," she said. Then, in case I'd missed the point, added, "I do a big shop, once a month."

I tossed the unopened packet of tampons back to her.

"And last month's batch were still in the bathroom cabinet, yeah?"

Sue nodded.

"She hasn't used any for a while, by the look of things. And she's been missing breakfast lately. I'd have spotted it sooner if I hadn't been so caught up with everything else."

"Has she been seeing Johnny?"

"He was round here a lot, he did a few bits of work for Dago. He was –" she held her arm out, as if curving it around someone's shoulders.

I could see Yakky didn't get the mime.

"Under Dago's wing," I explained.

"Yeah," Sue said. "He was one of his waifs and strays. He stayed in the spare room a couple of months back, while he got some money together for a bedsit."

The house boasted a spare room with its own bathroom and a lot of creature comforts. It serviced as a high-end crash pad for any Handsome London Boy who fell between the cracks. Or pissed off their old lady to the point that home became enemy territory. I'd spent a few nights there myself when my marriage was running aground.

"Timing's about right then." Yakky said. I made the spooling motion. "Morning sickness kicks in around six to eight weeks. If he was living here about two months ago…" he left me to fill in the blanks.

"And he now he's vanished," Sue said. "He hasn't been seen since Dago died. I thought he might just be licking his wounds, but not showing up for the funeral…" She left me to fill in the blanks as well.

Missing the president's funeral was a biggy. Not something to be done without good cause. To Sue it was proof positive.

"No one in the club's seen him?" I asked.

There was a blink-and-you'd-miss-it pause before Sue told me, no. I tried the reply with a little silence, to see if it teased anything more out into the open.

After a more generous pause she added, "Smudge said he'd been round to his bedsit today, but he wasn't there."

I remembered them talking on the door and Smudge's obvious frustration. I laid down a bit more silence but it brought out nothing.

"Well I'll do what I can, but this stuff don't come with a guarantee."

Sue said she understood and rounded up what details she had. It was more than we usually got. Dago's address book was a huge desktop volume, kept with a military precision he would have denied. It gave us Johnny's name, address, phone number and email. He'd also done a few bits of work for Dago, so should we need it, Sue assured us she could get his NI number and tax details. I don't know what she thought we could do with them.

For the most part, skip-tracing was glorified internet searching. If you knew where to look, or took the trouble to find out, you could usually pick up a trail of electronic footprints that would lead to a door to knock on or a number to ring. It wasn't rocket science, nor was it infallible.

Sue, in accordance with tradition, offered to pay us and we refused on the same grounds.

As I'd folded a copy of Johnny Simms into my wallet, Mary's teen musical had crescendoed with chaotic drums and high-pitched laughter. She joined us in the backroom and resumed the curled-up, little-girl, posture on the end of the sofa. Yakky gave her his awful impression of a smile and she nodded but didn't look at ease. She was still cuddling the oversized guinea pig.

I asked Sue if she had a photo of Johnny. In truth, I wouldn't have a lot of use for it, but I wanted to look like I was able to do something. Sue didn't have a photo to hand, which I could have guessed. She said that Dago would have taken a picture of him for his work security pass. The chances were, it would still be on the digital camera.

She went to get the camera and came back into the room looking puzzled.

"Mary, have you seen Dad's camera?"

"No."

Sue seemed cross at the response. "Well, where was it last?"

"I don't know," Mary said. Her voice was high and a little too loud.

"Look, don't sweat it," I said, trying to sound soothing. "I probably won't need it. If one turns up, let me know, if not, don't worry."

I think this pause in the momentum of the row was enough to restore calm because Sue nodded and disguised a sigh as a yawn.

"It'll be on his computer. I'll have to go into all that soon. Dago did all the bookkeeping and tax returns." She stopped talking abruptly as life handed her another reminder, that she was a widow. "I'm going to need to find an accountant."

I folded the sheet of paper with Johnny on it into my wallet and dug around in there until I found a business card.

"This fella's good, does my books. Rumour has it the tax office has a contract out on him."

Sue took the card and read it at arm's length. The look she gave me wasn't trusting.

"Is he legit? I don't want the Inland Revenue banging on the door."

"He's as straight as you want him to be. But if there's a way to avoid tax, he'll know it."

I didn't tell Sue he had property in South America and lived with his passport to hand.

She told me thanks and said, "Stop that, Mary," as she tucked the card into the cover of a small address book.

I glanced around and embarrassed Mary by seeing her take her thumb from her mouth.

"I like your guinea pig. Is she new?" I asked trying to leave the subject of thumbs behind.

She nodded and told me, "Daddy gave her to me."

"When?" Sue asked sharply.

"Today, at aunty Tanya's."

'Daddy' was Gavin Turnbull, Mary's biological father, and Sue's first husband. At the funeral that morning, Sue had been locked away in her own pain and Mary had been all but sitting on her aunt's lap. I hadn't been able to see, from where I'd been sitting, but I'd have put money down that Mary sucked her thumb all through the service.

Going back to her aunt's rather than attending the wake was a good call. Mary was struggling to make sense of things already; Dago's death becoming a party would have been too much.

Sue let me lead her out of the room and into the kitchen. She knew I was defusing a situation and she was holding it together enough to let me. We made more tea and she gave up the no-smoking-in-the-house rule.

"Sly little bastard." Her mouth had become a tight slit and the words did well to escape. "He rang me two nights ago, asked if Mary was going to the funeral. I told him she'd be leaving with Tanya straight after. I bet he was waiting outside her house."

She drew down too hard on the filter tip and coughed convulsively for a full minute. I slapped her on the back a couple of times and got her a glass of water that she waved away. When she'd finally stopped coughing, she pulled a tall stool from under one of the counters and sat down, wheezing. I spared her the lecture. Sue had stopped smoking for pleasure long ago and I doubted she currently had energy to fight addiction.

"*Daddy*." She said it in a way that made me glad I didn't have children. "Dago was her Daddy, not that wanker. Dago did everything for her, that worthless bastard's never done a thing." She took a last pull before flicking the butt across the room into the sink. I pulled up my own stool and waited to see if she'd finished venting.

I wanted her to cry, I was sure she hadn't and she needed too. Anger gets you so far but it's a short-term fix.

"Mary knows who her real father was," I said. "She calls Gavin Daddy, because that's what he's told her he is. She called Dago Dad, because that what he was, and she knows that."

The wheezing had eased enough to allow Sue a sigh. She was doing that too much.

"I know, I know. It's hard at the moment." I knew it was, and I knew it wouldn't get easier for a while yet. "There's something else I wanted to ask you, Doc. Dago had a gun. I want rid of it. I didn't like having in the house before, I really don't want it now."

"Not a legal gun I take it?"

She shook her head. "A sawn-off."

I had one of those already and didn't need another. I'd picked mine up years earlier when I was in a bad state of mind. I'd sit in the dark cradling it and picturing the man my wife had been sleeping with. Common sense, or something, held my hand. Apart from me, only Yakky knew I had it and, being Yakky, he'd never asked why.

The obvious answer was to throw Sue's gun in the Thames

but she didn't want to touch it, let alone drive around with it. I didn't either, but I told her I would. It was currently sitting under the loft insulation along with a box of shells. She said she'd get it when she had a chance, then call me. Sue could tell I wasn't happy about the arrangement but we'd just cremated someone we cared about, so happy wasn't an option anyway.

By the time Sue and I had finished in the kitchen, Yakky and Mary had moved to the room with the TV. A teenage actor, skin like silk, pouted in freeze frame.

Yakky was sketching out a likeness while Mary cooed over one he'd already produced. We killed twenty minutes and another round of teas while Mary hunted with the pause button for actors to pin on her wall. Before we left she asked Yakky if he could do some more for her and gave him the DVD, along with a list of portraits she wanted.

"That'll give me something to watch with Dad tonight," Yak said once we were outside with the bikes.

He tucked the DVD into his jacket, then spent five minutes mixing blasphemy and prayer on the altar of his start button.

It was still fairly early when I got home and I wasn't excited about an evening alone. I don't like autumn. Grey and damp, the season seeped into the flat and made me miserable. I debated going back out, finding a lively pub to sit in and drinking a few quiet ones to Dago's memory. Then the rain started lashing the windows again so I nixed the idea and just gritted my teeth.

My flat's stark and I won't quantify that statement. When we'd started the business, Gina, my then wife, and I lived in a tiny place a mile across town. The property above the shop we rented out. We'd agreed that living and working in the same space was a bad idea. The combination of a south-bound marriage and a tenant with rent arrears ended with the flat becoming my home.

The tenant hadn't wanted to pay his arrears or leave the flat. He also fancied himself as a barrack-room lawyer and started bleating about residents' rights. I told him to produce a contract; he changed tack and tried to claim squatters' rights. I told him he had one week to get out, or he'd be arguing the case with a friend of mine and his three Rottweilers.

He left the next day, after spraying various insults on all the walls and taking a shit in the kitchen sink. A bottle of bleach fixed the sink and I stripped the walls back to bare plaster. I pulled out the carpets and curtains and threw the lot into the shop's backyard.

I decided a fresh start was needed and, *as a physical manifestation of such, the flat could serve as a surrogate id.* I used to churn out essays with titles like that when I was a student. Only then I was sober and had no excuse.

I woke up with a hangover in a gutted flat. Of course, it had rained in the night and everything I'd thrown in the yard was sodden.

By the time I'd got my life back to the point where I had the energy to put things right, I'd got used to it being wrong. It was easy to keep clean and the feeling it gave me, of merely passing through, was close to a comfort.

I lit a candle with the image of Baron Semedi on the side and dropped a shot of spiced rum into one of the offering bowls on the altar. Plenty of Voodooists would baulk at the sloppiness of my practice but fuck 'em. The spirits can judge my devotion and I do it right when occasion demands.

After I'd made a pot of tea I opened the laptop and went to the people-tracker sites I subscribed to. I gleaned the same information Sue had given me already, plus Johnny's last address. Or at least the last address he'd cast a vote from. It had been in Southend, three years before. I looked it up on Google Street View and found the road where Johnny had lived was now behind a row of plywood hoardings. Signage promised luxury apartments were coming soon.

Skip-tracing's dirty little secret is this: most internet traces take less than an hour. If you want your customers to have the warm glow of satisfaction that comes with value for money, your wait a day or two before calling them with the info. That way they think you're been up all night earning your fee. That was why me and Yak did it – most of the time it was easy money. As a bonus, I got to play Miss Marple.

Having exhausted the marvels of the internet in less than fifteen minutes, I drummed my fingers for a bit and drank tea.

WWMMD: What would Miss Marple do?

If I'm honest I don't think Miss Marple would have dealt the tarot. But then, she didn't run a tattoo shop in north London so it's hard to draw direct comparisons.

I've got several tarot decks but only one I use for actual readings. It's an old pack that feels comfortable.

It didn't offer much comfort that night.

Sunday 17 September

I woke up late the next day and tried the mobile number I had for Johnny Simms. It rang a long time before going to voicemail. I hung up and tried a second time with the same result. I left a message asking him to ring either me or Sue.

Around noon, boredom coaxed me out into the rain. I struggled to get a pair of waterproofs over my jeans and rode over to Stonebridge Park and the address from Dago's phonebook.

The address was a shabby townhouse with eight doorbells. It had been built to house a big middle-class family and had birthed multiple bedsits. I thumbed bell 65E and waited, then thumbed it for a second time. When I got no answer, I pressed one bell after another and told the first person to answer I'd lost my key and asked them to buzz me in.

In the hallway, few of the original features had survived, but ornate cornicing suggested a history of elegance. Just inside the door, on the wall to the right, were a mass of consumer boxes and meters. To the left, at the foot of the unlit staircase, was a free-standing collection of pigeon holes for mail. It had been pulled from an office building or some such. Everything looked temporary and whoever had carried out the conversion work could have moonlighted as a butcher.

I checked the pigeon hole for 65E. It was empty. I gave the

others a quick look and not getting post was pretty well the norm. The floor was deep with junk mail and fliers, none of which had moved since being dumped there.

Johnny was on the first floor, or rather he wasn't. I spent a futile couple of minutes waiting outside his door between bouts of knocking. There was one other door on the landing and I knocked on it without much hope of getting an answer. As I was about to turn and leave, however, it opened a crack and a bloodshot eye appeared, along with a smell that would have stripped paint off the woodwork, if there'd been any left to strip. I asked the eye if it had seen its neighbour recently.

It took a long time to answer and when it did it said, "What?"

"Johnny Simms, he lives in flat E. Have you seen him recently?"

There was another painfully long wait, as the eye took a second swipe at processing the question.

"Johnny?"

I told the eye not to worry about it and went back into the rain to find a DIY store. Illegal entries weren't part of my skill set but it didn't look like the witnesses would be taking careful notes if I came back with a crowbar.

I picked up a flat section nail bar in bright yellow for under a tenner and as an afterthought bought a hi-vis waistcoat to match. People don't take notice of workmen in hi-vis jackets carrying hand tools.

Back at Johnny's door I knocked and pulled on a pair of latex gloves while I waited for no one to respond. In accordance with some regulation or another, the door was fire resistant and heavy-duty. The frame it sat in was on a par with the rest of the building. A sound system on the floor above covered most of the noise as I split the soft-wood jamb apart. I kicked the move obvious splinters into Johnny's hallway before closing the door behind me.

There weren't many doors inside. I stuck my head into the bathroom and decided whatever the landlord was charging was too much. The walls were tiled to waist height and mildewed from there up. The shower tray was buried in an inch of limescale. Other than a pair of dried cockroaches, up-ended in the sink, there was nothing in the room that wasn't fixed down.

No toothbrush, soap or towels, not even a toilet roll.

The kitchen carried on the mould and limescale motif but with the added attraction of a greasy cooker. When I opened the fridge, the smell of bleach made my eyes sting. Johnny wasn't a slob by choice. Three tins of protein shake and a screw top carton of milk were nesting in the door. I gave the milk a sniff and it was beginning to turn. In the cupboards there were a lot of tinned meals, soups, stews, things you could heat up in one pan. The draining board had a selection of crockery waiting on it, all of it clean and dry, as was the dish cloth hanging over the cold tap.

Kitchen and bedroom were in the same space. The bed was made up with a solitary sheet pinned with neat hospital corners. A tiny three-drawer desk and an old office chair completed the home comforts.

The bottom drawer had a towel and a cover for a single duvet; the other two held a small collection of clothes. I pulled out a couple of tee-shirts. They needed ironing but were carefully folded. They had a faint musty smell. It took me back to my student days, living in bug hutch accommodation and constantly fighting to keep clean. Getting clothes dried in limited space had been a losing struggle.

On top of the desk was a cardboard box with a collection of magazines in it, military history mixed with biker titles. The room's one window didn't have any curtains, but the sill had a small bunch of dead flowers in a glass jug, the stems still in forecourt cellophane. Judging by the tide mark, the water had been evaporating for at least a week.

Between the desk and bed, there was a calor-gas heater, nearly as old as the fireplace it was sitting in. The mantelpiece was doing service as a book case. The books, like the magazines, were military and motorcycle in equal parts. The bike titles were mainly exposures of 'notorious' outlaw clubs.

Turncoat members or undercover cops writing about their wild times down among the one-percenters. The military stuff was all memoirs, easy-read accounts of daring-do. On the wall above the row of books was a disposable carbon monoxide detector.

An address book would have been nice, but Johnny was the wrong generation to commit numbers to paper. Things don't get written down like they used to, mobiles hold three or four hundred numbers and e-mails replace letters. Even photo albums have been shunted to the margins by digital storage.

It didn't take long to search the bedsit. Or to draw a blank. Johnny's impact in the real world had been as light as his footprint on the virtual one.

Back at my flat I lit a candle to the spirit of Ezulie Dantor, the vengeful Voodoo spirit of women, lesbians, single mothers and children. Then I put the gas fire on and waited without much hope for the flat to warm up. I put some fish pieces in to cook and opened a carton of orange juice to ward off scurvy.

I didn't have a little black book to pull out. I page find by mental note. I remember numbers, orders of numbers, sequences of numbers, patterns. If I had Yakky's stone cold blank of a face I'd be world poker champion.

I dialled three numbers before one of guys I knew from the HLB picked up.

Jason had been on the run where Colin was reborn as Dago. He was a quiet, serious bloke until he'd had few then he was the life and soul, right up until the police arrived.

"Johnny Simms?" I heard Jason's lunch getting chewed; it didn't do a lot for my own appetite. "Don't know where he is, I missed him at the funeral, wondered if he was alright."

"Yeah, Sue was surprised he didn't show. She hasn't seen him for a while."

"Neither have I. She's asked you to have a look?"

I made a noncommittal noise.

"I was wondering if he might have headed back home."

"Derby? Doubt it, not the way he talked about his family. I've been shot at by people I think more of."

Jason paused, in the background I heard someone shouting, and a woman's voice shouted back *it was where they'd left it.* Wife, kids. Jason wasn't joking about being shot at. He'd nearly been killed in the Middle East, twice. After six months in a military nick, for punching one local too many, he spent his savings on a ticket back to civvy street. When he landed back in the UK, he did nine more months, this time as a civilian, for laying out a taxi driver who cut him up.

Meanwhile, I'd gone to university, bullshitted my way to a PhD in psychology. Did the whole bit, love, marriage, own business, letters after my name.

Jason was eating dinner in his family home and I was sat in a kitchen where someone had once shit in the sink.

"You spoken to Smudge?" Jason put on a little-girl voice, with a lisp, "Him and Johnny are bestest fwiends."

I assumed he was parodying one of his own brood.

"I haven't spoken with him, no. He sounded all set to give Johnny a hard time at the wake."

"That was just hot air. Smudge is working on his outlaw image." I made another noncommittal grunt and waited for Jason to make up his own question to answer. "Him and Dago went head to head over it more than once."

"*It* being?"

"Smudge keeps pushing to make us into a full patch club. He wants to go outlaw and wear a one percenter patch."

"Dago wasn't into it?"

"No, too old for that crap. Some of the younger guys are up for it though. I guess it'll go that way now."

"You think?"

I checked the fish pieces just as Jason started chewing in my ear again. The rain started hissing against the window.

"Yeah, the Handsome London was just us old bastards riding around with Dago really. Now he's gone it'll either change into something else entirely or just peter out. If it gets nasty about keeping hold of the name, I think the old guard will just let it go. Shame but there it is."

I agreed, both with his assessment of the outcome and the sentiment. The Handsome London Boys had always been a loose group, what used to be called a side-patch club. Like-minded people with a bit of common history. They'd never held a territory nor shown ambitions to. If the young bloods wanted to change the HLB, from a name to gather under into a flag to rally around, there wasn't a lot to stop them. The cooler, wiser heads would leave them to it and just remember the good times.

"I noticed there was a bit of a schism at the wake," I said.

I was thinking about the mosh-pit dance floor at The Jericho.

"Yeah, a lot of the guys left early. The younger fellas were trying to turn it into an all-nighter. I hung on 'till about eleven, chatting with Frenchy, then a fight started."

"Bad one?"

Jason made a disparaging noise. "Couple of half-cut wankers, thought they'd gate crash, once they'd called last orders in the main bar. Black Micky told them to fuck off and one of them took a swing."

I could guess how that one came out. Micky bounced for a living. I asked if the wankers had taken the hint.

"No. A couple of our lads run out to help and it got a bit silly. Me and Frenchy had to break it up."

"Anyone hurt?"

"Nothing much," he said, though we probably had different views on what *nothing much* meant. "Once the dust had settled I got the fuck out of Dodge. I don't need more time with the boys in blue."

Who does?

"Did the police turn up then?"

"I spoke to Frenchy today and he reckons there wasn't any fall out. He says he tore a strip off the twats that kicked off, said Black Micky's had a chat with them too. Oh, to be young eh?"

"Yeah. I'll let you get on with your dinner, mate. If you see

Johnny, tell him to give Sue a call and put her mind at rest, eh?"

"Yeah, will do. Frenchy might know more about Johnny's family if you want to try them. Johnny did a bit of work him, and he had a girlfriend on the go for a while come to think of it. Could be he's shacked up with her."

"You got name for her?"

Jason chewed while he tried to recall details.

"Ann or Anna, I think, something like that. Don't know her surname. Frenchy might, or Johnny's fwiend Smudge." He'd put on the little girl voice again.

I told him thanks and made two more calls before someone else picked up. A guy called Silk, who I knew through the shop more than through the HLB. He was another guy old enough to be gathered at the bar rather than standing around the dance floor.

Silk told me the same as Jason. He hadn't seen Johnny, couldn't believe he'd missed the funeral. By Silk's telling, Johnny was dedicated to The Handsome London Boys. If anything had The HLB in attendance, then he was there. Party, wedding, run down to the coast, his presence was a given. He told me about Johnny working for Frenchy as well.

"If he'd talk to anyone about taking off, it would be Frenchy. He loves that guy."

"Really?"

"Christ yeah. He's obsessed with the French Foreign Legion, never stopped asking Frenchy about it."

Something about that bothered me and I couldn't think what.

"Is Johnny one of the guys pushing to make The Handsome into a full house club?"

Silk didn't answer immediately and when he did, it sounded as if he was being careful what he said.

"Yeah, that guy's a true believer, he wants something to belong to. He calls everyone *brother*." He chuckled the way you do when someone tells you a joke you've already heard. "He's a bit keen if you know what I'm saying, tries too hard."

"Playing the tough nut?" I asked.

I wished I'd left the calls until I'd eaten. I didn't want to chew down the phone line and I could see my lunch getting cold.

"Not that so much, but he's struggling to make his mark. He always wants to talk army all the time. The older guys don't give a shit about that stuff and the younger guys are still raw from it. Dago only ever talked about the times he'd have to get ready for parade with a hangover and the young dudes go on about how much they hate officers. Course Johnny can't do that, so he ends up telling some story he's read in one of his bloody SAS books, or spouting shite about some bike club or other."

"So, why'd he miss the funeral?" I said it out loud but I was really talking to myself.

Silk answered anyway. "Don't know. I'm glad he did though. There was enough trouble as it was."

"I heard there was fight."

"More a stomping. Micky and me were by the door having a toke, couple of gobshites with a skinful tried it on. Me and Mick had it covered when bloody Smudge comes out and starts laying down the law. Course, once he came out, it was like the dam burst. The lairy one ended up on the deck, with his girlfriend on top of him, trying to shield him. Me, Jason and Frenchy ended up pulling our guys off before it went tits up big style."

"You reckon Johnny would have made it worse?"

"You know what it's like when someone thinks they've got something to prove. They're a liability when the shit hits the fan."

I asked about Johnny's possible girlfriend, but Silk knew less than Jason. He remembered Johnny turning up with a young woman on a few occasions but didn't have a name. He did recall nobody had taken to her.

I was winding up the call when Silk made a clicking noise with his tongue. It sounded like he was in two minds about saying something more, so I stayed quiet and waited him out.

Most people don't like silence, especially over the phone.

"Why'd you need to find Johnny, anyway?"

I skipped the clicking tongue routine, but my reply was no more off the cuff than the question.

"Sue mentioned she hadn't seen him. I said I'd keep my eye out. A lot of people pass my way, through the shop."

There was another pause, as Silk weighed up what to say next. I moved the mobile a little way from my mouth, to deepen the silence from my end of the line.

"I'd leave this alone, Doc."

I played the words back in my head, trying to decide if the words were a warning or a threat.

"Leave it alone, why?" I said, after what felt a long time but most likely wasn't.

"There's a lot of tension in the club, right now."

He wouldn't say anything more on the subject and we both made a point of talking about lighter stuff, as if nothing had been said. We ended the call, assuring each other that we'd get together for a drink sometime.

3.
Pastoral Views of Staples Corner

Monday 18 September

Dago's Harley had gouged the route of its last trip across the pavement and into the verge. Where it had come to rest, an angle-iron fence support was bent in a respectful bow.

There aren't many pastoral views around Staples Corner. The narrow strip of grass at the top of the T-junction, where Dago died, was as close as it got. I don't think it's where he'd have chosen to go down, but it made a strange kind of sense. At least to me. Under the sweep of the Edgware Road, by the roots of the M1, the air shook with the pulse of the city.

It wasn't Big Ben or the Houses of Parliament, not a slice of London people wanted to send home on a postcard, but it had the dirty back beat of the capital Dago had been a part of. The valley boy with a Spanish nickname and a Yankee bike. An outsider who, in the way of Shit City, was more London than every hipster, metrosexual and pearly king there'd ever been.

I hadn't intended stopping at the crash site. The carpet of wet card-stock and bouquets had made me pull over. There were a lot of tributes, Dago had been well liked, even outside of the HLB, and flowers and cards had been gathering for days. Maybe it was sentiment that drew me, maybe morbid curiosity.

I didn't realise I was crying until I made to put my crash helmet back on.

Before I went into Frenchy's office I took a minute to pull myself together. I wasn't embarrassed by the tears, but I didn't feel I'd earned the right to shed them in front of the man who'd found Dago's body.

The 'office' was a trio of portacabins, coupled together, in a corner of the scrapyard. The structure also served as break-room and changing-room. It permanently smelt of oil and cigarettes and in the rainy season, the odour of drying bike gear added to the mix.

Despite his surroundings, Frenchy was collared and tied. The white shirt and pressed trousers did nothing to water down his Parisian look, but, even freshly shaven, his jaw was five-o'clock-shadow blue. He acknowledged me with a nod that almost dislodged the telephone from the crook of his neck. I parked myself on a grime-black sofa and earwigged the conversation. The rapid fire French left my linguistic ambitions at the first curve. I speak a reasonable amount of Creole, bastard offspring of the mother tongue, but since he was talking about cars and not Voodoo, I was only getting one word in three. The call ended, and the phone rang again as soon as he put the receiver down. I waved off his eye-rolling apology and settled in to wait.

The cabin was messy in the way of most communal spaces. Half a dozen bike jackets littered the room and their HLB patches showed the provenance of the workforce. One corner, spread with a collection of mugs and plates, was given over to a tiny kitchenette. The fridge was plastered with the obligatory pin-ups as was the cabinet above the sink.

Wall space was more regimented. Schedules and instructions were encrypted on a poster-sized calendar and cork board. Behind Frenchy's desk, black-and-white prints dated back to his time in the legion.

Ideally, I would have been talking to Smudge, Johnny Simms' 'bestest fwiend'. But friendly as I was with many of its members, the HLB wasn't a capricious organisation and the awkward warning from Silk had me on my guard. I only knew Smudge from the peripheries of the club. He hadn't been one of the waifs and strays Dago seemed to attract but, like many of the Handsome London Boys, there was a slightly haunted feel about him. Going to Frenchy was a way of testing the waters and maybe getting a degree of grace.

The second call was brief and after he'd hung up Frenchy led me out into yard. The phone was rigged up to sound outside the cabin and the ringing tone followed us, but he seemed able to ignore it once we were out of the room.

The moment he'd crossed the threshold of his office, he pulled out a packet of cigarettes and lit up.

"You see all the flowers?" he asked.

With the switch back to English, his accent betrayed his Liverpool blood stock.

"Couldn't miss them. People still leaving stuff?"

"Yeah, it's getting on my nerves."

"Bringing back memories?"

He flicked the notion away with his hand. "I don't need reminders."

Frenchy had been the one to find Dago pinned under the wreckage of his Electra Glide. It was the small hours of a Friday morning and, measured by a clock, the ambulance would have made good time. Measured by the thoughts of a man waiting for his closest friend to die, it would have been an eternity.

"Is there any word from the police?"

Frenchy turned away from me and spat. It was answer enough. One more unsolved hit and run. Even if the scumbag was caught and convicted, the most he'd get would be four years. The maximum penalty for causing death by dangerous driving.

The yard's car compactor started up as Frenchy opened his mouth to say something. Rather than shout over the noise he motioned me to follow him and we walked around to the other side of the portacabins. The yard was an exercise in disorder. The only reflection on his history of military service were the uniform green overalls Frenchy made his men ware. I recognised faces from the dance floor of The Jericho, young guns with serious expressions.

At the far side of the yard, with the portacabins absorbing the sound, the compactor was reduced to a dull roar. Frenchy flicked aside the end of his cigarette. Before it hit the ground, he'd lit another. We'd stopped at an area hidden from general view. It served as a parking bay for the workforce and five motorcycles were huddled in it, sheltered by a lean-to. They all had the look of second bikes, which isn't to say any of them were cheap. The HLB young guns had a taste for big Harley Davidsons. The scrap metal business must have been good.

Standing away from the working machines was a twisted shape, wrapped in a tarp. Frenchy saw me glance at it and blew out a long stream of smoke, confirming what I'd thought, Dago's Glide.

"I told the police I'd store it here. Now the insurance assessors have finished with it, Sue wants it back. I didn't think she'd want to see it, I told her I'd scrap it for her, or sell it on. She's not ready for that…" He did one of his Gallic shrugs.

He wasn't looking at the wreckage. I was about to suggest moving somewhere else when he suddenly span and marched to the crippled bike. He moved like he was made entirely of nerve endings. The end of his cigarette glowed brightly as he grabbed the edge of the tarp.

"Breaks my heart," he said.

The '88 Electra Glide had been hit hard enough to tear the engine out of its forward mounts and fold the frame. Dago had shared my belief that motorcycles shouldn't be over dressed. He'd removed most of the usual polish and chrome clutter that Glide owners favour. What little he'd kept was now shattered. One of the panniers had been reduced to a tatter of fibreglass and the other was split and compressed. The lid jammed shut on the body, as if it were biting itself. There were divots of turf clinging to the shape edges.

The saddle and engine were streaked with soap residue, left over from a hasty clean. I assumed someone had taken the trouble to wash Dago's blood away. I hoped the task had fallen to a police technician and not Frenchy.

I put a hand on the fuel tank and wondered if Dago would have taken any comfort in dying with his bike. It was a stupid idea, designed to comfort the living. I shook my head and pulled the tarp back over the ruined bike.

"I told Sue I'd take it over to her garage this week. I'll do it while she's out," Frenchy said. "I'll get a couple of the lads to help me, get it squared away and covered up. She won't want to be seeing it all smashed in like this." Now he didn't seem able to look away. "I expect she'll get rid of it in time."

I thought about Dago's body laid out in the best room, waiting for Yakky's inks. The Electra Glide had been as much a part of the man as his tattoos or his scars.

"I wouldn't be surprised if she wants to keep it. Have it restored or something."

We both moved away from Dago's bike. The phone started up again and Frenchy looked pointedly in the direction of the ringing.

"That why you're here?"

"No," I said. "I'm looking for one of your lads. Johnny Simms?"

Despite all the noise in the yard, for a second, it felt quiet.

"He owe someone money?"

"Not that I know of. Sue's asked me to find him."

I didn't volunteer any more than that and Frenchy didn't make enquiries. He'd known Sue for as long as I had and if he was curious, he could ask at source. There was another moment where the two of us shared a bubble of silence. I guessed he had some idea of what would be on Sue's mind.

"Johnny's a big boy, he'll turn up when he's ready. He mentioned something about going to Derby a while ago. I think he's got family there."

"Wasn't he working for you?"

"He did a few bits and pieces for me, ran the crusher when we were pressed. Off the books, you know." He glanced around him, as if the tax man might have been close enough to overhear. Though any eavesdropper would have had their work cut out. The car compactor was going strong. "He did a bit for Dago now and then as well."

Dago's business had been security, much of it live-in guards. Most of his employees were ex-military and a few were HLB.

For a fee, Dago would provide a security guard who'd live in empty properties twenty-four seven, deterring squatters, arsonists and other problems. The amount of empty property around London produced a steady income.

The pay wasn't great. The draw of the work was free accommodation with the utilities paid for. How much they'd rough it varied from job to job. Sometimes there'd be a plush pad in Docklands, other times there'd be a dump, one step up from a squat.

"Smudge told me he'd been sniffing around him for some door work," Frenchy said. "You know Smudge looks after the door at that big nightclub? The one where they have the live bands, The House of Ice is it? They get a lot of trouble there since they got licensed. Five hundred teenyboppers plus alcohol." He did one of his Gallic shrugs and, Scouse accent or not, I mentally added a string of onions. "Plus, there's a few gangstas in the area that like to throw their weight about. Kids, really, but they egg each other on."

Take a venue full of hyped-up teens and twenty-somethings, marinate in hormones and booze for a few hours and it made sense to have a few people around to keep an eye on things. That increased by an order of magnitude if the local gangstas decided their honour was at stake.

"I don't think it came to anything," Frenchy added. "Probably for the best. I hear Smudge is a bastard to work for."

He flicked the end of his cigarette away. This time he didn't replace it. We began moving towards the office again.

"Don't Smudge and Johnny get on?"

Frenchy side stepped the question by rubbing his knee and sucking a breath through his teeth. I dutifully asked if he was okay.

"Always bad this time of year. I think it's the change in the weather. Damp."

I nodded in sympathy, then asked about Smudge and Johnny again. We were at the doorway of the office now. In line for the full blast of the compactor's din, we had to bellow at each other. He stood in the doorway and made no sign of letting me back in.

"They get on fine," he told me, "but Smudge keeps a tight ship, hard to get on the door there if he doesn't know who you are. He uses nearly all club guys."

"But Johnny didn't make it in?"

Frenchy shrugged. "Johnny didn't have experience on the door and he didn't come out the forces – and that went against him." I could tell there was an 'and' in the wings and I waited for it to come out. "Johnny was devoted to Dago. I don't think that helped, at least not lately."

I mentioned I'd heard Smudge and Dago didn't see eye to eye.

"Smudge's talking about back patches, sorting out the membership." Frenchy made a point of lifting his face into the drizzle that was beginning to get started. He lit up another cigarette. "It might go that way now. The older guys won't stick around if the youngsters start pushing for it en mass, and then the opposition goes."

The amplified ringtone stopped briefly then instantly started up again. Frenchy looked pointedly in the direction of his office. I told him I'd let him go and, as if it was an afterthought, mentioned that I might talk to Smudge. Frenchy shook his head and drew another breath in through his teeth.

"Everyone's wound up after the business with Dago, let it alone for a bit. Honestly, Doc, better to leave it. If Johnny's in trouble, let the club handle it."

"I heard Smudge say Johnny was going to get his arse kicked if he didn't show for the wake."

Frenchy did something halfway to a laugh. "That's just hot air. Smudge and Johnny…" He held up a hand with his fingers tightly crossed. "Big buddies."

"Not a big enough buddy to give him a job, though?"

I jerked when Frenchy flicked his half-finished cigarette past my head and into the yard. He took a moment so we could both acknowledge I'd flinched.

"Doc, leave it alone for now. Let things settle."

And I was standing in the drizzle looking at a closed door.

Ten thirty's the official opening time, though we often started earlier. Late, after talking with Frenchy, I found my first customer fidgeting as she waited. My apology and reassuring smile drained the blood from her face. Facial ink does that to some people. Though my smile had made people itch long before Yakky tattooed an extension to it.

It was her first tattoo, a straight forward piece of flash she'd pulled from the internet. I did my best to put her at ease, but it was an uphill struggle. Board stiff and paper white, she watched the butterfly take shape on her wrist without a flicker of pleasure. The process was a chore for both of us and the joylessness of it left a bad taste. Gina, my ex, had given up the ink, for good and all, once Yakky had gone full time. The vacuum she'd left had filled with his unsmiling soul and my freak show aesthetic. It wasn't to everyone's taste.

I finished the tattoo as quickly as I could and took my client through to the waiting room, to talk her through the aftercare. On the tail of my thoughts about the atmosphere in the shop, Smudge arrived. Like the confirmation of all my fears.

His open-piped Harley pulled up as the butterfly woman was exiting. They reached the door together and Smudge opened it, stepping to one side with a deep bow. There was something threatening about the elaborate show of chivalry that Yakky's next customer – a goth, young and timid under the eye-liner and black line – had picked up on. Black Micky pulled up a second later on his Moto Guzzi. Before stepping into the waiting room, both men scanned the road left to right.

Micky nodded to me but Smudge homed in on the young goth girl. She was sitting on one of the waiting room's two sofas. He ambled across with a cultivated gunslinger walk and executed another bow. In response, she shrank into the upholstery; he seemed pleased with the reaction.

When he looked my way his pale-blue gaze settled on a point just to my right.

"I hear you're one hell of a tattooist," he said and finally his eyes fixed on mine, though sighted might have been a better word. "That's what Johnny tells me."

4.
Tributes and Warnings

Smudge wanted a memorial to Dago on his forearm. He had no idea what he was looking for. It was just a pretext for his passive aggressive routine. I decided to call his bluff and pointed him to the books of sample work we kept in the waiting room. He dropped his bulk onto the threadbare sofa opposite the goth girl and started flicking through an album of tributes and memorials.

"If you want to book a date, it's a fifty-pound deposit, non-refundable. If you want it done straight away, it's cash in advance."

Without looking up, Smudge gave a dismissive wave the Queen Mother would have been proud of.

I didn't want to stand around waiting on his next move, so went and made the drinks. Yakky was changing needles when I put his coffee beside him. He must have heard something of the exchange because he nodded towards the waiting room and asked if there was a problem. I made some reassuring noises that Yakky knew didn't mean much.

I sat and finished my tea before going out to see Smudge again. With hindsight, I didn't use the time very wisely. I should have asked What Would Miss Marple Do, instead I meditated on being told to back off.

Smudge had shifted to the goth's sofa and was asking which of the designs she'd like to *see on him*. He was using the open pages as an excuse to lean into her space. As I got there, she picked out a piece of flash without showing a hint of interest. It wasn't lost on me or Smudge that she used her middle finger to jab the page. He gave an overly raucous laugh.

"If that's what the young lady says, then who am I to disagree? How much?"

I looked over the design. It was faux Victoriana style, a black ribbon entwining a scroll with In Memory of ______ at its centre. It wasn't totally dissimilar to the old Harley Davidson oak leaf badge. I priced it mentally and added twenty percent. Smudge dug into his leather, pulled a money clip out and peeled the notes away without comment.

Before I took him through to the backroom, he gave his leather to Micky. Micky, handling it like it was the Shroud of Turin, arranged it over one of the sofas, leaving the HLB patch on display.

Resplendent in a bodybuilder's shirt, Smudge lounged in my work chair like he owned it. His arms were thickly corded with muscle but the gym logo on the shirt was stretched across a growing beer gut. The bulk of his right bicep and deltoids was covered with a regimental insignia, a largely geometric design that wasn't sitting comfortably on the contoured skin. It looked to me as if it had been applied before he'd taken up weightlifting. Under the crest, in Gothic script, another stamp of ink read NEVER AGAIN, under that were two dates, four years apart. Dago's memorial was the first ink he'd be carrying below the elbow.

I shaved blonde peach fuzz from Smudge's forearm and cleaned the bald patch with an alcohol wipe.

"Not a good time?" I asked as I waited for the skin to dry. His drifting gaze settled briefly in my vicinity and looked blank. I nodded at the regimental colours. "The army."

"Had its moments." The pale-blue eyes moved on again, "But getting treated like shit wears thin pretty quick. I spent all my time counting, ten more days 'til a weekend pass, thirty more days 'til home leave, two hundred days and I'm out of this crap."

"We do cover-ups," I told him and nodded at the tattoo again.

"No thanks. Some things are part of you, they shouldn't be covered. Some people need to bear that in mind."

The restless gaze landed briefly on Yakky and his client. Without bothering to look up from his pasty white canvass, Yakky told him there were other tattoo shops in London, if he didn't like our attitude. He said it mildly enough but there was a certain quality to his voice. Tension tended to lodge in Yakky's shoulders and neck. Anger could thicken his raw meat accent to a grunt. By that point you'd probably left it too late to duck. In the silence that followed I fired up my tattoo gun. He didn't jump, but there was a decided twitch from Smudge as the needle started buzzing.

"You ready?"

Smudge nodded but I felt the muscles in his forearm bunch up. Not everyone takes to the needle. The old song about tattoos being addictive is just how the blank rationalise the illustrated. Some people suffer for my art. Normally, I do my best to put them at ease. Normally.

"Johnny rates our work, then?" I said, running the needle home.

"Oh, yeah. He's always showing off his latest tatt."

Johnny was a fairly regular customer, or had been. His tastes hadn't run to demanding pieces and he tended to land in whichever chair was free. By chance, that had mainly been Yakky's. That was why I hadn't recognised his name when Sue had first asked me about him. And, of course, in the shop we called him Knuckles. The first time he'd come to us, he'd wanted YOUR NEXT emblazoned across his knuckles. The ensuing grammar lesson had been painful in length.

I told Smudge I hadn't seen Johnny for a while.

"He'll turn up. He's probably gone up to Derby to see his folks."

He flattened the consonants of 'Derby' in a caricature of a Black Country accent.

"Odd he missed the funeral."

I was keeping my head bent to my work but I felt his gaze land on me again. Having nothing to hold on to, it slid away. People get fixated on eye contact when they have awkward conversations. It's a mistake. Nailing someone down with your sincerity just makes them twitch.

"That's a club issue," he said.

"So, what's that mean? Once Johnny rolls up he gets the bejeezus knocked out of him for missing the Prez's send off?"

"It means: it isn't your concern."

"I knew Dago when you were still swimming around in your dad's bollocks."

"Then you should know he was due some respect."

Smudge's languid reply came just as I was inking Dago's name and a flash of grief caught me off guard. I took the needle out of Smudge's skin because I didn't trust myself not to dig it in him.

"The reason the club started at all was because Dago cared about the people in it."

"It's still a club matter."

I pretended to adjust the seating of the needle, but by then my focus was on Yakky. On the edge of my vision, he'd repositioned himself so his back was to Smudge. The buzz of his tattoo gun had stopped. I wasn't surprised to see his free hand drift to the base of his customer's chair.

A lot of small business owners keep something behind the counter for those hard-to-please clients, pickaxe handles for example. I put my faith in personal charm and Ezulie Dantor. Yakky, faithless soul, offered communion with a claw hammer.

I told Smudge I got his point and gave him a quick flash of eye contact, so I'd look contrite. Though I was less worried about keeping him sweet than keeping Yakky out of prison. I started putting the ink in again. For a few beats the only sound in the backroom was my machine and the music from the shop's computer. Eventually, Yakky's tattoo gun started buzzing again; I figured he wasn't about to do something blunt and painful. The room was still strung ridged and, when I heard a yelp from the waiting room, I nearly leapt to the door. I took a moment to realise the noise had been laughter.

"Just Micky starting his routine," Smudge assured me.

My jumpiness hadn't been lost on him.

Micky must have cracked another joke because there was more giggling echoed by a new voice. I said I was going make myself another tea and went out to the front desk.

The young goth girl was still giggling, and had one hand over her mouth. The gesture ruined her undead aesthetic. The other laugh belonged to a woman who was flipping through an album of Yakky's designs. She was close to fifty, nearer to my age than Micky's, but his stream of patter had her giggling like a schoolgirl. The man himself was stationed at the window, his attention more on the road outside than on his audience.

I wondered why he wasn't sitting with his freshly minted fan club.

"Turning on the charm, Mick?" I said to get his attention.

He spoke without the passive aggressive bit and gave me a smile.

"Just can't turn it off, Doc."

The two women laughed again.

"Must be a curse," I told him flatly and his smile faltered.

I crossed to the front door and beckoned him to follow me out. I stood at the side of his Moto Guzzi, because if I was likely to take his bike over as I fell, he'd be less inclined to punch me out. Micky looked slightly baffled.

"Something up?"

"Yeah, something's up. I don't like being told where to get off and I particularly don't like being told it second-hand."

He still looked baffled and held his hands up, in a *whoa there* gesture.

"Doc, I don't know what you're talking about."

I squinted at him in silence for a couple of seconds and found I believed him. I took a deep breath.

"So, Frenchy's stepped up now?" He nodded. "Well, next time you see El Presidente, tell him if he's got something to say to me, he can come and tell me himself. I don't appreciate him sending errand boys. Got that?"

"I'll tell Frenchy what you said Doc, but I still don't know what the fuck you're talking about."

I was breathing hard and took another moment to calm down. There wasn't any mileage in getting stroppy with Micky. He had fifteen years and sixty kilos on me. He was also a veteran of two war zones.

"Nine o'clock this morning; I tell Frenchy I'm looking for Johnny, now Smudge is in my chair, telling me to stay out of club business. With you holding his hand."

The office of sergeant-at-arms didn't officially exist in the HLB. It hadn't been Dago's style. In as much as the role didn't exist, Micky wasn't it.

"A mate's getting a tattoo, I just came along for a ride. That's –"

He didn't finish the sentence. A couple of bikes pulled into the top of the road, moving fast. Black Micky's head snapped round in their direction. He didn't look scared, but his face was set and his pupils massively dilated. The bikes, crumbling dispatchers' hacks, rattled past the shop and out the other end of the road.

I left Micky to regain his cool and went back to finish Smudge's half-hearted tribute. The laughing and giggling started up again soon after, so I assumed Mick was back inside, doubtless stationed at the window. Back on hand-holding duty.

Yakky had a late evening client that kept him at the shop. I closed for business and spent an hour cleaning, tidying the books, keeping an eye on things and waiting for him to finish. I don't know what I was expecting to happen, but I started making him nervous and he finally told me to piss off.

I retreated to my flat and angled the better of my armchairs so it faced the wall. I sat and stared at the bare plasterwork as my tea went cold. Then I rounded up a few stray tarot packs, to cull some symbolism from, and took hold of a charcoal pencil.

I put a timeline on the wall. The first entry was September the eighth. The date Dago had died. Something about that didn't feel right. I rubbed until the date was a charcoal smudge and replaced it with August the seventeenth. That was when Dago had come to me about getting the cover-up. I added more dates, blue-tacked cards to the plaster to keep me on the path and committed to charcoal images that ground on my nerves.

A bunch of flowers and a carbon-monoxide detector.

A tin opener and a carton of milk.

A diamond with 1% written in it.

A little girl, hair in bunches, overkill cute. Somebody's 'bestest fwiend'.

I added a cluster of question marks. What they lacked baroque impact, they made up for in volume.

Yakky's caller ID appeared on my phone a little before ten o'clock. I don't have a doorbell, and no one can get to my flat unless I unlock the door to the shop's backyard. People who know me well enough to drop in know me well enough to ring ahead.

Yak made himself a tea and sat in the other armchair. He looked at the wall in silence for a while before speaking.

"Just to be sure we're on the same page, Doc. Smudge turned up at the shop today, with Black Micky in tow, to warn you off. That about right?"

"That's how I saw it, and I think he was sent here. So it's not just him telling me to back off, it's possibly the club."

"Any idea why?"

"I figure the Handsome London Boys are either protecting Johnny Simms or protecting themselves. Either way something's got them on edge."

"Traveling in pairs you mean? They might just be working on their tough guy image."

I told him about talking to Micky and the way he tensed when a couple of bikes appeared. Yakky made a grunt that could have meant anything, then pointed at the wall.

"Either way, you're not backing off, are you?" I shook my head. He produced another ambiguous grunt. "That might be a dangerous game."

"Dago thought the world of Mary. If he was still here, he'd be looking for Johnny."

"You weren't his only friend, Doc. Let Frenchy and his boys do it. They know Johnny better than either of us."

"Yeah, maybe you're right."

Yakky didn't say anything for a while then stood and shook his head.

"I'm talking to myself," he said and reached behind him. His jacket was draped over the back of his chair and he was feeling for a pocket. "Thought you might want to see this. I didn't get a chance to show you earlier."

What he finally extracted from his jacket was a bulky grey camera. It was the digital equivalent of a box-Brownie. I remembered Sue asking Mary if she'd seen Dago's camera. Yakky fiddled with buttons for a few moments and handed the camera to me. Johnny's face glared out from the screen on the back. It was a look-straight-ahead-and-don't-smile shot, as used on a million security passes. I scrolled the camera's memory and Johnny appear two more times. Similar pictures, though in the third he looked bored rather than hostile. I suspected he'd done his best to look hard for his ID badge.

"Mary?"

Yakky nodded. "She asked me if I could do a drawing of Johnny, made me promise not to tell her mum she'd given me the camera. I thought I'd slip it back to the house whenever we went back, that way it can be *found*."

"Have you done a portrait of him?"

"Didn't see what harm it would do. She can always throw darts at it if he has done a runner."

He started pulling his jacket on, getting ready to leave. He didn't look too enthusiastic about heading out and I asked him if he fancied breaking the journey home with a drink.

"Not tonight, I've got to get over to Chiswick."

"What's in Chiswick?"

"Some gay club Karla's heard about. Apparently they put on this cabaret and her friends are all raving about it."

He said *her friends* to rhyme with *bunch of assholes*. Icy sheets of rain greeted him at the front door as he left.

My workings on the wall loomed over me as I sat and finished my tea. They were doing nothing, other than reminding me that I didn't know where Johnny was.

It didn't take long to grate on my nerves and drive me out of the flat.

A surprising number of badass bikers switch to four wheels when it rains. I allowed myself a moment of smug righteousness at their expense. My Sportster brought the grand total of bikes in The Jericho's car park to three. I parked up close to the other two.

I knew both machines but took scant comfort in their recognition. One was another Sportster, younger than mine but beaten half to scrap. It belonged to Pete the Greek, long-time member of the Eight-Six MC.

The other was Johnny Simms' aging GSX.

5.
Eight-Six and 1%

In the early and mid-seventies, few tabloids went to press without some horror story about rampaging gangs of bikers. The flood of media excitement propagated any number of outlaw motorcycle clubs. Few of them outlasted their members' teenage acne. A handful were the real deal. The Eight-Six MC was among them.

While they'd based themselves on the stateside model – flying their colours as back patches, putting prospective members through the mill – they still managed a definite homegrown flavour. Unusually, the Eight-Six showed no inclination to grow and spread the brand. The London crew formed the first and only charter. For over thirty years they'd resisted, often violently, attempts at closure or absorption by the larger, national clubs.

I had a certain respect for them.

The eye naturally follows converging lines to their endpoint. If you want to lose yourself in a room, don't hide in a corner, take a position a little bit away. People's gaze will flow over you on the way to an endpoint. I slipped into The Jericho and scanned the crowd. Johnny's bike had made it there without him. Its new pilot was easy enough to spot though. He was next to Eddie the Greek, helping him prop the bar up.

Decked out in the obligatory black leather cut-off, he had the outlaw look down pat. But his stance was self-conscious, wearing it like a look rather than his skin. I wasn't surprised to see a white rectangular patch on the front of his jacket reading PROSPECT.

The prospect was eyeing the room, trying to catch people's attention so they'd look away. There weren't that many to catch. The rain was keeping a lot of the regulars at home. Most that had ventured out looked impossibly young, making Eddie the Greek stand out more than usual. Somewhere in his early fifties, he could have passed for late sixties. He was broad but not heavy, with a taste for amphetamines that kept him that way.

His back to the room, he displayed one of the few denim cut-offs still carrying colours. Round about the nineties, hacking the sleeves of a Levi jacket became passé and thick black leather was declared de rigueur. Some clubs insisted on it. Eddie's colours were his original set, which was probably why he was allowed to keep them. Crusted with countless miles and washed out by decades of rain, the patches themselves were almost illegible.

I appeared next to Eddie and said hello just as he'd got the barmaid's attention. He included me in the round, more or less on reflex. It's all in the timing. I pointed to the top shelf where the high-octane stuff lived and said I'd have a tequila. Eddie took the news of the cost with surprising grace.

"What's with the boat?"

He gestured at his own face, meaning mine. The tattoo work was new since I'd last seen him.

"Saves me the bother of smiling," I said.

He shook his head and laughed. "Fucking freak. You still tattooing then?"

I told him I was and he motioned us away from the bar. I felt the prospect's eyes on us but he made no move to follow.

"I might have a bit of work to put your way," he said, once we were sat alone at a table.

Eddie's accent was pure East End but with a strangely slow delivery. It's a trait I found peculiar to second generation London-Greeks. I draped my leather over the back of my chair where it dripped on the carpet. Though it was no drier than mine, Eddie kept his on and, again, he positioned himself with his back to the room. Club presence on parade.

"You got something special in mind?"

I hadn't put ink into one of the Eight-Six for years. Their current membership boasted one professional tattooist and a talented amateur. They offered club rates that ensured a closed shop.

Eddie leaned over his glass and stole a quick look to the bar, and the prospect.

"Might have a cover-up done. Club stuff."

He held my gaze for a little while, making sure the message had got through.

"You in bad standing?" I asked.

Eddie told me wasn't but not before taking another check on his prospect.

"It's just time to go."

The hordes of cyberbikers out there, riding their keyboards across the Badlands of the internet, provided plenty of stories about MC members who decide to leave. And what happened to their tattoos. Blow touches featured heavily. It has happened, most things have, but it's more myth than event. Attitudes to the ink allowed to ex-members vary from club to club. And differed depending on the manner of their leaving.

After three decades of riding under the same banner, Eddie the Greek was hanging up his spurs. I could understand that. People change, even if they don't want to. Bodies wear out, no getting away from it. Life in the fast lane and a taste for women half his age weren't taking any miles off Eddie's clock.

The cover-up idea I was struggling with. Up to a point I always would. I believed in tattoos like some people believe in marriage. It's all about commitment. Without devotion, loyalty, you might as well hang your ink on the wall. I wore my victories and defeats in the same shroud and they could sing my history clear and true.

But business is business.

I talked over a few ideas with Eddie. It was a back piece he wanted covered. The club colours had been set, full size, across his spine. The numerals eight and six in Gothic font, to their right, the letters MC, for motorcycle club. Below, in an upward arc like a cradle, the legend: LONDON. The Eight-Six had never bothered with the 1% diamond that most outlaw clubs carried.

The 1% handle dated back to the forties. A spokesman for the American Motorcycle Association had described the hell raisers appearing at bike events as the one percent of riders who gave the rest a bad name. In the way of shameful brands, it soon became a badge of honour.

I gave Eddie a ballpark figure for the work he was after. He pulled an unconvincing expression of horror. I didn't intend dropping the price. If he wanted discounts, he could take his chances with his club's needles.

Unbidden, the prospect appeared with a fresh drink the moment Eddie's empty glass touched the table. I waited for an introduction that wasn't forthcoming. When the prospect paused after delivering the drink, Eddie asked if he was *expecting a fucking tip*.

I watched the prospect make his way back to the bar and wondered how he came to be riding Johnny's GSX.

I asked if Eddie and the prospect were there to make a point.

Eddie shook his head.

"Just fancied a quiet drink on my lonesome." He followed a girl, barely out of her teens, across the room with his eyes. To his credit, he was looking more out of nostalgia than hope. He wasn't given to middle age delusions and knew his dog days were memories. I nodded in the direction of the silent prospect. Eddie shrugged and started on his fresh pint. "There's a bit of a flap on, something and nothing."

"What, if you're in your colours you go around in pairs?"

"Club policy at the moment."

"You hear about Dago?"

"What about him?" he said.

I looked for any tell he might have, but as far as I could see, he was genuine.

"He was killed. Couple of weeks back, some prick in a car hit him then left him for dead."

Genuine shock, too, I judged.

"I hadn't heard. That's gutting, that really is, I liked old Dago." We toasted Dago and Eddie slumped in his chair. He looked even older for a moment. "When was this?" I gave him the date and he nodded slowly. "I was over in Spain." He flicked his eyes to the ceiling. "Ironic in it?"

"Holiday?"

"Should have been." He stopped talking and I made a big thing about looking blank so he'd carry on. "Annual club run to the sun. All the lads take off to Madrid for a week. Meant to be a big family thing, all the old ladies, kids and all."

"What do you mean *meant* to be?"

"My boy's up north, at university, and couldn't go, my daughter's living with some prick in Bristol. I don't hear from her much."

I struggled to remember the name of the woman he'd been with when I'd last spoken to him. In the end, I had to play the pronoun game.

"What about the old lady?"

He shrugged. "Genie did a flit just after Christmas. Haven't heard from her since, not a word."

I guessed he hadn't been the only single bloke at the run but he was likely the most senior of them. Eddie was an old school party animal. Drink and screw until you collapse in a heap, then do it again. Sleep only happened to other people. Until the uppers ran out. It wasn't a lifestyle that came with a pension plan, or a lot in the way of fulfilment. Leading the life gave way to trying to keep up, and then to lagging behind. At some point the party turned into a chore. An aura of sadness hung around him. The smell of a retired war horse.

"I'm too old for this game," he said and hid behind his glass. "Time to let the young guns take it on."

"The scene's getting younger," I allowed.

He took another swallow of beer before answering. "Way it is, isn't it? It's all different these days anyway, not much of a laugh." I left the questions unsaid and he obliged by filling the empty space. "The guys coming into to it now, they're all different. Too much worry about money, take themselves too serious. You know what I mean?"

I thought about Johnny's GSX. I also wondered if some of the up and coming 'serious' guys had been online, reading about blow torches.

"You looking to cover-up the club tattoos before you tell anyone you're moving out?"

Eddie took my meaning and dismissed the idea with a grimace

"Nah, I've done twenty years plus. I'll be allowed to keep my tatts." He looked embarrassed. "I just want to draw a line under it and I fancy a big back piece. Wouldn't feel right asking Leigh or Portney to do it." I had no idea who Leigh or Portney were but assumed they'd be the club's resident tattoo artists. "Once I'm not paying club dues every month, I'll have a bit of cash spare."

I didn't ask what the monthly dues were; it wasn't my business and he wouldn't have told me.

I kept an eye on Eddie's glass and went to get my round in when it was down to the last couple of inches. I wasn't in any rush to lavish my money on Eddie's liver but I wanted a chat with the prospect.

I got Eddie yet another pint and restricted myself to a clear head and orange juice. When I asked the prospect what he was having he said lager and nodded his thanks.

"Is that your GSX out front?" I got an affirmative in the monosyllabic. It was hard to decide whether he was being evasive or just working on his attitude. "I love those old Suzukis," I lied. "What is it, an eighty-one?" I got another grudging yes. "It's in good nick, you had it long?"

He managed to join enough syllables together to tell me a *couple of years*, which made us both liars.

I gave Eddie one of my cards, knocked my orange juice back and called it a night.

Back home, I made a few additions and notations to the wall. It was still giving me more problems than solutions. After staring at it for an hour, I got into bed with Miss Marple.

At one in the morning my phone woke me up. It was Yakky calling to tell me Black Micky had been stabbed.

6.
Old Jokes and Employment References

Yakky had tried training as a nurse. He'd completed two years of the course before giving it up to sling ink for a living. That's how he met Karla. She'd been training at the same time and stayed for the duration. Even though he'd quit, Yak had spent enough time in hospitals to be left with a certain clinical detachment. With his natural deadpan demeanour, it made him look a cold-hearted bastard, on occasion.

From the account he gave me, it would have been easy to think he'd left Micky bleeding and headed out the door before the blue crew arrived. I knew Yakky well enough to know there'd be more to the story than that, so I didn't press him for mitigating details.

"Where are you now?"

"I'm back home. Karla's a bit upset so she's going to stay here tonight."

There was an indigent squeal in the background and I assumed Karla didn't want me being privy to her private life.

"Do you know what hospital they took him to?"

Yakky told me no, then something else was said in the background.

"Karla says the nearest A&E to the club is at the Royal Bailing." There was more noise and I heard Yakky put his hand over the phone. When he came back on the line he said, "I might be running a bit late tomorrow. I'll be in though. You okay with that?"

I told him I was and, before he hung up, I heard Karla call out again. It looked like his evening was going to be pleasantly exhausting or miserably draining. My money was on the latter.

On the basis he was single, I tried Silk's number. I didn't imagine I'd be thanked for waking Jason and his wife, in the small hours.

Silk picked up on the first ring, then took a long time to speak. I thought the line had been broken, but realised I could hear music softly playing.

Finally, he said, "Who is it?"

He sounded confused and, in a moment's panic, I pictured him bleeding from a head wound. Then he said *hellllooooo*, in a stern voice and burst out laughing. My imagination substituted the head wound for a haze of smoke.

The second time I told him Black Micky had been knifed, the message got through. I could almost hear the clang as his mood changed and the downer hit him. He had a couple beats of confusion and asked me what he should do before announcing, possibly to himself, that he'd call the hospital then get on to Frenchy.

Since the club was now informed, I decided I'd done my bit and hung up.

Tuesday 19 September

I let Yakky put a jug of coffee away before I asked him about the previous night. He'd come into the road doing sixty and laid seven foot of rubber down when he pulled up. He'd been on time, despite his warnings, but the aggressive ride had nothing to do with punctuality.

The club had been a place called The Salt Lick. Billed as a gay review bar, it was a money-making proposition in drag. The cabaret nights attracted a steady flow of single women looking a fun night out, minus the drunken advances. The Salt Lick wore its LGBT credentials as a seal of quality rather than as a commitment to a way of life.

Yakky had pulled a double take when he'd spotted Black Micky on the door.

"Micky's got to be the only bouncer in London who actually looks good in a tux." He made the low grating noise that he thought was a laugh. "He's stood there, all muscles and chiselled features, getting the glad eye off half the blokes going through the door. When he saw I'd recognised him, he nearly died of embarrassment."

I laughed too. Then remembered why we were talking about him.

"Did you see who shivved him?"

"Nah. Me and Karla were over the other side of the dance floor."

The crowd began to the thin as a knot of panic made its way to the doors. The strapping six-footer, doing the Madonna tribute, found he was singing acapella when the music stopped.

Karla, reverting to her day job, had gone into nurse mode and made her way to the bar. Yakky followed and they found Micky was the centre of attention once again. A second bouncer was kneeling at his back, sitting him up. Someone else was holding a bar towel to his side.

"There was nothing else we could do. I checked someone had called for a meat truck and told Karla we ought to vamoose. Bang," – he clicked his fingers – "suddenly I'm the bad guy."

Yakky had said he didn't want to spend the night waiting to tell the police he hadn't seen anything. Karla had consented to drive him back to his place, then sermonised about social duties all the way.

It struck me she'd had it both ways, enjoying the view from the moral high ground even as she drove away from it. I played the diplomat and kept my opinions private. Yakky, normally steady as Gibraltar, was often thrown off balance by his on-again-off-again fiancée. They'd been circling each other for years, getting further apart with each orbit. I thought it was time they called it a day. I kept that myself too. Relationships are like booze. No one can *tell* you you've got a problem, you need to see it for yourself.

"Anyway," Yakky said, still venting about Karla's moral posturing, "I'm not going to shed many tears over the likes of

Black Micky."

"What's the problem with Mick?"

"Nasty piece of work. He dragged Spooky round the back of some club a few weeks back and beat him witless."

"In aid of what?"

Yakky shrugged. "The way Spooky tells it, Micky caught him making a *big* sale. It was probably half an ounce of blow, you know what he's like."

Spooky was a part-time dealer who, from the seat of his minicab, talked like a one-man drugs cartel. The pittance he made dealing went, mostly, on pay-as-you-go mobiles that he called burners. He made a big thing of throwing one away every other week, so it couldn't be traced. The big talk had earned him police attention and a criminal record, which fuelled his delusions. A taste for Russian prison-style tattoos meant each stint of community service was celebrated in Cyrillic lettering. Sitting in Yakky's chair, he'd mistaken poker-faced indifference for respectful silence. And Yakky gained a regular.

"You reckon he gave Micky some lip?"

"More than likely, but it was still over the top. He had a face like a butcher's apron."

"Was this in Chiswick, the club you were at?"

"Nah, I think it was that one up the road, The House of Ice."

The club Smudge ran security for.

Towards the end of the day, I rang Frenchy's yard. After our last meeting I wasn't sure how we stood and the call was, at least in part, self-serving. Calling to ask about the health of Micky was a friendly gesture. It also reminded El Presidente that I'd been the one to inform the club it had happened.

"Why didn't you call me first?" Frenchy said, a pause and a sharp breath as he lit up. "Some bastard knifes one of my people and I don't get to hear about it 'til I get into work."

Leaving Silk to spread the news evidently hadn't been a wise move.

"I don't have your mobile number, how was I meant to tell you at one in the morning?"

"I was here, in the yard, until two."

"And I'm supposed to fucking know that, am I?"

Yakky's next client looked up from the tattoo magazine he'd been skimming. I mouthed an apology and took the phone call outside. Frenchy's answer was lost somewhere en route and, whatever it had been, I decided I could live without it.

I perched on the saddle of Yakky's bike, making the suspension sag.

"Anyway, how's Micky?"

I heard Frenchy take another draw on his cigarette, as he debated whether or not to answer.

"He'll be okay. Smudge got in to see him and said it wasn't that bad."

"He's allowed visitors?"

"Friends and family." He emphasised the words with a pause. "I was about to head over and see him myself."

There was another pause, so I'd know being on the phone was the only thing holding him back.

"I'll let you go, French, just give Micky my best, can you do that?"

He told me he would and hung up.

Yakky had asked if I wanted him to come with me to the hospital. I'm not sure what he thought was going to happen there. His default setting was mistrust, so I guessed he was expecting trouble. It was an offer I wanted to take up, but it was hard enough to keep a lid on my own paranoia without Yakky adding his to the brew.

Once the last customer had left, I nipped up to my flat and made a few offerings. Then I hid my right cheek under a layer of concealer. It made me look like I was covering a birthmark instead of frightening the horses. I dug out the chinos and long sleeve shirt that only my bank manager normally sees and rang for a minicab.

The dash, from the patient drop-off zone to the hospital

entrance, was enough to get me soaked. The Royal Bailing wouldn't be my first of choice of hospital. The entrance was a scuffed, grey atrium. It was dotted with posters telling you to get a flu jab, give up smoking and not beat up the staff.

A bored porter sat behind an oversized desk that blended organically with the floor. I told him a friend of mine had been brought in with a stab wound the night before, and then I told him again when he'd finished his text. After some guided computer work, he established Micky had been moved from the A&E department to the thoracic ward.

The porter pointed at the floor. It was inlayed with a dozen different strips of colour, like a map of the underground.

"Follow the blue line, until it becomes a green line, then follow the signs for the Randell ward." I assumed the instructions were meant for me, although they were addressed to the screen of his phone.

The line of blue vinyl I was meant to follow ran out after about three steps and the floor became a uniform grey. In the end I wandered around until I found someone in a white coat and asked them.

When I got to the Randell ward, a couple of posters asked me to not beat up the staff and to clean my hands with alcohol gel from the empty dispenser. Another sign said I should have visited six hours earlier. The doors were locked. I looked through the wire-enforced glass halfway along the tunnel of rooms. Half a dozen nurses and a pair of security guys were gathered at a desk.

If you wanted to get in after hours, there was an intercom affair with a camera lens poking out of it. My finger hovered over it briefly before I thought better of it. Outside of visiting hours, no doubt, there were rules about letting the general public onto the wards. With the number of staff around the reception desk, one of them was bound to want to play it by the book. It's easy to refuse a voice on an intercom.

There was a stack of plastic chairs in the corridor, should anyone want to sit and take in the view. I put one near the lift and sat down. When someone approached I'd hear their footsteps before they saw me. If they came in the lift I'd hear it rattle. I was just out of sight of the thoracic ward, but if the doors opened, I'd hear them pop.

One thing you could count on in the Bailing Royal was noise, every piece of equipment in it grumbled with age.

I didn't have long to wait. The lift arrived ten minutes later, sounding like it was sliding down a slipway into the ocean. I stood and did my best to look like I'd just arrived. A guy shouldered through the sluggish doors and struggled to pull a waste skip with him. The wheels caught on the ledge between the corridor and the lift floor.

I gave the hopper a tug and, between us, we got it out. He mumbled something I assumed was a thank you. I pointed towards the Randell ward, pulled an embarrassed face and flashed my driving licence. It showed him nothing but my photo, pre-facial tattoo, and the word 'Doctor' in front of my name.

"Couldn't let me in, could you? I've left my swipe card somewhere."

His flash card opened the doors with a grinding hiss, and I was in.

The knot of staff at the desk had diminished since I'd sat down. It was now three nurses and the security guys. I was saved the uncomfortable where-do-I-look bit as I walked towards them because they were chatting.

I headed for the bigger of the security guys and stood beside him at the desk, emphasising how small and harmless I was. I settled on the more senior nurse and did my best to appear embarrassed, again.

I explained Micky's mother was one of my *congregation* and she was understandably worried about her son. The poor lady also had a phobia about hospitals. I didn't put my hands up in a gesture of prayer, but I kept my fingertips together, slightly in front of my stomach. People heard the word 'congregation' and filled in the blanks how they thought best.

I was given five minutes.

The bay Micky was in had six beds, each with an occupant

boasting a big plastic bottle by their side. The bottles were filling with some sort of body fluid. Micky's was alone in being tinted with blood. And his beside cabinet was the only one draped with a leather cut-off.

The tube from Micky's bottle snaked under the sheets and into his right side. Physically he wasn't looking too bad. There was swelling at the corner of his mouth and a tiny split in his bottom lip. Other than that, and the tubing of course, he looked intact. But the bay was uncomfortably warm and he had the sheets and blankets pulled up to his chin, like a child. I touched his shoulder carefully and he jolted awake.

"It's alright Mick, it's just me."

Micky did a quick scan of the bay before acknowledging me. He asked me what time it was and I told him half-eight.

"I'm surprised they let you in."

His gaze flickered over the splodge of makeup.

I told him it was all down to good looks and charm. It got a smile. There weren't any chairs, so I squatted on my haunches, elbows on the edge of the bed and fingers laced together. From the door, it might have looked like I was praying. An activity people seldom interrupt.

"I heard you got shivved, what's the damage?"

He put on a face I couldn't read.

"Broken rib, punctured lung, that's what this is in aid of." He pointed awkwardly at bottle on the floor. "Reinflating the lung."

"Painful?"

"Not really, the cracked rib's the worst of it."

"So, what happened?"

He might have been aiming for nonchalance, because he tried shrugging, not a smart move with a busted rib. His breath caught, making him cough and causing another shock of pain.

When he told me the story he was still going for the too-hard-to-cry look. It didn't gel with way he jumped at every creak from the surrounding beds. Or with the way he kept an eye on the door. Or the way he had the sheets coyly pulled up to his chin. The Black Micky I knew would have been trying to impress the nurses with his six-pack.

He'd been working the door with another bouncer he didn't know very well. They'd been called inside to evict some minor problem – a couple of guys getting into it over something and nothing. Micky had held back, wanting to see how the other bouncer would handle it. When it was clear his presence wasn't needed, he headed back to the door and got sucker-punched as he turned. He thought he'd been winded, until the pain kicked in and someone screamed.

"Punch-knife, doctors said I was lucky it was the right side. If it'd had been the left…"

He didn't finish the sentence. Getting stuck with a punch-knife hard enough to break a rib means somebody meant business. A wound that deep in the left side would have had a good shot at finding the heart. I asked if he had any ideas who'd done it. He answered too quickly to be telling the truth.

"No idea. It was crowded, shit music and a lightshow."

No one else had seen anything either. In the way of most nightclub violence, by the time the blue crew turned up, the crowd had vanished. Yakky's exit had hardly been partisan.

"Was it just the two of you working the door?"

"Gay club," he said, as if that explained everything. I must have looked less than enlightened because he added, "Don't get much trouble. Most of the time, we're there to ward off the more obvious dealers. The wannabe hard cases don't want to be seen in a gay club, so it's an easy ride most of the time."

"You work it with Smudge?"

Micky laughed and the bottle on the floor bubbled, laughing hurt too so it didn't last long.

"Nah, not Smudge. He has his hands full with The House of Ice and that other place down the road. He pretty well runs the security entirely in those. If he'd been doing security at this place, this wouldn't have gone down."

I wondered if he was right about that.

"Frenchy told me Johnny was looking for door work."

"Did he?"

Expressionless response.

"Smudge gave him the knock back. That right?"

Micky shrugged again, then remembered it hurt. "Look, Doc, thanks for dropping by, but I'm kind of tired."

If he'd been able to roll over and turn his back on me, it might have ended there. But I was at his left side and he couldn't roll on to his right because of the lung drain.

"Now, I've heard off a few people Smudge and Johnny were tight. Johnny needs a job, goes to his best mate, best mate and club brother, and gets a *no*. How's that work?"

Micky had closed his eyes, but he was listening. I let the silence drag for a bit.

"Johnny didn't have the style. Working the doors is about stopping trouble. There's more to it than being good in a fight. Sometimes someone gets a smack, but mostly they get a warning. Johnny boy couldn't do that, he'd go in at ramming speed. And he lied about his CRB, told Smudge he was pure as the driven and he wasn't…isn't"

"He didn't think Smudge would check?"

"Well, he might not have done. A few of the regular crew have a shady history and, generally speaking, Smudge'll take club guys at their word." Micky hissed air through his teeth, then looked me in the eye. "Doc, you really need to leave this alone."

I waited and it became clear, Micky was willing to let the silence hang this time.

I leaned closer and told him softly, "That's where you are wrong, my friend. I don't *have to do* anything." I pointed at the cut-off, with its HLB patch, hanging on his cabinet. "'Cos I ain't wearing a little patch on the front of my jacket that says what I can and can't do. I'll tell you something else…brother…you want to think, long and hard about jacking that front patch up into a full back patch."

Flat lung or no, Micky was breathing pretty hard. Though, he'd lost the ability to blink it seemed. I decided to lighten the mood with a joke that had done the rounds when I was kid.

"Do you know why you don't get Mods in Belfast, Micky? 'Cos no bugger wants to walk down the Shankill Road with a target on their back. You want a target on your back, Mick?"

He didn't laugh. Must be the way I tell 'em.

"What's it to you what the club does?" he said.

"I'll level with you Mick: fuck all. But Dago was one of my oldest friends and his widow wants me to find one of the guys he'd taken under his wing."

I left out Sue's reasons for wanting Johnny Simms found.

Micky didn't say anything at first, then he barked out a laugh and had to clench his jaw. After a few slow breaths he gave me a nasty smile.

"Under Dago's wing? That shows what you fucking know. Oh yeah, Dago loved Johnny to bits. He told Smudge, he'd be idiot to employ him. Smudge wanted to give him a chance, Dago told him he'd throw him out the club if he did. Really looking out for him."

Some of what we were saying, or least the tone of it, must have been overheard. A nurse and one of the security guards came to tell me my time was up.

I got another taxi home and rang Yakky's mobile to find he was out with Karla. I don't know where they'd headed to, but it sounded quiet when he answered, so I guessed at a restaurant. If they'd gone from fun night of gay cabaret, to arguing, to quiet restaurant, then they were probably having a serious *adult talk* kind of an evening. I toyed with the idea of winding him up and decided against it. I'd generated enough bad feeling for one night. I told him Micky was okay but pointed out someone had taken a lot of trouble to shiv him.

"Is Spooky still dealing?" I asked.

Yakky took a beat to adjust to the change of tack. "He was the last time I saw him, why?"

"I need to get hold of some Billy."

7.
Billy Whizz and a Pain in the Neck

Friday 22 September

Yakky arrived at work in the back of Spooky's minicab that morning. He'd paid an uncommonly large fare but got to keep the plastic bag he'd found on the rear seat.

When I'd explain why I wanted five grams of Billy Whizz, Yakky had said he'd go along for the ride. I'd given it some thought before accepting the offer. Now we'd finished work for the day and were getting ready to head over to Kilburn.

"What the fuck are you doing?" Yakky asked.

It was a reasonable question. I'd taken a pinch of the dirty-white powder and was working it against the side of the sink, with my finger.

"Checking to see how much of this is Ajax."

There was limited impact on the tannin stains. I judged the amphetamine to be relatively free of scouring powder, one of the more common cutting agents. The kitchen sink test wouldn't rule out a thousand other impurities but there was only so much I could do.

"You want any of this before I mix it up?" I asked.

Yakky grunted and shook his head. I doubled the weight of the speed by folding it into a pile of self-raising flour. The plastic bag was bulging once I'd refilled it. It looked more generous. It was also a far less dirty white than what I'd started with. That made it look purer. I sealed the plastic bag and zipped it into a pocket of my bike jacket.

Yakky rode pillion with me over to his place to pick up his bike. I waited at the kerb while he went in to collect his keys and check on his old man. He was gone for a while and when he finally came out, his dad appeared in the front window, taking his cue to look forlorn.

Yakky unchained the Yamaha and began the ritual of getting it to start. He didn't look up at any point. His dad was still pressed up against the window as we rode off.

Spots was a twenty-four-hour pool hall with a drinks licence. It was an afterthought, tacked onto a members' only snooker club. Somewhere or other, it must have had a front door, but I'd never seen it. I always parked around the back and went up the fire escape. Spots was on the first floor.

The bulk of the machinery outside was made up of Eight-Sixers' bikes, Eddie's Sportster and Johnny's erstwhile GSX among them. Someone had sprayed painted '86MC'on the wall, under the Parking for Patrons Only sign. This added to the impression, which a lot of people had, that the building was an official clubhouse.

"Notice the guys in the shadows?" Yakky said quietly.

He was chaining his bike to mine and didn't look up as he spoke. I had seen them, two figures given away by the tips of their cigarettes. They were leant against the wall at the edge of the car park, maybe not hiding but certainly not putting themselves forward. A third man was standing at the top of the fire escape as we went in. I didn't recognise him, but his cut-off designated him as another Eight-Six prospect.

Spots had become more drinking den than pool hall, and the DNA of its origins leant to the under-the-counter feel of the place. The lighting arrays, swinging low over the tables, cast most of the room into shadow. The exception being the island of bright lights behind the tiny bar.

Speakers, lost in the darkness of the ceiling, were chucking out a song I didn't recognise. The volume was quite high, but still the space felt quiet, as if it was absorbing the sound. It had been a few years since I'd ventured in there. The atmosphere hadn't improved since my last visit.

I let my eyes adjust to the gloom and put the head count at around twenty. Only three of the dozen tables were in use, with most of the patrons sitting in a far corner. I spotted three or four people I knew but couldn't see Eddie. Yakky and me made our way over, aware that our progress was being monitored.

Ramsey, who'd gained a patch reading VICE PRESIDENT since we'd last met, shook my hand and his eyes flickered over my tattoo. I assumed Eddie had mentioned seeing me at The Jericho, because the first thing he said was, "You looking for the Bubble?"

Bubble and squeak: Greek.

"Yeah, got a little something might interest him."

I carefully scratched the side of my nose.

One side of Ramsey's mouth curved into the precursor of a smile, though he didn't tell me where Eddie was. His gaze found Yakky, then flicked back to me.

"This is Yakky," I told him. "He's a solid bloke. Yak, Ian Ramsey."

Yakky held out his hand and Ramsey waited a statesman's-like moment before extending his own. Sufficient to demonstrate rank, but not enough to give cause for offence.

Ramsey was gracious and made to lead us away to a door marked private. I could see the direction the vice-presidential parade was headed. We'd get to the door and Ramsey wouldn't let Yakky pass. Trivial power play. I proved myself equal to such pettiness by stealing his thunder; before we got to the door I sent Yakky off to rack up one of the pool tables.

The private door led to the snooker club proper. It was a scaled-up version of the room I'd left Yakky in, minus the crappy bar and air of neglect. Ramsey gave someone or other the nod and the door clicked shut behind me.

Eddie took a bit of finding; the space was huge and the herd of twelve-foot tables was doing good business. When I located him at the far end of the hall, he was playing alone. He acknowledged me, without smiling, and took his shot before speaking. The green banged off two cushions before dropping smoothly into a corner pocket.

"You up for a frame?" he asked. I told him cards were more my game. He nodded. "I had a feeling you'd be around."

"Fancied a chat," I told him and pulled out the bag of self-raising speed.

Eddie managed a smile at last.

I cupped my left hand around the line of powder and inhaled loudly, then I had to pinch the bridge of my nose. Eddie watched my amateurish snorting with indulgent good humour. While he watched my attempts not to sneeze, I smeared the portion of speed, I'd just palmed down the leg of my jeans. Eddie didn't bother with the subtleties of forming a neat line. He teased a pile of Billy from the bag and took it in with one deep snort.

"Smooth," he commented.

I told him I'd pass his compliments to the chef. He folded a stick of gum into his mouth and started chewing.

He knocked the remaining balls around the table for a couple of minutes while the speed kicked in. It didn't take long before his game dropped off and his mouth picked up.

"I hear the HLB are looking to up their rank," I said.

Eddie answered with a bark of laughter. "Yeah, they want to be big boys, big bad boys." He cannoned a red into a corner pocket. "I could have turned pro with this you know?"

"That why you and the prospect were in The Jericho the other night. Show of force?"

"No, not really. Well, yeah maybe, a bit." He hammered another red and missed. "Thing is, now Dago's shuffled off the moral coil, no one's negotiating, so we don't know where we stand. Just being careful."

"So, what was with the prospect rolling up on Johnny's bike?"

The rate of his chewing began to look comical as his brain worked.

"Who's Johnny?"

"Johnny Simms." More frantic chewing and a shake of the head. "He's one of the Handsome London Boys. He ain't been seen for a while and I'm looking to find him. That's his GSX outside."

The look of confusion flapped over Eddie face in a blur. Speed doesn't allow the luxury of confusion. It's a drug that deals exclusively in certainties.

"Give me two seconds," he barked and jittered across to the private door and out, before I could object.

I cursed myself and wondered if I was about to get on the blunt end of a good kicking. Eddie's two seconds became minutes. I debated going back into the pool hall but decided the snooker club contained more impartial witness. That might stop Ramsey and friends stomping me flat.

The snooker club side of things was quieter than the pool hall. Just the soft thud of balls colliding and the hush of serious gamesmanship. Little chit-chat and no music. I could hear the bass-line signature of the track playing on the other side of the door. If it turned sour for Yakky, I'd be able to hear that too. I told myself, if things went that way, I'd go in and help.

After what seemed like an age, Eddie reappeared, moving fast, with the prospect going double time to keep up. Ramsey and a big man I didn't recognise followed them both.

Later, Yakky told me that Eddie had skittered across the pool hall and out onto the fire escape. He bellowed down that China should *get his fucking arse up here*. China, according to Yakky, must have thrown himself up the stairs because he appeared in the doorway almost instantly. None of this was lost on Ramsey, who grabbed one of his men and followed Eddie and China straight back to me. On Yakky's side, another couple of the Eight-Six made sure the *private* door stayed that way.

The four men arrived at me, with Eddie in the lead. He was still chewing manically, and the smell of Juicy Fruit gum engulfed me. China stood slightly behind, looking confused.

"What's going on?" Ramsey demanded and Eddie, latching on to something he could explain, launched into a rapid monologue.

Ramsey had a fairly cool head. I could see why he'd moved up the ranks. He listened to Eddie and hushed him when he'd started to recycle the first telling. He turned to me.

"One of the Handsome Boy's gone AWOL, yeah?"

"Yeah. Johnny Simms, youngish guy, about thirty."

"And the HLB think we had something to do with it?"

"I don't know about that, but I've got my own reasons for wanting to find him. All I know is that's his GSX parked up outside."

Ramsey gave me the hard eye, but Eddie the Greek's tongue couldn't keep still any longer. He started demanding China tell him where he'd got the GSX. The prospect looked over to Ramsey, wanting to know if he should answer. Ramsey nodded, then told Eddie to shut up. Eddie stopped gabbing but started tapping a rhythm out on the side of his leg, counter pointing it with sharp head jerks.

"I lifted the bike about two weeks back. There's this row of condemned houses, opposite me granddad's crib, it was there. When I asked the old bastard about it, he started moaning about squatters. I didn't know it was an HLB bike. I thought it was some fucking hippy's rig."

I asked him for the name of the road. He told me Maple Blossom Parade. I couldn't place it and he said it was over towards Enfield.

Ramsey gave the prospect the hard eye treatment before muttering, "Fair enough." He turned back to me. "He didn't know it was an HLB bike. Call it an honest mistake."

"Looks that way. Can we talk?"

Ramsey gave it the consideration his office demanded and decreed a yes.

We left China and Eddie at the snooker table. Eddie was pulling out the bag of speed as we exited.

I steered Ramsey and the heavy towards the table where Yakky was knocking pool balls around. Yakky's face was his standard blank, though he'd have needed a hammer to hit the cue ball any harder. I'd hoped to make the gathering less confrontational, but it didn't go that way. Yakky and me stood on one side of the pool table, with Ramsey and his mate facing off from the other.

Ramsey didn't make an introduction and his friend didn't volunteer a name. He had a face built in a boxing ring and a patch on his cut-off reading ENFORCER. To drive the point home, he stood with his arms folded across his chest and only blinked on alternate days. I was conscious that Yakky had kept hold of his pool cue. I had my doubts that it would do any good.

I thanked Ramsey for agreeing to talk and his little half smile told me he'd seen through the flattery.

"What's this Johnny fella to you, anyway?" he asked before I could say anything else.

"A friend's daughter is going to be due some child maintenance in the near future. Guess what?"

Ramsey chuckled. "Daddy's done a bunk?"

"Bingo," Yakky told him.

Again, he chuckled. "Well, we've all been there."

"I'm just helping a mate out," I said. "Thing is, I'm being told, by the HLB, to leave Johnny Simms lost. Those guys I'm not going to sweat about, but if the Eight-Six have got Johnny under the wing, that changes things. I'll buy my mate some Mother Care vouchers and leave it at that."

Ramsey nodded, and his half smile made another appearance. Though Yakky and ENFORCER might not have felt it, the tension level dropped a few points.

"I hadn't even heard of Johnny…" He looked blank for comic effect.

"Simms."

"Johnny Simms. I certainly didn't know that was his motor outside. You want to find him, that's your lookout. We ain't going be wet nursing one of the Handsome Boys any time soon."

"So, there is friction then. I thought they seemed a bit edgy."

I thought the same about the Eight-Six but didn't say so.

"They're looking to join the premier league and fly a proper back patch." He grimaced and shook his head. "That went out the window when we found out Dago was dead."

"Was Dago into the back patch idea?"

"He was talking about patching the HLB over to us. Maybe setting them up as a second charter of Eight-Six." He sighed. "Only way it was going to work really. Now he's gone…" He shrugged.

"Now he's gone the HLB want to set up as an entirely separate outfit?"

Ramsey nodded. "Not going to happen. Anyhow, best of British finding Mr Simms." He slapped ENFORCER on the back and, as they walked away from the pool table, said pointedly, "I won't hold you up."

ENFORCER jerked his head in the direction of the door, in case we hadn't got the message.

On the way down the fire escape, I asked Yakky if he fancied a run over to a squat in Enfield.

The only appealing thing about Maple Blossom Parade was its name. The 'Parade' was a double row of terraces, seven to a side. It was part of a cluster of short roads, hemmed in by a convergence of railway lines.

We parked, just beyond the pool of light cast by the one working street lamp, and tried not to look furtive.

"Which one you reckon?" Yakky asked.

The condemned houses, where the GSX had briefly rested, formed a whole side of the street. Their inhabited brothers across the road weren't in much better shape.

We struck three of them off the list pretty quick, one was burnt out, the other two missing their roofs. The four remaining properties all had corrugated iron instead of doors and windows. On the second one we tried, the iron work on the front door had been buckled and pulled away from the frame. It opened like a tent flap. Behind the sheet metal the door was gone and I shone a light into an empty hall way. We'd made a stop for petrol on the way over and picked up a couple of cheap LED torches. I called out a hello that echoed back to me and something, too small to be human, rustled the darkness.

I went inside first and shone the torch up the staircase. Other than damp patches and peeling wallpaper, there wasn't much to see. I did a quick light up of the ceiling to be sure nothing was going to land on our heads. It sagged in places and, at the far end, was pregnant with slowly dripping water. The stink of damp and rot was overpowering and there was a cloying sweetness behind it. Not sweet in a pleasant way.

I rubbed dust off the top of the newel post at the foot of the stairs and hung my lid on it. Behind me Yakky fumbled with his jacket and another beam of light joined mine.

"Anyone home?" I called out, the damp and rot swallowed the words whole and nobody answered. "We're looking for a friend of ours; we'll look round then we're gone. We've not here to cause anyone problems."

We waited in silence and all we could hear was water dribbling out of the ceiling.

We started in the front room, because it was closest. At some point the house had had a visitor or two. The walls were coated with a spray can's worth of graffiti and, if the writing on the wall was to be believed, Jools and Susie were *4-ever*. Who says romance is dead?

I shone my torch across the floor, saw where somebody had ripped up some of the boards and yanked the copper central heating pipes up into view. If it was an attempt to strip the metal for scrap, it had been a fairly half-hearted one, or they'd been disturbed.

The backroom and kitchen were empty too, though somebody had taken the trouble to smash the cabinets.

We ducked carefully under the water filled bulge in the ceiling and started up the stairs. They were still carpeted, and the sodden fibre was slippery with mould. The treads held but the big one at the top, where the stairs turned ninety degrees to meet the landing, creaked and gave slightly.

I called out another warning of our presence when I was on the landing. I didn't want to startle some meth's drinker into making his last stand.

The doors on the top floor were all intact, but the ceiling

plaster was gaping away like a skin condition. The thick, sweet smell was more obvious.

The first door Yakky nudged open, using his boot, was the bathroom. The smell was horrendous. Somebody had used the toilet and tried to flush it by pouring a bottle of water into the pan. The empty plastic bottle lay on the floor. Yakky made a disgusted noise and pulled the door closed again, the smell lingered on the landing.

Yakky, because he was closest, pushed open the door of the back bedroom. Now we knew someone had been there, recently, he was very cautious. When the door was open enough to see into the room, but not wide enough to let anyone come flying out, Yak called out, not too loud,

"If there's anyone here, stay calm, we're just look…" The sudden silence was very loud but short lived. Yakky muttered, "Christ," and kicked the door back against the wall.

He barrelled in, scanning the room with his torch. I followed with no idea of what he'd found. The smell in the room was worse than the toilet.

Yakky was kneeling by the far wall, playing the torch over a slumped shape that turned out to be Johnny. As I recognised this, Yakky stood and backed away.

"Is he…" I didn't want to say dead, but it was the obvious line of inquiry. Yakky took the light away from the body and led us back to the landing.

"We need to get out of here," he said. "He's been garrotted."

I nodded and grabbed hold of the banister, until the tremor stopped. I could hear Yakky breathing, deep and very slow. Carefully controlled.

"I want to have a look around," I told him.

"What Would Miss Marple Do?"

"Something like that, yeah."

Yakky barked out a laugh, much higher than his normal growl. He cut it off, before it took on a life of its own.

"You're mad as a shithouse rat, you know that?"

I turned and edged the beam of my torch slowly towards

the doorway of the back bedroom. Matters of my sanity aside, we had to make sure he was dead. I kept the torch low and lit the body, a bit at a time. Feet, legs, torso and then the neck.

Johnny Simms was very dead.

The garrotte had been made from a strand of thick wire with its ends twisted around two lengths of dowel – they looked like cut-offs from a broom handle – to act as grips. The wire was only visible near the handles. Where it had been wrapped around his neck it was too deeply buried to be seen. I estimated the meat of Johnny's neck had been cinched in at least an inch.

I played the light around the room, still keeping it low.

There was a camping stove in one corner with a solitary saucepan, empty and clean. Johnny's body was slumped on a camo-patterned sleeping bag. The bag had been unrolled on a layer of plastic sheeting. It seemed improbably bulky and, when I took a closer look, I saw it had been lined with a single devout. Like the kind I hadn't found at the bedsit. An upturned milk crate was acting as a table with a wash bag and an electric lantern standing on it. A full-face crash helmet with a pair of winter riding gloves were stowed in one corner. Next to them was a six-pack of Australian lagers and a stack of canned food. Along with the tin opener that had bothered me so much.

Johnny's face was discoloured and barely recognisable. I'd know him by the tattoos on his knuckles. The day he'd come to the shop, after we'd explained the difference between YOUR NEXT and YOU'RE NEXT, he'd settled on another design: HAND SOME.

The sound of Yakky stepping into the room broke me from my contemplation of Johnny's hands. I realised the foul smell was coming directly from the body.

"Bowels probably opened as he was choked," Yakky said. "Poor bastard."

I nodded my agreement and as I did I heard a siren. It was a long way off and nothing to do with us, still it reminded me that we were knee-deep in a crime scene.

"We better get gone, Yakky."

We left separately. I let Yakky go first, on the basis that my bike could be relied on to start and not leave me stranded. Before he slipped through the gap in the corrugated iron, he told me to go home via his place.

Yakky's bike cooperated for once and I heard it clatter out the end of the road. I forced myself to wait ten minutes before following. It was possibly too late to worry about such precautions, but paranoia plays a seductive song. When I eventually left the house, I turned right and walked away from my bike. I took a stroll around the block, passed another ten minutes in the dark and came to my bike from the opposite end of the street. I rode to Yakky's place with one eye on the speedo and the other on the legions of traffic cameras.

Yakky opened his door before I'd shut my engine down. He told me he'd been getting worried and I explained my long-winded journey. I was ushered into the kitchen and, at the speed of a miracle, a mug of tea appeared in front of me. I let myself soak up the warmth and light and, for the first time, it struck me what we'd seen.

Johnny Simms wasn't even Yakky's age. In a different life I might have had a son that old. And he'd been left to rot, sat in his own shit.

Yakky was frying bacon.

I felt I could have easily never touch food again. Then I surprised myself by eating the sandwiches he supplied. Neither of us said anything about Maple Blossom Parade until we'd finished and then Yakky said what I'd been thinking.

"What do we do now?"

"Good question."

I reached into my leather and took out my tarot.

Yakky, as ever, kept his poker face but the muscles around his neck clenched.

If you're a white European practicing Voodoo and tarot, it doesn't serve you well to take censure to heart. If people offered me their disapproval, I tended to rub their faces in it.

Yakky seldom asked questions about my beliefs and, because it was Yakky, his opinion was almost impossible to gauge. But the tension he was carrying suggested there'd been enough time outside the comfort zone for one night. I held off on dealing the cards but let them travel through my repertoire of one-handed cuts.

"Police?" Yakky said, throwing the idea up like a clay pigeon.

I shook my head without giving it much thought.

"What do we tell them, when they ask us what we were doing there?"

"Anonymous call?"

"We just trampled over the crime scene, Yak. We've been asking about Johnny all over town, Christ, I even broke into his bedsit. Don't matter how we involve the blue crew, they're likely to return the favour with a set of handcuffs."

Yakky nodded slowly; he'd known that already.

"Alright, but what then? He's got family somewhere, they've got a right to know he's dead."

That was something *I'd* already known. To the list I also added Sue, not just because she'd been the one who asked us to find Johnny, but because of Mary. If Johnny was the father of the baby she was carrying, then she needed to know as well. Whatever Johnny may have thought of what had gone down, I suspected Mary regarded it as far more than just a leg over. Asking Yakky for a portrait of Johnny suggested a chapter of her life she'd yet to close.

Sue was due another painful conversation with her daughter.

"Won't Sue just go to the police if you tell her?"

I shrugged, a careless gesture, an attempt to fool me as much as Yakky.

"I don't think she will, not if she thinks it'll drop you and me in the shit."

Yakky decided he wasn't hyped up enough and started making a pot of coffee. I put a bid in for another tea. As he waited for the kettle to boil, Yakky leant against the sink staring into space.

After a minute or so he said, "The police could be the least of our worries."

"Meaning?"

"Johnny didn't garrotte himself. The HLB didn't want us looking for him and the Eight-Six didn't exactly warm to us. They were on edge too; I counted three guys watching the car park. And Ramsey and his pet thug really hustled to get over to you in that snooker club." He broke off to get the kettle when it came to the boil. "If Johnny getting snuffed is down to some club action, whoever did it will have lot of backup. If they get it into their head we know something …"

He left the rest unsaid.

"I don't think we need to worry about Johnny's killer coming after us," I said. I didn't really want to explain more. It felt disloyal, but respect for the dead falls way behind consideration of the living my book. "I'm pretty sure Dago killed him."

Yakky didn't say anything. There was a cheap pleasure to be had in seeing him nonplussed. Any reaction from him was a rarity.

"For getting Mary in the family way?" I nodded. "That's a hell of a leap, Doc."

"It's a motive. Mary's a vulnerable young woman and Dago always did look out for underdogs. And he considered her his own daughter, his little girl in fact. Now she's up the stick. People have died on account of less."

Yakky still wasn't convinced. He said it seemed thin.

"Three things they look for in a guilty party," I counted them off on my fingers, "The motive, the means and the opportunity."

Motive was covered; if anything, means was easier. Dago was an army brat. Born in Aldershot and surrounded by a family obsessed with its military heritage. His older brother had ten years on him and spent most of them beating his sibling up. Dago had idolised him. Come 1982, big brother did his bit for Margaret Thatcher in the Faulklands. He came home somebody different. By then Dago had followed his example and was two years into his regular army contract.

He'd told me once that he'd been marched into the presence of an officer and stood to attention. Then the officer told him of his brother's suicide.

One bottle of Scotch, three boxes of paracetamol and cue the last post.

Dago's initial four-year contract was followed by a second. Army life fuelled the anger and deployment gave opportunities to use it. I believed Dago was a good man, but I didn't doubt for a moment that he'd know how use a garrotte.

I laid it out and Yakky's only comment was, "Opportunity?"

"Black Micky reckons Smudge was warned off putting Johnny on the doors. So, Johnny's out of work. Maybe Dago tells him he's got a rush job: *get your gear together quick and get to this address.* All he has to do is wait until dark, Johnny lets him in and…"

I'd hoped saying it out loud would make it sound ridiculous. I waited for Yakky to pick holes in what I'd said. He knew I wanted to be proved wrong. He did his best.

"Not buying the motive. Not for a calculated murder. Dago finds out his little girl's been defiled and kills Johnny in a fit of rage, now that I can see. But going into his shed, cutting up a broom handle and making a garrotte, then luring Johnny over to Enfield? Too cold."

I shook my head, it wasn't enough.

"Dago could burn slow," I said. "You saw what he'd done to himself when he came to arrange that cover-up. He had his troubles, but he wasn't a loose cannon."

The regimental tattoo, with its gouge marks and cigarette burns, bore witness. Others would have closed the book with a removal or underlined their contempt with a dismissive NEVER AGAIN, a la Smudge. Dago had chosen to punish the memory.

Yakky shrugged. Counsel for defence admitting defeat.

"You plan on telling this to Sue?"

"I can't see what it's going to achieve, connecting her husband to a murder, I'd sooner let her think it was just a random bit of violence in a squat. Nothing to do with her, no connection to her family. I'm thinking it might be worth telling Frenchy, though."

"Lost me on that one," Yakky said.

"Firstly, if we have a discreet word with El Presidente, it could improve our relations with the HLB. Second, if the HLB have been assuming Johnny going AWOL was down to the Eight-Six, Frenchy knowing otherwise might stop a lot of bloodshed. It also puts the ball for dealing with Johnny's family into the club's hands and it keeps Dago's memory out of it, at least publicly. The Handsome Boys ain't going to go to the cops, so there's a good chance the crime scene will just vanish."

Yakky, who was no one's fool, worked the third point out for himself.

"Along with any evidence that we were ever there."

8.

Birthday Cake and French Polish

Saturday 23 September

I left Yakky's and headed for home at around one in the morning, burnt a few candles and filled the offering bowls. Then I slept for about four hours and went to work.

Life goes on.

Next morning, I found Yakky in the shop before me and two thirds down his first pot of coffee. I told him I was going to see Sue after work, to tell her I'd found Johnny.

"And Frenchy?"

"I'm going to ring him later, try and sort out a sit down with him. It's not something I want to go into over the phone. I wouldn't mind a bit of company, to be honest."

"Frenchy? Sure."

"I was thinking more of Sue. I don't know how she's going to take it. If it gets a bit tearful, I'd rather Mary was occupied. I take it you've got a few more pictures for her collection?"

"And a camera to return."

I got hold of Frenchy on his work number after five attempts. He held the professional air of politeness until he realised it wasn't a business call, then he just sounded harassed. I explained, there was something I needed tell him that shouldn't be aired in public. We arranged for me to call at his house that evening.

After we'd shut up shop, me and Yak headed across the river to Kew. We got to Sue's, complete with agenda, ahead of the first wave of evening traffic.

The lights were on downstairs when we rolled onto the end of the driveway. We could hear the music before we knocked on the door. More of Mary's sugar-sweet pop.

The door snapped open like a mouse trap in reverse and, until she saw it was us, Sue's expression was about as welcoming. There was a cigarette hanging from her mouth, its filter pinched flat. Unrepaired makeup traced the course of her mood.

"Bad time?" I asked.

Sue shook her head and led us to the kitchen. She put the kettle on without asking if I wanted tea and I felt a wash of something close to sadness. Seemed these days the only women I knew put the border sign up at the point of knowing what I drank. Maybe I spent too much time keeping out of sight.

The kitchen was full of the music, leaking in from the front room. The tracks would jump halfway through and a new one would start up. Yakky unslung the document tube from his shoulder and rapped it with his knuckles, making mute enquiry. Sue, face tight, pointed in the direction of the noise.

Yakky left us to deliver the portrait of a dead man.

Sue, wordlessly, picked up the mugs she'd filled and led me to the quiet of the TV room. I jumped ship briefly to look in on Mary.

She was bopping around in the living room, her excited rhythm badly matched to the goth look she was still trying for. The coffee table had been banished to the sidelines. On top of it, lying on its side, was a gold foil bag. At least a dozen CD boxes had escaped from it and little puffs of crumbled cellophane littered the floor. Mary didn't see me and I decided against drawing attention to my presence. She clipped another song off mid-verse and it was replaced with something that I couldn't tell from the first. Yakky was perched on the arm the sofa and I wasn't entirely sure Mary had noticed he was there. I caught his eye, and he gave me a thumbs-up and carried on waiting for Mary to calm down. The tension of her excitement bounced around the room.

Sue was on her next cigarette. Her tobacco habit was as frantic her daughter's musical appreciation. There was a TV guide on the floor, its cover painted with ash and lipstick-smeared dogends. The glow of the table lamp turned the low hanging haze of smoke into a silvery fog, but the air smelt mainly of exhaustion. Alongside the improvised ashtray was a small plate with a shower of crumbs and over bright icing on it.

I sank onto the other end of the sofa, the one nearest the TV, and waited. Sue all but sheared through her new filter tip with the edge of her lips.

"Mary's birthday." The words were intoned to make 'birthday' sound like an obscenity. I guessed the crumbs and icing had been a cake. "Gavin turned up. First time he's remembered in bloody years."

She took another bite of smoke and let most of it get away with an angry hiss.

"What happened?"

"Oh, he turned up with a bag full of CDs and now he's the best Daddy in the universe." She put a slightly hysterical twang on the word 'universe'. I jumped before realising it was an imitation of Mary's excitement. 'Universe' had always been one of her favourite words. Things were always the biggest or best in the universe.

I could see there was more to Sue's mood than having to listen to her daughter's taste in music. I took a swig of my tea to cover up the fact I wasn't saying anything and, before long, Sue filled me in.

"He's sniffing around for money again."

She carefully deposited a soft tube of ash onto the magazine. There was more to come, but I could tell she'd reached some internal debate and was either going to fill in the blanks, or not. She gritted her teeth when the sugary track from the living room was cut in favour of some more menacing drum and bass.

"Gavin didn't take long to start pouncing again, did he?" I said, to short circuit the diatribe that was likely to be the counterpoint to Mary's sound track.

"He always needs money. He could lose a bet in a one-horse

race." That had been one of Dago's sayings. I saw Sue's throat working. She made another heroic swallow of smoke and carefully tapped the new ash away. "I've been giving him handouts for years."

That was news to me. I'd known Gavin was a ponce, I thought he'd been scared off though. And I'd never marked Sue as a soft touch, but then Gavin was Mary's natural father, even if he was a piss-poor example of the breed. I wondered if Sue knew that Dago had once beaten him unconscious.

"Big handouts?" I asked, out of curiosity.

Sue shrugged. "Couple of hundred now and then. He used to appear when I was picking Mary up from school, or he'd try and catch me when he knew Dago was out."

She fell silent and finished her cigarette. The filter joined the gathering on the magazine cover, they'd left a gap in Sue's lipstick and the centre portion of her lips looked pale and cold.

"He wanted more this time." She pulled a fresh cigarette from the pack as she spoke. "I half thought he would. Now Dago's gone, he thinks he safe." I noted the inflection she put on 'safe'. "Smudge was around earlier, with a present for Mary. Gavin knocked on the door, about a minute after he'd gone. I bet he was waiting for him to leave."

The volume of the music went up a couple of notches and Sue screamed to turn it down. When it didn't, she made to get up, I got there first and told her I'd do it.

Mary was close to manic. The last of the birthday cake was on a side table. I assumed Sue and Gavin would have had a slice each, or maybe two. It looked like Mary had worked her way through a good half of it. The smell of the sugar would have killed a diabetic at twenty paces. I tuned the hi-fi down to a reasonable level then took the edge off the intrusion by cutting some of my sweet dance moves, which made her laugh.

"Happy birthday," I told her and asked her which one it was, as if I didn't know. She told me twenty-two and I admired her CDs. "New sounds?"

I didn't recognise a single group or artist on any of the

covers, but I let her talk me and Yakky through the finer points of their talents. Gavin had made a good selection it appeared, Mary was genuinely pleased with the set. And quite possibly wracked with guilt for enjoying them when Dago was dead.

Mary confided she wanted to buy a ghetto blaster for her room with the next instalment of her student loan. Sue was currently getting the bad guy role for injecting the idea of financial restraint into her birthday. She told me her dad *going was* going to buy her one, stumbled on the tense and changed it to *had been*. There was a brittle segment of silence, despite the noise from the hi-fi. I deflected the moment by randomly picking one of the new CDs.

"What are these guys like?"

There was enough of the adult about Mary that she grabbed the distraction, and enthused about the disc, before putting it into the player for me to listen to. Thankfully, I'd chosen a group more taken by ballads than bass and I listened to a track with her before heading back to Sue. As I left, Yakky was unloading the contents of the document tube.

Sue was lighting another cigarette. After coming from the other room, the smell of stale smoke was overpowering. The scent of the cleaning products she'd been using to wash away the impact of widowhood was lost now. The cleaning obsession trumped by addiction. She'd aged in the last few weeks and I wondered if she was sleeping.

"How much did Gavin want?" I asked, taking up the conversation where we'd left off.

Sue rolled her eyes and the hint of a smile tugged one side of her mouth.

"Five grand."

"Cheeky bastard." Sue nodded, agreeing with my assessment. "You going to lend it to him?"

The smile managed to break through this time. It wasn't an expression of affection.

"Am I fuck." And I was glad to see a flash of Sue's old hardness. "If he thinks he can show up here with a few birthday presents and get me writing cheques, he can bloody well think again." She blew a smoke ring and watched it fade before speaking again. "He must have guessed Dago would have seen us right."

I nodded, I was thinking that as well.

"Does he know about Mary's student loan money?" Sue looked startled and I realised she was wondering how *I* knew about it. "She mentioned she wanted to use some of it to buy a boom box."

Sue frowned as the implications of Mary's blabbing about having access to money sunk in.

She said, "Even Gavin wouldn't sink that low." But, obviously, I'd just given her something new to worry about. "I think I'll let her buy herself a hi-fi. She can keep *that* in her room then." The volume had crept up again, but it was less obnoxious. The aggressive drums had segued into teenage love songs. "Dago was talking about getting her a system for her birthday." Sue stared at the blank TV screen and blew another smoke ring. She shook her head clear after a while and asked, "Why did you drop by?"

I came close to not telling her. She'd had enough for one day, but I didn't want her finding out about Johnny via the HLB or out of the blue from a chance news report. She also had to be prepared for the fall out if the news reached Mary. When I told her about Johnny's body, sitting in an Enfield squat, she winced and rubbed her eyes with the heel of her hand.

"That's horrible."

It was the reaction I'd expect to the death of a casual acquaintance. It didn't surprise me particularly. Like many spouses on the fringes of male-dominated arenas, she'd occupied a position of trusted outsider. And her concerns about Johnny's whereabouts hadn't been out of affection. I suspected an element of it had been a displacement strategy. I took the digital camera out of my jacket and brought the murder a bit closer to home.

I explained about Yakky's recent commission.

"Oh, that little shit. She must have thought it was going to be flowers and romance." She worked the heel of her hand into her eyes some more. "Bloody men. Even when they're dead I've got to clean up after them."

"Have you spoken to her about it yet?"

"No. I keep putting it off. I thought things would be hard enough with her birthday. You know, the first one without Dago being around."

Another cigarette took its toll on her lipstick. It looked like she was about to go on the warpath and I braced myself to try and stop her. Then she slumped in on herself, too worn out to take action, or maybe even to care.

I made tea.

The latest cigarette went largely unsmoked. It smouldered to ash in Sue's fist then collapsed under its own weight. She brushed half-heartedly at the grey smudge on the sofa.

"You been struggling today?" I asked, nodding in the direction of the music.

Sue grimaced.

"We were okay until Gavin showed up. Said: We needed cheering up."

The mood was maudlin all of a sudden, instead of angry. It was a relief. Mary's first birthday without Dago, her real Dad by any measure that mattered, should have been a little sombre. Not a frenzy of music and sugar. Mary couldn't understand why she wasn't feeling good about feeling happy. She was still a child in some ways. Her 'father' didn't have that excuse. In the normal course of events, I'd have trusted Sue to handle the likes of Gavin, but I resented the fact she should have to at a time like this. I stayed for another tea and watched Sue put another nail into her lungs, then made a move.

I popped my head in to say goodbye to Mary and collect Yakky. I found them sitting on the floor with their backs against the sofa. The manic energy was mostly spent now and she looked ready to sleep. I noticed she'd put all the CDs back in their cases and put them in the foil bag. Gavin might kid himself that he had a daughter, but she was Sue and Dago's child. I sat next to her for a bit and pretended to appreciate the music, as it hit another high C.

Yakky had spread the drawings over the floor. Most of them were competent likenesses of characters from Mary's DVDs, but the portrait of Johnny Simms was something else again.

It takes an exacting talent to execute a good portrait from a photograph, particularly a bland ID shot. Yakky had pulled the stops out and given Johnny a depth and nobility I suspected he'd never had. As tributes went, it was pretty good.

Before we left I asked Mary if I could borrow her phone and went into the kitchen. Once I was out of sight, I scrolled through her contacts and committed the number for 'Daddy G' to memory.

There were two bikes parked on the road outside Frenchy's house. I recognised Silk's weather-beaten BMW, so I figured El Presidente had wanted some of his men around him. Yakky clocked the bikes too. As we parked up, we exchanged looks.

It was Silk that let us in. It was tempting to make a remark about being promoted to butler.

"Evening, Doc."

I nodded a response and we followed him along the hall. It was a long walk. Frenchy was doing himself alright.

The man himself was seated at one end of a highly polished dining table big enough to host board meetings. To his left was an ashtray and a short glass, to his right, a pile of notes and coins. Jason was also at the table. He too, had a pile of cash at hand. His was a lot smaller. A third pile of stake money and a pack of playing cards indicated Silk's place, along with three crushed beer cans and a fourth awaiting its demise.

Frenchy gestured to me and Yakky to sit and asked if we wanted a drink. Yakky passed but I said I'd have a beer, curious to see if Silk would be despatched to fetch it. Frenchy called over his shoulder, to the adjacent room that I supposed was the kitchen. A young woman about Mary's age with an expression as blank as Yakky's, appeared with a tin, put it on the table and walked out again without speaking. The smell of burnt hemp followed her in and out.

I'd taken the seat next to Jason and absently picked up the deck of cards.

I asked what the game was.

"Poker," Frenchy told me. "Texas hold 'em. Opening bid's five quid. You want to sit in?"

I trooped the cards through a few different cuts and put them down in front of Silk again.

"No thanks, it looks like you're having all the luck tonight."

I nodded at Frenchy's stack of notes.

"Yeah, tell me about it," Jason moaned. "The wife's going to skin me alive when she finds out how much I've dropped this evening."

Silk laughed and told him, "Scared money never wins."

Frenchy just gave one of his Gallic shrugs.

"You wanted to see me, Doc?"

"Johnny Simms."

I let the name fall so I could gauge the reaction. The room didn't explode, but I felt any good humour evaporate.

"What about him?" Frenchy asked.

"Me and Yakky found him. He's over in Enfield, sitting in a squat with a garrotte round his windpipe."

No one said anything for a few beats. Jason broke the silence with a soft curse that unfroze the tableau. Frenchy and Silk both asked, at once, for the news in black and white.

"Is he dead?"

"Has been for a while judging by the smell," I said.

Jason cursed again and one of his hands went to the front of his neck. It stopped short of making contact and retreated to the table instead. Then he concentrated on putting away what was left of his stake money. Frenchy nodded, took the cue and did the same. Squaring away his pile took longer, there was more of it and he tidied the cards away first.

Silk hadn't taken his eyes of me since I'd dropped my little bombshell. He took a pull from his can of beer; his hand was steadier than Jason's had been.

"Johnny didn't…was it murder?"

"Garrotte," I told him again.

Jason swallowed loudly and this time his hand made it to his throat.

He didn't curse again, just muttered, "Poor kid."

"There wasn't much sign of a struggle," Yakky told him. "It looks like he was taken by surprise." Jason turned to look at him, he was still rubbing his neck and wincing. "I mean, it was quick."

"You think?" Jason asked.

"The garrotte was in bloody deep. No blood to the brain, he'd have blacked out after thirty seconds or so."

It was lucky that Frenchy had gone in for a big table. Jason's chair tipped over but came up short against the wall. The obstacle it made of itself, slowed him on his way to get at Yakky.

"Why don't I put you in a fucking choke hold? Then you can see how quick thirty seconds feels, you cunt."

Yakky got to his feet with less drama but more speed. Silk, who may have spotted the way things were going, was actually on his feet before anyone else.

"Alright Jason, at ease, son. He didn't mean anything by it. So, just chill mate, okay?"

El Presidente, also on his feet, blocked Jason's anti-clockwise path around the table. I pushed my chair away from the polished surface, annexing the clockwise option. Playing roadblock from a seated position made sense. It would have taken him longer to climb over me then to knock me down. And, if I was about to hit the floor face first, I wouldn't have so far to go.

Yakky was the usual stone-cold blank; it wasn't helping Jason get a perspective on things. To people used to a degree of respect, or at least fear, Yakky's unresponsive features could come across as a 'fuck you'.

Then it was over.

Jason was as quick to repent as he was to anger. He righted his chair and sat down again, then avoided looking at anyone. The glance he cut across to Yakky, was shamefaced rather than apologetic. Yakky accepted the offer of his embarrassment with a nod.

"I'm sorry about Johnny being killed. I didn't mean to sound callous."

Jason's muttered reply was lost in the general clatter of everyone settling down again. By unspoken agreement, we were waiting for him for pull himself together and no one said anything for a while. Finally, Silk, who'd got to the bottom of his last can and was crimping it carefully into a ball, looked from me to Yakky and back again.

"So, how did you two find him?"

"Prospect with the Eight-Six was tooling around on Johnny's GSX. I had a word with Eddie the Greek, him and Ramsey pulled the prospect in. The prospect told me where he'd pinched it from." The mundane chain of events made the murder feel depressing instead of terrible. Maybe sitting at Frenchy's table was playing with my memory, turning what was hideous into something merely squalid. I sighed, "It was a straight lift, he said he didn't know it was an HLB bike."

"And you believed him?" Jason sounded controlled now, but the words were an uneven mix of question and accusation.

Silk answered for me, "If the Eight-Six had taken Johnny out, they wouldn't go telling Doc where they'd left his body."

Jason wasn't ready to let the idea go.

"They've been putting themselves about lately. Maybe they're sending a message."

"Then why would they go all coy about it when Doc asked? Anyway, that's not how the Eight-Six operate is it?"

The Eight-Six had taken their name from an urban myth, or possibly truth, about the good old days when Las Vegas was run by mobsters wearing pinstripe suits. The story went that losers who couldn't settle the line of credit they'd squandered were prone to vanishing without a trace. Common wisdom had it that they'd been taken eight miles out of town and buried six feet deep. The lack of evidence only increased the fear of being eighty-sixed.

Likewise, the Eight-Six MC knew the value of keeping

things close to home and letting people's imaginations fill in the blanks. That they were capable of violence, extreme violence at times, wasn't in doubt, but leaving proof wasn't their style.

"Who then?" Jason demanded.

Silk rolled his eyes in reply: *how should I know*. More silence. Frenchy poked a hole in it by snapping open his lighter and incinerating a third of a cigarette with one draw. It was a pretty good attention grabber, and suddenly he was the focus of the room. The moment was spoiled slightly by the young woman in the kitchen, dropping something, and then giggling about it for too long. Once she'd finished, and the lack of noise had had time to feel odd; Frenchy stared at me through the fog of tobacco.

"Over to you, Doc. You seem to be the expert all of a sudden. If it wasn't the Eight-Six, then who did do it?"

It wasn't a power play precisely. In that setting, at that time, I was too far down the food chain to be worth picking off. But I think he was eager to shoo me away from the club. His problem was I'd turned up with more information than the club was privy to. So, the balance had to be reset. I think he'd expected me to roll my eyes, like Silk, and tell everyone I'd given them all I had to give. Then I'd be redundant, an outsider sitting at the table and wearing my welcome thin.

"You ain't going to like this," I told him.

He laughed and smoke escaped his pursed lips in a fan shaped stutter.

"You think we like any of this?"

Silk and Jason both grumbled an agreement.

I laid it out for them as it had come to me. Dago's over protection of his step-daughter. Her confused attempts to become an adult, the fixation on Johnny's image in the camera. Johnny needing work badly and the job offer that was a trap. Frenchy surprised me by nodding. He lit his next cigarette from the dying end of the previous one.

"I knew something was wrong with Dago. Those last couple of weeks, he wasn't himself. I thought it was just the business with the guys pushing for back patches." He did his Gallic shoulder shrug. "Does Sue know?"

"I don't plan on telling her. She's got enough to deal with. So's Mary."

Frenchy nodded again and looked around the table, meeting the eye of everyone in turn.

"I think we should keep this to ourselves. Having the club know Dago killed Johnny won't achieve anything. I think we should let the news about Johnny just filter down through the natural channels."

Jason shook his head, his voice was quiet, he sounded exhausted. "We can't just leave him to sit in some bloody squat. We can't do that to him. He lived for the club, we can't do that."

Frenchy leaned over and put a hand on Jason's shoulder. It only just fit, I'd never noticed how big his hands were before. He spoke gently, and I think he picked up a trace of a French accent, but that might have been my imagination.

"Jason, it's the club I'm thinking of. It's a bad time for us right now. A lot is happening. Dago's gone, Black Micky's in hospital. Losing Johnny, having the police sniffing around, maybe finding out what Dago did? Not now. Johnny was a good solider. He would have understood, for the good of the club. He'll be found, at some point he'll come back to us. When that happens we'll do it right, give him the club send-off he would have wanted. If we're a patch club by then, we'll bury him in full colours. But, for the club, it has to wait. For now, it doesn't leave this room."

Jason's breathing was uneven. I was braced for him to kick off again, but it didn't happen. After a couple of deep breaths, he stood and walked out of the room, into the kitchen. We heard him say something and get an answer that was somewhere between a giggle and a yawn. He came back in holding a cluster of beers, the cans still tethered at their necks by their plastic net. He stayed on his feet, pulled a can free and threw it to Silk before opening one of his own.

"Okay," he said, "we keep schtum about Dago topping him

and we don't make any announcements, but" – he emphasized the pause with a swig from his beer – "I'm telling Smudge. Smudge should know."

He looked between Silk and Frenchy, ready to beat down any objections. Frenchy hissed, one of his Parisian mannerisms, but before he could speak, Silk held up a hand. It was meant like a halt sign, to cut Frenchy off. To me, it looked like he was raising his hand in class.

"Smudge is going out of his mind. Jason's right, he needs to know Johnny's dead and he needs to know it's not down to the Eight-Six. If he takes off on one, we could wind up in real trouble –"

He stopped, silenced himself, and I guessed he was roaming into club business. I wasn't that interested anymore. I'd found the body, even worked out who did it. Now I'd given the loose ends to the HLB to deal with.

Johnny *shouldn't* have been my problem anymore.

"Well, gentleman," I stood up and Yakky followed suit, "I'll wish you a good night. Thanks for the beer. We'll see ourselves out."

"You got any cash on you?" I asked Yakky.

Without comment, he pulled his wallet from the side of his boot, thumbed through it and found three twenties. I told him I'd pay him back the next day, and folded the notes into my pocket, along with the ton-twenty already there.

Yakky's bike must have had a taste for damp weather because it started with minimal drama. When I didn't make a move to pull away, he asked if I was waiting for something.

"Jason," I said pointing at Frenchy's door. "He's made his stand, I don't think he'll be long."

Not quite on cue – we had a minute or so to wait – the door opened, and Jason came out. He closed it behind him very slowly, working hard not to slam it. His bike, a nondescript Jap, was next to my Sportster. Evidently still embarrassed about his outburst at Yakky, he busied himself with the chain securing his wheels. I'd had enough tip-toeing for one night and asked him outright how much he'd lost. He straightened to his full height, maybe trying to look unrepentant.

"Best part of three hundred. Kim's going to do her biscuits. You wouldn't believe the luck I've had tonight."

Kim was Jason's wife. The only person I'd ever known him to back down from. I took the sheaf of notes from my wallet and handed them to him.

"Hundred and eighty, all I got on me." In accordance with tradition, he asked if I was sure. "Yeah, pay me back when you're straight again."

"Thanks, Doc. Look I'm sorry about –" He turned to Yakky and looked helpless, which in many ways he was.

I waited until the notes had been shut away before asking, "Smudge and Johnny, close were they?"

Jason had been one of the first people I'd spoken to, regarding Johnny. I remembered him telling me Smudge and Johnny were 'bestest fwiends'. Saying it in a little-girl falsetto. It had jarred with me at the time.

"Best mates," Jason told me again.

He didn't do the silly voice.

"But Smudge wouldn't give him a try out on the door?"

Jason's hand was still in his pocket, reminding him how friends treat each other.

"Not here, alright?"

"My place is nearest," Yakky said.

The light was still on downstairs when we got to Yakky's. He swore under his breath and told me to give him five minutes. Jason and I waited in the drizzle while Yakky played a round of silly buggers with his dad. Family life: a game of nerve end attrition for two or more players.

We were finally ushered through the door and led straight to the kitchen. The coffee was already brewing and the back door was wide open, trying to dump some of the heat. Yakky's old man felt the cold and liked the central heating on full, day and night. We all had black coffee. The devastation in the kitchen sink included a collection of empty milk cartons.

Jason wrapped his hands around a mug and hunched forward. I had the feeling this was the view Kim was given when he confessed his loses.

He wasn't volunteering anything, so I asked, "Why the knock back on the job front?"

"Smudge runs a tight ship. He likes pros, Johnny was too eager to go in swinging. Too eager for trouble."

I waited, gave him the chance to stop stalling of his own volition. We all got fed up waiting. I asked him if he knew Spooky. He made the face people make when they're pretending to think, then shook his head.

"Small-time dealer," I told him, "and I do mean small. The average Girl Guide's probably got a bigger stash. Black Micky damn near put him through the Pearly Gates for trying to unload an ounce of puff. I'm finding it hard to tally that up with Smudge nixing Johnny for being too violent."

"Smudge was probably worried he'd get hurt."

"Johnny would get hurt you mean?" Jason nodded. "Worried beyond the point of one brother looking out for another?"

"Different sort of worried."

I'd known this was where the conversation was headed, but wanted it confirmed. Mentally, I ticked off one of the drawings on my wall. The overkill-cute little girl. The antithesis of masculine.

Jason didn't want to talk about Smudge, but he'd taken my coin and now he owed me. He'd also gone for Yakky and had his conscience to appease. I've known a lot of a people from that cast – tempers on a hair trigger and regrets on standby.

"What do you want me to say? Johnny was Smudge's best mate."

"Bestest fwiends?" I attempted to do the camp little girl's voice. The way Jason had during the phone call days before. He sighed again. I wondered if he felt guilty for betraying Smudge now or for making fun of him then.

"What do you want me to say, Doc?"

"You think Johnny and Smudge were more than *just*

friends?"

Jason shook his head. "Nothing…happened. You know what I mean." He used his coffee as a prop to stall. Then bought more time by waiting for me, then Yakky, to agree that we did know what he meant. "I don't know if Johnny ever picked up on it, he's…he was…thick as shit, but Smudge thought the sun shone out of him. Smudge is the only reason he got in the club at all. Dago found him somewhere or other, you know what he was like, introduced him to the lads."

He took another taste of coffee and grimaced. I sympathised – Yakky's coffee could strip paint.

According to Jason, there'd been no expectation that the newcomer would be asked to join the HLB. He'd always lived on Civvy Street and didn't have too much about him. Gradually though, he became a fixture. The Jericho became his local and he rode Smudge's coat-tails into private parties and club runs. Smudge put him forward for membership, Dago seconded it. It wasn't a pedigree many objected to.

"Give him his due, he tried hard," Jason said. "He never missed a meeting and he paid his dues on time."

"But?" said Yakky, because one of us had to.

"He was over the top with it. Slightest thing anyone, outside of the club, said would get his backup. It's true what I said, he was a loose cannon, but it was like he was working at it. Like he'd written himself a script to act out."

"And he didn't get his marching orders?"

"End of the day, he'd do anything for the club and that made him useful. Some of the guys took the piss with that a bit. And of course, he'd come into the club via the Pres and he was best mates with Smudge. He got along with Frenchy too. French'd lay out his spiel about the Foreign Legion and Johnny would be lapping it up. That was the plus side of having him around; the rest of us didn't have to fucking hear it." He took another mouthful of coffee. "Got anything stronger?"

It might have been a joke about the coffee, but Yakky evidently thought he was talking about booze. He asked if tequila was alright. While he was out of the room, I asked Jason if Frenchy talked about the legion often. He didn't elaborate hugely, just rolled his eyes and nodded.

What Yakky was holding when he came back, was a bottle of oak-aged Highland No. 1 Reposado. It had been due to be my birthday present apparently. On my list of things to sing praise to, it was up there with Ezulie Dantor and Harley Davidson. Yakky found a couple of glasses as I cracked the seal. As it was technically mine, I poured one generous measure and two reasonable ones.

The first sip is always the best. I savoured the slight buttery flavour and waited for the trace of pine to settle on my tongue, before allowing myself another taste. Jason up ended his glass into his coffee.

There's no hell in the Voodoo tradition. For some things there should be.

"So, you get to tell Smudge his boyfriend's dead." I said.

The comment earned me a sour look that I probably deserved. Jason took a swig from his mug and smacked his lips.

"I think it's best he hears it from me."

Yakky, who was sipping from his glass the way I'd taught him, said, "Are you the only one knows the score?"

"There've been a lot of digs made, lots of wind-ups. Smudge'd walk in and someone would tell Johnny his missus had arrived, shit like that. Smudge would laugh about it, but you could tell it riled him. I think that's why he started giving Johnny a hard time."

"Distancing himself you mean?" Yakky asked.

Jason shrugged and helped himself to another shot of the tequila, for his coffee.

"Maybe, but he still stuck to Johnny like shit on a blanket, only it was different. He started riding him about being a stand-up member of the club, telling him he'd have to knock himself into shape when the HLB went to a full patch." Jason finished the contents of the mug. He sat upright at last and opened his arms. I wasn't sure what the gesture was meant to mean. "I don't know what it was with Smudge and Johnny, I don't think Smudge does either. He'd hang around the guy like he was a bitch on heat, but if either of them is bent, Smudge'd be the last to admit it. Probably be the last to know. Now I've got to tell him Johnny's dead. He's going to go off the fucking scale."

"If you do tell him, you got to make sure he knows it wasn't the Eight-Six."

"I'm going to tell him what you've told me: it was Dago. It won't go any further than him, not if Frenchy's saying it's to be kept quiet. Once he's finished shouting the odds, he's going to be gutted." He stood up abruptly and grabbed his crash helmet. "Thanks for the cash injection. I'll pay you back in a week or so if that's alright."

I told him there was no rush.

As he left, Jason commented, "I had some good hands tonight, Frenchy's got the luck of the devil."

I sat at the table with Yakky again and finished off my measure of Reposado. I examined the bottle. It wasn't something you'd come across in most off-licences. A thoughtful gift.

"Thanks for this man, top present."

The muscles along one side of Yakky's jaw tightened. You might almost call it a smile.

"Your face when he topped up his coffee."

"Pearls before swine. I nearly asked for my money back."

"You think you'll ever see that again?"

I shook my head. I'd already written the money off as expenses.

"If he keeps playing poker with Frenchy he'll need all the money he can get." Yakky made a twirling motion with his fingers. "Didn't you notice the table? All that polishing?" I mimed dealing out a hand of poker. "Angle the cards right and keep your eyes on the table. When it's your turn to deal, you get an idea what everyone else is holding. You're not going to be able to see every card, but the obvious patterns, kings, queens, aces…you'll see them."

"Or maybe he just likes shiny things."

I let Yakky have one of my more annoying grins. "That pack of cards he was so eager to tidy away? They were marked."

"So much for brotherhood."

I left Yakky's soon after Jason. When I got home, I poured a shot of the high-end tequila into an offering bowl and lit a candle for Ezulie Dantor. The ritual I enacted was to ask her to watch over Sue and Mary. I poured another shot for my own consumption and sat facing the wall. In the flicker of candlelight, I couldn't really see the details. It didn't matter. There were questions on the wall that hadn't been answered but now they were curiosities and not pressing matters.

I felt deflated in a way I couldn't place. At first, I thought it was the unfinished feel to the wall. Putting my thoughts into pictures and symbols was something I did a lot. Normally it worked for me. This time felt different. The jottings I'd put on the wall, the dates, the tarot cards and disconnected sketches, had become a rat's nest. Loose ends. And the solution had arrived without explaining any of them. Case closed. Johnny Simms was dead and his murderer was beyond justice.

And that murderer was the real issue.

I'd never been under the illusion that Dago was a choir boy. I had believed he was one of the good guys. That was hard to reconcile with a homemade garrotte buried in a man's neck.

I'd scrub the plaster clean tomorrow and move on to the next thing.

The next thing, after slinging ink and making a living, was going to be Gavin. I didn't closely question my motives for what I was going to do. I wanted to think I was doing it for Sue and Mary because Dago wasn't there to do it for them. At the other end of the scale was the possibility that I was grieving twice over. Once for the friend I'd lost and then again for the memory of the person I'd thought he was. I was looking to spread the hurt around, and Gavin seemed a deserving case.

Somewhere in the middle, and probably the closest to the truth, was a nagging feeling that I'd missed something.

9.
Knowledge, Belief and Pizza Delivery

Monday 25 September

Yakky, as seemed to be the norm now, was in the shop when I got there. The place smelt of coffee and the music was set to awful. I told him about Gavin sniffing around for money. He whistled at the mention of the five grand Gavin had been trying to tap.

"Hell of a sum to want out of the blue."

"Sue's been drip feeding him for years. Now Dago's out of the picture, he's got a free hand. Or thinks he has. Plus, Dago was insured to the hilt, so there's a lot of money floating about."

Yakky shook his head. "Did he know Dago had himself insured?"

I felt someone walking over my grave. I hadn't thought in that direction at all, I'd just assumed Gavin would take it as read that Dago would look after his family. Now the idea was there it took hold. Gavin wouldn't assume anybody would look after their family.

Worthless piles like him inhabited a space somewhere beyond the normal confines of selfishness. Other people's problems were outside the frame of reference. I tried some logic on the idea: how would Gavin have known about Dago's insurance plans? I couldn't think of a way but something turned around in the back of my mind, refusing to come out into the light where it could be seen.

I turned to the cards, cleared a space on the table in the waiting room and began to deal. I didn't get as far as laying the full spread. The third card I put down was the High Priestess. The giver of hidden knowledge. The thing at the back of my mind came into the light. Singing a high C.

"I think I'm going to pay Gavin a social call, this very evening," I told Yakky.

When Yakky had decided on tattooing rather than a steady career in the NHS, Karla hadn't been what you'd call overjoyed. I'd been included in her displeasure by extension. His involvement with my occasional skip-tracing hadn't eased relations any. So, asking Yakky to ring her for help had, at least in part, been an attempt at bridge building.

Mostly though, it had been expedient.

I needed to tease an address from a mobile number and that was easier if you had the right voice. To be frank about it, men are more likely to fall for a soft female voice than my north London growl.

"I'll call her if you want," Yakky said, "but you're wasting your time."

I asked him to humour me; he shrugged and pulled out his phone. I didn't hear what was said – he knew I'd have listened and took the call outside, out of earshot and into the rain. When he came back into the shop, he made an exaggerated gesture of surrender.

"She's not on shift today, she'll be over about one. Perhaps you're on to something with your poxy Voodoo."

I blew a kiss to the picture of Ezulie Dantor on the waiting room wall and gave Yakky an innocent smile. The reality was less romantic. Karla had, more than once, dismissed the skip-tracing as *grown men playing cops and robbers.* That was before she'd been invited to join in the game.

Karla didn't want me to see it, but she was excited. I didn't blame her for that, the cloak-and-dagger stuff was kind of fun.

She made the call from the shop landline, blocking the number so it wouldn't appear on Gavin's screen. He picked up on the second attempt, a little after one o'clock. I assumed he was on his lunch break, which was no bad thing. It helped with the food motif.

Karla had rehearsed her part well. She told him good afternoon and said she was calling on behalf of Pizza Hut Restaurant Group. If he could spare two minutes to answer three questions, Pizza Hut Restaurant Group would send him two vouchers, each redeemable against a sixteen-inch pizza with the topping of his choice and an accompanying soft drink or glass of wine. No purchase required.

"How often, in the last six months have you eaten at one of our restaurants?"

Then she asked him how often he ordered a take away Pizza. Third and final question: Which pizza base do you prefer, thin and crispy, thick base or deep pan? We listened to the answers without interest and failed to note them down. Karla told him thanks.

"Thank you, that's great. Now, if you can give me your home address, one of our delivery boys will bring the vouchers around to you personally, within the next thirty-six hours."

The address *was* noted down. Then she asked him to repeat it, to be sure.

"Will you be in this evening? At what sort of time?" There was a pause and Karla forced a laugh. "No, I won't be bringing them personally, but I'll try and get one of our people to you tonight."

She told him thank you, one last time, and hang up with a grimace.

The address we had for Gavin was in a block of flats that didn't look much better than the ruin we'd found Johnny's body in. I'd been intending to go and see him on my own, but Yakky had volunteered to come along and I didn't see any harm in going mob handed. I didn't have any plans that involved subtly.

The rain had held off, but Gavin's street seemed to hold the memory of cold and damp like a bolster against false hope. We parked up a little way out of sight of the block and chained the bikes together.

The rough-cast concrete steps into the block were carpeted with roundels of chewing gum and spray-painted tags reading ZitskY. The same tag was repeated mindlessly along the corridors. If the smell was anything to go by, someone had made a bid to claim ZitskY's patch by pissing in all the corners. The lift must have been a similarly prized piece of real estate and the ambience encouraged use of the stairs.

Gavin's flat was on the third floor, one of a dozen or so recessed into a concrete and rubber-matted walkway. I hung back from view of the fisheye-peephole mounted under the door number. The door also boasted a horseshoe nailed under the letter slot. If its previous owner had been as lucky, it was due to be boiled down for glue.

There wasn't an immediate answer to Yakky's knock but the faint luminesce of the peephole lens vanished, so we guessed Gavin, or at least someone on the other side of the door, had their face pressed to it.

Yakky knocked again, louder, and bellowed, "I've got your pizza vouchers."

He brought his crash hat into view to cement the idea that a pizza delivery moped was parked outside. The door cracked open just enough to give a side shot of Gavin. He clocked my presence but Yakky diverted him by telling him he had to sign for the vouchers, "Or the boss assumes I just nick them."

Gavin, as chance would have it, was left-handed. The side I could see through the crack in the door was his right. To free up his left hand to sign, he had to open the door completely. As he swung the door inward, I registered his shoulder twitch and heard something land beside him, with a soft *doink* sound. There followed another *doink* as Yakky's helmet hit the floor and rolled towards me. Yak had let go of it and slammed into Gavin, with a bunch of nylon shirt material in each hand. The next noise was the back of Gavin's head, bouncing off the wall.

The front door swung into a hallway barely deep enough to let it fully open. Yakky, dragging Gavin, went left and I followed behind, surprised at the turn of events. I'd picked up

Yak's lid and cast a quick look around to see if we'd been observed. As far as I could tell, the recessed doorway had kept us off the radar. Not that I had the impression of community spirt and people watching out for their neighbours.

As I closed the door behind me, I saw what Gavin had been holding in his left hand. A two-foot length of pine, two by one. It was an ill-advised weapon. Too light to do much more than piss someone off and too long to wield in the confines of the doorway. I suspected Yakky, seeing Gavin shedding it, had mistaken the move for an attack.

Gavin was wheezing, his breath high-pitched and laboured. Yakky had him pinned to the wall and he was making no move to fight back. This, if you knew Yakky, was a smartish move, but struck me as odd given that two strangers had broken in. The odds weren't that long and, since he'd taken the trouble to bring a baton to the party, I'd have expected more of a defence.

I waited for Gavin to turn his head towards me.

"We're friends of Sue's and I want to ask you a few questions." I gave him a moment to digest this and carried on when he nodded his understanding. He'd calmed at the mention of Sue. "Now, I would like to talk to you, in a civilized manner, over a cup of tea. If you don't fancy tea of course, I'll step outside and leave you to chat with my friend here. How would you like to do it?"

"Tea."

"Good man."

I smiled and scared him all over again.

Yakky let go of Gavin's shirt front slowly, then asked him if he had an inhaler. Gavin nodded and pointed at a cheap car-dealer's sheepskin hanging on the wall. Yakky stepped to one side and Gavin fumbled in one of the pockets. He found a small blue aerosol that he sucked on with relief. I gave Yakky a questioning look as Gavin's breathing levelled out and gave way to the shakiness of fright. Yakky mouthed the word 'asthma' at me.

I dispatched Gavin to the kitchen and told him milk, no

sugar. I heard scrubbing and figured finding three clean mugs wasn't a usual event. I sat on a chocolate-coloured sofa that was flaccid with use.

The flat's living room was painted in the municipal palate of mid-eighties beiges. The artexed ceiling was yellowed with nicotine, but there were more ashtrays than dogends in the room. I didn't see Gavin being a slave to restraint and guessed the habit was controlled by funding, rather than willpower. The furthest wall was a perfect square with a single pane of rectangular glass set in it, like a gun emplacement. Under the window was a low, mid-nineties shelving unit with a tiny TV on it. Along with six champagne bottles. All empty. Yakky, who was standing next to the doorway leading to the kitchen, saw I'd noticed the bottles and he pointed at the wall to my left.

Each bottle starred in its own framed photograph. The earliest one featured Gavin, booted and suited for what looked like a wedding. The wooden circle of a winning post told the truth. Next to him, slightly in the background, was a very young Sue. She was dressed in the same mode as the last time I'd seen her. The tight and short tailoring was more effective when she'd been in her twenties. Brassy suited her. Gavin was smiling, open-mouthed, at the camera; his hands a blur as he shook the bottle to produce a spray of fizzing wine.

Sue looked happy in the background. Out for a day at the races and wining big enough to get the fizzing bottle and the photograph. The marriage was young enough that such scenes were a treat and not a death knell.

She was absent from the other five pictures and after the second one, the morning-suited glory gave way to the working-day clothes of a man just doing when he did. By the fourth photo, Gavin's lady-killer good looks had faded into history. The cocky smile as the champagne flowed stayed the same. The grin of entitlement a winner wears because they knew all along that's what would happen.

One of my customers was a professional poker player and sometimes pool hustler. He made a living and paid the bills.

He maintained the difference between a professional and a compulsive gambler was the difference between *knowledge* and *belief*. The pro *knew* a loss was inevitable at some point and braced for a fall. The compulsive *believed* the big win was the next one and bet the bank.

Gavin came in and handed teas around, then sat as far away from me as the L-shaped sofa would allow. He had to move aside several copies of the *Horse Racing Almanac*. He put them on top of a box that, according to the printing, contained a Sony ghetto blaster with a wide selection of whistles and bells.

"Who are you guys?"

Yakky ignored the question and I repeated we were friends of Sue. "You know, the woman in the photograph?"

I pointed at his first big win, the snide comment went over his head or he chose not to react.

"What do you want?"

I leaned forward and produced a smile. "I want to know the name of just one of those CDs you gave to Mary. Just one."

I held up my index finger to illustrate the point.

Gavin said, "What?"

I didn't repeat myself, he'd heard me and was flapping his lips in a bid for more time. All three of us knew it. When it was clear he couldn't answer my starter for ten, I sat back and watched him sweat for a bit. He managed to slop tea down his shirt; I hoped it wasn't his best one.

I pointed at the row of photos on the wall, again. "I bet you remember the name and the odds on every one of those horses, don't you?" He nodded that he did and looked as if he might recite them if I asked. "But you forget your daughter's birthday, year after year. Until now. This year you turn up with a hundred quid's worth CDs and they're all spot on, just what she wanted. You know something, Gavin? I'm forty-eight and not once in those forty-eight years have my parents failed to send me a birthday card and a little something, a little token. Never forgotten, not once in forty-eight years, isn't that nice?" Gavin slopped more tea, agreeing it was. "But here's the thing, Gavin. My parents could no more pick out a song that I'd like than they could fly to the moon." I took the grin away. "Now, tell me your secret, Gavin, and please don't lie to me."

I took a sip of my own tea and had to choke back a gag reflex.

"Dago come over, told me not to forget Mary's birthday."

"And you splashed out a ton on CDs, just on the off chance?"

Gavin actually had the nerve to look shamefaced. "He gave them to me, said they were groups she was into."

Dago had what he'd called 'open ears' – he'd listen to any music and find something to like in it. I could imagine him and Mary discussing modern bands that most parents would ban from the house. In spite of the taste, I had to take another swallow of the tea.

"Is that all you wanted?" Gavin asked, then jumped slightly.

Yakky had peeled himself away from the wall and stood nearer the centre of the room. Too close to Gavin for comfort.

"I don't see you as a big music fan, Gavin. No CDs, no albums, no tapes."

I waved a hand at the rest of the room. Gavin shrugged,

"Not my thing."

"Then why the ghetto blaster?" I asked, and we both looked at the box on the floor, with the almanacs resting on it.

Gavin tried flicking his gaze between me and Yakky. He took longer than most people would to realize that neither of us would help him out.

"I picked it up cheap. I was going to sell it on."

I thought about Sue going nuts with Mary's CDs blasting her and the argument they were about to have, about Mary spending her loan money. The dawning light sometime shows you things you'd rather not see.

"Picked it up where?"

I could see thoughts running across Gavin's face and shook my head at him, so he'd not bother lying again.

"Dago."

He sighed deeply, and I saw his throat working, I think he

was fighting the urge to throw up. In the silence I could hear Yakky breathing, he was still blank-faced, but maybe being asthmatic had tuned Gavin into breathing patterns. He stopped avoiding my eye and tried to blot Yakky out of the picture entirely. He took another hit from the blue inhaler.

"How often has this happened?" I asked softly. I didn't give a damn about Gavin's state of mind quite frankly, but I didn't want Yakky going off half-cocked. Gavin didn't understand the question or pretended not to. "How many times did Dago give you presents to give to Mary. And how often did you sell them on?"

"He's never done it before, never. This was the first time he's ever been around here. Never done it before."

Lucky for everyone in the room, I'd expected Yakky to lose it and I managed to put myself in front of Gavin.

"Easy, Yakky, easy." I put a hand up to stop him advancing anymore. He'd picked one of the champagne bottles off the shelving unit and I didn't doubt its next stop was going to be Gavin's head. Gavin had curled into a foetal ball on the end of the sofa. It was a hard decision to back Yakky down rather than just arrange an alibi.

"I need the money," Gavin was whimpering, like a scratched record, "I need the money."

I ignored him until I was sure Yakky had pulled himself back together. Finally, he gave me the tiniest of nods and stepped backward to the wall. He crossed his arms and looked at Gavin with a blank expression that wasn't fooling anyone.

I sat Gavin back up and waited for him to focus on me.

"You're willingly to steal the last present Dago bought for Mary, and you answer the door with a chuck of wood in one hand." I looked in his eyes and nearly fell into the desperation. "Who do you owe money to?"

The answer was most of north London. He'd run out of friends, credit and licensed bookies who'd take his bets. The unlicensed ones gave credit, but with repayment plans that gave A&E departments a lot of business.

"How much you owe?"

I wasn't surprised when he said five k. I stood up to leave and Yakky pulled himself away from the wall again. He shook his head in answer to my silent question.

"How much?"

He nodded at the box with Dago's last gift in it.

Gavin, who was the colour of milk, managed to pale even more and whimpered, "Just take it."

Yakky pulled his wallet from the side of his boot and counted out four twenties and a pair of tens. He left the notes alongside the empty victory bottles, picked up the box and left the flat.

Gavin didn't take the money straight away; he looked across at me to check it was safe. I wondered which horse he was going to invest it in. I told him I would be telling Sue about the little chat we'd had, and warned him against using Mary as leverage in his next attempt to ponce money.

"Understand this, Gavin, if I hear you've been upsetting Sue and Mary then I'm going to arrange a party and all twenty or thirty guests will swear blind, on a stack of bibles, that me and my friend were there having a good time. Only we won't be. Are we on the same page?"

He said we were and I saw no reason not to believe him.

"Why did Dago come to see you? Were you touching him for money?"

Gavin shook his head and let out a shaking breath. I guessed he was thinking he was back on level ground and didn't have to expel energy on watching how he told me things.

"I don't know. Honestly, I don't. He showed up one night, out of the blue, gave me the stuff for Mary and told me not to forget her birthday." I sat back down again and realized Gavin must have been sweating badly. The peppery smell of him cooling down was too close in the confines of flat.

"Was he threatening you?"

Gavin began patting down his pockets. I told him I didn't smoke, and he gave up the charade of looking for the cigarettes we both knew he didn't have.

"He didn't threaten me, no. He was upset, sort of sad. He

told me if anything happened, he'd made sure Sue was alright, but I'd need to clean up my act, because Mary would still need a father."

Yakky was securing the boom box to the back of his bike with a tangle of bungee cords and loops of duct tape. I asked him if he was alright. People didn't always see it with Yakky's poker straight face, but his bursts of anger troubled him deeply.

"Yeah, I'm fine."

"What you planning to do with that?"

He wound one last loop of tape over the box and shook it to test its seating.

"It's for Mary. You give it to her, yeah? I don't know them well enough, it'd look odd."

I told him it was cool, and he followed me back to my place, so I could take it off him. I offered to give him half the money for it. When he refused, I didn't argue the point. I think paying over the odds for Mary's birthday present made him feel better about threatening Gavin. Not a gesture I thought was called for, but it was Yakky's conscience, so I let him square it how he saw fit.

10.
Smoking, Swearing and The Cracks between Logic

Wednesday 27 September

Life went on. After breakfast I went to work and opened the shop. Slung ink around and earned a living. That was the routine, life going on. But it felt as if I was moving under water. Maybe something more viscous. I'd sit in my flat looking at the wall.

It was meaningless.

The tarot had lost structure and issued random cards and values.

The spirits took my offerings and gave nothing in return.

My friend: the slaughter man.

I finished work early on the Wednesday, after seeing Gavin, and cleared the wall. It didn't clean up well. The charcoal markings were eager to lose their form but insisted on leaving their mark. My notations and sketched queries become a mottled, grey plane. I put the damp towel through the wash and then stared at the blank space. It hadn't been a successful cleansing in any way.

My lack of thought was interrupted by a phone call. It made me jump and I jumped again when I saw it was getting dark. According to the numbers on my mobile, it was six in the evening.

The voice on the other end of the line was Sue's. She wanted to know if I was still willing to dispose of Dago's shotgun. Mention of the gun made something skitter across the back of my mind. But it hid under a stone before I got a good look at it, then refused to come out,

I told Sue I was still willing to do the deed and apologised for letting it slip my mind. With a pregnant daughter to contend with, Sue had forgotten the gun too. She'd remembered it that morning, talking to her sister.

The phrase *shotgun wedding* had been used.

I told her I'd come right over and hung up.

Cracks. Gaps in logic and reason, where things can get lost. Things like three hours of your life, where you stare at a charcoal-stained wall.

It's worth remembering, if a crack's big enough to *lose* things in, then it's big enough to *find* things in.

As I pocketed my phone, I saw the wall wasn't blank anymore. At some point in those lost hours, a single word had been added. Dead centre and no bigger than a signature on the back of a credit card.

MONEY

Whoever had put it there had used my handwriting.

I broke some eggs into the offering bowls and added a few shots of spiced rum. I thanked whoever might be listening and headed out to Sue's, taking the ghetto blaster with me.

It was a shame Yakky wasn't there. He missed Mary's excitement when I handed her the ghetto blaster. Sue asked its provenance, of course. I told her Yakky had come across a deal too good to miss. She'd kept enough bad company in her life not to ask too many questions.

Mary's delight with the boom box increased in volume once she'd plugged it in. Sue suggested we retreat to the attic and retrieve the gun.

The trapdoor to the loft was held shut by a turn catch, it needed a tool, on the end of a stick, to unlock it. Sue went into what had been Dago's office to look for it. When she didn't come out immediately, I followed.

The office bore the marks of Pedro's military upbringing and the level of order would have pleased even the most demanding sergeant major. It was like the business suit he'd been cremated in. Not a side of the man everybody was privy to. Looking around the room I felt a twinge of regret. This was yet another part of my friend that I'd never known.

Sue was squatting behind an over-sized, leather-top desk. Her back was to me as she felt along the rear of some low shelving.

She'd heard me come in, or felt me watching her, because she said, "I can't find the hook thing. Dago normally kept it up there." She flicked a hand in the general direction of the higher shelves. "Maybe Ranjit moved it."

Hearing my accountant's name gave me a moment of confusion. I'd forgotten that I'd recommended him.

"You got him in to do the books, then?"

"Yeah. He did a wonderful job. I thought Dago knew a few tricks, but that fella of yours, acts like he's at war with the inland revenue." Sue made a sound between a sigh and a groan. "I can't find the bloody thing."

She used the edge of a shelf to pull herself upright, then sat heavily into Dago's old swivel chair. With the expanse of the desk in front of her, she looked very small, almost as if she was sinking.

"Have you told the police about Johnny?" she asked, seemingly out of the blue. I told her I hadn't.

"I trampled all over the crime scene, setting the police to work on it wasn't high on my to-do list."

Sue nodded, then put a cigarette between her lips but didn't light it. We were in Dago's inner sanctum. He'd been a clean air zealot in the way only an ex-smoker could be. Sue caught my scrutiny and, very deliberately, fired-up the filter tip. The lines down the side of her mouth deepened with each drag. The I'm-coping-with-it gesture did little to reassure me.

"One of the things Ranjit flagged up was a list of people Dago was paying. A few of the jobs Dago had on the go were for friends, I guess, the payments coming *in* were in cash." She inflected the statement like a question and gave the impression she was unsure about it. I assumed she was parroting an explanation Ranjit had given her. "That's not a problem, apparently, but the wages being paid *out*, to the guys working the jobs, are all above board. All Dago's fellas are clear and clean, regarding tax, and their wages are paid by direct debits.

There's no paperwork, at least none Ranjit can find, saying if the jobs are still ongoing. I could be paying out wages for a job that's finished."

"What's this got to do with Johnny and the police?"

"Johnny's still being paid. His job was one of these cash set-ups. I don't want to cancel the direct debit until I'm officially told he's dead. I don't want someone asking me how I suddenly knew to stop paying him."

I had the feeling again of having missed something and the image of the word money neatly written on my wall popped into my head. Sue took my lack of response as a sign that she was on her own. She blew smoke at the ceiling and watched it dissipate.

"There's only two things give you trouble in this life. Money and men."

As the subjects had come up – and I was feeling useless – I told her that Yakky and I had been to see Gavin.

She closed her eyes and exhaled more smoke, this time in a fast jet.

"I can handle Gavin."

"He claims Dago went around there a few weeks ago and reminded him about Mary's birthday."

"Figures. Useless bastard wouldn't remember any other way."

"Dago told him he had to get his act together. Said if anything happened to him, you'd be taken care of, but Mary would still need a father."

Sue's lips became a hard line. She took a huge drag on her cigarette, so the end glowed a deep red. Then she ground it out on the leather desktop. The burn mark hadn't stopped smoking before she had her lighter out again.

"Bloody…men."

She tried to draw on the fresh cigarette but was holding it so tight, it had split. She slammed it into the desktop with the flat of her hand.

"He was trying to do the right thing, Sue. He thought he was looking out for you and Mary."

Lucky for me, looks don't kill.

"So, he goes to bloody Gavin? I can't count the times that arsehole gambled away the rent then lost the housekeeping trying to win it back. I'd have been better off as a single mother. As it was I had to look after two bloody kids: Gavin and Mary. I told Dago that. He knew what Gavin was like. He'd seen what he was like."

The music from the living room changed, mid-track, and heavy bass notes slapped against our feet. Soul grindingly relentless. Sue's eyes, her whole face, closed tightly for a dozen beats. Then she lit a fresh cigarette, with cold precision, and blew a pencil thin stream of smoke at the burn mark she'd made.

"You know why I started smoking?" I didn't think she'd expected an answer but when I didn't respond she repeated the question. I shook my head. "I was thirteen, desperate to grow up. Me and my friends would hang around the local park. Smoke and swear. 'Cos that's what the grown-ups did." She angled her wrist and carefully burned another hole into the leather. Her words were less clipped when she spoke again. I wouldn't have said calm, more weary. "But after a while we really did grow up. At least the girls did. Most of the boys didn't bother. You have that option. Men get the choice.

"The girls have to grow up. 'Cos we have to raise the children and teach them to stay safe. We get to clean away the mess and do the waiting up late and worrying ourselves to sleep at nights. And the men keep right on smoking and swearing and thinking that's all they have to do. Move on to a bigger playground somewhere and kid on that they're all grown up because sometimes people get hurt."

She studied the pattern she'd burned into the desktop, drew hard on the filter again and began adding another scorch mark.

"When my sister's husband got tired of hitting her and started on the kids, when she finally went to the police, you know what they said?"

I took a guess, "Domestic?"

"Domestic," Sue confirmed. "Some fresh-faced prick who had his mum iron his uniform. I could see what was going through his mind: *if the silly bitch doesn't like it, why doesn't she leave?*"

The answer had been as obvious as it was commonplace. Two kids to raise, no viable means of support and a violent husband, who'd make it a point of 'honour' to find her. I remembered Dago telling me about the situation. I remembered his solution too.

Sue's brother-in-law had been bundled into the back of a van by two men he hadn't been able to describe. They'd driven him to a hospital. Eventually.

Soon after, Sue's sister had a clean, uncontested divorce. Her ex never missed a maintenance payment and never walked without a stick again.

Every member of the HLB had been at a club event on the night in question.

Sue may have read my thoughts because she gave me a withering looked.

"I know what Dago and Silk did. And that bastard deserved all he got and more, but it was still just one step up from the playground. They all thought they were cock of the walk after that. All of them. Even the gobshites that just spent the night round Frenchy's flat, swilling beer. Heroes every one of them. Swaggering about like they were bloody John Wayne. If Linda had put a carving knife in that bastard the first time he hit her, would they have called her a hero? Would they fuck, they'd have called her a crazy bitch.

"That's men in a nutshell, you know that? You swagger about 'cos you're the big protectors looking after the little woman. Or you're knocking the shit out of some silly bitch that hasn't got the sense to run away. You get to play heroes and we get to be little girls, grateful for the protection, or silly bitches that take the abuse. Well there's more to it than that. It takes…more."

The music skipped mid-track again. More hammer-fist bass. Sue dropped the still lit cigarette on the desk. She rubbed her temple as if trying to ease a headache.

"Mary has to grow up. Dago couldn't see that. All he wanted to do was knock over anyone who'd hurt her. Men all think they're immortal. They can't imagine the world can exist if they're not in it. Well he's not here now." She rubbed at her temple again. "Oh, that bloody noise."

She stood up suddenly and I thought she was about to storm downstairs. Instead she went into what must have been Mary's room and dragged out a shocking-pink chair. It gave her the extra height to reach the loft hatch, and I steadied it while she fumbled with the pull-down ladder.

As with the office, Dago's mark had been evident in the loft space. Cast-offs and scraps of domestic history were stacked in plastic storage bins. Dust sheets shrouded items too bulky to be corralled in boxes. But it was still an attic and Dago's need for order hadn't extended to dusting it.

After an hour of searching, Sue and I were covered in streaks of grime. Pulling up tracts of loft insulation had left my skin on edge and I was raw from scratching.

Most people over estimate their cunning, and the space where the gun was meant to have been would have been spotted by any cop at ten paces. Except, there was nothing to spot.

At first, Sue had gone into the attic alone. Standing at the base of the ladder, I heard her grunt as she moved something aside. She said something to herself that I didn't catch, then tutted and swore. After a minute or two of listening to more things being shifted around, I climbed up after her.

"He must have moved it," she said, her back was to me as she pulled up a strip of dirty insulation.

The rock-wool lagging lay in the troughs formed between rafters. Most of the rafters had had boards nailed over them to form a floor, so the insulation was largely hidden. Most of what could be seen, Sue had already pulled aside and the light, from a pair of unshaded bulbs, glittered with clouds of dust.

To the right of the loft hatch, within reach of the ladder, a flap of rock-wool had been neatly folded back. It was a contrast to the disarray Sue was leaving in her wake. I glanced into the exposed hide space. There was a small box that had once contained twenty-five shells of number nine birdshot. I was careful not to leave fingerprints on it when I picked it up. I gave it a shake and it rattled. Some of the shells were missing.

"He must have moved it," Sue said again.

Now I was primed for it, I could hear the edge of unease.

"Was the insulation pulled back when you came up here?"

"Yeah," she said. Then, again, asserted *Dago must have moved it,* before the logic of her answer took hold.

There didn't seem any point in telling Sue what she already knew, so I helped with the futile search.

If Dago had moved the gun to a new location, he'd have taken the ammo with it, at the very least he'd have put the insulation back in place.

When Sue started backtracking and sifting through the rock-wool again, I guided her to the stacks of storage tubs and told her *I'd* double check the lagging. Under the guise of searching I reinsulated her aloft. Finally, she stopped insisting the gun had been moved and accepted it was gone.

"What in God's name was he thinking?"

It was more curse than question.

"Don't know," I told her, which was half true at best.

Sawn-off shot guns have a limited range of uses. None of them required much imagination.

Sue was surrounded by a tide of debris. Her search of the tubs had amounted to up-ending the first half-dozen she came to. She began putting it back to rights. Before going to help her, I took the box of cartridges from their hiding space. They had a date with the Thames.

Sue was crying. Like the hard-faced mare she was, she did it quietly and without fuss. I let her get on with it. It wasn't surprising; everything we touched was a reminder of her time with Dago. One box had been filled with Mary's old school books, and the crying became more earnest.

"He would have loved being a granddad," she said.

We spent another half hour in the attic while Sue got herself back together. When she'd finished crying, she'd wiped her eyes with the back of her hand. The smears of dust mixed with the make-up and looked like camo gear.

"I was all for taking this stuff down the tip." She waved vaguely at the freshly stacked memories. "Dago complained about lugging it all up here, but he couldn't face throwing it out." She shook her head and added, softly, "Men."

My skin held the memory of the loft insulation. Even after twenty minutes in the shower, it felt like my tattoos were trying to crawl away. Clothing made it worse, so I ignored the temperature of my living room and paced back and forth in my pants.

The remainder of Dago's shells had gone over the side of Kew Bridge but not before I'd ripped the top off the box. Now it was pinned to my wall, next to the word 'money', like a Post-it note. An ugly Post-it note, at least to my mind.

The more I dug into Dago's memory, the less certain I was of things. The markers of the life he'd lived were taking my friend from me far more successfully than his death had.

I waited until the small hours before getting dressed and heading back to Enfield.

11.
Burning Questions

Thursday 28 September

"What's up?" Yakky asked me before saying anything else.

I was in the shop before him, rarity enough to raise questions. I told him about my run over to Enfield.

Since my last visit, Maple Blossom Parade was a property down on the deal. Number five had been burnt out. The roof and upper story had collapsed. What little remained was locked away behind steel mesh fencing and its own little parade of plastic ribbon. Blue-and-white stripes, emblazoned with the Met's insignia.

I'd ridden past the end of the street without any perceptible drop in velocity. It was still there long enough to catch the bitter signature of wet soot in the air.

"Pretty much what we expected," Yakky said. "What's the problem?"

"Dago was paying Johnny Simms via direct debit." Somehow Yakky made his blank expression blanker still. "So, we've gone from an unconnected dead body halfway across town, in an empty house, to an employee of a security firm that specialises in placing people in empty houses. An employee on the books, under the gaze of God, the Devil and the all-seeing eye of the inland revenue. I'm beginning to think I was wrong about Dago killing him."

"That why you went back to Enfield?"

I nodded. I'd wanted to take another look around, see if I'd missed something. Only now the crime scene was a pile of ash. Thanks largely to me.

"It doesn't follow that Dago's in the clear just because he left a trail," Yakky said. He was busy with the coffee machine.

"You said yourself: means, motive and opportunity. He still had all three. If this was going to court, I'd say there's a good chance he'd be convicted."

"That's a different argument. I'm not talking about the cops clearing their books, I'm talking about guilt. You've seen Dago's house. Order. Discipline. He may have wound up hating the army, but he carried it with him. He was trained and disciplined and smart. If he'd wanted someone killed, he wouldn't have left a paper trail to follow. Certainly not one that'd lead back to his own home. The more I look at it, the less I see him doing it."

"Doc, I hear what you're saying. Soldier, business man, club prez. Knew how to get stuff done and keep it all tight. But he'd been through the mill. You saw his chest. What he'd done to that tattoo, what he'd done to himself. I counted five cigarette burns, five. And a lot of those scars weren't that old. Perhaps he had Johnny lined up for work. Johnny settled in to that dump in Enfield. Then Dago found out Mary was pregnant and" – he snapped his fingers – "whatever had been going on in his head, that was the final straw."

I shook my head, then nodded.

"Maybe. I don't know."

I kept coming back to the position of Johnny when we'd found him. Sitting up in his makeshift bed. From what I'd been hearing, about his gung-ho attitude, it wasn't how he'd have greeted an intruder. Whoever had killed Johnny had had his trust. And who would Johnny trust more than his own club's president?

I hadn't slept much after getting back from Enfield. What I was hearing from Yakky, I'd already heard from myself, on repeat. Like a bad song. I took a coffee to keep me awake, then slumped in one of the sofas wishing my mind would shut up for a bit.

I was still slumped on the sofa, largely out of sight from the street, when Spooky appeared.

Mid-morning, he parked his minicab on the opposite side

of the road and crossed to the shop, frowning and scanning the street like an extra in a film about Vietnam. Unaware that I'd already seen him, he pulled one of his 'burners' out as he got to the door and pressed it to his ear.

"Yeah … yeah. Look don't give me that crap. I know a load came through customs last week. Well, tell him it's me he'll be sweet."

He did another *Apocalypse Now* style glance behind him, then ruined it all when he failed to see me and cut his dealer chat off too soon. He rallied briefly when he spotted his audience, directing a terse, "Laters, bro," into the phone.

I noticed the screen on the mobile was dark as he slipped it into his pocket.

"Looking for Yak?" I asked.

Spooky gave me a silent, serious-business-type nod.

Yakky was busy stitching PRINCESS, in heavy Germanic script, across a nineteen-year-old proletariat. I thought the font was more suited to a gangsta-style piece. Maybe it was meant to be ironic. He grabbed a break and went to see what Spooky wanted.

I took a seat behind the counter and manned the phone in case it rang. Staying out of sight was purely habit, as was ear wigging. I don't think Spooky knew I was listening, but Yak did. There wasn't much got past him.

Spooky wanted another tattoo for his collection. Given that I ran a tattoo shop, that wasn't ground-breaking news. The kind he wanted made my ears prick up.

"Dagger through the neck," Yakky repeated back to him. "Russian-prison style again?"

Russian-prison style was what used to be known as jailhouse style. Images produced in black with a single needle, detailing done with lines or dotting. The way a tattoo would be produced in a cell, using lashed together equipment. Few of the Russian-prison style pieces you'd see in Europe had any connection to the work produced in Eastern Bloc nicks. Those had defined meanings and overtones.

I knew what the dagger through the neck was reputed to

mean. I assumed Yakky did too because he asked Spooky if he was sure, and that was something he almost never did. Spooky assured him he was. It seemed he had a point to make.

Yakky told him if he wanted to come back that evening, after six, he could do it then. Spooky strutted back to his cab, his attempts to look clandestine standing out a mile.

Yakky caught my eye.

"What you make of that?" he asked.

I didn't go through the motions of pretending I hadn't listened in.

"He's taking his self-image to another level."

"Maybe," Yakky said. I made the spooling motion with my index finger. He looked into the backroom to check his German princess wasn't listening. "I was thinking about the hiding he got off Micky the other week."

London's best dressed bouncer has been laid low, and London's least discreet dealer was looking for a dagger tattoo.

The dagger piecing the neck, so legend had it, meant the wearer had killed and was willing to do it again. I told Yakky I'd stay and keep him company when he started work on Spooky.

"How you want to play it?" Yakky asked.

"Try and get him on side," I told him. "You catch more flies with sugar than salt."

Of course, if sugar didn't work, we could accommodate a taste for salt.

I'd tried to bet a tenner that Spooky would come through the door with a phone in his hand. Yakky had ignored me. He wasn't one of life's gamblers, at least not with me. Smart.

"Yeah…course I can, how much you want? No problem." Spooky tucked the phone away before the door had swung shut behind him. The screen was still dark.

Yakky ushered him through to the backroom and, ever the pro, showed him the drawings he'd run up in his lunch hour. I locked the front door and closed down the lights in the waiting room.

The evening traffic was commuter heavy and the streetlamps glistened with icy rain water. If you were making a film, you might have squeezed in a nicely threatening roll of thunder. I realised I wasn't worried about what Yakky and I might be about to do. Maybe good solid London-in-autumn dreariness was what was called for.

Spooky okayed the drawings. I didn't think they were Yakky's best work, but then I wasn't sure they were even going to get used. Straight lifts from a web-search of 'prison ink'. I cleaned up around my work station as Spooky made himself comfortable in Yakky's chair. A throwaway phone placed carefully on his lap should he have an urgent call. I also lit a candle to Ezulie Dantor and caught Yakky watching me from the corner of his eye.

When the buzz of the tattoo gun started, I settled myself and watched Yak work. He started at the base of Spooky's neck and, just above his collar bone, quickly outlined the handle of a dagger. The only tattooist I knew who could work faster than Yakky, without producing a mess, was Gina, my ex-wife. She'd given up tattooing the year before in favour of *real* art. The sort people like enough to put on their walls but not enough to bury in their skin.

"So, what's this one in aid of?" Yak asked quietly. He had begun some details on the handle of the dagger. He'd given the image a more European look, it possibly wasn't what Spooky had in mind. The result would look more old-school tribute than authentic Russian lock-up. In the event that Spooky found himself inside, the difference might get him an easier time in the showers.

"Oh, you know, business stuff," Spooky told him.

I suggested it looked like a heavy sort of business and Yakky grunted an agreement. Spooky looked like he was about to smile, then caught himself, and produced a grim frown. He sighed heavily.

"It can be. Sometimes people get hurt." Yakky didn't answer and Spooky filled the silence with, "Some people need to be taught who they shouldn't mess with. Some people need to learn the hard way." He sighed again and added, "Nature of the business; someone gets out of order, they need to be put straight."

The candle to Ezulie Dantor guttered as the dagger took shape. Yakky inked in silence for a while then fixed Spooky with an unblinking eye.

"So, who you been putting in order, Spooky?"

I could see Spooky struggling with his new-found role of hard case. He'd suddenly realised that he was locked inside a silent shop with a man holding a needle an inch away from his neck.

I put a little sugar on.

"You can tell us Spooky, we all know the score."

He grabbed the lifebelt of camaraderie with both lips.

"Some stroppy bouncer over in Chiswick."

"Black Micky?" Yakky asked.

"That's the guy."

"Works the door at The House of Ice too, doesn't he?"

Spooky eased back into his chair a little; he probably hadn't realised how tensed he'd been.

"That's him, cocky little sod."

"You put a shiv in Black Micky?" I asked. "You better pray he didn't recognise you – the crew he rides with will stomp you into the ground." I left him a second to digest the change in emphasis. "Ex-army boys, very thorough hombres."

Yakky fired up the tattoo gun again. Spooky didn't jump, but there was a decided twitch.

"Yeah, you might want to be careful where you show this off, Spooky." He nodded at the nearly finished tattoo. "You might find you're wearing the three-D version".

Bravado proved to be a harder nut than the man wearing it and Spooky managed a laugh.

"Who's Black Micky's obbo, Yak? Smudge is it?" Yakky nodded. "You know him?" I addressed this to Spooky, who obviously *did* to judge by his complexion. "Runs security at The House of Ice. Pure bastard."

Spooky still wasn't getting the idea. Yakky turned to look at me and I shrugged. Sometimes sugar melts in the mouth and other times it dissolves in the mists of delusion. Yakky sat back on his stool and quietly regarded his client.

"Spook, you start telling people you know something about Black Micky getting knifed, and you'll be up to your neck in shite. Think about it, you're a cabby, you'll get a call to an address some night and wind up with no kneecaps. You hearing me?"

Spooky opened his mouth to speak but closed it again without a sound. I could see his throat working as he tried to moisten his tongue.

"I didn't say I stabbed him."

When Yakky didn't respond, Spooky's eye fell on me and he repeated the statement. I left the silence to contract around him a bit longer.

"So, what's with the ink?" Yakky finally asked and punctuated the sentence by starting with tattoo gun again. The needle pinned Spooky like he was a butterfly

"It's just a tattoo," he protested.

Without looking up from the blade tip he was inking, Yakky said, "It's a prison tattoo, a prison tattoo that sends a message. It's your choice man, but if I was part of a crew that had taken out one of Smudge's men, I'd be a bit more discreet."

Spooky managed not to back pedal entirely, he was trapped in the fantasy he'd built for himself, though he did allow he wasn't part of the crew at the nightclub. But if he wanted to be a part of an all-powerful drugs cartel, stepping the razor's edge in London's underworld, then he had to believe that world existed. Which it doubtless did, even if not in the manner Spooky would like to think.

We allowed him to think he'd chanced upon the world of shadowy figures, watching and thirsting for vengeance at every slight. We all sat without speaking and listened to the buzzing needle song, as Yakky applied an ill-considered boast. It was a shame that Spooky would probably be too frightened to show it to anybody. Yakky did damn nice work.

Once the tension had plateaued and I judged Yakky was

close to finishing, I asked Spooky the thirty-thousand-dollar question,

"So, who did shiv Black Micky?"

Whether he answered through fear or because he was in character I couldn't say. The important thing was that he did. He almost gabbled the response but managed to stop himself.

"It was a couple of guys from Harlesden. They used to move a lot of gear at The House of Ice, only Micky and Smudge muscled in. Then the same thing started again at that gay club, and they'd been shifting poppers over there like no one's business."

He petered out.

"So why Micky, he's not the only bouncer there?" Yakky asked, the needle had gone quiet again. I could see he'd finished, but he didn't look like he was going to tell Spooky that until he was ready.

"Micky and Smudge wanted the whole thing."

I didn't get what he meant and leaned in a bit closer to him. "Meaning what, exactly?"

He glanced at Yakky, an appeal, and Yakky motioned me to back off.

"The House of Ice is a closed shop now. If Smudge doesn't control it, it don't get shifted. You can still deal at that gay club, but, if you don't give them a cut, you get a kicking."

"And the Harlesden boys weren't happy about that?"

Spooky shook his head. "It's just not getting a cut to turn a blind eye, it's like a takeover. The gay club's getting like The House of Ice. They were probably too scared to make a move at the House, that's all Smudge's guys there. The gay club has its own people, less risky".

Yakky dressed the fresh tattoo. The violent imagery looked stupid on the obviously terrified Spooky, but the ink was nicely vivid against the fish-belly white. He'd asked us, a dozen times, not to tell *anyone* that he'd given us what he knew. We assured him we wouldn't.

Yakky had refused payment and told him he'd owe him a favour. I think the hint of underworld bonhomie did as much to calm him as our assurances that we keep quiet.

When the north London drug baron had driven his minicab away, Yakky rubbed the tips of his finger and thumb together. The universal sign language for money. Where there's drugs, money's usually close behind.

"That could explain the push to make the Handsome London Boys a full patch club," Yakky offered.

The dope peddler hanging around the school gates was a tabloid wet dream, designed to sell papers. It was as much a myth as the *altered consciousness* spiel, designed to sell drugs. Narcotics, like every commodity, have a price and need a buyer to pay it. Until little Janet and John leave school and start earning, they don't represent much of a profit margin.

Pubs, raves and festivals provide a more lucrative market than most classrooms. Nightclubs also feature high on the list. If you controlled the door on the club, you could dictate what got sold and who by. You'd make a few friends and a lot of enemies. A reliable and visible crew, to help mark your ground, made good business sense.

Keeping the competition under control was another good idea. And in the drugs trade, corporate takeovers tended to be aggressive by nature.

Money.

12.
HAND SOME

Friday 29 September

Smudge was waiting outside the shop the next morning before we opened. I'd heard his Harley pulling in as I was having breakfast. I decided caution was the better part of valour and waited for the sound of Yakky's engine before leaving my flat.

It was raining but Smudge, sat on his bike, was indifferent to the downpour. As I'd drawn level to him, Yakky had sidestepped, putting himself between us. Smudge's drifting gaze slid across him and onto to me. The manoeuvre hadn't been lost on him. We all exchanged nods and he climbed off his bike, moving like a man in his nineties. It was twenty minutes before we officially opened to the public, but I didn't have the heart to leave him outside.

Yakky put the kettle on while I fired the heating up. Smudge peeled his jacket off and, not bothering to arrange a display of HLB insignia, draped it over the back of a sofa. The rain had soaked through his leather and the lumberjack's shirt he wore underneath. The material across his chest and shoulders was heavy and dark. It matched the circles under his eyes. He sat down the way a puppet would if you cut the strings. Yakky asked if he wanted tea and he shook his head, then changed his mind and said yes as if he hadn't really heard the question.

I sat on the opposite sofa and waited for Smudge's restless gaze to find me.

"Help you?"

Smudge nodded, again as if he wasn't really listening. He asked if we could fit him in that day. Yakky caught my eye from behind the counter and nodded, he had the appointments book in front of him.

"You don't have anyone until half twelve."

I asked Smudge what he wanted to have done. He held his hands up, clenched loosely into fists, one against the other. I knew what he was going to say.

"Handsome."

"Across the knuckles? The way Johnny had it?"

He nodded. "Yeah. He'd have liked that. How much?"

"Nothing. I won't charge you for that."

Smudge's eyes had barely been registering anything above knee height and I almost jumped when they locked onto my face.

"I know what's being said, alright. It's bollocks. I ain't a poof neither was Johnny. We just…I mean…"

The flash of anger, or energy, deserted him and the words trailed off. His gaze began floating again.

"I don't give a damn what people are saying. Someone you cared about is gone. I know what that feels like."

I also knew what guilt felt like. I could cut it how I liked but Johnny's body, sat in its own shit in a condemned house, had been burned to anonymous charcoal because of me. Inking a tribute onto someone who loved him was the least I could do in his memory.

The tattoo was a straightforward piece. Eight letters in a basic Gothic font, matching the lettering of the HLB patch.

The broken puppet drop he'd made into the sofa wasn't repeated for the dentist's chair, instead Smudge lowered himself into it with a fragile dignity. It was how I'd imagine aristocrats ascended the guillotine. I remembered his aversion to the needle and warned him work on the fingers wasn't pleasant. He shrugged and said he knew, Johnny had told him.

I spent a lot of time positioning the templates and getting the letters lined up. Smudge's input was minimal. Now and then he'd grip the armrests of the chair but other than that he was impassive.

"When did Jason speak to you?" I asked.

"Saturday morning. I still can't take it in."

Toneless. Flat.

"Yeah. I get that." I loaded the needle with ink and set it buzzing. Smudge's grip on the arms of the chair eased slightly. I think he wanted the discomfort. It made the feelings he was grappling with physical and more palpable. "You ready?"

"Yeah." I touched the needle to the little finger on the right and began outlining the H. "I'm glad you found him, Doc. You did well, thanks." The words came out quickly, like he didn't want to give himself time to change his mind. "He'd have wanted to be found. He wasn't a loner. Couldn't stand being on his own."

I didn't know how what to say to that, so just nodded and kept my head bowed to the ink. His grip on the chair tighten again as I started putting the N over the bony ridge of his middle finger. I asked after Black Micky, to get him talking again.

"Not good. He's out the hospital but he's really shaken up. Says he'll be back at work in a couple of weeks but I'm not sure."

"Does he know about Johnny?"

I felt him shake his head.

"Frenchy wants the news to filter out naturally."

The silence fell again. It began to get to me and I called out to Yakky to pull some music up on the computer. Two of the tracks, of whatever he'd chosen, ground into my nerves and then I heard him greeting a customer. Still Smudge didn't speak. I finished up the right hand and moved across to the left. I asked him again if he was ready and got a slow nod in answer. I nearly made the old joke about changing hands, but it wasn't the time or place.

Yakky's customer came in wearing Day-Glo Lycra and a cloud of jittery chatter. She was wire thin apart from her legs which were composed from twisted sheets of muscle. Full-length leg tattoos on London's cyclists were becoming as common as full sleeves amongst bikers. Both demographics came with a coating of road grime. I welcomed the lively presence, but Smudge drew himself down another level.

I finished up as Yakky began outlining a chain and sprocket on his cyclist's calf. Back in the waiting room I made Smudge listen to the standard lecture on tattoo aftercare. A surprising number of people don't take any notice of it and I could tell he was one of them. But that was his choice. Once a tattoo leaves the shop it stops being mine, until that point I do my best to keep it safe.

Smudge asked again if I wanted payment and thanked me when I told him no. He briefly held my gaze and I thought he was about to say something more, but he abruptly pulled on his sodden jacket and walked out the shop. The noise of his Harley starting up shook the street, then suddenly cut out. When I looked up to see what had happened, Smudge was sat on the silenced machine, staring back at me through the window. He glanced quickly around him before dismounting and coming back to the shop. Glancing about him again he stopped just inside the door and beckoned me over.

"Jason told me what you said about Dago." He kept his voice low as if the room was full of people. When I didn't answer he added, "About him killing Johnny. Well you got it wrong, he can't have."

I wasn't sure how I wanted to play it with the HLB, and with the likes of Smudge in particular, so I stayed quiet. Again, he looked over his shoulder. I don't imagine he thought anyone was listening in. I think he was struggling with own his loyalties.

"I saw Johnny after Dago was killed."

Smudge obviously had something to say and wanted to talk. I didn't want to hold the conversation in whispers and, clearly, he didn't want to try his hand at public speaking. I suggested going up to my flat where we could get some privacy. Yakky didn't notice me leave the shop. He had a few choice words for me when I eventually returned.

I led Smudge straight to the kitchen and, once the kettle was on, I sat across from him at the pine table that served as my dining room.

"You saw Johnny Simms alive, after Dago was killed?"

Smudge nodded. It was a relief. In my own mind I'd already been doubting the solidity of my verdict, but it was still a relief. It also raised other possibilities.

"The day Frenchy told us about finding Dago," Smudge said. "I'd seen Johnny caning it down the North Circ."

"What time?"

"About five. Five in the morning."

Dago had been found by Frenchy at around two a.m. He'd made the nine-nine-nine call, knowing the ambulance was blue lighting its way to a lost cause.

I asked Smudge if he was sure it was Johnny. I felt bad for asking when I saw his expression.

"I'm sure. He saw me and…" Smudge lifted his left arm and made a clenched fist salute. He brought the hand down and pressed the back of it to his mouth, like he was about to be sick. "That was the last time I saw him. I pretended I hadn't, just ignored him. Drove past."

Smudge, Black Micky and Reggie – a Handsome London Boy I didn't know – had been working security at The House of Ice the night before. The shift, Thursday into Friday, had been largely trouble free and, with time on his hands, Micky had spread some of his charm around a drunken hen night. The bride-to-be and most of the party had staggered off around midnight. Four hardcore party girls had made to through until closing time and one of them suggested they take the celebrations back to their flat.

Back at the flat the party hadn't come to much. The drinking picked up where it had left off at the club, now augmented by various pharmaceuticals. One of the women passed out soon after landing and two others vanished into a bedroom with Black Micky. Reggie's chemical handouts kept the fourth hen-nighter entertained.

"So, you're left twiddling your thumbs?"

Smudge shrugged. "I had a toke. Listened to the shit Reggie's bint was spouting, I don't know what he was handing out, but they were both high as kites."

"You weren't?"

"Bit of puff. That was it for me, that and a tin of larger. I knew I had to get everyone back home in the morning, we were using my car. I didn't want to risk getting pulled and losing me licence, not for a shot at some rough old skank."

"A shot you didn't get anyway."

"Oh, don't you believe it, it was on the table if I wanted it."

There was a flash of arrogance in his response. For a moment he was back to the malign presence he'd been the last time I'd seen him.

"But you didn't? Want it I mean."

Smudge snorted. "One was out cold. Micky had sloped off with both the lookers. The last one standing had brought her guts up before we left the club, then started on a bottle of Bacardi the minute she got in the flat. She stank to high heaven, and Reggie had already been through her."

"Not your style?"

"I told you already, I'm no fucking queer."

The words were harsh but quietly said.

"Is that why you pretended not to see Johnny?"

I was caught in the crosshairs of Smudge's gaze again. It didn't last long. The spark of anger vanished, and he looked away. It wasn't his usual condescension; this time, he was avoiding eye contact. When he spoke again his tone had changed. It was a confession.

The Handsome Boys had taken their cue to leave the flat around four. One of the women who'd teamed up with Micky had made a post-coital dash from the bedroom, too embarrassed to show her face. Reggie's match had begun frantically snatching at the air in front of her trying to catch things only she was seeing. Reggie was high enough himself to find the whole scene manically funny. Smudge had exercised leadership by means of jangling his car keys.

Black Micky had to be extracted from the bedroom where he was sat naked, sending a text, while the remaining woman snored. He'd left the room without a backward glance and tried to doze in the car, half collapsed across the back seat.

Reggie, pupils the size of pinheads, had fired questions at him about the ménage a trios. Discretion or fatigue had largely held Micky's tongue. Reggie started talking to Smudge instead. The blokey banter quickly found its way to his score of zero the previous night.

As they pulled onto the North Circ someone remarked it was a pity the *Missus* hadn't been there.

"The Missus being Johnny?" Smudge nodded. "Meaning your Missus, I suppose?"

"Yeah. It was a standing wind-up."

"Who was it meant to wind-up, you or Johnny?"

"Either one of us. I think Jason started it, he was joking, but Johnny didn't see the funny side and went into one. So of course, everyone picked up on it. The old guys, Silk, Jason, that crowd, they could still get away with it, but the young guys let up on him pretty quick." He frowned to himself. "Johnny dished out a couple of slaps and people decided getting a cheap laugh wasn't worth the fight. He had a short fuse about anything like that."

"Anything like what?" In answer Smudge raised a hand from the table letting it hang limply at the wrist. "Gays?"

"Hated them."

"Is that why you didn't take him on for the door work?"

I was thinking of the clientele of The Salt Lick, where Micky had been stabbed.

Smudge graced me with another moment of full eye contact.

"He told me he didn't have a police record. Turned out he had a conviction for assault, back when he was living in Southend. It wasn't anything major, someone lost a couple of teeth. When I asked him about it he told me, some nancy boy had tried it on."

It sounded like there was something being left unsaid.

"You believed him?"

"Yeah. But…the way he said it, he was really pissed off. At the time I thought it was because he knew he wasn't getting the job but…I don't know. I think it was more than just that."

"You were still getting the wind-ups?"

"At first it wasn't about me, it was like I was in on the joke. That was changing though. I don't think anybody really thought I was queer for Johnny, but I kept getting the comments, getting the needle put in."

The round of comments in the car came just as Johnny Simms rode past. Micky was trying to sleep and Reggie, head down with a lap full of tobacco, was struggling to roll a fag. Only Smudge saw Johnny's clenched fist salute, rather than draw attention to himself, he chose to ignore it.

Smudge had his hands flat on the table. His gaze had finally settled on the clear dressings I'd put around the new tattoos. His homage to Johnny Simms.

"Then, that night, Frenchy told us Dago had been killed." Smudge grimaced and closed his eyes tight.

"Did he get everyone together to tell them?"

"He called an extra ordinary meeting. That's when I started wondering about Johnny, when he didn't appear."

"Did everyone else show?"

"We all got a text or a message: T-U-E." I shook my head to show I didn't understand. "Turn up or else. The only other no-show was Paddy. He was laid up in hospital having his knee replaced."

"Did anyone notice Johnny wasn't there?"

"Not really, it was all pretty messy. Frenchy made a sort of formal announcement at the next regular meeting, but that night, he told the first few people who got there and it filtered through as more guys turned up. People drifted in and out, it was easy to miss faces, we didn't take a roll call. I was one of the first to get there and I stayed until the end, waiting for Johnny."

"Have you told Frenchy this, about you seeing Johnny that morning?"

"No, I didn't realise at first, I didn't put the times together. And no one's talking about it, for the moment we're keeping everything quiet."

"Why?"

Smudge actually looked at me, trying to size me up. At that

moment my mobile started ringing and I fished it out of my pocket. He took the interruption as an opportunity to look away.

"Why?" I asked again once I'd turned my phone off.

"No one knows about Johnny yet. But when the news gets out, Frenchy doesn't want anyone drawing conclusions about anything. He worried about someone starting something with the Eight-Six. The less people know the better."

He shrugged. El Presidente had spoken. It was time for all good soldiers to follow orders.

"You think that's the right decision?"

"For the good of the club, yes."

"You think Dago and Johnny would have seen it that way?"

"Yes. I do. I knew Johnny, he'd have done anything for the good of the Handsome London Boys, anything."

"So, why are you telling me?"

Smudge picked up the mug of tea I'd put in front of him and took a long draught before answering.

"Because you found Johnny. No one else even thought to look for him and all the time he was fucking dead. I know you and Dago went back a long way, he had a lot of time for you. He didn't kill Johnny. I think you're entitled to know that."

I thanked him. Then I asked if he knew of anybody who would have wanted Johnny dead.

"No. I'm sure he made enemies, he was an easy bloke to start a fight with but…" Smudge shook his head and went back to staring at his hands. "I'd like to know who did it though, I really would."

The words were barely audible but the feeling behind them was loud enough.

"You think there's any connection with the guys that shivved Black Micky?"

Smudge snorted a laugh. "Nah. Anyway, they're dealt with."

"Harlesden crew?"

There was more than a little satisfaction watching him fail to hide his surprise. "How the fuck'd you know that?"

I shrugged and tried to look relaxed. Not an easy task as,

once again, I was in the crosshairs of his attention.

"I went to see Micky, in hospital. From what he described, it sounded like he was set up. So, probably more than one person involved. I ask you about the *guys* who put the shiv in, and you say *they've* been taken care of. Plurals. That confirms it. Micky also told me the door at The Salt Lick wasn't under your control, not like The House of Ice. I know dealing in The House of Ice is a fool's game, without your say so. People get hurt."

I could see Smudge slipping, from his comfort zone of hostility into the cold waters of puzzlement. That was the speciality of the house. I gave him my Cheshire Cat smile.

"So, a violent crew with a score to settle. I figure that score was more likely racked up locally, at The House of Ice, than over in Chiswick, during the gay cabaret. Crew, local to Harlesden, looking to repay a favour. They jump in a car and nip over to The Salt Lick where London's best dress bouncer won't have anyone much watching his back."

I left out the bit where London's least successful drugs baron dropped in for a tattoo and told me and Yakky all of the above. Leaving Spooky's name out of it was a nod to his continued good health.

And avoiding full disclosure made me look smarter than I was.

"Clever fucker ain't you?" Smudge told me after a suitably aggressive pause.

"Must be true," I told him. "Everyone says the same thing."

He didn't smile back. He put on the faux Jamaican accent you hear bounced around north London's school yards.

"*Ay mon, ya work it bout. Micky 'im get stab up by a couple of gangstas from the Harlesden massiffe.* Well bully for you. So, fucking what?"

I gave him a moment or two of my own brand of silence then leant in closer. Not right into his personal space, just a bit nearer. Enough to not make it cosy.

"I'll tell you, *so fucking what.* You want to know who murdered Johnny. Well how do you plan on finding out?"

Smudge's gaze had slid away again. I wanted to grab hold of his throat and twist his face around. But I had a shrewd idea how that'd turn out. "Did you know Dago had lined Johnny up with a live-in security gig, over the other side of town?"

He spared me a glance.

"No."

"No. You were probably his closest friend and even you didn't know. But some other bastard did."

Smudge was still finding interesting things to look at over my shoulder, but at the words 'closest friend', he turned back to me.

"You don't know shit. Maybe he just walked in on some crackhead and…boom."

I shook my head. "He'd got there and got it set up. His gear was laid out, tins of food, camping stove, sleeping bag. He'd even had time to take a shit and find out the toilet didn't flush. There hadn't been a struggle. If someone came at me with a garrotte I'd move around a bit. I found his body propped up in a corner, on his sleeping bag. Right opposite the door, like he'd sat there while someone just walked in the room. Him and his killer knew each other."

"Why are you telling me this?"

"I'm the best chance of finding who did this, but I want to know where your loyalties are. What's the big issue for you? Your club or your friend's life?"

13.
Three Handsome London Boys

Smudge didn't speak as we walked back to his Harley. He had a lot to think about and, I suspected within the confines of the life he lived, a hard decision to make. Before he dropped the clutch and pulled away he turned and nodded at me. It might have been nothing more than a hands-free parting wave, but I chose to take it as a good omen.

Yakky met me at the door.

"You alright? I rang, but you didn't answer."

I assured him I was fine and told him Smudge had seen Johnny alive and well, four hours after Dago was killed. Yakky nodded and then looked over his shoulder, back into the shop. It wasn't the subtlest of hints, but I pretended I hadn't seen it.

"Can you manage without me for a while? There's something I need to do."

"Want to tell me what?"

In answer I tapped my right arm and the tattoo of Baron Semedi. Yakky didn't roll his eyes, but I took his exasperation as read.

The Voodoo tradition has several names and forms for the spirit of the dead. My favourite was Baron Semedi. A cigar-chomping skeleton with a taste for spiced rum, dressed in a funeral suit and sporting a top hat. Grinning and laughing at death, because that's the only thing it makes sense to do. His tattoo was also a reminder of my marriage. It was the last one Gina had done for me.

In the court of law that ran inside my head, Dago had been declared not guilty. Now there was *my* guilt to deal with. I'd paid respects to my friend as his body was burned and then accused his memory of murder. So, I rode out to Staples Corner to make some sort of peace.

The rain had been fairly constant for the past week. Most of the flowers and cards left on the smear of grass had turned to colourless pulp. There were a few bright spots, some people had renewed their tributes and others had come late to the party. Bound to a lamppost with duct tape was a modest but fresh bouquet. The attached card was printed with the colours of the Eight-Six MC and bore the handwritten message: *With Respect.* The lettering was a finely executed copperplate and I wondered if it was the work of one the club's tattooists.

I carried out the sort of thing I do and part of me was comforted by the thought that Dago might be aware of my contrition. That gap in logic again, the crack where intellect stops and something else happens. Instinct, intuition, the subconscious. Some people talk about *gut feelings* and *things coming out of the blue.* Or they commune with their muse. For me, wedged tightly in that gap – and too deep to be coaxed into the light – is belief, ritual, the Voodoo laws and the faces of the tarot.

Think you've been away from the cave too long to trouble with such nonsense? Next time you hear a creak on the stairs at four in the morning, will it be logic driving your fear?

When I finished, I stood for a while staring along the way the hit-and-run driver would have come. It felt like a long time, but I doubt it was even a full minute. A car transporter, with a trio of crumpled hatchbacks riding on it – likely on route for Frenchy's compactor – laboured down the road. As the driver worked the gears, to make the right turn, he took in the scene. The motorcycle at the kerb, a man standing by a pile of dead flowers. He caught my eye and bowed his head, in acknowledgment of what he thought he was seeing. I found it a strangely touching gesture and lifted a hand in return.

As the transporter hauled through the turn something rolled over in the back of my mind. I felt cold. Not because of the weather or my damp leathers.

I walked back and forth across the junction two or three times. Watched different vehicles taking the route the transporter had taken. Then I rode back to my flat.

Back to the altar and the wall. Then, finally, back to logic.

Yakky called me from the shop before he locked up for the night. He asked if I was alright. He'd heard me ride up the alley at the side of the shop when I'd returned mid-afternoon. I hadn't checked in and now it was seven in the evening.

"Yeah," I told him, "I'm fine. Any chance you can come up? Got something to show you."

"Yeah, will do."

He was longer than I'd expected. He'd come by way of the local pizza shop and handed me a flat box spotted with grease.

"Figured you wouldn't have eaten."

He followed me into the living room and collapsed into one of the armchairs. He didn't comment on the wall until he'd finished his first slice of pizza.

At last, he pointed and said, "Is that where Dago got taken out?"

It was. Three-foot square and drawn as if the viewer were standing ten foot back from the mouth of the junction. I'd portrayed a dark sky, the industrial units gleaming under security floodlights and the verge illuminated by a lamppost. I'd omitted the flowers and cards but left in the gouge marks on the kerb and the damaged fencing.

To the left of the drawing was a smaller, schematic version of the same scene. An aerial view with the addition of two rectangles, one impacting the other. Dago's Electra Glide and whatever had hit it. X marked the point of landing.

Yakky started on another slice of pizza without further comment. He was looking over the revamped wall and giving no indication of what he thought. His eye settled on the sketch of the room with Johnny's body in it. I asked if that was how he remembered it. He nodded then looked away.

"So, what's this in aid of now?" He pointed at the drawing of the junction.

I knew he was purposely avoiding the rest of the wall. And the tarot cards spread on the floor. That was okay, there was logic showing its head now. Enough logic to ruin anyone's sleep.

I stood up and tapped one of the notes on the wall: 870 lbs.

"That's what an Electra Glide weighs. Dago's was stripped back a bit, but it still came in at over a quarter of a ton."

Another note read: TEN FEET. I pointed at my picture of the crash scene, the gouge marks in the kerb.

"That's where the Glide mounted the pavement." I rapped a knuckle on the bent over section of fencing. "That's where it landed. Ten feet away."

"That driver must have been shifting."

"Yeah, but that's not all."

I took a pencil and, on the overhead view, drew a line from where the bike had landed to the point where it had taken a chunk out of the kerb. I kept the line going. As the crow flies, it went from the fence, through the witness marks on the kerb, through the mouth of the junction and straight along the road.

"Eight ball in the side pocket," Yakky said. He still had a slice of pizza in his hand, but he'd stopped eating. He realised I was waiting for him to say something else. "Am I missing something here? Nasty accident and all that but…what?"

"The position of the bike's all wrong. To take the route it did, Dago's Glide must have been directly opposite the mouth of the junction when it was hit, agreed?" Yakky nodded. "If he was heading in the direction of Frenchy's unit he'd have been pulling a right. I didn't think of it until I was there today and saw a lorry making the turn. As you come out of the junction, you move in an arc. The only way Dago would have been there" – I tapped the impact spot on the bigger drawing – "would be if he was crossing the mouth of the junction, or if he was parked up. And he can't have been crossing the junction because the road's been blocked off."

On the map the two roads formed a T-junction. In reality, the left hander had been sealed off with a preformed concrete barricade.

"So why would he park up in an industrial estate, at night, less than a mile from Frenchy's unit?" I asked.

"Because someone asked him to meet them there."

"Exactly." I rapped the wall with my knuckles again. This time on the drawing of the flood-lit industrial unit. "So, after dark, he's parked up particularly underneath a streetlight and, as a back drop, he's got sixty square foot of pale grey, pressed-steel wall. Which is lit up by no less than four security lights. Stevie Wonder would have had a job not to see him."

"Yet he gets rammed hard enough to punch a quarter of a ton of steel into a fence that's ten foot away." Yakky swore under his breath. "This wasn't a hit-and-run."

"No," I agreed. "It was an execution."

Yakky started chewing on his dinner again. He saw me looking at him and jabbed a finger at my own pizza. Or rather the box I'd yet to open.

"Being hungry won't change any of this. Eat."

I slumped into the other armchair and did as he suggested. Yakky asked if I could guess the topping without reading the scrawled description on the box. I couldn't. About halfway through, I went to the kitchen and made tea, mainly to get rid of the taste of dinner. When I came back, Yakky had finished eating and was sat on the edge of his chair, studying one of my notations on the wall.

It was a trio of interlocking circles. I'd pinned the Ten of Swords in one of them: Johnny Simms. Dago was represented by the Magican. Black Micky I'd simply designated MB.

Three Handsome London Boys, not quite, sitting in a row.

Where the three circles overlapped I'd written,

- HLB
- PLANNED
- EIGHT-SIX?
- MONEY?

-Dealers?

"You think someone's gunning for the HLB?" Yakky asked.

"Might be. Dago and Johnny, both murdered. Micky stabbed."

"You going to tell Frenchy, about Dago's *accident*?"

"Not at the moment. The Eight-Six and the Handsome Boys are both hyped up. For now, Frenchy's keeping a lid on things. I think that's for the best, I don't want a war on my doorstep."

Yakky resumed chewing his pizza, after another mouthful he shook his head.

"Surely, if he knows Dago didn't kill Johnny, it's academic?"

"He doesn't know. Smudge didn't twig about the times straight away, he hasn't told anyone else yet."

"He will though," Yak said.

I suspected the story Smudge had told me wasn't something he could easily recount in the context of his club. Whatever the truth of his relationship with Johnny, it was something he felt threatened by.

"I've asked him not to."

"And he agreed?"

"He's thinking about it. He said if he decides El Presidente needs to hear about it, he'll let me know."

I was currently in credit for locating Johnny's earthly remains. I wasn't under any illusion that my credit would prove any more fireproof. Yakky's thoughts were probably following the same line because he shrugged and pointed at the wall, leaving the subject alone.

"The Magican's Dago. That right?" I nodded. "Why?"

"Wisdom. Hidden knowledge. If Ramsey was being straight with us, then Dago was negotiating the Handsome Boys dropping their patches and taking up Eight-Six colours instead. I don't think that was common knowledge around the HLB."

Yakky nodded at the listed items in the overlap.

"That's the similarities between the…attacks?"

"Yeah. They were all different but none of them were spontaneous. From what Micky told me, whoever put the shiv in waited until the other bouncer was busy and drawing a crowd. Might even have been someone staging some trouble, to draw him away. Planned."

"Spooky's Harlesden crew?"

"Maybe. Smudge didn't disagree when I suggested that, said they'd been dealt with. You think Spooky was on the level with that story?"

"I think he believed it. But I've got to wonder, how many real players would Spooky know? He might have just been regurgitating somebody else's line of bullshit." Yakky slumped back into his chair. He was reading the list again, or at least looking at it. "Whatever the truth of it, this looks like trouble."

I couldn't help but agree. The question was, did we make it our trouble or leave it for someone else to sweat on?

"We could just walk away," I said. "Sue asked us to find Johnny Simms. Job done. Nothing we do is going to bring Dago back."

Yakky gave me a long, expressionless look and finally shook his head.

"You ain't going to walk away."

"No."

Yakky didn't leave until the small hours. Then, alone in the flat again, with the wall staring back at me, I was hit by a fresh wave of emotion.

Grief normally comes with a side order of anger. It tends to be formless with nowhere to go. People we care about die and that makes us angry. And the universe shrugs its shoulders and says: tough, deal with it. What I had then, sat in my armchair, full of bile and bad pizza, was different.

I sorted through a tarot pack until I found the eighth card of the Major Arcana. Justice. I set it high on the wall. Then I took up the offering bowls and sacrificed what remained of the night to Ezulie Dantor.

Someone had murdered my friend and, one way or another, they going to get what was coming to them.

14.
The Reigning Pool Champion of the Four Leaf

Saturday 30 September

I can't remember what had been happening nationally that week, but, news wise, it had eclipsed the fire in Enfield. Not that it would have taken a great deal. Even with the added excitement of a body in the ashes a condemned building catching fire was hardly a scoop.

Most of the local Enfield press were happy to ignore the first report. The two online rags that did carry it put it behind coverage of a juicy car crash.

That changed when the fire brigade found evidence of *the use of an accelerant.* Human tragedy was news, provided someone had taken the trouble to soak it with petrol first. It still wasn't enough to make the nationals, but the bigger local papers got all excited for a couple of days. They didn't go so far as to use the word *murder*, though they used the word *suspicious* with gay abandon. There was the obligatory number to call if you had any information. By day three, they'd gone back to cat-stuck-in-a-tree dramas.

Checking the news feeds had been the last thing I'd done before going to the shop.

No one had put a name to the body.

After I'd handed most of my clients to Yakky, I'd called Eddie the Greek. Another night of minimal sleep, and a pint of Yakky's high-octane coffee, meant I wasn't fit to work. At least not with a tattoo gun.

Eddie answered his mobile on the third ring and before he said anything I heard him suck in a breath. He managed to say hello while he was still inhaling. I couldn't remember what he did for a living, whatever it was, he fitted it in around fag breaks.

"Hello, Eddie, it's Doc. We need to have a talk, mate."

"Oh yeah, about what?"

"A deal on a Suzuki."

There was a pause, long enough to make me wonder if he knew what I was talking about.

Finally, he said, "Problem?" I told him it was possibly a big problem. There was another pause and I heard him drawing on his cigarette again. "Okay."

"Can you meet me in The Jericho, about eight?"

There was another round of nicotine addiction then, "Not The Jericho. The Four Leaf."

"That's fine. You might want to bring that prospect with you."

"China? Alright."

"Okay, The Four Leaf at eight. I'll get 'em in."

I hung up and Yakky asked me where The Four Leaf was.

The Four Leaf Clover, to give it its full name, hadn't existed for over a decade. After many years of defending its reputation as the roughest pub in London, last orders had been called on it in 2003. It was reborn two years later with a self-consciously trendy name and a different slice of the market. It was still known as The Four Leaf, or The Fours to the older guys like me and Eddie. Some people had a certain nostalgia for its past glory. I didn't recall it with any affection.

I couldn't remember its new name and described it to Yakky as the place opposite the big Ikea store. He nodded but couldn't remember the name either.

"I'll go with you."

I told him I'd known Eddie for years and that I'd be alright. Yakky shook his head.

"What about his prospect? Or what if he turns up with half the club in tow?"

I had thought about that. Me and Yakky, hand-to-hand with the might of the Eight-Six. All *that* meant was we'd *both* get the shit kicked out of us. I told him as much, and he didn't like my views on damage limitation. He tried to insist he'd come along

"I appreciate your concern Yak, but it's more likely to kick off if you're there. If it looks like I've turned up expecting trouble, I'm likely to get it."

"We'll go in separately, I can go in first see the lay of the land."

"If they're keyed up, just seeing you will be enough to turn it sour."

Yakky turned on his heel and went back to his customer. "Have it your way."

I got to The Four Leaf at eight. I hadn't expected Eddie to be punctual, but his beaten-up Sportster was already outside. Standing next to it was a late model Triumph. I assumed that belonged to China because there was no sign of Johnny's GSX. I did a quick scan of the car park as I secured my own Sportster, next to Eddie's. I didn't see any other motorcycles, but there were a pair of anonymous-looking white vans that gave me pause. If the Eight-Six had decided to turn up mob handed, they were less likely to arrive on a fleet of bikes than in the back of a van.

I could see the Eight-Six hadn't arrived en mass as soon as I walked through the door. The clientele the remodelled Four Leaf was attracting looked young enough to be buying their first legal round. The volume of everything, the music, the laughter, the calls for drinks, was moronically loud. I might have been casting my own feelings on the gathering, but the atmosphere felt desperate rather than happy. It reminded me of Dago's wake. That same manic need to show how wild and full of living they all were.

Eddie and China were both propped at the bar. Neither of them were wearing colours, but even without their club finery, they stood out a mile. They also radiated hostility. The prospect was clearly working at it; for Eddie it as close and natural as a scar.

The pair of bouncers on the door had exchanged a look as

I walked in. I don't suppose I was considered much of a threat, but I could see them calculating the odds of trouble. I put it somewhere around even money. There was a moat of floor space around Eddie and China and a couple of the young bucks were trying to psych themselves up.

It was still early but I didn't think the first bad judgement of the night was many drinks away. Spotting Yakky hunched over the pool table didn't make me feel any more optimistic.

I offered Eddie my hand and he shook it without smiling. The prospect did the same. I got the drinks in and steered us to a table across the room from the pool table. I took the seat against the wall and Eddie put himself dead opposite. China stayed on his feet, slightly to Eddie's left and sideways on, so he could watch me and the crowd.

"This place has gone to the fucking dogs." Other than telling me what he wanted to drink, it was the first thing Eddie had said.

"I haven't been here since it reopened. It's changed a bit."

"Gone to the fucking dogs," he repeated. He took a pull on his pint and grimaced. I tasted mine and there was nothing wrong with it. "What's this all about, Doc?"

"The GSX? Your mucker there" – I motioned to the prospect with my pint – "needs to lose it. Let's say it's packing quite a story, not one either of you want to be a page of."

Eddie glanced up at the prospect and said something. I didn't catch what China said in reply but the way he said it came across. He wasn't worried.

"It's been taken care of," Eddie said.

I shook my head. "No, it hasn't been. Not if you're talking about grinding a few numbers off the frame and giving it a re-spray."

Eddie put his best poker face on. It was enough to tell me the GSX was sitting in someone's lock-up, waiting for the paint to dry. With the noise level China couldn't have caught much of what we'd said, but he wasn't stupid. The exchange hadn't been lost on him and now he was watching us closely.

"He should hear this," I told Eddie.

He pointed the prospect at a chair. China gave the room a last baleful scan before sitting with us. He spun the chair round, so its back was against the edge of our table, then straddled it like a horse. It put me in mind of that black-and-white photo of Christine Keeler. I doubted it was the look he'd been trying for.

"Doc thinks that GSX is going to bite you on arse."

"Says who?"

This was addressed to me. China all but bared his teeth.

"Don't shoot the messenger. I'm just warning you, that bike could drop you in it up to your neck."

China was still giving me his best ugly-when-I'm-angry look. I folded my hands on the table and leant forward. Cast a meaningful look around the pub's customers. When we all had our heads together in a degree of privacy, I gave China the provenance of his new ride. I could see he was more excited than concerned. Perhaps dead bodies gave chasing his patch some validity, made it something more serious than just joining a club. Eddie, who'd been round the block a few more times – and seen his share of police interview rooms – was more circumspect.

"You're sure this guy was murdered? He didn't just take too many of the happy pills or something."

I told him happy pills hadn't entered into it.

"Someone topped him. And they meant to do it, it wasn't any kind of accident."

Eddie shrugged and turned to the prospect. "Cut it up and lose it."

It obviously wasn't what China had been expecting to hear.

"You got to be fucking joking. Why should I?"

Eddie rolled his eyes. It clearly wasn't the first time he'd asked God to give him strength.

"Have you listened to anything we've been saying, here? The guy you nicked that poxy bike off was murdered in the fucking street you took it from."

China pulled his own exasperated expression. "Yeah, in Enfield. How's that going to land on me?"

"Doc joined the dots and found out. You really think the police won't?"

China might have been thinking about his chances of getting a full patch. He stopped giving Eddie the hard eye and turned it on safer pastures: me.

"And how the police going to find out anything, you plan on telling them?"

I let the insult hang for a bit before standing up. "I've had enough of this. I'm trying to do you a favour son, and you call me a grass. Fuck you."

The prospect made to spring out of his seat, but Eddie grabbed his shoulder and wrenched him back into his chair. With his free hand, he made calming motions at me.

"No one's calling you a grass, Doc. Sit yourself down. China," he let go of the prospect's shoulder, "get another round in. Get Doc a tequila, 'cos you owe him."

China left enough of a pause to signal his displeasure before going to the bar. I noticed Yakky was already there. He didn't blend in any better than me or the pair of Eight-Six.

"Okay," Eddie said, "now the average IQ at this table has gone up, what's your game?"

"Like I said, I'm doing your boy over there a favour. When he took that bike, no one knew its owner's body was twenty foot away. Since then, some bright spark's torched the place and now the police are wondering whose ashes they've found."

"Who lit the match, you?"

I shook my head impatiently. "Why would I do it?"

"Same reason I would, if I'd been trampling all over a crime scene." I was surprised how quickly Eddie had worked that one out. It must have shown because he laughed. "Trouble with clever buggers like you, Doc, is you get to thinking you've got the only brain in the room."

"Alright," I told him, "I'll give you that one. But that fire weren't down to me."

"I'd guess it was whoever killed him then."

I shrugged.

"To be brutal about it, that ain't my problem." Eddie didn't say anything for a moment, just looked at me through narrowed eyes. "What? I'm trying to do you a favour here and you're giving me grief."

He smiled and looked past me, to a point over my right shoulder.

"You know, Doc, this innocent spiel would be lot more convincing if you hadn't brought your heavy with you."

He nodded to whatever he was looking at. I turned and realised the window behind me, looking out onto a pitch-black car park, was effectively a mirror. Even with his back to the bar, Eddie's view of Yakky was as good as mine.

"Yakky's not a heavy."

"No? Well he must be one hell of pool player if he's gonna take a shot from over here."

Putting distance between me and Yakky hadn't been my brightest move. I should have known he'd migrate across to us, known too that he'd keep hold of his cue.

"He was with me when I found Johnny. I told him I was going to talk to you and China, about losing the GSX. He was worried it wouldn't go down too well." I nodded at China, who was making his way back. "I'd say he had a point, your little prospect's not exactly open to friendly advice."

Eddie smiled. "No, fair point."

China arrived at the table with the drinks, he hadn't got one for himself. When he put mine down he managed to slop most of it out of the glass. It was no loss. I'd seen the bottle it came out of, acid house label and a cap shaped like a sombrero. The barmaid had even perched a slice of lime over the rim.

Eddie waited until China was sat down again before turning and beckoning Yakky over. He did the formal introductions and Yakky had to tuck the pool cue under his arm to shake hands. There was another comic moment as Yakky sat down and had to find a place to put the thing.

"Reminds me of the good old days," Eddie told me, looking at the cue now propped against a fire extinguisher. "Makes me feel almost nostalgic."

He fell silent and returned his gaze to me, waiting for me to take up the story.

"Back in the day," I told Yakky, "when this was The Four Leaf Clover, on Friday nights they'd bring in a couple of barrels. A man would stand in each barrel and they'd both get a pool cue. Someone would shout go and they'd beat seven bells out of each other. Bouts tended to be decided by a knockout. The lovely Eddie, here, was The Four Leaf's reigning pool champion."

"Still got the winner's trophy," Eddie said and pulled back a sweep of hair, displaying a scar running around the back of his right ear.

Bringing it up was a political move on Eddie's part and me doing the story-time bit was an act of diplomacy. Yakky needed to have his card marked. The message needed to be sent that Eddie the Greek and, by extension, the Eight-Six weren't cowed. It also served to save any face that might have been lost by Eddie's next move.

"Thanks for the tip off, Doc. We'll see the bike's dealt with. We appreciate you contacting us."

He made a gesture, opening his hands, as if offering something. Or putting something in my court. *Are we all happy now?* I nodded and held up the bloody awful tequila, in a silent toast.

Politics can be a subtle game. It was lost on China.

"I'm still losing out here. I'm the one scrapping a good bike, on this arsehole's say so."

I handed narrative duties back to Eddie. He sighed deeply, before attempting to explain the birds and bees, again.

"You're not losing a good bike. You're losing a connection to a murder. And you're not doing it on this arsehole's say so. You're doing it on my say so. If it falls on you, it falls on the club. Even if the police don't get involved, the Handsome Boys ain't going to be too chuffed about seeing someone, tooling around, on one of their guy's bikes. Not when word filters back he's been topped."

China shook his head, not meeting Eddie's eye. "Seriously?

I've got to throw away my rig, in case we upset the HLB? You think the club can't take those pussies out?"

Eddie pulled the God-give-me-strength face again and took a pull on his beer.

"You're an educated man, Doc, you explain it to him."

It was an insult, asking someone outside the club to put a prospect right. I wondered if it was just apathy on Eddie's part, now he'd decided to quit the Eight-Six, or the slight was calculated. China was baring his teeth again. I trod carefully.

"No one's saying the Eight-Six should back down from the Handsome Boys. We all know you guys can handle yourselves, but the HLB wouldn't just roll over. People would get hurt, on both sides, and that draws heat." China wasn't listening. Or at least he was making a display of not listening. I leant in closer than I wanted to. It wasn't a move I'd have made if Eddie hadn't been there. "You fancy your chances of flying a patch? Well you better get this through your head: the club isn't your private army. You're a prospect for the club, not vice versa. Even if you make it to full member, you look after the interests of your club. It's not all about you."

China didn't bother looking at me. He turned to Eddie, maybe to gauge how he was expected to act. Eddie nodded and raised his glass; he might have been toasting the sentiment I'd expressed or just using it to single me out.

He told China, "Brotherhood. That's the whole point."

The prospect shook his head again, stood and left the table. He went back to propping the bar up. From the corner of my eye, I saw Yakky sit back further into his chair. Eddie glanced at me and didn't quite smile.

"You're going to have trouble with that one," I commented and tilted my head in the direction of the bar.

Eddie shrugged. "I'll be out the club before he gets voted in, 'til then –" he flickered his hand in the air as if he was brushing a fly away "– I'll see to it that GSX gets proper lost, okay?"

"Fine."

Eddie gave me another shadow of a smile. "So, is that it?

Or, do you want to tell me what you want?"

I thought about trying for a laugh. Lighten the mood. Eddie's almost-smile didn't encourage the move, so I played it straight.

"I want to find out who killed Johnny Simms. When we talked with your mate over there at Spots the other night, he said his granddad lived opposite the squat."

"And?"

"I want to talk to him, see if he saw anything. As you pointed out, I've already trampled over the crime scene. I'd sooner be up front with him than risk getting his antenna up with a load of jive."

Eddie nodded slowly and shrugged. "Alright. I'll talk to China, get him to sort it. I'll ring you tomorrow, give you the details. Give him the night to calm down."

We had another round of handshaking before we left. China pointedly ignored Yakky and me. I decided I could live with it.

15.
My Solider Boy. X

After leaving the warm embrace of China and Eddie, Yakky asked if I fancied a quick one at The Jericho. I'd been intending to head straight home to bed, but I suspected Yakky was offering an apology for his impromptu appearance at the Four Leaf. I knew, by tacit agreement, it wasn't something we'd speak about.

There were a few bikes already parked outside The Jericho, one of them was Silk's Beemer. I saw Yakky taking stock of the other machines, doubtless toting up the number of Handsome Boy rides. I'd done the same. We'd both had enough tip-toeing around club sensibilities for one night.

Club presence was minimal when we got inside. Silk was busy pumping coins into in a slot machine and two younger guys I recognised from the funeral were at the bar. The pair at the bar turned as we entered, but that was the extent of it. It looked like all was quiet on the western front. I slipped into a table that wasn't in clear view of anyone and left Yakky to get the drinks.

He came back with a double of the good stuff and put it in front of me. After a moment of awkward silence, without taking his eyes off the two HLB at the bar, he asked if really thought I could trust Smudge.

"Yeah," I said. "He wants to know who murdered Johnny."

"Maybe, but that isn't your agenda, is it? You're after whoever killed Dago."

"If someone's gunning for the HLB, then they're probably one in the same."

"And if there not?"

"Smudge still wants to know who did Johnny and he's not going to the police, any sooner than we are. So, he's got two options: us or the club. At the moment Frenchy's looking out for the interests of the club, over and above anything else. I'm happy with that; I'm hoping he can keep a lid on things and stop people doing anything stupid."

"Meanwhile, Smudge gives you another set of ears and eyes?"

I shrugged. "Maybe. Really I just wanted the inside line on the HLB going for the full patch club gig."

According to Smudge, Dago had been dead against the idea from the start. I'd asked Smudge where he stood on the matter of going outlaw.

"I'm for it," he said. "I've never made a secret of it."

I asked why, and he rolled out the well-worn clichés about brotherhood and freedom and the way of life. I let him wind down and left a pause, before telling him he was full of shit.

"You're elbowing out the local dealers. You got The House of Ice nailed down, The Salt Lick's close on its heels. I don't doubt you've got an eye on some others."

He didn't deny it. "That's just business."

"It's the business that put Micky in hospital."

"That was dealt with. We sent a message."

"Is that what your brotherhood amounts to, Smudge? Using your friends as muscle to backup your 'business' dealings?"

He didn't answer immediately, and I got the impression he was weighing up his options. After a while he pulled his chair nearer the table and closed in on me. He kept eye contact for a long time, at least by his standards. He wasn't entirely comfortable with confiding in me.

"Do you know how many members the HLB has?" He answered the question before I had a chance to tell him I didn't. "Without Johnny and Dago, we've got twenty-three men, and, most of them make their living inside the club. A couple of them work in Frenchy's yard, another couple did the live-in security bit for Dago, so right now they're up in air, wondering what's about to happen. About ten of them work with me on the doors. My gig's where the money is. Thing is, it's not lying around waiting to be picked up. If the HLB step up, do it right, get their presence known and felt, then all the guys benefit. That's what brotherhood means to me, taking care of my people. But I need to know the people I'm looking after will look out for each other, not just themselves."

"And you think going outlaw's the way to do it?"

Smudge nodded. "On-one gets a free ride, everyone proves their worth and earns their place. That way, we'll end up with a rock-solid team. Call it tough love."

I called it self-serving bullshit, an opinion I kept to myself. Not least of all because I suspected Smudge was a true believer. Faith takes many forms.

"The money isn't in working the door though, is it? It's in the drugs."

Smudge shook his head. "Not drugs. Control. I'm not interested in dealing. Let the muppets and the gangstas do the ten-stretch for carrying. The HLB stay clean." He allowed himself a laugh. "Cleanish. We say who deals on our patch and we take a percentage. By regulating who deals and how much, we keep the squabbles over territory off the dance floors and people stay safe."

I told him that was very public-spirited of him. He'd laughed again.

Yakky took a pull on the pint he was holding. He glanced across at the bar again and sighed. Silk had persuaded the fruit machine to give up a win and the two young guns gave a cheer of solidarity.

"I think you made a mistake talking to him, Doc. The club is always going to be his first consideration. If finding out who killed Dago and Johnny conflicts with that, he'll be on the side of HLB."

When telling Yakky about my conversation with Smudge, I'd left out as much as I could about his emotional state. It wasn't exactly patient confidentiality, but I figured, whatever internal struggles Smudge was having, they were his business.

"I think Smudge had a vision of himself and Johnny riding

along with the same patch on their backs. That way he'd have context for what he felt. That depth of emotion he had would be brotherly love. A valid way to feel in the microcosm of an outlaw club." Out loud it sounded like the self-important guff I'd crammed into my first-year essays. Aiming for a cheap laugh I added, "Been a lot simpler to just slip him one."

Yakky didn't laugh.

"Maybe he tried that, and it didn't work." I made the spooling motion with my fingers, *carry on*. "Maybe, Johnny tells his big buddy Smudge, that he's got a job looking after some dingy pit over in Enfield. Smudge goes over one night to give him a bit of company. Bit of puff, bit of booze, just the two of them, miles from their usual stomping ground. Smudge puts on the moves."

"Only Johnny doesn't go for it and Smudge can't risk it getting back to everyone?" Yakky nodded. "I don't know. I keep coming back to the garrotte. Who carries a garrotte for fuck's sake?"

"Okay, maybe Johnny did go for it. The scales fall from his eyes and he's ready to declare their love to the world. Only once the afterglow's worn off, Smudge is all guilt and panic. He tells Johnny he'll be back the next night. Then he goes home and gets busy with the bailing wire."

Johnny's body had been slumped on his arrangement of sleeping bag and duvet. In effect, lying on his bed. Whoever had garrotted him had been trusted to come up on him from behind.

I still wasn't convinced.

"But then Jason tells him Dago killed Johnny. Instead of breathing a sigh of relief, he tells me Dago's in the clear, and loses the best cover story he'll ever have?"

"Yeah, but think about *why* Jason told him Dago did it."

It had been a peace-keeping move. The assumption had been that Smudge was a hot head, likely to lead a revenge attack without thought for the outcome. Putting Dago in the frame moved other considerations, such the Eight-Six, out of it. Maybe an internal club matter didn't suit Smudge's ambitions and passing the blame for Johnny's death onto Dago wasn't his best option.

Sunday 1 October

I got a phone call from Eddie the Greek the next evening. He was somewhere loud and was shouting down the phone.

"Doc, you still want to talk to China's granddad?" I told him I did. "Good. Good, good." His voice was too fast, and I could hear the wet snap of gum being chewed. "China says the old bastard never goes out, so you can catch him anytime. He's in number six. You can't miss it; the house dead opposite has burned down."

He thought this was a great one-liner and repeated it after he'd finished cackling.

"Listen, Eddie, what's this guy's name?"

"Peter." A great cheer went up from wherever he was calling from and he started cackling again. Another cheer went up and something about it told me there was a strip show or a pole dance going on. "Peter Barnes."

"Does he know I want to speak to him?"

"Nah. No point telling him. China says the old bastard'll talk your ear off anyway. Never stops moaning...Wahhay!" The last was a shout and my mobile translated it into a hissing crackle. "You ought to get over here Doc. It's all happening." The speed-fuelled idea took hold and he invited me again, "Bring that miserable-looking mate of yours with you. Might put a smile on his face."

He gave another whooping cheer and I heard glass breaking.

"Not tonight, thanks."

"Nah, don't say that, get yourself down here." The noises in the background were getting less inviting by the moment. "Get yourself down here, it's only up the road from you."

"Where are you, Eddie?"

"That big nightclub, The House of Ice."

I gave up trying to disengage from Eddie's top-speed phone call. In the end I told him I was losing the signal and hung up.

Whether he noticed and stopped talking was anyone's guess.

I rang Yakky and told him he'd be holding the fort again the next day.

Monday 2 October

The rain had dampened the smell of the burnt timbers, at last. It was an improvement, though there was still a way to go before you'd call Maple Blossom Parade up and coming. I parked the Sportster a couple of streets away and walked around to see China's grandad. I'd borrowed Yakky's jacket for the ride over. His was a traditional black leather and less likely to be noticed than my oddball, white item. I'd smeared a layer of concealer over my jaw tattoo before leaving my flat.

Six Maple Blossom Parade had been treated to a sheet of stone cladding. The crofter's cottage look was topped off with aluminium double glazing. The home improvements, unsympathetic or not, were part of the property's history; currently it was a monument to neglect. Peter Barnes, when he finally answered the door, was much the same. He was wearing a cap-sleeve shirt that was riding up the swell of his gut, but, under the fat, I could just make out the chassis of muscle his bulk had once been. The effort of walking the length of his hallway had left him red in the face. It clashed with his nicotine-yellow beard and teeth. He didn't offer me a welcoming smile.

Before I had a chance to explain why I was there, he asked me if I was from the council. There was a definite note of disapproval in his voice, so I took a punt on him having a beef with local government.

"The council? God no. Do I look that big a wanker?" It turned out to be the right answer and I let him vent for ten minutes about the bins, the hospital waiting lists and, of course, immigration. When the record started to repeat, I guided the subject away from racial purity and into the direction of house fires.

"Bloody kids," was his pronouncement. He waved a hand,

enthusiastically, at the wreckage of the short terrace. "Always messing about in there."

I judged him to be a badly persevered sixty, and suspected he'd consider anybody without grey hair to be a kid.

"Did you see them? I mean on the night of the fire."

I could only hope I wasn't opening a can of worms. One that would wind up with me, and Yakky, front and centre in his mind.

"Always messing about, bloody people in and out, all the time."

I asked him what he thought they were doing in there and, as he ran the more intriguing possibility through his imagination, his eyes misted over. When he'd come back from whatever disturbing plane he was exploring, he shook his head: *didn't know.*

"Were there many over there, about three or four weeks ago?" I asked, thinking about Johnny on guard duty. Nicotine Santa shook his head and regarded me for a second before answering. He'd finally stopped talking long enough to listen and was beginning to wonder why I'd knocked on his door.

"One of them turned up on a motorbike. Woke me up in the middle of the night." He pulled a face. "Noisy bloody things."

"Just one guy?"

I was thinking about me and Yak on the night we found Johnny and wondering if he'd seen us. I didn't get an answer.

"If you're not from the council, what's it to you?"

"A friend of mine had his bike nicked about a month back. I was talking to China about it. He said you'd told him some squatters had turned up with something that sounded like it." Evoking China's name failed to draw a look of recognition and I realised his nickname was the only handle I had for him. "You're Peter Barnes, right? China's grandad?"

"Yeah," he stretched the answer out, like elastic. It wasn't the sound of a proud grandparent. "Charlie's my eldest's boy. His friends call him China."

It started to drizzle with rain. Peter Barnes gave no

indication that he was about to invite me in.

"My friend's bike was an old Suzuki." Blank look. "Pale blue."

"That was a blue bike out there." He waved across at the blackened gap opposite. "Weeks ago. It's gone now."

"Was it there long?"

"No." He shook his head. "Gone the next day. Good riddance. Noisy bloody things."

"They have many bikes over there?"

He may have had some notion of his grandson's activities, and a degree of discretion, because he suddenly went all coy. I guessed I was on a hiding to nothing asking him anything else, so I told him thanks and left him to his rants about the council. Then I knocked on his neighbour's door.

Number four wasn't any more loved than number six, but its original features were intact, which leant some charm to the neglect. My knock was answered by a pair of eyes peering through the letter box. When I squatted down to peer back, there was a snot-glazed child of about four mutely staring out. What I could see of the hall behind him looked like a war zone. I asked if his mum was home; he nodded solemnly and carried on staring at me.

"Could you go and get her?"

The flap on the letterbox clanged shut and I heard him running down the hall.

I'd given up waiting and had turned to leave when someone called out, "Who is it?"

The letterbox flap was pushed open again. This time there was an adult on the other side. I gave her the reassuring smile I kept for nervous customers and repeated the story about my friend's bike. The eyes vanished from behind the slot and the door opened a crack. The woman looked suspicious rather than scared and when I repeated the line, about my friend's stolen bike, she asked if I was the police. My laugh was sufficient to convince her otherwise and she opened the door enough that we could communicate. The smell that wafted out of the hallway was a blend of stale cooking oil and damp.

"When was it pinched?" She asked. She was dressed like she was barely out of her twenties and in good light could have passed for forty. She had the telltale ridge of a healed break across the bridge of her nose.

"A while ago," I said. "Someone told me they'd seen one like it, around here about a month ago. They said it was outside number five. Long shot, I know."

The woman looked over my shoulder to the burnt-out house.

"Was it your friend they found in there?"

She sounded eager.

"No. I don't know who that poor sod was." I cast a glance to the ruin myself. To keep the morbidly curious at bay, the police, or the fire brigade, had fixed up wire-mesh security fences. Someone had attached a bouquet to one of them. "You ever see anyone over there messing about with bikes?"

"Nah." She shook her head and looked disappointed that I wasn't connected to the local tragedy. "Only bike I've seen round here is China's. He drops in to look in on –" I guessed she didn't know Peter Barnes' name because she just jerked her hand at her neighbour's door. "He's a good lad that China. Most people wouldn't bother with the old man."

I asked her if it was China that had put the flowers outside number five. She said no, some girl had dropped them off. She hadn't recognised her, but thought she'd been a social worker.

"A social worker?"

The woman shrugged. "Yeah, she had that look, you know?"

Somewhere behind her, the little boy started crying and I let her go.

Before I went back to my bike, I crossed over and checked the flowers. It had been raining on and off most of the week, but they were fairly intact and still had some colour. They must have been reasonably fresh and probably weren't picked up on the cheap to start with. There was a small white card hanging from the stems, written in green ink was the legend:

My Solider Boy. X.

16.
Do-Gooders, Marked Cards and Matters of Style

The traffic coming out of Enfield doubled the journey time and I got back to the shop later than I'd expected. Yakky was still working, presumably on the slack he'd picked up in my absence. I went up to the flat and, after I'd changed into dry clothes, rang him to apologise. After assuring him I'd be there shortly, I got waylaid by the wall. By the time I made an appearance, Yakky had put out the CLOSED sign and was cashing up.

"I rescheduled your appointments where I could," he said in greeting, "but you're beginning to upset people. This isn't the only tattoo shop in town."

I told him I knew and apologised again.

"I think I might have something to go on though, you want to come up and have a look?"

Yakky arched his back, grimacing. "Nah. I'm knackered, I need to get home, get in the bath and soak this back. Just give me the highlights."

He'd taken his crash helmet from under the counter and kept hold of it as he carefully lowered himself into one of the sofas, letting me know he was done for the day. I sat opposite and realised he wasn't being precious about needing a bath. I could smell the hours of work on him. Coffee, sweat and tiredness.

I told him about the bouquet and card left in memory of Johnny.

"When all this started, and Johnny was just a skip-trace, a couple of people mentioned he'd had a girlfriend. I think the flowers were from her."

"How do you work that out?"

"I spoke to this woman on the other side of the road. She said whoever left the flowers had the look of a social worker. This is from someone living in a shithole and peering through the letter box before opening the door. I reckon she's met a few social workers and I don't think they did her much good. What's the negative stereotype of a social worker?"

"Middle-class do-gooder, straight out of uni and setting the plebs to rights. Until they get bored."

It was a picture about as accurate as any the media would use to sell a story. A description many people would recognise.

"The card on the flowers reads: *My Solider Boy.* To me, that sounds patronising, it's only one step up from being, *my little man.*"

"So, where does this connect with Johnny's anonymous girlfriend?"

"Silk and Jason couldn't even remember her name. All they knew was nobody had taken to her. Plain Jane turns up, then starts talking down to people." I shrugged. "I can't see anyone I know in the HLB welcoming her to the fold."

"Why'd you say Plain Jane?"

"If she'd been a stunner, she'd have lodged in Silk and Jason's minds."

Like Sue said: men. Yakky nodded slowly, acknowledging what I'd put forward.

"And you think she knows something?"

"There was over a week between us finding Johnny and the news of a body in the ashes. Someone joined up the dots, worked out whose ashes they were, just from hearing where they were. I'm thinking, our social-worker type knew that's where Johnny had been, but she didn't know he was dead until it made the news. I think Johnny told her about the security gig and when she heard a body had been found, she put two and two together."

From the impression I'd been given by others, and what I'd known of the man himself, Johnny wasn't the sharpest tool in the box. And there was a bit too much of the macho prick about him for my liking. I could quite easily picture him holding force to his girlfriend. What I was wondering, was why he told her.

"Expect he was hoping for a bit of company on the long cold nights," Yakky said.

The pit we'd found Johnny in wouldn't be my choice for a romantic liaison. However, I was nearing fifty and roughing it wasn't on my list of things to do anymore. At Johnny's age, my joints, and libido, had been considerably more resilient. Still, I had my doubts.

"I don't know. If she knew where Johnny was and if he'd told her so she'd go and see him, then she'd have found the body not us. The cops would have been all over the place before Frenchy's boys had a chance to light the blue touch paper."

"Maybe he extended the invite and she didn't go for it. Like you said, she hears the news about the pile of ashes turning up in Maple Blossom Parade and makes the connection. Until then she didn't know anything was wrong."

I wasn't buying that.

"This is someone who cared about Johnny. I don't think she'd have ignored an invitation to keep him company. So, now she's putting flowers where he died, but it don't look like she's gone to the plod."

The flowers had been on that fence for a few days at least. If the police had been told the identity of the body and who it was associated with, they would have been knocking on HLB's doors already. They weren't and that suggested whoever had left the flowers to their Solider Boy had kept quiet. And that implied they were scared of something.

"You want to risk asking questions around the club, again?"

"Don't see that going anywhere. And to be blunt about it, I want to distance us from what happened in Enfield. It'll get out about Johnny at some point. I'd sooner no one, clubs or blue crew, has us in mind when it does." Mentally, I took a deep breath. "Which is why I need you to ask Karla to do us a favour."

"Us?"

Yakky's expression had sailed beyond blank, into the icy waters of a dead calm.

"Alright, do *me* a favour. I don't think Johnny and Dago getting killed, and Black Micky getting shivved, are unconnected. If it's the beginnings of a turf war, the HLB can look out for themselves, but even so, I want to know who murdered Dago."

"Then what?" I told him I hadn't thought that far ahead. Yakky left a long pause to let me know that he knew bullshit when he heard it. "So, where does Karla come into this?"

"I'm going to try and get into Frenchy's next poker school. While the men are busy getting fleeced, I thought Karla could have a chat with Frenchy's lady friend."

"The dope head in the kitchen? Even if she's there again, why would she talk to Karla?"

I mimed someone taking a hit off a joint. The poker night we'd interrupted ended with Jason blowing his stack and the young woman in the kitchen hadn't even registered it. My plan was to put some more business Spooky's way. I wanted to ensure relations, away from the table, stayed amicable. And not too intellectual.

Yak's face still hadn't moved. My eyes began to water in sympathy.

"All I want her to do is go to a poker game. Worst case, Frenchy's bit of stuff ain't even there and Karla gets to sit through an evening of second-rate poker. Best case, she has a friendly chat in the kitchen and gets a bit of info about Johnny's girlfriend."

"And what if things kick off?"

"I'll be there." Yakky finally blinked. "Okay, why would there be trouble? It's just a poker game, the money on the table is all anyone's going to be interested in."

There was another round of not blinking.

"I'll ask her," Yakky said at last. "If she's up for it, fine, but I come along too, so I can keep an eye on things."

"Like you did at the Four Leaf?"

"Fuck you. If I'm there as well, it'll look less suspicious; no one's going to buy Karla turning up with *you*."

I conceded that was a good point.

"Okay, if I can get you a seat at the game, you'll talk to Karla?"

"I'll talk to her, yeah. One other thing." He pointed to the ceiling and the flat above. "That gun you've got under your floorboards; you give it to me to look after."

"What do you want it for?"

"I don't want it. I just want to make sure you're not holding it when you find out who topped Dago."

I nodded and Yakky surprised me by holding his hand out. We shook on it.

That was fine. There were other weapons in the world.

Tuesday 3 October

I caught Jason before he left work. He said hello and asked what I wanted in the same breath.

"How often does Frenchy have his poker games?"

There was a lot of noise in the background, the metallic clatter of a shift ending. Jason asked me to repeat myself. I had the feeling he was stalling and waited, in silence, until he'd remembered he owed me money.

"Every couple of weeks."

"This week?"

He told me yes, stretching the word out. "There's a game on this Friday. You looking for a seat?"

"I'm looking for two, Yakky plays a bit."

Jason told me he'd okay it with Frenchy and call me back.

I got the presidential seal of approval later that night and rang Yakky at home. There was a certain malicious humour in his voice when he told me he didn't know how to play poker.

Wednesday 4 October

I'd drawn a hand so bad I'd folded on the first round. Yakky, poker-faced by birth, was nevertheless proving to be a bloody awful card player and, player three, who didn't exist, won another pot.

"I can't believe people do this for fun," Yak grumbled, as I pushed the pile of notes to the imaginary player.

The money was from the day's takings and it was going back in the cash box at the end of the night. Whatever humour he'd extracted from telling me he couldn't play Texas hold 'em had evaporated half an hour into his crash course on cardsmanship.

"Your deal," I said. "Deal in a fourth player this time. Lower," I added when he flicked the cards a full foot from the tabletop. "I can see half the cards your dealing."

I could hear the edge in my voice. Yakky told to keep my hair on, but he dealt the remainder of the hand by skimming the cards across the surface of the table. I told him: *better*.

While Yakky studied his cards, I looked at the three hands I'd be playing. It took me longer than I'd have liked to decipher the markings on their backs.

Marked playing cards are easy enough to get hold of. I'd ordered a deck the previous evening after I'd got the seats at Frenchy's table. It had taken about thirty minutes online to find the same pack he used. Paying the premium rate to ensure next-day delivery doubled the purchase price. It cost the better part of a night's sleep to commit the marks to memory. Yakky's lesson was an opportunity to practice the art.

I asked him what cards he had. He told me the seven of diamonds and the queen of hearts.

"So, what can you make with that?"

Yakky recited the best hands he might get and the likelihood of seeing them beat. Then we played the hand out and player three took him to the cleaners again. He muttered a curse as he watched the winnings move to the other side of his kitchen table.

"I'm going to get eaten alive."

"That's pretty much the game plan," I told him.

I took the deal and had to remind Yakky to pick up his cards as soon as they landed. The more time they spent on show, the better Frenchy's chances of reading the marks. Yak snatched the next card before it had stopped moving.

"If I'm meant to lose, what does it matter how I handle the cards?"

We'd been playing for more than two hours. We'd spent an hour before that going over the rules and structure. All the while, Yakky's old man interrupted us, bleating for attention. It hadn't been a relaxing evening.

"People home in on the weakest player. That's just the way of it. Frenchy's going to be over you like a rash, but I want him to have to concentrate. I don't want him reading your deals off his polished tabletop and I don't want you to give him a clear view of his marked cards. You're bait, you're not a gift, he'll have to work at it. Anyway, what are you worried about, you'll be playing with my money?"

Yakky glanced at his cards and put them down again, covering them with his hand, the way I'd taught him. He'd developed at least one good habit.

"You know what I'm fucking worried about."

"Yeah, okay. I get it, but the more money at stake on that table, the less anyone's going to wonder what Karla's chatting about in the kitchen. The fact you'll be keeping everyone's attention off what I'm doing is a bonus."

"And what will you be doing?"

"Cheating better than Frenchy."

Texas hold 'em, like all variants of poker, is deceptively simple and it's easy to think you're good at it. It's easier still to lose your shirt. I've met a lot of people who've done just that because they thought they were players. They normally talked a lot about 'tells' and 'bluffing'. They watched a lot of gangster films and won a lot of money online from the bank of make-believe. And they usually had a lucky tie or hat or ritual. And crucially, they only ever remembered the times they'd won.

Players, I mean real players, don't talk about tells, or know all the slang names movie directors give playing cards. What they do know is how many packs of cards make up a dealer's shoe and how many times the queen of hearts has come up in the last eighteen hands. They notice that the three of clubs or seven of diamonds has a tiny dent on its top edge and that the guy opposite never raises on anything lower than a flush. And they don't talk about these things either.

By one a.m. Yakky's head was swimming with numbers. We called it a night and, before I went, I handed over my sawn-off. I warned him he was looking at five years if he was caught in possession of it. He told me he understood.

I don't consider myself a player. I think to be a real player, you should win without cheating.

And that's never been my style.

17.
Small Blind, Big Blind, Flop

Friday 6 October

There are people in the world who, if you give them a watch, will prise the back off so they can see how it works. Nine times out of ten, those same people will end up fiddling with the works and fucking things up.

I'm much the same with human beings and, in my eagerness to unpick their mysteries, I'll sometimes forget they work best left in one piece.

For someone like me, a guy like Yakky could be an irresistible challenge. And whereas the watch stoppers tend to make their investigations with a screwdriver, I favour putting the needle in. The difference with trying to get into Yakky's workings was that if you got it wrong, there was a good chance you'd be one to get fucked up.

I'd sometimes forget that too.

"I'm not happy about this," Yakky said, for what felt like the hundredth time. His voice was low. I didn't know if it was tension building in his throat or just a precaution against Karla hearing the conversation.

We were in her flat. She split the rent three ways, with a pair of students working on sports degrees. The open-plan living-room-come-kitchen was common ground and, since it was everyone's job to keep it tidy, nobody did. The layers of debris alternated sweat-stained running gear with take-away cartons and the space smelt like a gym's changing room.

Yakky had tried to pace up and down, but there wasn't enough floor available. He'd compromised by standing with his back to the wall and, at irregular intervals, updating me on his emotional state.

"I'm not happy about this," he stated yet again.

The last word was clipped because Karla had come out of her room in another outfit. Loose-fitting combats, artfully ripped at the knees, and a vest top that showed off her cleavage. She stood in her doorway and pulled a sarcastic twirl. This was the third change of clothes.

Yakky had vetoed the first two attempts on grounds of road safety. The miniskirt would have been too cold for riding pillion and the shorts-and-tights combo wouldn't protect against gravel rash. Neither would the light cotton combats with the compromised knees, but Yakky was okay with them. The drop-neck top was another matter.

Karla told him it would have to do, adding, "My habit's in the wash."

Agitated or not, Yakky conceded defeat with a nod. Karla slipped back into her room and closed the door behind her. I had the feeling they'd have been arguing loudly if I hadn't been there as a witness.

"I'm not happy about this."

"Relax, she's a big girl," I told him, then put on my watchmaker's hat and best Cheshire Cat smile. "As that outfit shows."

In watchmaker terms, it was the point where you go in too hard with the screwdriver and a delicately balanced timepiece becomes an explosion. I was sitting across the room from Yakky when his mainspring went. He covered the space in a remarkably short time.

"You make all the smartarse remarks you want, but she'd better not get fucking hurt." His voice was barely a hiss. It didn't need to be loud, his face was an inch from mine. "You hearing me?"

"You think I want her to get hurt? Really?"

Yakky backed away, two maybe three millimetres. I hoped it was a good sign; I could still feel his body heat.

"I think you get caught up in your own games. Two people are dead. This isn't a fucking joke."

"One of my oldest friends has been murdered, Yak. You

think I'm doing this for a laugh?" I put a hand on his shoulder and eased him out of my space. He let himself be pushed away but his voice was still constricted.

"If she gets hurt..."

He didn't finish the statement and I didn't have anything to say in return. Despite the fizzing silence, neither of us heard Karla coming back into the room. We only noticed her when something bounced off Yakky's face and left a bright red line across his cheekbone.

"And since when did I need your protection, or your bloody permission?" Karla had added a bike jacket to her outfit. It was an old one and far too big for her, probably a hand-me-down from Yakky. "Who the hell do you think you are?"

Her voice had become shrill, though there was nothing comic about it.

Yakky's response to the tsunami was an unreadable blank face. Something else flew across the room, barely missed him and shattered on the wall in a pale-brown cloud. Karla spat a round of insults at Yakky, or maybe him and me both, then left, slamming the door behind her.

The brown explosion had been some kind of make-up. I was relieved to see the vivid red gash along Yakky's face was lipstick.

It was clear Karla wasn't going to be getting on Yakky's bike that evening. When we followed her out of the flat, she was standing resolutely next to my Sportster and daring anyone to say anything about it. It was not a good way to start.

All three of us were on edge by that stage and, very briefly, I considered nixing the whole idea. Then Yakky's bike started first go and I decided to take it as a good sign.

Frenchy's door was opened by one of the HLB young guns. I remembered seeing him at the wake and, again, working at Frenchy's yard. It gave me another second's pause. I'd been counting on just the inner circle being there.

The new spanner in the works was decked out in the regulation black leather cut-off and bad-ass expression. He did his best to look like he was expecting trouble but wasn't overly convincing. I told him we were there for the poker game and he told us to hang on. He closed the door in our faces and doubtless scurried away to check we were expected. Yakky muttered something under his breath, I didn't catch what. He obviously wasn't impressed with the posturing.

When the door opened again it was Smudge behind it. He did one of his ironic bows, to Karla, and I assumed we were due an evening of his club persona. I let Yakky and Karla go in first, ensuring they gained a pace or two on me. When they followed Smudge into the room with the polished table, I paused again before going after them, hoping to emphasise their arrival as a pair. Yakky's comment, that no one would believe Karla was with me, was valid. Arriving beside him slotted her neatly into the role of attached female and, to the men at the table, she'd hopefully become largely invisible – cleavage or no. Turning up behind an old bag of bones like me might have raised questions.

The game was already in progress. Silk wasn't there this time, but Jason was back, ready to sacrifice his wages to the Gods of Luck. Smudge was at Frenchy's left. The guy who'd opened the door was introduced as Vic. The stacks of money everyone sat behind were still fairly even, so I guessed we'd only missed a few hands. The table was already crowned with a drift of cigarette smoke.

Yakky and I took our seats. Karla asked where the fridge was, holding up a bag with a pair of six-packs in it.

Frenchy pointed to the kitchen door with his thumb and said, "Through there."

He was courteous enough to wait for her to leave the room before giving me a quizzical look.

"Yakky thinks she's lucky," I offered in explanation.

All eyes settled on Yak. It fell to Vic to say something. He was the new guy and wasn't entirely sure of the lay of the land, or the status of the man he was addressing. There was an over long pause while he decided tactics. He went for tough but reasonable.

"I admire your taste in lucky charms, mate. But if she's not in the kitchen, she better be standing behind you. Fair enough?"

"Sure."

Yakky pulled a roll of notes from the side of his boot and dropped it on the table, like it wasn't important. To him, it wasn't. All sixty of the crisp new fivers were mine.

With no further discussion Smudge dealt us each a pair of cards. He had Yak's one-time habit of holding the pack too high. I glimpsed a red ace, winging its way to Jason, and assumed Frenchy had seen it too.

Vic picked up his cards with an insolent slowness, too casual to be natural. He held them tight to his chest, like Paul Newman in *The Sting*. When he put them face down on the table, the marks told me he was holding a queen.

I heard someone laugh delightedly in the kitchen. The sound caught Vic's attention and he called out for a beer. It was Karla who brought it to him. Though he thanked her as she leaned across the table, his manners didn't extend to not leering down her top. I took a quick sidelong look at Yakky, but of course his face told me nothing.

Karla, playing along nicely, didn't comment, other than to ask if anybody else wanted a drink. When no one did she headed back to the kitchen. The woman who'd been in attendance at the last poker night met her in the doorway and asked if she had a light.

Yakky had managed to minimise costs on the night's other expenditure. He'd rung the latest number he had for Spooky and told him we'd managed to deflect the attentions of the HLB away from him. Spooky's relief translated into a good price on a lump of the Lebanon's highest earning export.

We checked the two cards we'd each been dealt. The way Texas hold 'em works is this, each player is dealt two cards of their own and the first player puts down a bet, called the small blind then the second player doubles it, the big blind. If the remaining players want to stay in for the rest of the hand, they have to match the big blind and any subsequent raises.

We all threw in a fiver and Smudge dealt three cards to the centre of the table, face up, the flop.

The two cards you're dealt don't mean a great deal until you know which three cards are in the flop. Novice players watch the flop being laid the way rabbits stare at headlights. Mistake. Those three cards aren't going anywhere and it's a better use of your time to watch the other players.

Jason, who'd played and lost enough to know better, scrutinised the flop one card at a time as Smudge put them down. He kept a deliberate poker face on that made me think he had nothing. I glanced across at Frenchy; he wasn't watching the flop, but I hadn't expected him to. I wanted to see who he was checking out. His eye fell briefly on Vic, or rather his cards, then moved on to Yakky.

Yakky's grabbed his cards off the table as soon as they landed. He looked at them once then put them down, hiding their treacherous backs from view using his forearm. It was good method, though executed without elegance. Yakky was clearly a fresh fish to the school, but he wasn't about to be a pushover.

The second round of betting began. Vic raised to the max and continued to practice his Hollywood cards sharp poses. I was holding next to nothing and folded. Yakky did the same. There's ten or eleven hands you want to throw money at. I'd told Yak what they were and told him to sit tight unless he had one of them. Silk and Smudge matched Vic's bet. Frenchy thought about it and matched it too. His hand currently beat Vic's but that could change. After the flop and the second round of betting, the fourth card was dealt to the table, the turn. That could transform your three of a kind into four of a kind or an outside change into a sure thing.

Poker, the action of dealing a random – supposedly random – selection of playing cards doesn't hold my interest. The people and their reactions, how they deal with what they're dealt, that's where the fascination is. Cheating's just one more reaction and I can respect a good cheat, especially when it comes to poker. For me, the money's a side issue, it's not the point.

That doesn't mean I won't cheat back.

I was confident that Frenchy's level of skill, with the marked deck, would outstrip mine, but I had the advantage of knowing someone else at the table was playing dirty. Frenchy wasn't taking the trouble to keep his cards from the sight line of other unprincipled players. He had made the age-old mistake of assuming he was the only one in the know. Strangely, a lot of cheats do.

The fourth card turned Frenchy's hand into a winner. Vic was novice enough to raise the max again and scared Smudge and Silk away; the table was reduced to just him and Frenchy. He'd not be getting nominated for an Oscar anytime soon, but Frenchy's impression of a man debating whether or not to match a bet was passable. It helped that it was what Vic wanted to see.

The last card of the hand, the river, was laid face up on the table and changed nothing. Vic raised the last bet to the max one more time and Frenchy raised in turn.

Most people lose track of the money. There was eight hundred and fifty-five pounds on the table. If you'd asked everyone what was in the pot at that point, most of them would underestimate. Ask them how much they'd put in personally and they'd underestimate again. If you want a fair assessment of how much a gambler's lost, the best one to ask is his wife. The rule is pretty much reversed when they think they're about to win. In Vic's mind, the pot in front of him was huge, towering over his hopes and desires like the New York skyline. But you don't win the pot, even when you do. What you win is the pot minus however much you've put into it. Vic had contributed more to the pot than any other player. It would cost him eight-sixty to see Frenchy. The game frankly wasn't worth the candle.

Easy for me to be smug of course. I knew the cards were marked. Vic paid to be beat and displayed a good working knowledge of Anglo-Saxon. Frenchy pulled the money towards him and gave one of his Gallic shrugs. Vic tried to save face by showing everyone how close to winning he'd come and flicked both his cards over for all to see.

They say if you can't see the sucker sitting at the table, it's because it's you. Vic wasn't seeing the sucker.

It was my turn to deal. I flicked the cards out fast, keeping them low to the table and making them spin, reducing the odds of Frenchy reading the marks. I hadn't waited for him to square away his winnings. Someone with a big pot to put away, or to arrange in front of them, concentrates on the money, not the cards. It's as close to a universal trait as I've ever found.

I wanted Vic out of the way. I sacrificed a few chucks of my hard earned to a couple of pots, hoping to bankrupt him quicker. In remarkably short time, he lost another grand, most of it to Frenchy. Annoyingly, he then pulled out his wallet and thumbed out a wad of twenties to start over. It was a flamboyant move. Flashy and stupid.

"You look like you came loaded for a serious game," I said.

He shrugged and tried to look nonchalant, like the high roller he wasn't.

"No point coming to a game without a stake."

"Any danger of raising the limit?" I was talking to Frenchy, not Vic.

Yet another Gallic shoulder hitch. "I've got no problem with that." He looked around the table in mute enquiry and, when no one raised an objection, said, "Maximum raise is double the pot. Everyone okay with that?"

Vic's overly intent eye contact betrayed his sinking heart, but with my help, he'd backed himself into a corner and couldn't stand down. Three hands later and most of his new stake was piled in the centre of the table, looking for a new home. Vic was waiting on the river card, hoping and betting, and possibly praying, on a queen of diamonds. He'd have had a long wait on that one. Both red queens had found their way into my procession. Along with the jack of spades and the ace of hearts.

Having an ace up your sleeve is an often-misunderstood

concept. You don't hide high cards, so you can use them later, you hide them, so you know nobody else will.

It was a stupid mistake, made in desperation. With the queen he had a good hand, without it, nothing. With six players at the table, the chances of a specific card coming out on the river are less than three percent. Betting on that kind of deal is a bad idea, plain and simple. Vic raised, I matched, the river was dealt, and he raised again.

Bluffing is the wasteland where the desperate go to die. Everyone's seen *Cool Hand Luke* and thinks they can break the bank with a pair of threes and an air of confidence. They're wrong.

When I showed my ten-high straight flush and took the pot, Vic made his biggest mistake of the night. As appeared to be his habit, he flipped over his cards to show off his losing hand.

"Fucking look at that."

He was drunk. As his losses had started to pile up, he began sliding the lagers down. The first couple he'd shouted for had been brought in by the young woman that haunted the kitchen. The first time she was giggling to herself, the second time she was chewing on a Mars bar. Karla had brought the lagers to the table after that. The pile of empties had grown as his pile of money shrank.

Smudge looked at Vic's cards.

"Not your night is it, bro?"

"Yeah, pity your mate Johnny weren't here, eh?"

Smudge didn't answer immediately, everyone except Vic heard the silence. Then, "What's that meant supposed to mean?"

"Just saying, I could have done with a queen."

Frenchy and Jason both moved fast, but Smudge moved faster. Vic didn't have a chance to get out of the way. They were both big men, but Smudge had the advantage of practice and rage. He grabbed Vic's cut-off and hauled him out of his seat, square into a head butt. The noise it made was a wet crack and Vic's nose streamed blood. I don't think he'd fully registered what was happening before Smudge slammed him onto the table and started punching him. The blows all came from the shoulder, brutally efficient. If Frenchy hadn't got to him and pulled him into a bear hug, we'd have been witnessing a murder.

Jason stepped behind me and put himself at Frenchy's back. Frenchy had his weight against Smudge's chest, pressing him to the wall. Smudge had calmed down, or at least wasn't struggling. There was blood on his forehead from Vic's busted nose.

Yakky and me checked on the wounded, who was still face up on the table. He was making an effort to stand, but it wasn't going well. Between us we got him to a chair. His left eye was swelling shut and his top lip had split against his teeth. He coughed and sprayed Yakky with blood.

"He's going to need stitches," Yakky said, wiping at his face with the back of one hand.

Karla had come into the room at some point with a wet tea towel folded into a compress.

She handed it to Yakky who held it to the man's damaged mouth. She asked if she should call an ambulance.

"Harri can drive him to A&E," Frenchy said.

I looked round at him. He was still keeping Smudge against the wall but was no longer holding him. Smudge was coolly regarding us as we tended to Vic. He wasn't trying to get at him, neither was he showing any remorse.

"Harri's not fit to drive," Karla announced, and I guessed Harri was the woman in the kitchen.

Yakky was still pressing the tea towel in place and limiting the blood flow. Without looking up, he suggested calling Spooky. Frenchy cast his own eye over the casualty and grunted agreement, before patting him on the shoulder and telling him he'd be fine. In the same breath and without turning around, he told Smudge to go. Silently, Smudge complied. We listened to the open pipes of his Harley, leaving the street at speed.

Frenchy left Vic's side and began gathering together the detritus of the poker game that had been knocked off the table. Given his less than honest tactics, I made sure I collected my money from the floor before he got close to it.

I also made sure Frenchy saw the wad of notes I was holding. Then I asked if anyone else wanted to carry on the game.

Spooky knocked on the door just as we'd got the table set up again. We'd waited ten minutes for him to get there, which was less than a meat truck from the Royal Bailing would have taken. Vic was sitting upright without aid and Karla had gone back to the kitchen to get him a fresh tea towel. I followed her, on the pretence of getting a drink.

The kitchen was a big room and well equipped, but it didn't look like it worked very hard. When I opened the fridge, it was filled with a mixture of beer and processed food. Frenchy obviously wasn't a Gourmont chef.

The room was dominated by an island unit with a herd of stools circling it. Harri was sat on one of them with her forearms on the work surface. She was smiling to herself and made an effort to follow me with her eyes. Once my trajectory took me to a point that required turning her head, she gave up. The litter of Rizla papers and gutted cigarettes told the anticipated story.

Karla was wringing cold water from a clean towel. Her hands were rock steady, and some internal shutter had come down. I began to see why she and Yak kept drifting back together.

"Spooky's here to take him to hospital. Do me a favour, volunteer to go with him, to the hospital."

I kept my voice low. Harri didn't look like she could understand what I was saying, let alone remember it, but paranoia gets to be a habit.

"Why?"

"I want to keep Jason and Frenchy here." I nodded in the direction of Harri. "Talkative sort?"

Karla told me she was. I grabbed a quad of lagers from the fridge and headed back to the game.

With Vic out of the way, Frenchy concentrated on Yakky, as did Jason. When it was my turn to deal, I offered the pack to Yakky. He rapped the top of the deck with a knuckle, universal sign that he didn't want to cut the cards. I shrugged and cut them myself before flicking the cards across the table.

There are a number of false cuts. I only know one but it's practically undetectable if you do it right, and I do.

In the wake of the fight, and with the speed I dealt the hands, no one noticed I dealt my cards from the bottom.

We put the first round of betting down and I dealt the flop. I had a mild coughing fit when I saw the favours it did Frenchy. There's a lot less luck in poker than people like to think. Still, having fate smile on you now and then doesn't hurt at all.

Yakky raised. We all matched his bet then he raised again, and Jason folded. Frenchy, as I'd hoped, took it down to the wire, matching all of Yakky's raises. On his last go Yakky doubled the pot, then folded when he was matched, once again. Frenchy and me, mano e mano, wound up duelling over a pot of epic proportions. After Frenchy paid stupid money to see my cards, I collected my winnings.

"I'm out of this," Jason announced. "Too heavy for me."

"You and me both," Yakky told him and took the ashes of his stake off the table. "You've got the luck of the devil," he told me. Exactly as scripted.

I blessed Frenchy with my Cheshire Cat smile.

"The devil don't come into it. It's all about knowing the cards."

I was holding the pack in front of me with the backs facing out. As I spoke, I tapped a finger on the corner of the top card. The spot where the telltale marks live. Other than his pupils dilating a fraction, Frenchy's face didn't move.

I dropped the deck in the centre of the table and piled my winnings into a neat stack.

"I take it Smudge is still upset about Johnny?"

Frenchy lit a cigarette and shrugged. I had the feeling the shrug was in recognition that I had the upper hand. For now.

"Looks that way. I should pull his patch for that."

He waved at the side of the table where Vic had got the sense knocked out of him. He'd landed on his pile of lager cans and the polished mahogany had a cluster of scratches, commemorating the event. I didn't know if Frenchy was concerned about the damage to one of his men or to his furniture.

"Does he know Johnny's gone up in smoke?"

Frenchy nodded and used his cigarette to point at Jason.

"Jason told him. I think it was a mistake." He looked pointedly at the damage on the table. "I should pull his patch."

"It wasn't a mistake," Jason said flatly. "I said he'd be in a state, and he is. If we'd left him find out about Johnny, out of the blue, he'd have gone off half-cocked and started a war with the Eight-Six."

"I doubt it'll change much now," I said.

"Meaning."

"Dago was talking with the Eight-Six about the HLB stepping up to a full-blown outlaw club. If no one's talking to them now, then you're going to get a war anyway. They won't let another patch club just pop up without their say so."

"I don't know why we're even considering this patch club crap. Tell Smudge and his crew, if they want all that bullshit, they can go and do it under their own flag." Jason was looking at me but the words were for Frenchy.

"If I do that we'll lose half the club, probably more."

"Then someone needs to talk to the Eight-Six."

Frenchy dropped the end of his cigarette into his empty lager tin. He listened to the faint hiss before replying.

"This club means too much to me to let it become a lap dog to the Eight-Six."

"It was Dago's club and he was talking to them."

Frenchy gave Jason a long look and finally told him, "Dago isn't the president anymore, I am."

"You might have a more immediate problem," I said and they both turned to me. I had the feeling I wouldn't be getting invited to the next poker night. "I don't think Smudge is too stable at the moment."

Jason laughed. "No shit Sherlock. Do you think that's why Vic just got carted off to A&E?"

"Smudge did that to him about five seconds after he was commiserating on his losses and calling him 'bro'. Then he walked out of here and rode out of the street, doing about ninety. He was going somewhere in a hurry."

"Where do you think he's headed?"

It was Jason that spoke. Frenchy was squinting at me from behind another shroud of smoke.

"You told him about the house in Enfield getting torched. Does he know who actually lit the match? 'Cos if he does, I'd say they're in danger."

Frenchy laughed. "You're not as clever you think, Doc."

"No?"

He shook his head, strangely delighted.

"No. Smudge was the one who lit the fire. He said he *wanted* to be the one to do it."

18.
Family

The route back to my flat passed Yakky's house, so I pulled in behind him and scrounged a brew. I'd have preferred a belt of tequila to a cup of tea, but I wanted to see how the land lay between us.

He didn't mention how close Karla had been to the violence at Frenchy's and, as he showed no signs of setting me up to keep Vic company, I assumed we were on an even keel.

Sat at his kitchen table, as ever, he asked how much money I'd taken. I dropped the block of notes in front of him, and he whistled through his teeth.

"I'm surprised you bother running a tattoo shop."

"You seldom find a group of players, that bad, willing to bet so much. And anyway, even with all the cheating, we were lucky tonight."

The good hand I'd given myself in the last game would have counted for nought if Frenchy hadn't been holding something worth betting on. Holding the winning hand wouldn't do you any good if nobody else was putting money down. My coughing fit, when I saw how well Frenchy was set up, was Yakky's cue to start raising. I'd suspected Frenchy would go after him. We'd arranged the signal beforehand, along with instructions on when to fold.

"I'm going to give it back anyway."

"Why?"

"I've got something on Frenchy now, that was the point really. It meant we could talk about club matters, a bit, find out who torched the squat. Let's call giving him his money back a gesture of goodwill."

"I doubt he'd do the same in your place."

"Maybe not, but I haven't got a private army behind me. I suspect a lot of the HLB would cheerfully break my legs on presidential decree. Gesture of goodwill seems a good idea."

"Shame, fucker had coming."

I was about to agree with him when his mobile went off. It sounded like Karla was calling from a karaoke bar. Busy night at A&E.

"We've only just been seen." She had to repeat herself because the first attempt was lost in a chorus of drunken yowling. "They're going to keep him in overnight but it's just a precaution. You'll have to come and pick me up, I don't have any money on me."

I followed Yakky out of the house and we rode off in opposite directions. When I got to my flat I felt tired. It wasn't particularly late but the intensity of the evening at Frenchy's had ground into me. Sleep was elusive though and my bed felt uncomfortable; it didn't take me long to give up on the idea.

I lit a few candles on the altar and was pacing the front room when Karla rang. She apologised for calling late in a tone that made me doubt her sincerity. I told her not to worry.

"Yakky got you home alright?"

She said 'yes' in the same off-key tone. I left a gap for her to add something, but she didn't.

"You spoke to Harri?"

"I spoke to Harriot." It took me a moment to match *Harriot* to Harri, the dope head in the kitchen. "We were best friends, once we'd skinned up."

There was another pause. Normally I let pauses blossom into uncomfortable silences, that people rushed to fill. I could tell that wasn't going to work here.

"I was right about the dope breaking the ice, then?"

"Yes. Well done you."

"And?"

"And…next time you can do your own dirty work. Leave me out of it."

"Do you want to tell me what the problem is here, Karla?

You didn't have a gun at your head when I asked for help. I don't expect Harriot needed one at hers when you offered her a smoke."

"Have you ever spoken to that girl?" The question came in a rush, and she didn't give me a chance to answer it. "She's barely out of her twenties, for Christ's sake."

I knew from Yakky that Karla was twenty-eight, a year younger than him. A fully paid up nurse for two years, three years in training before that. When she'd been *barely out of her twenties,* she'd been learning how to keep people alive. Nobody had put a gun at her head then either.

"She's not a *girl*, she's a woman."

My phone translated Karla's anger into a squeal of feedback and the subtleties of her response were lost to me. The gist of it was *don't pull the feminist card on me.*

"She's practically a child. What the hell is she doing, shacked up with some thug, old enough to be her father?"

I couldn't help but think of the beginning of the evening with Yakky an inch away from my face, snarling his disapproval. I wasn't entirely convinced I needed a proxy to shore up my moral code and I was damned if I wanted two of the them.

"You'd have to ask her that. I know any number of people, men and women, in lousy relationships. It doesn't stop them being adults."

For a moment, all I heard from her end of the line was breathing, high pitched and nasal. I could picture her mouth pressed into a thin line as she fumed. When she spoke again, her voice was too reasonable to be anything other than furious.

"This has got nothing to do with me and Andy."

The remark made no sense to me, partly because the name, Andy, didn't register straight away. Aside from Karla, no-one I knew ever used Yakky's given name – also, my comment hadn't been meant in reference to their relationship. I felt a wave of sympathy for the woman and a fresh prickling of guilt. I pushed both into a mental file, labelled: *not now.*

For a short time neither of us spoke. I had to remind myself that Karla didn't fully understand the stakes we were playing for. She was still under the impression I was doing nothing more than a skip-trace.

"When you were in A&E, did Vic tell you why his mate beat him half witless?"

"No."

"No. He wouldn't have, because that's not how it works. He made a joke that Smudge took offence at and that was the price he paid. That's the playing field we're on at the moment. And I'm trying to find someone who doesn't want to found." Which was the truth. If not actually honest. "The safest way to do that, is on the sly.

"Yakky didn't want you involved in this, in case you got hurt. You can call that being over protective or just old-fashioned sexism if you want, but the fact is, he's got a point, this isn't a game. If giving some doper a lump of brain rot so they'll think you're their mate is going to keep you awake at night, then you need to bow out."

Another pause, then, "Nice speech. Did you rehearse it?"

"Yeah. I'm available for bat mitzvahs and weddings if you're interested."

She didn't laugh.

"I get your point. I don't like it though, and I don't like Andy being dragged down to your level."

"Noted. Now, do you want to tell me what Harri said, or have we all wasted our time?"

There was a long silence and I thought she was about hang up on me or explode again. I wondered if Yakky was with her, and if that was making matters better or worse.

Finally, she said, "Harri told me Johnny had turned up a few times with a woman about my age. She was called Christine – not Chris or Chrissie, she was very particular about it. Harriot said she didn't last long. She didn't fit in."

Which was the sum amount of what I'd heard about her.

"Did she say what the problem with her was?"

"I think Harriot liked her, it was the other women in the

club. They thought she was full of herself. I thought they might have been jealous or something like that, but apparently, she was wasn't exactly a temptress. Harriot said, *she dressed like she worked in Oxfam*."

"Meow."

"I asked if anyone had spoken to her about where Johnny might have gone." There was another one of those pauses. "She said she hadn't spoken to her *lately*. So, I guessed she might have a number for her. Only I couldn't see any way to get it without sounding weird. She was stoned and all, but I didn't know how much she'd remember when she was straight again."

"Don't beat yourself up. You did okay, we know more than we did."

"It's not that," she snapped the words out and I sat through another pause before she added. "When the fight happened, she didn't even notice, so I stole her phone. It was sitting on the countertop. It's not something I'm proud of."

"Don't worry about that, I'll get it back to her somehow. Is there a number for a Christine?"

Karla made a hissing noise, and I suspected my take on the mother confessor role needed some work.

"There's one for Chris. That might be it, should I ring it?"

"Not now, we need to give it some thought. Is Yakky with you?"

"Yeah."

"Let him have the phone and he can give it to me tomorrow."

I was intending to say 'thank you', but she hung up before I could.

I didn't have Smudge's number, so I rang Jason. The tension, from his end of the call, leaked into my flat. I could hear one of his kids crying. He grunted when I asked if it was a bad time.

After I'd got off the phone with Karla, I'd jotted the name Christine on the wall and treated myself to a shot of tequila.

It wasn't much, but a name, and possibly a phone number, could be seen as progress. If you squinted a bit. I was still squinting when my mobile went off again. Yakky's voice was the usual desert of emotion.

"Karla spoken to you?"

"Just got off the phone. I thought you were with her."

"I nipped out to get some milk. Did she tell you about the Handsome Boys turning up?"

As he'd left the hospital with Karla, four guys on Harleys had been pulling in. He hadn't recognised anyone, but they were wearing HLB patches. And, as Yakky put it, *no bugger was carrying grapes.*

"You got a phone number for Smudge?" I asked Jason. He told me to hold on and while he consulted his contacts list, a door slammed. It took three attempts to get the number because his wife was shouting at him. I couldn't make out what was being said. At a guess, it involved poker.

Smudge's phone manner could have used a little polishing. He picked it up first ring and snapped, "What?"

"It's Doc here, any chance we can get together? I'm in the mood for a chat."

He gave me his address and told me to come over. The connection was broken without another word.

Smudge's property was a terrace, not dissimilar to Yakky's place. In most parts of the country it would have been a cheap place to live. Being so far inside of the M25 put it beyond a lot of people's reach. I parked up next to the canvas-wrapped shape of Smudge's Harley, and the front door opened before I could knock.

Though Smudge lacked the OCD that Dago imposed on his environment, the house was tidier than most bachelor pads. The front and backrooms had been knocked into one, and the space was dressed for gatherings. High-end stereo speakers were putting out something soft but powerful. I wouldn't have marked Smudge as a Billie Holiday fan. That may have said more about me than him.

Like Dago's living room, much of the wall space had been given over to photos of parties and club events. On one wall a collection of pictures, framed in black, remembered dead members. Dago's photo was mounted highest, as befitted his rank. The latest edition, of course, was Johnny Simms.

There wasn't a photograph, instead the black frame held the portrait Mary had commissioned Yakky to produce. Next to his picture, a coat hanger had been mounted, a black leather cut-off hanging from it. It smelt faintly of damp and worse.

"Johnny's?" I asked.

Smudge nodded and sat heavily in an expensive office chair.

"When we go to full-back patches, the first set go to Johnny."

There was an edge of aggression in his tone, a challenge to question the statement. He'd been drinking.

"He'd have liked that," I said, which was what I believed.

Smudge nodded again and the chair creaked as he settled into it. He waved a hand in the direction of a low table loaded with bottles. Most of them had been intended for an optic's rack, their provenance was betrayed by their inverted labels. I helped myself to a mixer can of coke.

"*That* might be a problem, if the police start sniffing around."

I pointed at the cut-off with the hand holding my drink. Smudge seemed to mistake the movement for a toast, and mirrored it with a glass he picked up from the floor. He drained the measure of amber liquid in one hit.

"Don't see the police ID-ing him anytime soon."

I didn't have Smudge marked as an idiot, so I put it down to the drink talking.

"You need to bear in mind, Smudge, I found him. The cops won't take that long to back engineer whose body they pulled from the ash. Don't forget, he had a police record."

He let Billie Holiday finish her verse before answering softly, "I won't forget." He stood up and went to the drinks table. The fresh measure he poured himself was modest and he took a sip, not a belt. "I did a very thorough job – they'll have their work cut out finding a name."

He shook his head and left the glass, unfinished, on the table. I suspected the details of the 'thorough job' were something else he wasn't going to forget.

"I'm sorry you had to do that. It shouldn't have fallen to you."

"I told Frenchy, I wouldn't let anyone else do it," he said. It was a definite end to the subject. "You said you wanted a chat. What's up?"

"We put Vic in a taxi and Karla took him over to A&E. Yakky went to pick her up about half hour ago. As they were leaving, a group of HLB guys turned up. I thought you might want to know."

Smudge made a noise that could have been a sigh or a laugh. "Sounds like Frenchy's boys."

"Inner circle?"

"Nothing like that. Some of the guys work for me, doing the doors, there's another contingent working with Frenchy. It's not a problem."

"You might not hold that opinion if you were the one stuck in the Royal Bailing."

Smudge shook his head and told me not to worry about it, then added it was a club matter. I didn't bother raising an objection, and he read more into it than my indifference to his health. As Billie Holiday oozed into the next track, he fixed me with a look and pointed at one the speakers.

"Did you know she was a smackhead?"

"Smack, booze. Dead at forty-four. Terrible waste."

Smudge was still looking at me, not quite steadily – he was drunker than I'd first thought – he shook his head. I was missing the point.

"Drugs and booze was the least of it. Her life was complete crap from the minute she drew breath. But just listen to that voice. She became so much more than the shit she came from. Imagine if she'd survived."

"How's this connected with you and Vic?"

Smudge smiled, the way parents do when their children are

still young enough to appear innocent, rather than stupid. "What she went through made her great. But there was no one looking out for her. Her family used her as a meal ticket, the government locked her up for being an addict, for being sick. One man after another, used her as a punch bag. If she'd had us…" He waved at the surrounding walls and the pictures of HLB unity. "…she would have survived."

"What are you telling me Smudge, Billie Holiday should have jointed a bike club?"

He found the remark funny and laughed; it was the first time I'd seen him express any genuine amusement. Briefly, it overrode his baseline antagonism.

"I'm saying being mollycoddled isn't the same as being loved." He waved at the speaker again. "If she'd been wrapped in cotton-wool, they'd be playing her music on smooth FM and no one would give a fuck. She needed people to keep her alive, not make her soft. Family."

Fortune smiled on his little speech and the track ended, at exactly the right point, to lend it gravitas.

"Smudge, that is bullshit. You can die tonight, knowing a million people love your records, or you can die in fifty years, in a soft bed, with a full belly. If someone had given Billie Holiday that choice, you think we'd be listening to her now?"

Smudge laughed again. He was back to his usual snide mockery. "No one, fucking *no one*, gets that choice. If we can get this set up properly, then we're all there for each other. We get to have those fifty years. And," his teeth were bared, "people will still know who we are: the Handsome London Boys." The music wasn't so accommodating this time and the cry of *Handsome London Boys* had to compete with a trumpet solo. He nodded at Johnny's cut-off. "First set of colours, they're Johnny's. Brotherhood, family."

Embarrassed by his grandstanding or maybe the soul baring, Smudge got out of his chair and squared his shoulders. He asked me if I wanted a proper drink. I told him I was fine with the Coke.

"What about Johnny's family? His parents don't even know

he's dead."

Smudge retrieved the glass he'd abandoned earlier, he took a measured sip. His self-control impressed me. He obviously wanted to knock it back.

"Where were his fucking family when he was arrested?" He picked up a bottle of Southern Comfort, then put it down again without opening it. "Johnny told me, when he left school, his old man told him to go down the DSS, with a walking stick, and try to get himself registered as unfit to work. Told him, if he could get full disability allowance, he'd be set for life. That's what his poxy family wanted for him, to pretend to be a cripple. That's what they thought he was worth. He never had a good word to say about any of them. Not many of us do. That's the point of it, of the club, to be a family."

"You sound like a purist."

Smudge took one of the mixer cans for himself and sat down again. It was a relief. I was sitting on one of three sofas in the room; it was in bad shape and I'd sunk low in its embrace. Having Smudge towering over me wasn't exactly relaxing.

"I believe it's more than swanning around on a Harley, trying to look hard. If you keep it tight, keep everyone on the ball, then it's something else. Something worth fighting for."

"Did you know Dago had been negotiating with the Eight-Six, talking about patching the HLB over?"

"No. That's news to me."

"Would the HLB go for that?"

"They might have done, but I can't see Frenchy putting any time into trying to broker a deal with another club. He's not bothered, one way or the other, about the back patch thing. I think he'll just put it to the vote, see if it goes through and then worry about the details. I'm not going to go crawling to the Eight-Six, asking for a set of hand-me-down colours."

"What if they've got something to say about a new club starting up? I heard there was trouble at The House of Ice last Sunday."

He didn't bother pinning me with his sniper's eye, but the bark of laughter was no warmer. "Do you know what Dago used to say about you? He said, if you followed someone into a revolving door, you'd walk out in front of them. He thought a lot of you."

The way Smudge said it implied he was less enamoured. I pressed the point about the trouble at the nightclub. He'd only concede that the Eight-Six had been around on the previous Sunday. What I'd heard, in the background of the phone conversation with Eddie, had been a snippet of a stag night.

I didn't see The House of Ice topping the list of stag venues for anyone I'd ever known in the Eight-Six. If there was any truth in Smudge's story, then some pretty young twenty-somethings had probably had their party highjacked.

"You think a vote would go your way?" I asked.

Smudge nodded. "Oh, yeah. There's a good fourteen or fifteen guys who want to go there. It's going to happen. Sooner rather than later now."

"Why now? What's changed?"

"Dago's gone."

"He was blocking it?"

Smudge shrugged, then changed his mind about the Southern Comfort. He fumbled with the cap slightly and I noticed the knuckles of his right hand were coloured with bruising.

"He wasn't big on the idea."

"Frenchy's into it more?"

Another shrug. "Like I said, I don't think he's bothered one way or the other. He doesn't really get it."

"It?"

Smudge waved at the walls again. "The idea of brotherhood."

"I think he might. He did do fifteen years in the French Foreign Legion."

"Yeah. Between eighty and ninety-five." Smudge laughed again, probably at my blank expression. "There was fuck all happening then. The legion went into Iraq, *after* someone else had been bombing it for a month; they all but walked into Al Salman airport. The nearest Frenchy came to any real action was losing his foot when that jeep flipped over, and that was 'cos the driver was high as a kite. All he'd have done for fifteen years was the three pees: polishing, parading and pissing it up."

19.
Grown-ups, Men and the Proud-Snake Shuffle

Saturday 7 October

Too wide for a residential road, Maraton Way, had become a rat-run for commuters and couriers. The rich crop of speed bumps the council had sown along it did little to slow the traffic, and the pedestrian crossings at either end were decorated with generations of floral tributes.

Christine West lived at number sixteen. More accurately sixteen B. And she was pretending to be out.

Sixteen B had once been a small garage, now it was a tiny flat. I'd seen the lights were on from the road, but when I pulled up on the hardstanding it all went dark. I knocked on the door and got no reply. Calling hello through the letter box was equally productive. What finally got her to the door was the assurance that I had her vouchers for the free pizzas.

Yakky had appeared at my flat early that morning and given me Harri's phone. I used the telephone questionnaire ploy again to glean an address from the number for 'Chris'. I made the call using my 'posh' voice and a stammer. Because I didn't have her second name, I told her I wasn't sure I had the right person and asked her to confirm the number I'd just dialled. I told her there was possibly a fault with our database but assured her she could still have vouchers for two free pizzas of her choice.

Affecting a stammer kept her on the line. Very few people are willing to hang up on a man straggling with a speech impediment.

A security chain rattled into place and the door to sixteen B opened enough to let a blade of light escape. A small face appeared diagonally in the gap. I looked into my cupped hand, pretended to read something.

"Christine West?" The face nodded and I tried to smile without using too many teeth. "I'm going to need your autograph, for the vouchers. If I don't get a signature the boss thinks I flog them on eBay."

The slanted face relaxed, or possibly tightened, into a gently sympathetic smile. The door was pushed closed and the chain rattled some more. When it opened again, I quietly put my foot over the threshold and handed her the card with, *My Solider Boy. X*, written on it.

Even in the evening gloom I saw her face whiten. She tried to slam the door and for a moment – when it bounced off my steel-toe cap – I thought she was going to scream.

"Christine, I'm not going to hurt you. I just want to ask you about Johnny."

She lost another shade of colour and her mouth opened and closed convulsively. Turned out she wasn't a screamer, thankfully.

I stepped inside, and she backed away, badly frightened. Both hands in the air, I told her, again, that I wasn't about to hurt her. She didn't look convinced but after another couple of gaping fish impressions, she found enough oxygen to ask what I wanted.

"I want to know how you knew it was Johnny Simms' body in that fire."

"I don't know any Johnny Simms." She tried to pass the card back to me. "I don't know what this is about."

I'd wondered how many more bad poker players I was due to meet. I took the card back and told her I was trying to find out who had murdered her Solider Boy. She told me she'd call the police if I didn't leave.

"The time to call the police was when they appealed for information about the fire. But if you want to do it now, go ahead. I'll wait. And we'll see who talks their way out of trouble quickest."

She was smart enough to know her bluff had been called. She sagged slightly, as if she'd just noticed she was exhausted.

"Who are you, are you from Johnny's club?"

"I'm not from any club." I offered her my hand, which she either ignored or didn't notice. "My name's James Slidesmith. I knew Johnny, through a good friend of mine."

I saw Christine look at the tattoo on my face and jerk slightly as she made the connection. Up until then she'd been too scared to think straight.

"Slidesmith. You're the tattooist?"

"At your service. Can we talk now?"

If Christine West had been an actress, she'd have had a career playing intense, well-meaning types. To say she looked like a social worker wasn't totally unfair. And, unkind as it was, I could see where Harri's assessment of her dress sense had been coming from. Christine was overly fond of careworn textiles that she wore with a proprietary air, the way a lot of bikers wear knackered leathers. She also – when she'd calmed down a bit – held eye contact too long. I forgave these failings when she offered me tea.

As the tea brewed, she asked me how I'd known Johnny was living in the abandoned house. She asked the question with her back turned to me, which required no small effort. The kitchen was a length of work surface, attached to a corner of the tiny flat, and causally avoiding your guests took planning.

I told her the bare bones of tracing the stolen GSX and finding the body, I left Yakky's presence out of the narrative. There wasn't any reason to recount the details, but I told her what I'd found was a murder scene. When she handed me a mug of tea, her hand was shaking.

"It wasn't an accident," she said. I was caught in the glare of her overly sincere eye contact again, but she'd made the statement to herself. "I thought it might have been an accident or...or something."

Christine had perched on the edge of a straight-back chair, sitting next to a drop-leaf table. I'd sat on an ancient sofa that left me a full foot lower than her.

"No accident," I told her. "Someone went there intending

to kill him."

"Why?"

"That's the big question, but your starter for ten is this: how did you know he was there?"

"He told me he was going to be there. He told me he'd been given an *assignment.* He said he'd be lying low for a while, afterwards."

She pulled the same sympathetic smile she'd given me at the door, when I'd been pretending to have trouble reading. I pointed out he hadn't laid low enough, and the soupy grin died where it fell.

I could see why she and Johnny had wound up together. He was easy to feel superior to and likely to mistake patronising indulgence for admiration. It wasn't hard to see why she hadn't been a hit with the rest of the HLB.

"So, what was this assignment he was on about?"

She didn't know. All Johnny would tell her was he'd been tasked with an assignment or, sometimes, a *mission.* Clearly, he'd wanted to be asked about it, but only so he could say he couldn't talk about it. Reading between the lines, Christine had been happy to play along.

I asked her when this had started, and she said Tuesday the fourth.

I pointed out that was a very exact date.

She nodded and looked miserable, "It was the day before my nephew's birthday. I was rushing to wrap his present and get it to him. My sister was taking him paintballing early the next morning. I mentioned it to Johnny and it started him talking about the army and the Foreign Legion. He worked it around to this assignment."

That would have been four days before Smudge saw Johnny, for the last time, riding in the direction of Enfield.

"And he told you where he'd be?"

"Not then, that was later, it was the last time I spoke to him. I hadn't seen him for a few days, he was doing things with that club of his. We went out together on the Thursday, he was very quiet. Something was upsetting him. We came back here, and I thought he'd stay the night, but he told me he had his assignment to take care of. He gave me the address of that place in Enfield, said it was a safe-house and made me swear I wouldn't tell anyone about it."

"Why did he tell you?"

"He didn't say as much but, I think, he wanted me to go over and spend time with him. He couldn't stand being on his own and he'd frightened himself. He was in a bit of a state when he left. I tried to persuade him to stay, but he wouldn't, he said he needed to go. It was for the good of the club."

"But, he still wouldn't say what he was doing?"

Christine shook her head. She was still keeping up the eye contact and I could see she was close to crying.

"He wouldn't tell me." The tears didn't come, but they were close. "I lost patience a bit. I was fed up hearing about the club, every five minutes. I said he didn't have to do anything if he didn't want to, I said something unkind, about boys and their toys. He said it was more than that. It was a band of brothers, it was a regiment and sometimes sacrifices had to be made. For the good of the club. I thought…" She trailed off, unable to articulate what she thought. "I didn't think he was being serious. But, now, I think he knew he was going to die. I think he was willing to die. For the good of that stupid club."

Other than she was scared, she knew little else. I offered her what comfort could and before I left, I gave her one of my cards. If anything happened, or she remembered something she thought was important, I told her to call me. I told her to keep her head down otherwise. It was hardly reassuring, but people had died. I didn't want her convincing herself that she was jumping at shadows.

Sunday 8 October

Around four, I tacked my last customer onto Yakky's list and left work early, heading towards Kew.

For Sue, finding Johnny had been about collaring the father of Mary's child, and his murder had made the exercise redundant. I doubted Sue would be interested in what Johnny's girlfriend had to say, but it provided a reasonable pretext to drop by and see how she was getting on. I also craved some female company. I'd been passively inhaling testosterone for too long and the smell was getting to me.

When I got to Sue's, there was a car on the drive, parked behind her BMW. I didn't recognise it and was edgy enough to give it the once over. There was nothing more sinister to be seen than a collection of sweet wrappers and a child's backpack on the rear seat.

Mary opened the front door wearing black leggings and a vest top, both items were close fitting. She'd inherited her natural father's whip-cord build and, like her clothing, it left nowhere for the growing bump to hide. She told me Mum was in the garden and led me to the house.

The living room had been turned into a temporary beauty parlour. I assumed the customer was the owner of the backpack in the car. Even in school uniform, with her hair teased into an elaborate plait, she bore a startling resemblance to Jason. Giggling along with Mary, as her session resumed, she ignored my scrutiny. I made my way to the patio.

The rain had stopped around one o'clock, but the sky had stayed the colour of lead. Apart from the table, with its umbrella, all the garden furniture was still glossed with moisture. Sue and Jason's wife, Kim, both had their coats on and sat drawn tightly into themselves. The damp air magnified the stink of wet dogends.

The skin around Kim's eyes was dark and, at first sight, I thought she'd been punched. When she glanced up at my approach however, I saw it was fatigue and I wondered when she'd last slept. The look she gave me was cool, to say the least. I guessed Jason had told her about my night at the poker table.

As I slid the patio door closed, Sue dropped a fresh cigarette butt into the ashtray. It hissed a goodbye.

"She says it's not Johnny's." It wasn't clear who she was speaking to, but Kim replied with a long *tsss*, as if she was doing a duet with Sue's dogend.

"Of course it is, that's why the little sod's done a runner."

"Mary says it isn't."

"Oh, come on." Kim glanced over her shoulder, to the living room. Mary was undoing the fancy plait she'd put in her daughter's hair and was starting over. Both were laughing. "Of course it was Johnny, who else would –"

She bit the sentence off and buried her face behind a mug of coffee. I could see Sue had caught the implication. She'd had two decades of people writing her daughter off, once they'd labelled her as, *a learning difficulty*. It was water off a duck's back.

For me, the comment rankled. Yakky's carefully executed portrait of Johnny was hanging on Smudge's wall. I didn't see it getting there by any route other than gifting. There's more to humanity than intellect and, to my mind, Mary's sensitivity meant more than a few IQ points.

"Why would she lie about it?" Sue asked.

Kim pulled a face rather than answer and, when she looked up from her mug, she homed in on me.

"I hear you had a good time the other night."

"Yeah, I was lucky."

"I'll tell the bailiffs that when they came round."

"How much did he lose this time?" Sue asked.

"Four hundred pounds."

Kim's posture changed as she reported the crime, she pulled herself more upright, her shoulders rocking. The effect made her look like a snake. It was hard to tell if she was trying to hold her head high or boast about how hard she was having it. Sue shot the words through with a whistle of cigarette smoke.

The money I'd taken from Frenchy was in my pocket, waiting to be put back on his polished table. I decided he could handle a short fall better than Jason's family. Kim watched me as I counted off a wad off notes. She shook her head when I made to hand them to her.

"I don't want your money." She did her proud-snake shuffle

again. "I don't know how you all sleep at night, taking his wages like that, I really don't."

Kim came closer than she knew to winning the moral high ground and losing the money. Pride I've got a little time for – though only a little – martyrdom I can't be doing with. I put the stack of notes on the table, in front of her.

"I sleep just fine and I didn't *take* his money, I *won* it. I won it because Jason's one of the worst poker player's I've ever seen and because he's dumb enough to keep on losing. So, either take the money and pay your bills or give it back and be a martyr. Either way, don't have a dig at me because you married a mug. I'm going to have a word with Mary."

I got up from the table and managed to cut Sue a look. She gave me the tiniest of nods, letting me know she'd persuade Kim to accept the cash.

Mary and her client were having a better time than I was, out on the patio. Both were giggling and excited, and one of Mary's teen musicals was in the DVD player, being ignored. I asked if I could book in for perm, and they giggled some more. When I patted my stomach and pointed at Mary's growing bump, there was a quick flash of suspicion before she broke into a huge smile and told me she was going to be a mum.

"How's your mother feel about being called Granny?"

Mary hooted with laughter and Kim's little girl – too young to get the joke – did the same, a beat late. I gave Mary my congratulations and hoped I wasn't the first to think of doing so. I told them I was going to put the kettle and, from the kitchen, heard the patio door slide open and Mary asking 'Granny' if she wanted tea. By the time I'd found a pot, the choruses of Granny were in full swing. When Sue joined me in the kitchen, she thanked me for giving my winnings back.

"She's taken the money then?"

Sue rolled her eyes. "Of course she did. She just wanted to give you a hard time about it first."

When we went back with the tea, Kim was still confusing pride with martyrdom. The pile of five-pound notes, much reduced, landed in front of me as I sat down.

"Jason said four hundred." She left a primly dramatic pause. "I don't want your charity."

I weighed up the satisfaction of taking the money back against the urge to throw it in her face. In the end I did neither. I didn't know Kim particularly well, but I was aware she'd come up by a similar route to Sue. Husband number one had left her high, dry and broke. Jason had displayed more staying power, but life was never easy. Like Sue, she'd hardened. Like her husband, she couldn't spot a bluff. I tidied the pile of notes and put them in the centre of the table.

"I don't care what Jason told you, I'm giving you what I saw him drop into the pot last night. If your pride's more important than putting food on your family's table then fine, I'll put that in my pocket and let you worry about your kids."

Kim's lips tensed across her teeth in a string of silent curses, and she picked the money up. Rather than thanks, I was given an assurance that she'd kill her husband.

She left soon after, telling Sue she'd pick Jackie up the next morning. I toyed with the idea of ringing Jason and warning him about the evening ahead, then decided he had it coming. He also needed a wakeup call.

From the side of her mouth that wasn't clamping on a fresh cigarette, Sue told me I been a bit hard on her.

"I handed her over five hundred quid. A word of thanks would have been nice."

She squinted as the wind carried a waft of smoke into her eyes. Crow's feet and bags drove home what the last months had been like.

"She was embarrassed."

"Yeah, pride'll do that to you. You believe Mary?"

Sue sighed, though I couldn't have said whether she wanted to avoid the subject or had more to say about Kim.

"I can't see why she'd lie. But that business with the camera was funny."

I told her that Yakky's commission was currently in Smudge's house. She wasn't greatly surprised. Handsome London Boys were a fairly constant presence in Mary's life.

The respect, extended to the presidential family, ensured she'd only ever seen them at their best.

"Johnny was always good with her." She sighed again and a set of frown lines joined the crow's feet. "I know what Kim meant, in some ways Johnny was on her level. Where Johnny was, you'd normally find Smudge close behind."

"Have you asked who the father is?"

"Yeah, she wouldn't tell me. She said it was a secret."

"Shall I try and have a word with her about it?"

I'd thought she'd to want me to, but Sue shook her head. "It's nothing to do with you, Doc. Mary's a grown woman and now she's about to be a mother. So, treat her like a grown-up and respect her privacy."

She held my eye waiting for my agreement.

"What about the father? Shouldn't he be acting like a grown-up too?"

She shook her head again, hissing smoke.

"He won't be a grown-up, Doc, he'll be a man."

Her face was hard set. I knew she wasn't going to change her mind, not then at any rate, and the best I'd achieve was an argument. I didn't have any desire to poke into Mary's private affairs, though her turn of phrase worried me: *it's a secret.* There's a difference between privacy and secrecy. When a young woman's found to be pregnant *her* secret's already out. After that, she's keeping somebody else's secret. It was hard to think of a good scenario to connect that story to.

I held my hands up and Sue acknowledged the surrender with a nod. But she looked away from me and, as she finished her cigarette, I knew we were thinking along the same lines.

20.
Mediation and Other Games of Chance

Monday 9 October

The phone in Frenchy's office hadn't started up for the day and he wasn't in work mode. He sat behind his desk, regarding me over the rim of his mug. El Presidente hadn't offered me a seat and one of us needed to blink first. I placed the envelope of money on his desktop. I was small-minded enough to put it slightly out of his reach. To claim it he had to lean forward in his chair, ruining the cut of his presidential repose.

"I've kept my money, everyone else's is there, apart from Jason's, that went to his old lady. That way she can feed the kids."

Frenchy thumbed the wad and had the nerve to ask me if my conscious was bothering me. I told him no and took out the cards I'd palmed from his deck. I dropped them on the desk, within reach this time. The move caught him sufficiently unawares that he dropped the blank look he was trying for and rolled his eyes.

"Dago told me once, 'don't ever pay cards with Doc'."

I took the seat I hadn't been offered and gave him a knowing grin. Not that I knew anything. I never had played cards with Dago and the comment made me wonder if he'd just assumed I'd cheat. Surprisingly, the thought stung. Nevertheless, I told Frenchy it was sound advice, then asked him where he'd learned to play with a marked deck.

Frenchy crumpled the stray playing cards into a ball and threw them, over arm, into a wastepaper bin.

"Back in the legion, in the eighties. Polish guy in Algiers had a pack of the things. He stripped me raw for the first three months I was posted there."

"Welcoming the new guy?"

"Something like that. Then he told me what was happening, after that we'd go and fleece the local Arabs." Arabs pronounced with a hard A so it became eh-rabs.

Frenchy left his seat and stood at the end of the desk, signalling the meeting was over. I didn't move.

"Did he give you your money back?" I asked.

He still held the cash in his hand. I could see he wanted to put it in his pocket. I'd called Frenchy out on being a cheat. Keeping that secret was doubtless on his mind, but it possibly wasn't the first order of business. Before negotiating my silence, he wanted to justify his poker tactics. Most people like to imagine their souls are new and improved bio-wash white, rather than dishcloth grey.

"I made more from what he taught me than I ever lost to him."

"So, getting mugged was a tuition fee?" I suggested.

He nodded, and the notes vanished into his hip pocket. It wasn't a bad conscious soother, if you've a taste for such things. Should I ever feel the need to align self-image with reality, I might try it.

Frenchy tried the silent treatment again and sighed when I sat right through it.

"What do you want, Doc?"

"Jason. He can't afford your tuition fees."

Frenchy rolled his eyes again. "He's a grown man."

I thought about referring him to Sue for her opinions on grown men.

"The HLB's not the legion, Frenchy. No one's giving Jason, or his wife and kids, food and shelter, that's what his wages are for. Tell him he's not part of the card school anymore."

Left unsaid was my agreement to keep schtum about Frenchy's crooked, if beautifully polished, table.

"Okay, it that's what you want. But it's not the only game in town. If you're a mug there'll always going somebody willing to wring you out."

I let him have his extra grain of vindication.

"Has it crossed your mind that Dago was run down deliberately?"

"Jesus Christ." He shook his head and a frown twisted the corners of his mouth. "You're so full of your own shit, Doc, you even believe it yourself. It was an RTA, alright? Arsehole in a car with a skinful. Happens all the time."

"That's the official club line, is it?"

Frenchy shifted back into his chair and drew hard on the last half-inch of his cigarette. Most of the smoke he let back out came my way. He was pleased to have the chance to get angry.

"If, *if* you're right, can you imagine how that'd go down at the moment? As it stands, most of the guys think Johnny's gone AWOL. The news is going to break at some point, someone's going to work out whose body they've found. When it does, if people get to thinking that it ties in with Black Micky getting stabbed, people are going to start getting jumpy. You start dropping in half-arsed bullshit about Dago and it'll kick right off. Then what do I do? Calm things down by telling everyone, *the Eight-Six didn't kill Johnny, Dago did...just before somebody else did him.*"

He flicked the stub of his cigarette across the room, aiming at the sink in the corner. He pulled out another but couldn't keep his mouth still long enough to light it.

"You saw what it's like at the moment, Doc. Vic says the wrong thing and Smudge half kills him. I've got twenty-plus men in the Handsome London, if they all get it into their heads members are being targeted, it's only a matter of time before someone does something stupid. The Eight-Six are flexing their muscle as it is, I don't need someone handing them an excuse."

As he finished talking, the side of the industrial unit shook as a pair of open-piped Harleys ripped past it. The engine noise cut out as they parked up. Frenchy glanced in the direction of the noise. It seemed to settle him, and he put a flame to the end of his fresh cigarette.

"Look, I'll tell Jason I'm not having him at my table again, alright? But do something for me, alright? Keep your stories about Dago to yourself."

I nodded and told him okay. He started telling me he had to get on with work, but I was already on my way to the door.

I rode away from Frenchy's yard gingerly. The road out front was wet and coloured with rainbows of diesel oil. I kept the speed down most of the way home, watching my rearview mirror as much as the road.

Turning off the A3 and sighting The Jericho usually gave me the sense of being home. That day it was more a feeling of leaving hostile territory. As I rode past the front of the pub, I raised a hand to Spooky's blue Nissan, which had been pacing me since Staples Corner, then I slipped the Sportster between some gaps in the traffic.

Yakky's bike was chained to the lamppost outside the shop when I got there. My own bike I normally kept tucked away in my backyard, under cover and out of sight. That morning I locked it to next to the scruffy black Yamaha with an air of defiance. Maybe all the bullshit, about brotherhood and the crap it brings with it, was getting to me.

Threading the bike between lanes had gained me quite a lead and by the time Spooky's Nissan pulled up across the road, I'd made tea. I poured one for Yakky as he climbed out of the passenger side door. He bent at the waist and spoke briefly with Spooky before the car pulled away.

"Frenchy give you any trouble?" Yakky asked, as he came in the door.

"Not really, but I left when the workforce started to arrive. I didn't want to push my luck."

Yakky took the mug of tea and tilted it towards me, in a toast.

"Amen to that."

"How did Spooky take to undercover work?"

We'd decided if things went south with Frenchy, I'd like some company. Since rolling up with Yakky in tow wasn't likely to lower the tensions, I suggested he stay outside and look harmless. The plan had evolved slightly and Yakky had waited across the road, sitting low, in Spooky's minicab.

"He didn't think much of getting up before midday. Did you actually get anything out of Frenchy?"

"Nothing much. One thing though, it sounds like Smudge hasn't told him about seeing Johnny. He still thinks Dago's in the frame."

Yakky peeled his jacket off and draped it over a radiator.

"So, Smudge isn't that taken with the new management?"

"Looks that way. Of course, it could all be down to my personal charm. I told Frenchy I thought Dago was murdered, he wasn't having it. It clashes with his idea of what's good for the club."

"Brotherhood," Yakky commented.

The list that day was busy, mostly with new customers who all seemed to need reassuring. Or, failing that, a slap. Yakky did his usual tuning out act, losing himself in the needle song, and I spent most of the day telling people it wouldn't hurt.

At half five, when Jason came in for a showdown, I was almost pleased. He waited until my customer had paid up and left before striding across to the counter and calling me a cunt. I didn't bother telling him otherwise.

Jason didn't do slow burn. His temper had been either on or off for as long as I'd known him and the fact he'd finished work before coming to the shop probably meant he was going to leave my teeth intact.

"You want to keep your nose out of my business." The countertop was still between us and he leant over it to jab his finger against my chest. I batted his hand away and told him he should grateful. "Grateful? I had Kim on my back all bloody night. She didn't pause for breath. Four in the morning she started up again. I had it all under control, until you went and grassed me out."

I saw Jason's attention flit away to my right. He hadn't been shouting, but his voice was loud enough to have been heard over the shop's sound system. Now Yakky was standing in the doorway to the backroom. Blank-faced and silent, he was keeping his hands out of sight. His presence worried me more than Jason's, at that point.

"Back in your kennel, Fido. If I was going to hit him I'd have done it by now."

Yak ignored, or maybe filed the insult, and turned to me. I told him I was alright, and he nodded once before slipping back to his client. I waited for the sound of his needle starting up again.

"Alright, Jason, I'm running a business here so let's take this discussion upstairs."

Jason was rapidly deflating. He sighed and asked what the fuck there was to discuss. I told him we could start with how he intended repaying the seven hundred odd quid, he owed me.

Jason was installed in the better of my two armchairs, the one facing the wall with my rendering of Ezulie Dantor on it. I left him looking for somewhere neutral to settle his eye. He was staring at the ceiling when I came back with a mug of tea.

He broke the silence first, "I'll pay you back, Doc."

"With what? Next week's winnings?"

He didn't reply. The stress or anger, whatever he'd been running on until then, had hit empty. I pulled a card out of my pocket and flicked it across to him. It landed in his lap; he frowned when he picked it up.

It was the joker from my own pack of marked cards. I'd written *Get Out of Gaol Free* like a halo around Harlequin's belled cap. He gave me a puzzled look then, probably without knowing, glanced at the room around him, as if checking the walls were where he'd left them.

"What is this?"

"I'm clearing your debt, at least the part of it you owe to me."

Jason shared his wife's delusions of pride and he flicked the card back towards me. There's a knack to that trick and he didn't have it. The card fluttered and landed at his feet.

"I don't need your charity."

"No? You think anyone else is going to give you any? How much shit are you in Jason, really?"

Jason licked his lips and avoided my eye. His mental calculations must have equalled something he couldn't cope with, and he put his face in his hands. I waited quietly for him to come out again.

"That bad, eh?"

"It's not the amount, that ain't so bad." He sighed and closed his eyes. "I've cleared out the savings. It wasn't that much but…"

"But Kim doesn't know?"

He nodded. "When she finds out, I think she'll walk and probably take the kids with her. The courts won't give me a look in, not with my record."

I asked if it had all gone into the poker pot and he told me no, that had only been the swansong. Like most gambling stories, Jason's had started with a win. Some muppet he worked with had a system. The system applied to horse racing and the first tip he'd handed out came in at fifteen to one. Jason had prepaid the tax and handed over a tenner. The hundred and fifty he got back made turf look like a wise investment.

Despite odds of thirty-three to one, the next tip was a 'stone cold cert'. This time Jason prepaid the tax on a grand. Pinkham's Twist fell at the first and was destroyed. Jason's days of dabbling in horse flesh ended there and then. Only now, he had a savings account with a hole in it.

"One of the younger guys in the club, one of Smudge's lot, told me about the poker school. He said there was big money changing hands."

That had been about three months before. The savings account had borne the brunt of Jason's cards playing prowess. Donating his wages had been a more recent attempt to recoup losses.

I picked up the playing card by Jason's feet and handed it to him. He hesitated, still not happy about it.

"I've already had this conversation with Kim. What do you want to feed more, your kids or your pride?"

He took the card and nodded. There was a tremor in the breath he let out, and he tried to coax it into a laugh.

"Get out of gaol free, eh?" He folded the joker in two and tucked it into a pocket of his cut-off. Accepting it, owning it and knowing nothing is ever, really, free.

"The guy who put you on to the card school, is he still playing?"

"Yeah, luckier than me I guess."

"Better able to wear the losses I expect. What's he ride?"

"Two-year-old Harley Fat Bob."

"One of Smudge's boys, you said?"

Jason nodded. "Most of the regular players are. Them and the guys working at Frenchy's." He tried to laugh again, but what he said wasn't funny. "Those buggers can afford it."

The night I'd been at the table, the only bike I'd not known was another late model Harley. I could have sold my '78 Sportster three times over and still not raised enough to buy it. Jason confirmed it had been Vic's bike.

"And what's that about?" I pointed at a line of pinholes on the front of his cut-off, outlining the absence of the HLB patch.

"Handed it in last night. We had the vote. It's official, the Handsome London Boys are about to become a back patch club. The Handsome Boys MC, London." He lifted his mug in a sarcastic toast. "Good luck to them. They're going to need it."

"Who else took a walk?"

"Paddy's gone. Silk didn't vote for it, but he's thinking about staying. There's a week for everyone to decide. A couple of Smudge's boys are going to have to prospect. Black Micky's not sure. Smudge was working on him when I left."

"Frenchy?"

"He's all for it."

"Still El Presidente?" Jason gave an elaborate salute by way of answer. "Whose up for vice?"

"I left before they got into any of that. Not my club anymore, is it?"

"Sorry man, must be a wrench."

Jason shrugged. "Not enough of a wrench to take on the Eight-Six. I'll give it six months, then…" He spread the fingers of his right hand, wide. Like a conjurer making something disappear.

In my opinion, he was being optimistic.

"Six months on the outside. If they're lucky and if they keep their heads down."

"It might be too late for that already. Couple of Smudge's boys caught someone on Johnny's GSX."

"According to the guy I heard it from, they didn't know China was prospecting for the Eight-Six. He wasn't wearing colours. All they saw was someone on Johnny's bike."

It didn't look as if Eddie the Greek was listening to me, but he'd taken a long time over the shot he was lining up. Finally, he bounced the yellow ball off three cushions and we watched it sink into a corner pocket. The ball had traversed the full twelve foot of the table. I told him it was a nice shot.

Eddie sighed and abandoned his practice.

"Trick shots are just for show. The real trick's not needing them."

He racked his cue and sat heavily on the bench-seat that ran the length of the wall. It was a relief to join him, the island of light around the snooker table made me think of rabbits frozen in place by headlights. We both pretended we weren't keeping one eye on the door.

The car park, at the back of Spots pool hall, had been mostly empty. Eddie's Sportster was chained up near the foot of the fire escape. The only other bike was a much cleaner Jap; I didn't recognise it and it didn't have any club markings on display. The shadows and fire escape were free of prospects.

The pool hall itself was no busier than the car park and the connecting door to the snooker club was unguarded. The ownership of a ten-pound note was briefly discussed with the man behind the bar, and the private door duly swung open.

Eddie had been playing at the same table as the last time I'd been there. I'd said hello and he didn't seem surprised to see me approach.

"Johnny's GSX turned up again. Couple of the Handsome Boys reclaimed it and dished out a kicking." Eddie waited for me to ask the question. "China?"

Eddie nodded and started lining up his trick shot while I made my little speech of mitigation.

The story from Eddie was broadly the same as the one I'd had from Jason. Crucially, they agreed on the point about China not wearing his colours.

"How badly did they work him over?"

"Couple of broken ribs and a lot of bruises." Eddie shrugged. "He'll be pissing blood for a couple of days, but we've all done that."

I'd somehow missed out on that part of life's rich pageant. I decided I'd live with the regret.

"You don't seem overly concerned."

"He brought it on himself. You warned him that bike was bad news. I flat out told him to lose it. Any other time, we'd probably give him another hiding and tell him to go prospect somewhere else." He held his thumb and finger half an inch apart and squinted at me through the gap. "I was that close to handing over me patches and being on me way."

He shook his head in disgust.

The timing was bad for pretty well everyone. Under normal circumstances, China's ill-advised decision to ride the stolen bike through HLB heartland might have come under the heading *club discipline.* Riding without his colours would have meant the matter of his beating could be ignored without the Eight-Six losing face. His time as a prospect might have lengthened, or become more arduous, but the matter would have stayed in-house.

Now, with an upstart club making noises about raising their game, nothing could be ignored. That had a knock-on effect for Eddie the Greek. Leaving your club brothers in times of peace, after decades of loyal service, was one thing. With trouble on the way, an honourable discharge began to look like an abandoning rat. Leaving the Eight-Six in bad standing wasn't something to take lightly.

"You think there's going to be a backlash?"

Eddie laughed at the question. "Oh yeah. There'll be a backlash. The only question is, how many people the HLB are willing to lose before they take the hint."

"What about the negotiations Dago was working on?"

Eddie made a similar hand gesture to the one Jason had made earlier. POOF: *all gone.*

"Dago was the only one talking, and he's dead now. Frenchy don't want to know."

As he stood to retrieve his cue, he rolled his shoulders, making the faded cut-off shift on his back. It looked like he was setting his patches more firmly into place.

"Look Eddie, as far as I can tell, the Handsome Boys haven't settled on who's who yet. There's no vice pres in place and their sergeant-at-arms doesn't know if he's in or out. If I have a word with a few of the possibles, see if they're willing to talk, would your guys sit down with them?"

There was another long lining up session before Eddie potted a red in a centre pocket.

"You'll have to be quick. If the Pretty Boys start mincing around with a set of three-piece patches, it could all go south, big style."

"How does the club feel about that?"

He unconsciously glanced to the connecting door before answering and miscued his next shot.

"Nobody wants it to go that way, except a few of the real hot heads, and China, of course." I waited for the 'but' that was standing in the wings. It was the one I'd expected. "But nobody wants to back down."

I sighed and rolled my eyes. The macho man stuff had always grated on me.

"And what about you?"

Eddie didn't answer for a long time. He was agonising over another shot, one he could have snapped off with his eyes shut. Once the ball was finally down, he turned to me with a mildly embarrassed expression.

"I want to get out, clean. I want to patch things up with my daughter, spend a bit of time with me boy." He fired the next shot off and missed. "I can't do that from a coffin or a cell."

"You think it'll get that bad?"

"I do. You do as well."

I nodded. Feelings were already running high. Johnny's death wasn't going to stay secret indefinitely and, if beating up the guy who'd appeared on his bike earned the disapproval of the Eight-Six, people were likely to put two and two together and make five. I could sympathise with Frenchy wanting to keep a rein on the information he held, but his timing was off.

"So, which of your guys would be willing to talk first and shoot later?"

"Ramsey probably would, he doesn't go in for cracking heads if he can help it. And where he goes, Maccy follows."

"Maccy?"

"Club enforcer." Eddie gave a sly smile. "You met him last time you dropped in."

"Short hair, folded arms, never blinks?"

"That's him." He'd not struck me as a man with a talent for diplomacy. Eddie guessed my train of thought and nodded. "Cracking heads is his first response but –" he emphasised the word by striking the cue ball "– as far as he's concerned, if Ramsey says it, it's gospel. And Maccy's the man you'll need on side, if you want the hot heads kept in check."

I made a note of the way Maccy was the man *I'd* need.

"You want to talk to Ramsey?"

Eddie shook his head at the notion. "Right now, I'm in the doghouse. China's my prospect, he fucks up, it reflects on me."

"Can you put us in touch?"

"Yeah, I've got your number."

I'd been glad of the rain. People don't tend to go looking for trouble when it's pelting down sideways. So, I was surprised to see the spread of expensive machinery sitting outside The Jericho as I rode past. Both Vic and Smudge's Harleys were there, parked up and flanking Silk's BMW. Rather than carry on for home, I pulled in to check out the ambience.

There was a knot of the older hands clustered at the bar, and two of the young guns were stationed at the door. As I'd gone in, a trio of people had been leaving. All four of us were given the hard eye treatment. The unofficial doormen must have been great for business.

I exchanged nods with a couple of the guys I knew, but clearly wasn't part of their conversation. At the far end of the room Vic and Smudge were propping up the bar. Smudge's ever roaming scrutiny flickered across me and he lifted a hand, acknowledging my presence. Like the group of older drinkers, the two younger men weren't inviting company. Vic's face still looked like a side of beef.

I ordered two pints and wandered over to the pool table. Silk was alone, knocking the balls around the cushions. His skill with a cue didn't match Eddie the Greek's.

I put a pint on the edge of the table and watched Silk miss another shot.

"Mind not on the game?"

The sarcasm wasn't lost on him and he scowled at me before abandoning the frame. As well as skill, he lacked respect for the baize and all but threw the cue onto the table.

After claiming the drink I'd bought him, he joined me in one of the empty corners. I told him about my chat with Eddie the Greek and confirmed what he'd probably guessed.

"That guy who took a kicking was an Eight-Six prospect."

Silk groaned. "Fan-fucking-tastic." He gave the pair on the door a dirty look. "Tweedle Dumb and Tweedle Dee, useless bastards."

He didn't add anything more, but I guessed they'd been the ones dishing out the justice. I noted Silk didn't ask how badly China had been hurt.

"I hear you're in two minds about the back patch idea."

He pulled a face. "I don't see what we gain, going the full outlaw route, but since it's happening anyway..." He shrugged.

"Not a good way to start, getting on the wrong side of the Eight-Six."

"Don't I fucking know it."

"Okay, walk away, while you've still got a pair of working knees."

He cast another dirty look at the door.

"Thing is, it's between me and Smudge for the vice president's seat. If Black Micky had left, Smudge would have been the obvious choice for sergeant-at-arms, but Mick says he's in, so..."

"So, what? You fancy working your way up the ranks?"

The comment earned me a pained expression. "Ideally, Frenchy wants one of us old bastards sat at his right hand. Cooler head, you know?" He pointed discreetly at the bar and the huddle of older drinkers. "No one's really that interested."

I knew most of the guys he was pointing at. They were cut from a similar cloth as Eddie the Greek, old-school party animals. Some of them could be hard as nails, when the occasion arose, but they were into having a good time more than anything else. From my seat across the room, I couldn't hear their conversation, but I could see the tension running through it.

"So, El Presidente's asking you to step up?"

"More or less. It's a promotion I could do without, honestly."

"How long have you got to think about it?"

"Next meeting's the last one as a side patch club."

Less than a week. After that The Handsome London Boys would be The Handsome Boys MC, London, and you were either in or out.

I looked around, to make sure we weren't being overheard.

"Eddie the Greek thinks Ramsey might be willing to talk, keep things peaceful. Only it won't be happening if the HLB start strutting their stuff too soon. Have a word with Ramsey, vice to vice as it were. If it looks like you can work together, accept Frenchy's offer. You might be able to stop some grieving before it starts."

"If we can't work together?"

I pointed at the rectangle of cloth on the front of his leather cut-off.

"Then hand your patch in at the next meeting and walk away. You've got kneecaps to look after. What's Smudge's poison?"

I bought my way into Smudge's company, with a double Bourbon, and he was gracious enough to accept the exchange. I asked Vic what he was drinking. He shook his head without breaking eye contact. The swelling, on the left side of his face, meant he only had one eye to do it with, so the effect was lost somewhat.

"Congratulations," I raised my glass to Smudge. "I hear the club's stepping up."

"Yeah, all going down good."

"Black Micky on board?"

"What's it to you?" Vic snapped.

I was standing closer to Vic than I was to Smudge, and he leant into my space, still going for the hard-case Cyclops look. If we'd been alone, or better yet, I'd had Yakky at my back, I'd have been tempted to grab his nose and see if it had set. Smudge put a hand on his shoulder.

"Doc's a friend of the club." He patted, gently, "He's alright, Vic, okay?"

Vic allowed himself to be brought to heel, making sure everyone could see what an effort is was. He tried one last baleful stare before stalking over to the door, and the other two wannabe tough guys.

"You two kiss and make and up?" I asked when he'd gone. Smudge sipped his bourbon and cracked a thin-ice smile.

"Yeah, we're good. That's what I was trying to explain to you, about being part of something. People give up on friends all the time." He said *friends* as if the word couldn't be trusted. "Family, you stick with." His gaze skimmed towards Vic, standing by the door. "We can clash, come to blows, but we're still brothers. That's the point."

Vic was listening, intently, to something one the Tweedles was saying. A car must have swung around in front of the pub because he was briefly lit up in a wash of high beams. The tighten skin of his injured face shone in the glare.

"Makes me glad I'm an only child."

Smudge snorted. "You don't get it, do you?"

"Not as often as I'd like, no. So, is Micky in?"

Smudge's attention, or at least his focus, wasn't on me any longer. "That's club business."

"A minute ago you were telling Vic I was a friend of the club."

Smudge made eye contact at last. "And I told you, *people give up on friends all the time*." This time he managed to make *friend* sound like an insult. I returned the favour.

"Okay, *friend*, file this under business failings: your two brothers over by the door kicked seven shades out of an Eight-Six prospect. The Eight-Six have been riding around, with bottom rockers reading LONDON for nigh on thirty years. They didn't manage that by being a pushover. If you ain't got the sense to smooth the way a bit, your brothers won't be wearing colours, they'll be wearing targets."

He finished the short and put the glass on the bar behind him.

Without looking at me he said, "Thanks for the drink."

I could have said more but there was no point, he wasn't listening. Silk, who'd returned to the pool table, looked up as I retrieved my lid. He must have seen the way the exchange had gone from my expression.

"If you can set up a meet with Ramsey, I'll do what I can, okay?"

"Good. Any idea where I'll find Black Micky tonight?"

"Working the door at The Ice House."

I assumed Silk had meant The House of Ice, and backtracked five miles in the rain. As with a lot of London, the short distance seemed to encompass a hidden border crossing. Small businesses, locked behind shutters for the night, were inched out by brightly lit boutiques. And the roads used speed bumps to hinder traffic flow, instead of potholes.

The House of Ice had once been an ambitious department store, if the frontage was anything to go by. There was a lot of ornate brick work and carefully fashioned mouldings. Most of them had been painted acid-house colours and picked out with blue spotlights. The pavement outside was crowded with fresh-faced clubbers, undeterred by either the rain or the god-awful noise leaking through the doors.

Too old to be mistaken for a queue jumper, no one bothered commenting as I went to the head of a corralled line where I'd spotted Black Micky. He was patting down teenagers, working so fast that the patrons barely had time to object before they were inside. The searches were unlikely to find anything.

Micky jumped when I touched his arm and the girl he was vetting squealed. He apologised and gave her one of his heartbreaker smiles before waving her, and her boyfriend, inside. The boyfriend gave him a nasty look, once he was sure it wouldn't be seen.

"You got a minute?"

I had to raise my voice to be heard. This close to the doors, the bass pulse from the club rewrote all other sound. The ceaseless four-four signature also put me on edge; I chalked that one up to middle age. Micky asked me what I wanted, but I pointed at my ears and shook my head, pretending not to hear. There was a minute or so of semaphore before he led me to a break room that doubled as a store cupboard.

"What's up?"

"I hear you're climbing on board with the MC idea."

Micky narrowed his eyes. "And?"

"And I found Johnny Simms."

The change of tack put him on the back foot and, for a moment, he looked comically startled.

"Where?"

"He'd been doing a spot of live-in security for Dago's firm. When I found him, he was sitting in a puddle of his own shit, with a garrotte round his neck."

Micky looked startled all over again, this time sans the comic effect. He opened his mouth two or three times before anything came out.

Tarot cards don't tell you when to expect a phone call but, studying the spread on my kitchen table an hour later, I wasn't surprised when my mobile rang. Or when it was Silk on the line.

"Doc, I just had a call off Black Micky. He's in. He reckons between us, we can bring Smudge round. If you can arrange a meet with the Eight-Six, I'll sit down with them."

I told him I'd be in touch and hung up.

I turned a fresh card and wasn't surprised when my mobile rang again, and it was Ramsey.

21.
Sans the Knifeman

Tuesday 10 October

I'd made a dozen phone calls back and forth, setting things in motion. Because both sides wanted to play it like a cold war movie, we wasted time on formalities. Neutral ground was agreed and the numbers involved decided. And the roll call of personnel.

I'd assumed Eddie the Greek would be doing a double act with Ramsey, but he was vetoed in favour of Maccy, the enforcer. The HLB's contingent was finally settled on as Silk and Black Micky. Neither club was intending to wheel out the president. The Eight-Six were undoubtedly scoring a political point, but I suspected Silk and Black Micky were acting outside the chain of command.

The meeting was set for Friday. That was only two days before the HLB were planning to start flying their new MC regalia. There was no way that birth was going to be stopped. I was hoping that the sit down might at least reduce the labour pains.

When Silk phoned the shop to say it had all gone tits up, I was out buying a pizza. Yakky had taken the call and told me Silk had sounded agitated. When he'd asked Yakky how many people had found out about Johnny's death from us, it was as much accusation as question.

The news was out. Somehow or other, the police had worked out, or been told, the identity of the pile of charcoal they'd found in Enfield. Despite Smudge's efforts, the police had also made the connection to the HLB. Silk had already had half a dozen calls from Handsome Boys, telling various tales of inquisitive uniforms. Tweedle Dum and Tweedle Dee had put two and two together and naturally, made five. Now they were beating themselves up for letting Johnny's killer go. They were also looking to improve their standing by tracking him down and balancing the books.

"Frenchy's called a special meeting tonight," Yakky reported. "Silk, reckons this is it, in or out time."

"Did Silk say what Frenchy thought about all this?"

"According to Silk, all he said was, c'est la vie."

It is the life.

Doubtless he added a Gallic shrug.

"If Silk's right, and tonight is make your mind up time?"

"Then Silk says he's walking."

I didn't blame him.

The meeting duly delivered its ultimatum and Silk walked away. I heard from Smudge that the Patches would be handed out the next day, but before that, the first set would be sewn onto Johnny cut-off.

The following morning, someone set The House of Ice alight.

Wednesday 11 October

News of the attack was broken to me by Silk, whose route to work to took him past the nightclub. I wasn't sure of his motives for ringing me. He was concerned and angry in equal measure.

"I think it's kicking off already," he told me the second I picked up.

"And good morning to you too."

I checked the time, it wasn't seven.

"Yeah, yeah, morning. I just went past that club Smudge runs. It looks like some arsehole torched it."

I asked if anyone had been hurt. Before he answered, a car horn blared and Silk bellowed 'fuck you'. I guessed he was still driving as he called. It wasn't the time to deliver a lecture on road safety.

"I got no idea, Doc. I just rang Frenchy up to see if everyone was alright. You know what that little prick told me? He told me it was *club business.* Can you believe that?"

Sadly, I could. I let Silk fret and vent at me for a while before easing the call to an end. I told him I'd find out what I could and ring him back. Then I did what he'd have done himself, if he'd been less pissed off. I called the police. I said I'd just been told about the fire and was concerned because my step daughter might have been there with friends the night before. I was duly assured, no one had been hurt in the blaze.

The story began to filter down to the internet a few hours later. Although no bodies had been pulled from the soot, the press took more interest in the nightclub fire than they had in the one at Enfield. Probably because the fire and ice motif provided catchy headlines. That and the surge of interest on social media. Within hours of the smoke clearing, hundreds of 'likes' had been awarded to Facebook postings, cataloguing people's near misses: *The House of Ice! OMG! I was there just TWO DAYS AGO*, followed by more exclamation marks and illustrated by a snapshot of the ruined frontage. Usually, the fire-damaged building was serving as a backdrop to a pouting selfie.

The fire had started sometime in the early morning, when the club had been empty, and the police were treating it as arson. Damage was mainly confined to the area around the front door and was dramatic rather than major. A spokesman for the London Fire Brigade explained the blaze had been exacerbated by cleaning solvents stored in a room that doubled as a staff rest area. If I'd ever taken the trouble to post on Facebook, I could have told friends, far and wide, that I'd been *exactly* there, just forty-eight hours ago. OM-bloody-G.

I got to the shop before Yakky and when he rolled in he asked if he was late. I called him a sarcastic git and brought him up to speed. He made the same calculation Silk had.

"Eight-Six?"

"Don't know, but I'd lay money that's what the Handsome Boys are thinking. Can you get hold of Spooky?"

The latest number Yak had for Spooky went straight to voicemail, he left a message saying we wanted a word.

Spooky's *burners* tended to be discreetly retired, in as flamboyant a manner as possible. His mobiles had a shelf life of about two weeks, less if he wanted to impress someone. The message could well have been awaiting retrieval from the bottom of the Thames.

"Give it a few hours," Yakky suggested, as I cursed Spooky's paranoid fantasies. "Leaving his feather before noon brings him out in a rash."

Spooky's cab pulled up outside the shop about half two. He gave both lengths of the street careful appraisal, before leaving the car. His pre-entry check of the waiting room was quick but thorough. His act was getting better.

I called to Yakky. He took a five-minute break and led Spooky around to the side of the shop, for some privacy. While he was gone I made his client a cup of tea and admired the fresh work on her shoulder. Yak had always had the goods when it came to the needle, but the hours he'd put in over the last twelve months had taken his skill to a new level. People talk about talent as if it arrives at birth, fully formed and ready to go. All the talent in the world counts for nought if you don't put in the hours. I wondered how long before Yakky moved on. He was rapidly outgrowing his humble beginnings.

They kept it short and sweet, and Yakky reappeared in the doorway a few minutes later. He raised a hand to Spooky as he got back behind the wheel.

I heard Spooky call out, "Laters bruv," before he pulled away.

The gist of what Spooky told Yak was that the bouncers at The House of Ice, in particular Black Micky, were upping the pressure on *unsanctioned* dealers. The blessed few were allowed to rent a lane of lucrative traffic. Anyone venturing in from the wilderness got discouragement in the shape of a fist.

"Does he know who set the fire?"

Yakky jiggled his hand in a *maybe* gesture.

"He told me he didn't, but he was shaken up about something. Did you notice he had a fat lip?" I nodded, I'd seen the swelling when he pulled up. "I think he knows more than he'd like to, and he's scared to talk."

Which was possibly a good thing. If it was someone on Spooky's radar, then it was more likely a dealer than the Eight-Six. I could pass that on to the HLB.

"I wonder if it was the same crew who put the shiv in Micky."

Yakky shook his head.

"I asked the same thing. According to Spook they've dropped off the radar. Delivered unto them was a kicking of goodly proportions. Looks like they took the hint and closed up shop."

"Smudge told me they'd been dealt with."

There was a blink-and-you'd-missed-it pause. By Yakky's standards it was an expression of profound concern.

"Well, what Spooky heard – and let's bear in mind his visits to plant Earth are few and far between – is that the whole crew got bundled into the back of a van. They all got worked over, with a pickaxe handle, until they gave up the one who knifed Micky. Then they got dumped, on some building site on the M25, sans the knifeman – he's still in the back when the van drives off."

"And no one's seen him since, right?"

Yakky nodded.

The gospel according to Spooky, one-man drugs cartel and occasional visitor to plant Earth. Yet, it was a piece of scripture I found strangely plausible.

Black Micky listened, but his impatience was almost radiant.

It was the first time I'd been in his flat. It was an odd mixture of squalor and splendour. Furniture most people would have taken down the tip, under cover of darkness, was draped with Germaine-Street shirts and tailor-made suits. The curtainless wire, strung along the top of the window, fluttered with a dozen silk ties. The only free-standing item not acting as a clothes horse was a home multi-gym.

"You still need to have the meeting," I told him, again.

"After what they've done?"

"I don't think it was the Eight-Six."

Micky gritted his teeth and the muscles along his jaw stood out and caught the light. He'd been getting ready to go when I'd called. He smelt of expensive cologne and his face still shone from the razor.

"Doc, at six o'clock we all go to Frenchy's and give our decisions and make it official. The HLB is now an MC." He lifted an index finger to mark point number one. The nail gleamed as if it had been manicured, which it probably had. "Seven o'clock, a load of the guys are down The Jericho, celebrating. Secret's out, public knowledge." He flicked up another polished finger for point two. "And then, less than twelve hours later," point, and finger, number three, "the best money earner the club has is set alight."

He'd kept his voice level, but his breathing was shallow and fast. The last finger he'd lifted was bitten to the quick.

"I know the deal with the door work, Micky. Other people risk their neck, selling junk to the brain dead, but *you* say which people." I held up a hand to forestall the bullshit about club business. "You've pushed too hard and too fast and you've upset a lot of people. The chances are, some dealer got sick of getting hit, and had a busy night with the petrol."

Micky was close to losing it. There was a bead of sweat worming its way down the side of his face and his pupils where wide.

"This ain't your fucking business."

He picked up a low table, with a pile of folded shirts on it, and threw the lot across the room. I'd seen it coming and put myself a foot to the right before it reached me.

I put my hands up, in surrender, and left him to clear up the mess.

It was close to the last straw. I'd had worse things than Micky's temper tantrums happen to me over the years, but generally, I'd get into trouble on the back of my own stupidity.

Not other people's.

I rode home and, on medical grounds, put another dent into my best tequila. I'd half decided I was ready to wash my hands of the whole business when Black Micky rang me and apologised. There was an edge of desperation in his tone that was covering real fear.

"You been like this since the stabbing?" I asked him.

"Like what?"

If we'd been having the conversation face to face I'd have kept quiet, letting the tension do the work, but I was scared Micky would hang up if the going got tough.

"On a hair trigger. You're a hard man Micky, but you're not a thug. Army days coming back to you?"

There was a juddering sigh from the other end of the line. It was enough to tell me I'd hit the target. I risked a dose of silence.

"After that wanker knifed me, the bad dreams started again. I've been jumpy ever since, it's like watching a telly when the settings are all wrong. Everything too bright and too loud."

"Did you get any counselling, when you left the army?"

"Some."

"You got contact numbers, a help line or something?"

Another juddering breath. "Somewhere."

"You need to ring them. Will you do that?" He told me he would. I wasn't convinced. "Mick, this might not be the best time to sign up as sergeant-at-arms in a patch club."

"I know, I know. But I can't do anything else, they need me."

"Okay, I can see that, but they need *you*, not your muscle. The Handsome Boys won't make it, not if they go head-to-head with the Eight-Six and every drug dealer in town. You need to cut a deal with them. You know that, don't you?"

"Yeah. I know. I'll work on it, Doc. I'll get Smudge on board, we can sort this."

"Ring those numbers, Micky, okay?"

"Okay."

22.
Three's the Magic Number

Thursday 12 October

Things started happening fast. The next day, Vic appeared in the shop, wanting to know if, as a friend of the club, I gave members a discount. It told him no and expected him to leave without further ado. He surprised me with a good-natured chuckle.

"Worth a try. How much to do this, as a back piece?"

He turned to show the back of his jacket. He craned his head to see my reaction. The gesture made him look guileless, he was waiting for some sort of approval.

"Nice," I said obligingly. "Who came up with the design?"

"Terry's old lady, she's at art school."

For the sake of her degree, I hoped she upped her game. The patches were the accepted outlaw design, which had meant a change of nomenclature. The standard layout was a top rocker with the club's name under that the club emblem and under that, the bottom rocker with the chapter's location. To avoid the cut-offs bearing the clumsy legend, *Handsome London Boys, London*, the top rocker simply read, *Handsome Boys.* It took the whole business a little further from the original HLB and, in a way, I was glad. I couldn't imagine the strutting gobshite in front of me was what Dago had envisioned as a legacy.

The emblem was a cold grey heart, with a jagged blue crack running through it. It took me a moment to see the crack was, in fact, the Thames. To the right of the heart was a yellow on blue *MC* patch, to the left: *1%*, set in a diamond.

I quoted a high price for turning Vic's new patches into ink. Partly, I wanted it known that I didn't do discounts in my shop, no matter what you joined. Partly, I hoped to dissuade him. The Handsome Boys MC would be lucky to see the new year, I didn't particularly want a hand in producing tattoos to commemorate their failure.

Business is business though, so, when he asked how soon I could book him in, I took a deposit and we arranged the following Tuesday.

Ramsey called me that night. There was flat-sounding music in the background and the occasional sharp crack of a cue ball making contact. I assumed he was ringing from Spots. I took that as a good sign; it meant he wasn't trying to keep anything secret from his club. In effect, it was an official call.

"Hello, Doc. You heard there's a new set of patches riding around?"

"Seen it with my own eyes. You still willing to talk to them?" I'd been expecting to wait for an answer but Ramsey didn't bother with a portentous silence, and simply said 'yes'. He went up in my estimations.

"The question is, are they willing to talk back?"

I explained the situation with Silk quitting.

"Black Micky sees it makes sense to sit at the table, he's trying to get the new VP on board. As soon as he gets back to me, I'll let you know. Can your guys keep a lid on it, until I hear?"

"Depends on the Pretty Boys. A few of the lads are all ready to cut them down to size. If they start flying their patches in the wrong part of town, it might kick off."

He pronounced *town* as *toon*, the hint he'd retained of his native Glasgow accent becoming a distinct twang. I hoped it wasn't a sign of stress.

I made a pot of tea and shuffled my tarot cards. They didn't tell me anything I didn't know already, but at least the bad news was picturesque. I made a couple of calls to Black Micky and another to Smudge. Neither of them were picking up. I guessed they were working the doors, keeping the lines of supply and demand open.

Smudge rang me back in the small hours and I pointed out it was two a.m. He offered a half-hearted apology for disturbing me. I didn't bother telling him I was already awake and hoping for his call. I've been told I'm not good looking enough to play hard to get, but I choose not to believe it. Smudge said if the Eight-Six were still willing to talk, he'd sit down with them. I offered up a prayer of thanks to whoever might be listening.

"I'll let Ramsey know. You going to be there as the new VP?"

He said he was and I told him congratulations. Smudge was smarter than Vic and recognised irony when he heard it. He told me to go fuck myself.

Friday 13 October

I'd been surprised when all four of them arrived on time. I'd been expecting some kind of childish power play, with at least one side showing late, if at all. We'd met up in the waiting room and I led them to my flat. I told them to hang on when we reached the hallway and I dipped into the living room. Out of sight of prying eyes, I grabbed a couple of magazine off the table that had been left there earlier. I rolled them into tight a tube, the way you do if you don't want the covers to be seen. I shuffled back into the hallway. Smudge's ever drifting gaze caught me stuffing the magazines into my back pocket. He cocked an eyebrow.

"Granny porn," I told him, forcing a smile.

"Aye, good choice," Ramsey commented, evenly. There was a ripple of laughter.

I led them into the living room, told them where the toilet was and where to find the tea bags.

"Room next door's my bedroom. I'd appreciate you all respecting my privacy. And, if this goes tits up and you start punching each other, try and bleed on the altar, eh? Every little helps. Pull the front door shut when you leave."

I sat behind the counter in the shop. Now and again there'd be the sound of a chair being pushed back from the floor above. I'd been glib with Yakky about the arrangement, but leaving the four men alone in my home wasn't sitting well with me. Since my marriage failed, solitude had become a habit and I'd become used to the privacy it brought, without realising how much I valued it. When I heard footsteps above, I wondered where they were heading.

I tried distracting myself with the computer's play list and found myself switching tracks before any of them finished. After I'd started editing a selection of AC/DC numbers, Yakky bellowed from the backroom to *leave the fucking music alone.*

Yakky was working late again. It had been a last-minute booking and, I suspected, he'd taken it because plans had fallen through. He hadn't mentioned Karla in a few days and that usually meant the on-off romance was off. I set the computer to play a long album of acoustic blues standards because I knew he'd hate it. When I started singing along, he put his head around the door.

"Doc, why don't you go for a pint or something?" He pointed at the ceiling and the meeting happening on the other side of it. "If anything occurs, I can call you."

He'd changed the music before I'd got my jacket on. His selection did nothing to delay my departure.

If music was the food of love, he was destined for the life of a bachelor.

I'd headed for The Jericho. When I'd got there, the figures of Tweedle Dum and Tweedle Dee skulking around the doorway put me off. Part of me wanted the meeting in my flat to go badly. I wasn't overly pleased that my stamping ground was hosting the HLB's ascension to the outlaw league. Having ringside seats, as the wet-behind-the-ears patch club was stamped into oblivion, wasn't without its appeal. Then the memory of finding Johnny's body reminded me what that might entail. Thoughts of Johnny got me to thinking about Sue and Mary.

I swung the bike around and headed for Kew Bridge.

Sue was better than I'd seen her for a while. The house looked better too. It didn't have the appalling gleam of obsessive cleaning. Or the feel of hopelessness. I put on my psychologist's hat for a few minutes and decided she'd started the grieving process proper. The anger and denial were done with and now she could see what she'd lost and know it had been worth having. It wasn't the same as happiness, but it was a step on the way.

"You want tea? Silly question."

Sue led me to the kitchen and set the kettle to work. The smell of nicotine was still with her, as ever it would be, but it wasn't overpowering, which made me think she'd at least stopped chain smoking.

Music was on upstairs, the dull bass repeat was audible but, like the cigarette smell, not all conquering. When we took our mugs into the living room, there was a litter of magazines over the coffee table. Mother-to-be and newborn titles. There was also a paperback, in a plastic library cover, listing baby names. I asked if Mary was getting excited about becoming a mother.

"Yeah. I am too, now the shock's worn off. I dug out some of Mary's baby pictures. I'd forgotten how much fun they can be." She looked into the middle distance for a couple of beats. "It's such a shame Dago didn't live to see this. He missed all that with Mary."

By the time Dago was on the scene, Mary was a toddler. He missed quite a few of the milestone moments. As had her biological father – the difference was Dago had cared.

Sue made a noise somewhere between a sigh and a laugh.

"And this might have finally made him see his little girl is growing up. Though, there'd have been hell to pay, for the dad."

"Has Mary told you who it is, then?"

Sue shook her head and waved a hand at the idea; it was unimportant. Whoever daddy was, he'd done his part and his presence was no longer required. "Dago wouldn't have let it go. He would have badgered it out of her, then…" She finished the sentence by rolling her eyes.

It didn't take much imagination to work out the implication. Dago was a good man, that didn't mean he wasn't without his demons. They'd get out from time to time. The phrase *shotgun wedding* popped into my head and I wondered again, where the sawn-off had got to. Sue might have read my mind.

"I went through the garage, looking for that gun of his. Didn't find it. Makes me think, maybe he did know." She pointed to the ceiling, meaning Mary, meaning the father.

"You think he decided, someone wasn't son-in-law material and perforated him?" I tried to make it sound stupid. "Body with bloody great holes in it? Somebody would have noticed."

Sue laughed. "Is that the best you can do? You must be getting old, Doc."

I'd noticed the photos on the walls had been thinned slightly. The endless pictures, of club runs and events, had been reduced to a more focused collection of closer friends and family. Even so, that left a hefty gallery of alibis, should Dago have needed them. Sue knew that as well as I did. Bodies could be vanished, witnesses arranged. Wannabe gangstas from Harlesden could disappear into bottomless transit vans.

"Why dwell on it? What's done is done. Anyway, for all we know, he sold it on. I'm sure Smudge, or Vic, could find a place in their hearts for such an item."

She shook her head.

"That's why he wouldn't have sold it to them. That's why I asked you to lose it, rather than go to the club."

I was spared anymore desperate bullshitting by Mary's appearance. I was surprised by how much her bump had grown, until I realised she was thrusting her belly forward and walking with her palms pressed into the small of her back. I played along and gave her my seat and put her feet up. Sue was right, Dago would have lapped all that up.

Mary sat with a theatrical sigh and laced her hands together over the growing bulge, though it was nowhere big enough for the pose.

"There's no sign of it kicking," she told me.

I told her not to worry, "That'll come."

Sue laughed. "Along with acid indigestion and swollen feet."

Mary poked her tongue out at her and reached forward for the book of baby names, forgetting to flounder for the moment. Sue caught my eye and smiled.

"We've narrowed it down to the final hundred or so," she told me and won herself another sighting of her daughter's tongue.

Mary asked what I thought of Margot, mispronouncing it.

"Mar-go," Sue corrected. "You don't pronounce the tee, it's French."

"I know," Mary said. "I like French names, they sound cool."

"What if it's a boy?"

Sue shook her head at the notion. "Scan says we've got a sensible one."

I asked if she'd heard about the HLB rebranding itself as the Handsome Boys MC. She nodded and glanced towards one of the bigger photos. It showed Dago and Jason, helpless with laughter while a grinning bystander watched them. Obviously not in on the joke, he was still caught up in the moment of good humour.

"Dago must be turning –" She cut the sentence short, probably for Mary's sake.

"I heard he was talking with the Eight-Six, trying to arrange a deal."

"I know, he wasn't happy with the way the club was heading. He didn't really talk about it though."

While Mary's attention was on the book of baby names, Sue mimed drawing on a cigarette and stubbing it out on her chest. I winced, remembering the scars on the tattoo Yakky had covered up.

I used the excuse of more tea to carry the talk into the kitchen. As Sue filled the kettle I asked her for what little Dago had said about the HLB.

"He thought it was getting out of control. He didn't say so

directly but I think the amounts of money people were flashing around bothered him. He thought if the patch club thing went through, it'd get worse. He hated the whole patch club move."

"So, why was he talking with the Eight-Six?"

Sue perched herself on a chrome stool and we watched the kettle boil.

"He'd given up trying to talk the fellas out of it, at least if the Eight-Six had a hand on the reins, there was a chance of no one ending up dead or behind bars. He always said the Eights were a smart outfit. I don't think he would have stayed around." She mimed burning herself with a dogend again. "He was sick of the whole thing, the club, the 'brotherhood'," she used finger quotes, "looking out for everyone. It was getting to be all one way. He felt let down. We both did."

"Sounds like depression."

Sue shook her head, adamant. "He had his bad times, but it wasn't that. He just wanted out and he couldn't walk away and leave them to it. Wasn't in his nature."

"You know it's all gone ahead? The Handsome Boys are swanning around in three patch cut-offs and flashing a one percent diamond."

She nodded and poured water into the teapot. "Smudge popped round yesterday. I saw his colours. He didn't know about the baby." She rolled her eyes. "He wanted to know if I needed 'anyone put straight'."

More finger quotes.

I didn't bother to ask what she'd told him.

"People keeping in touch?"

"Not the younger guys, apart from Smudge. I still see Kim and Jackie quite a bit." Jason and Silk's old ladies. "Other than that…"

I wasn't surprised. The shift in the Handsome Boys from close-knit group to macho unit had made it more insular. The closer the links to club brothers became, the tighter the controls on who was in or out. It was an environment where loyalty and commitment could be rationed. Only those with membership were entitled to a share.

"I can't say I'm sorry," Sue told me. "When it all goes wrong, I don't want to be part of it. This would have broken Dago's heart. It did break his heart."

I had the tea and admired the baby scan Mary showed me. She pointed at different parts of the white-on-black blurs and told me what they were, head, spine, feet. It was nice to see her enthusiasm. At the back of my mind, I couldn't help wondering if Dago had met the father before he died.

When I had a phone call from Yakky telling me the meeting in my flat had gone off without any major problems, I made my excuses and bade them both good night. Before I left, Mary asked me if I thought Yakky could do her a drawing of some actress I hadn't heard of. I asked if she had a picture to work from and she'd run up to her room to retrieve a magazine. Sue called after her to be careful on the stairs.

The magazine was a colour supplement with the actress on the cover, airbrushed into impossible beauty. She didn't know it, but her name had been entered into the pool of chic possibilities.

The meeting hadn't lasted that long, according to Yakky. That could have been a good or a bad sign. More encouraging was his report that the four men had ridden away with the minimum of drama.

My flat was as I'd left it, other than smelling like an ashtray. Yakky helped me shuffle the table back into the kitchen and watched impassively as I retrieved the Dictaphone taped to its underside.

"That was a hell of a risk," he commented.

I pressed the rewind button and gave him my Cheshire Cat smile.

"What would life be without the occasional risk?"

"Safer and longer?"

I let him have that point.

"What time did they leave?"

"They were here about forty minutes. How long was that

thing running before they sat down?"

"I slipped into room just ahead of them to turn it on. Pretended I was clearing away my porn stash."

The tapes ran thirty minutes a side. Knock off five or ten minutes for people getting settled and fidgeting, and I might be lucky to have twenty minutes of audible recording.

I hit the play button and winced at the sound of my own voice.

23.
Game and Candle

…goes tits up and you start punching each other, try and bleed on the altar, eh? Every little helps. Pull the front door shut when you leave.

(Sound of the living room door closing then chairs scraping as people take their seats.)

RAMSEY – Okay, I think you both know me, name's Ramsey, vice president of the Eight-Six motorcycle club. This is Maccy, he's in charge of club discipline and security.

MACCY – Evening.

SMUDGE – Smudge, vice pres of the Handsome Boys MC. This is Black Micky, our sergeant-at-arms.

RAMSEY – Good to meet you. To be sure we're all on the same page here, this meeting is to discuss your club's arrival on our patch. I don't have the absolute authority of my club to make any offers or concessions. Whatever we might decide here tonight will be reported to my president and the club, and will have to be approved. I can say that the Eight-Six have always regarded violence as a last resort but that is not be taken as a sign of weakness. The Eight-Six would also like to officially extend its condolences, on the death of Dago. He was well known and respected.

SMUDGE – Thank you for that. I think we're on the same page. It's not the intention of our club to cause trouble for the Eight-Six. I don't believe any of us want to shed any blood, least of all into Doc's altar.

RAMSEY – Aye, was that mad bugger serious, do you think?

BLACK MICKY – God only knows, but if he lives like this, he must be halfway crazy. I think he likes putting the wind up people.

RAMSEY – Well he's going the right way about it; this place gives me the shits.

(Laughter)

SMUDGE — If he lives like this, I'd say he's taking it seriously.

MACCY – Let's get on with this, eh?

SMUDGE – Alright, what's your objection to our club? The Handsome London Boys have been around a good while. Relations with the Eight-Six have always been good. What's the problem?

RAMSEY – Don't come the innocent with me. The Handsome London Boys was a side patch club. Now you're wearing top and bottom rockers and a one percent diamond. That sends a message, that changes things. The fact that you're sitting there, wearing colours right now, puts everything in a new light. You knew that would be taken as an act of provocation. This meeting wasn't meant to be between two back patch clubs.

SMUDGE – You need to understand something: this meeting was never about our club's existence. That decision was never in your hands and it's not up for discussion now. The Handsome Boys MC is a fact. We're here to discuss the best way to keep the peace. Assuming that's the way you want it.

MACCY – Watch it, sonny.

RAMSEY – Take it easy Mac, alright? Listen, Smudge, I've known the Handsome Boys a long time, I knew Dago and Frenchy before you were on the scene. If you think you're the first bunch of pretenders to buy a few pretty cut-offs, you can think again. What was the last lot called?

MACCY – The River Men.

RAMSEY – Aye, that's right, the River Men M-bloody-C. You ever see their colours?

(No answer)

RAMSEY – No? Well you would nay, they're not around more. As far as I know, the only set of their colours left in existence are hanging in Maccy's trophy room. Along with a good few other clubs that are no longer out and about. And you need to know, some of those patches came off the hard way.

(Sound of slow clapping)

SMUDGE – That was very good. If I hadn't been to the Gulf and got shot at by the Taliban, I might even be scared. But I'm not scared, so don't bother with the veiled threats.

RAMSEY – I know about the HLB, I know more than half of you are ex-military and I know some of your men are right hard bastards. But do you think that all there is to it? And do you think me and Maccy are going to be your biggest problem if you start making too many ripples?

BLACK MICKY – And what's that meant to mean?

RAMSEY – The Eight-Six in one small club, no support clubs giving us backup, no other chapters, just us. And we've survived three decades. You think the big international clubs are scared of us?

BLACK MICKY – So, what, you're a puppet club?

MACCY – The only club I support is my own.

RAMSEY – We're an independent club. We don't have to live up to some corporate image or take orders from some mother chapter in the states. We run our club, by our rules. But that comes at a price. We don't live in a vacuum, there's other clubs out there, bigger players. The little wannabes we can grind under our heels, but the international clubs, the ones with the support clubs, doing the dirty work? Different sort of game. It comes down to balance, too small and we get rolled over, too big and we become a threat. You'll be just the same, only you're already too big to be swatted.

SMUDGE – I still don't get what your concern is. Our club is currently smaller than yours. If one of the big clubs wants to swat someone, surely, we're the ones who have to worry about it.

RAMSEY – The Eight-Six is old school, bikes, booze and birds. A couple of the guys run their own businesses, but that's about it. Wiping us out won't make any money. Our turf doesn't represent a financial acquisition. But you fellas are coming at it from a different angle.

SMUDGE – Unless our members' business interests overlap with any of yours, how we generate income is none of your concern.

MACCY – Well, just take it as read that we're making it our concern.

RAMSEY – Take it easy, Mac, this is the time for talking. We don't want to risk ruining the good Doctor's elegant abode with a punch-up do we? Anyone got a light?

BLACK MICKY – Here.

RAMSEY – Much obliged. You want one of these?

BLACK MICKY – Thanks.

SMUDGE – I quit.

RAMSEY – You had your fill of smoke, have you?

SMUDGE – You talking about The House of Ice?

(Sound of a chair scraping on the floor followed by laughter, possibly from Maccy)

RAMSEY – I'll tell you what Smudge, since you and me are getting on so well, I'll let you in on a little secret. The Handsome Boys aren't the only club with a few ex-army types in the ranks. One of our boys was a Royal Engineer. He wasn't the type of engineer that put thing together mind, he was the type that fucked them up. Now, take my word for it, you wouldn't have had a wee fire in a broom closet if that had been us. Your bit of smoke damage will be down to one the dealers you're putting out of business. That's what I mean about making ripples. Anyway, I was nay talking about your nightclub.

BLACK MICKY – You got something to say, why don't you just say it?

RAMSEY – Tension getting to you is it? Alight, here's what I'm saying, stop me if you'd heard it by the way. One of our prospects, and between you and me, a right useless one, takes a fancy to a bike he spots outside a house in Enfield. Now, he's a stupid bastard, but he's got a real talent for lifting the old bikes, so away it goes. No big deal, except, suddenly there's a lot of interest in that machine, people asking where he got it and the like. And not so long after that, whoosh, a house in Enfield goes up in smoke, along with some poor fucker's body that was inside it. Then our prospect gets the shit kicked out of him, by a couple of you Handsome types.

Oh, yeah, while we're on the subject of things that goes whoosh in the night, here's another story for you. Once upon a time there was a little drugs dealer in Harlesden, who ignored what his mammy telled him, about nay getting into vans wi' strangers. And he was never seen again. But a van, very much like the one he took a ride in, appeared in a field down Southend way, only this van had been in a nasty fire.

SMUDGE – Your prospect, who is a very stupid bastard, turned up on one of our guy's bikes. Our boys just took it back and dealt out a bit of karma. And they didn't know he was one of your lot, he wasn't wearing any patches. We were just taking back a member's property. The rest of what you're saying means nothing to me.

MACCY – Tell it to the judge.

RAMSEY – Or better yet, tell it to the next dealer in the chain. All the small fish you're throwing out of the water get their gear somewhere. It's just a matter of time before you upset one of the big fish.

BLACK MICKY – Which still isn't your problem.

RAMSEY – That's where you're wrong, because you fellas running around, like a bunch of kiddies playing cowboys and Indians, drop us all in the shite. Now, you can deny it all you want, but I know, right enough, your outfit topped that little gobshite the other night. Now, personally, I don't have much time for drugs or the wankers that sell them. I'm no shedding tears over a dealer getting snuffed. But, the point is, everybody's heard about it, the word is out. That's the trouble with building yourselves a reputation, see? If people don't hear about it, it don't work. We're lucky, all we're to do is say 'leave us alone'. We dish out the odd slap and people get the idea. You guys are needing a cooperate identity. The sort of stuff you'll need to do can put you inside for a ten stretch. With stretches like that on the cards, the polars start getting excited and then everybody's life gets to being a misery.

SMUDGE – The way you're telling it, the biggest problem you'll get off the police is being pulled over on your way to choir practice.

RAMSEY – Aye, pure as the driven, that's us right enough. If you start wiping away all the little dealers, what's left?

(Silence finally broken by Maccy)

MACCY – One big dealership.

RAMSEY – As it stands, this little patch is hardly worth a fight. The Eight-Six have survived so long on simple mathematics, the hassle it would require to get shot of us is simply not worth the gains to be made by doing so. The game, my friend, is not worth the candle. What you guys are all about could change that. I see it like this, you put the word out that you're real hard asses, don't-mess-with-us types. You put your backs in to it and whip all the dealers into line – one way or another – and maybe you take the message up to the next tier of chemists. You'll make money, so you will, big money. But you'll have to bear a lot of pressure. The people whose livelihood you'll be taking won't be the sort to just hand it over. And all the while, the polars will be sniffing around, looking to put people away for a nice ten to fifteen. You'll be flat out staying ahead of the game. And at that point, someone's likely to decide that what you've got is worth taking. Next thing you know, one of the big clubs, or one of their support clubs, declares open season on Handsome Boys. The long and short of it is this: The Handsome Boys MC will cease to exist, and the Eight-Six will have a major club, right up-close and looking to protect its new assets.

BLACK MICKY – Who says this big club's going to be able to take us down?

MACCY – Christ almighty, listen to it. What have you got, twenty people?

RAMSEY – Nay, Maccy, they got sixteen full patches and two prospects.

MACCY – Jesus, and you seriously think you're going to see off a national outfit? You're minor league, barely even that.

SMUDGE – If we're such little fish, why are we you sitting at this table? Why hasn't my club been eighty-sixed?

RAMSEY – Like I told you, I've known the HLB a long time. I had a lot of respect for Dago, I have no desire to see what he built destroyed. And, I say this in the spirit of full disclosure, I don't imagine for a second that you boys would give in without a fight. We'd win, don't doubt that for a minute, but it would cost us, people get hurt, or worse. The polars would have a field day nicking everybody in sight. Chances are we'd get rid of you, then get picked off some poxy support club while we were trying to recuperate.

SMUDGE – The Handsome Boys MC is a fact. We are not going to drop our patches without a fight. We'll defend our colours, against you or any other club.

RAMSEY – I didn't suggest otherwise.

BLACK MICKY – So why are we here?

MACCY – We need to set boundaries.

BLACK MICKY – We're not answering to the Eight-Six

RAMSEY – That's not what we're saying. But you need to understand: if you shit on your own doorstep, we live close enough to tread in it too. What I'm proposing is this: both clubs are free to fly their patches, but we show a little respect, a bit of restraint and decorum. I don't want HLB rolling up to Spots, not without prior notice. The Eight-Six will treat The

Jericho in the same way. Your little enterprises on the nightclub doors, you take to another area. Keep it over Chiswick way maybe. That way, any fallout lands on you without impacting us.

BLACK MICKY – If, *if*, we agree to this, I think we should have assurances that the Eight-Six won't turn up en-mass at any venues the Handsome Boys run. At least not without prior agreement.

RAMSEY – I think that can –

(tape cuts out).

24.

Silence and Laundry

Tuesday 17 October

I'd put the tape in the back of a drawer. It wasn't labelled, but mentally I filed it under, 'possible leverage material'. Which is how I take the edge of words like *blackmail.* Nothing I'd heard put me any closer to knowing who'd murdered Dago, or why, but it was some comfort to know a turf war, on my doorstep, might be avoided.

When Vic appeared, to begin the work on his back piece, he had one of the prospects with him. The prospect positioned himself in the doorway and looked set to practice his glare on passers-by. I told Vic his pet monkey could sit down, if it was house trained, or it could wait outside.

"I'm not having him standing there, scaring business away."

Vic directed Tweedle Dum, or possibly Dee, to one of the sofas. He used the opportunity to flex his full patch status, and didn't bother speaking, just clicked his fingers and pointed. The pet monkey obeyed.

Vic was easier to tattoo than Smudge had been. He sat backwards on the chair, barely flinching while I worked. I asked him why he'd brought Tweedle Dum along.

"Just the way it is at the movement. We don't travel alone if we're wearing patches."

It occurred to me I might rename the tape, 'futile attempt'.

Once I'd finished with Vic I rang Smudge. I told him I'd just had a full set of patches in the shop, one that apparently required a bodyguard. He didn't want to talk over the phone.

There were no soothing Billie Holiday tracks playing at Smudge's house this time. The volume on his hi-fi was low but the sound managed to fill a lot of space. It had the tortured quality Yakky favoured in his music.

In the front room on the wall, Johnny's cut-off was resplendent with its new colours. There was something about the crisp new patches that was slightly tragic and, much as I hated to admit it, I found the sight quite moving. Whatever my thoughts on the Handsome Boys' new identity, I didn't doubt the sincerity of Smudge's tribute.

"Yakky had the impression the talks went well the other night."

Smudge was dressed for work, his cut-off at odds with the two-piece suit and clip-on tie. He yawned and dry washed his face with one hand. There was a rasping noise from his stubble.

"Frenchy wouldn't wear it."

"What was his problem?"

Smudge dry washed his face again. "He's not convinced the Eight-Six didn't have something to do with the fire, at The House of Ice. Plus, he's come round to *your* way of thinking, about Dago's *accident*."

"Only he thinks the Eight-Six killed Dago?"

"He's not saying that, but he not ready to trust them." I asked him what his take on it was, and he shrugged. "There's a chain of command."

"You mean, El Presidente has spoken and that's it?"

He squared his shoulders and looked me full in the face for a moment.

"It went to a vote."

"Why would the Eight-Six take Dago out? He was the only one talking to them."

Smudge held his hands up, pacifying. It was an unexpected gesture coming from him.

"*I* don't think they did have anything to do with Dago getting killed. But it's not just about what I think. The club voted on what to do regarding the Eight-Six. My hands are tied."

"If you don't work with the Eight-Six, you'll be working against them."

He held his hands up again.

"What do you want me to do, Doc? I've got to respect the club's decision."

"It's the wrong decision. It's going to get people hurt, people in your club. What's the point, respecting the *club*, if that means your *brothers* end up bleeding?"

Smudge turned to face me, his movements were too fast and betrayed the stress he was carrying. I expected him to tell me to fuck off or, at least, shout me down. He gained some respect from me by doing neither. The cheap suit strained as he took a deep breath. When he sat down, it was obvious he was making a huge effect to stay calm.

"Who's that woman you got across the wall in your flat? Julie…"

"Ezulie," I corrected, "Ezulie Danter."

"She's the Goddess you worship yeah, part of the Voodoo?"

She was a spirit, a lwa, not a Goddess and worship wasn't a part of my practice, but I nodded anyway. The terms were as close as Smudge needed. And I got his point. Voodoo, serving Ezulie Danter, was what I did. It provided a structure to anchor my life to. Others' beliefs, or understanding, where irrelevant.

What Smudge believed in was his club.

The way sea captains believed in their ships. The same ones they went down with.

"Okay Smudge, okay. I get it. I'm not part of the club but I've got a connection to it, friends in it. I don't want to sit back and watch people die. I don't want to have to see *that*, again."

I pointed at Johnny Simms' patches, hanging on the memorial wall.

Smudge nodded and stood so he could reach the cut-off. It was an unguarded moment, an indication of how tired he was. He stroked the brightly fresh emblems of the club. Touching all that remained of his friend's existence seemed to calm him.

"I understand that, Doc. I appreciate it. But what can I do?" He patted the top rocker on Johnny's cut-off. "This is what it's all about, we can't just drop them. I can't back out and leave my brothers, to carry the slack. What can I do?"

"Do you trust me?"

"Yeah, I do."

It wasn't an immediate answer, he'd given the question a lot of thought. I wasn't offended. Most people who knew me wouldn't trust me.

"Then just keep me in the loop, okay?"

"What are you going to do?"

"Same as I've been trying to do all along, find out who did kill Dago and Johnny."

Tweedle Dum, or possibly Dee, was arrested the next week, for possession of a firearm. It didn't make a splash of any kind in the news. I'd noticed he wasn't at his usual place, on the door of The Jericho, but hadn't thought much of it.

Despite Smudge's agreement to keep me in the loop, the news had filtered down to me via Spooky. Yak had told him to keep us updated on the situation around the clubs Smudge ran. In return, he'd been promised some credit when it came to time under Yakky's needle. Spooky's eyes had glazed over, as he began concocting a dozen dreams. Yakky had brought him back to terra firma by clicking his fingers in his face.

"What you tell us best be true, Spook. You understand?"

What colour there was in Spooky's face fell out of it.

He'd surprised both of us by appearing at the shop on a daily basis with a notebook. The contents were dull enough to be believable. His thoroughness was impressive. Yakky grumbled that he'd be *tattooing the skinny fucker for free* until he retired.

Ramsey's suggestion, that the HLB move their door work out of the immediate area, had been ignored. The deal, whatever the full story had been, seemed to have gone to the wall. Business at The House of Ice continued largely unchanged. The knock-on effect, at least according to Spooky, was the fast-track growth of the five or six favoured dealers. Muscles were being flexed. Spooky was complaining that business was suffering.

I asked if the guys on the doors were still stomping people into the ground.

"It's calmed down a bit. Most people have got the message now and don't even try. Now and then someone gets caught, trying to sell a bit, and gets smacked. Other than that…" He finished the sentence with a shrug. "It's better now that black bastard's not on the door."

"Black Micky?" Spooky nodded. "He's not working The House of Ice anymore?"

"He hasn't been seen this week. Might be on holiday or something. If he is, I hope his plane crashes."

After Spooky had scampered back to his cab, I rang Micky's mobile and it went straight to voicemail.

Thursday 26 October

Micky opened his door and peered at me through the crack.

"Alright, Mick?"

Without replying, he pulled the door open and walked away, down the short hall. I took it as an invite and pulled the front door shut behind me. I caught up with Micky in his living room. He was stretched along the multi-gym, pumping a set of weights. He wasn't shaved and the tee-shirt he was wearing had a coffee stain across the chest. The smell in the room suggested the workouts were outpacing the showers.

The mixture of squalor and splendour in Micky's flat had shifted more towards the squalor end of the market. The expensive clothes were still in evidence, but they'd been joined by crumpled laundry and a few days' worth of dirty plates. Micky pumped iron and showed no interest in speaking to me.

"You not working the doors anymore?" He managed to shake his head, mid-lift. I waited but he still didn't speak. "What's Smudge got to say about that?"

Big as he was, even Micky couldn't lift barbells and shrug. He set the weights on their rest and sat up. I guessed he'd been at for a while; there was a noticeable tremor along the muscles in his arms.

"I don't exist to him anymore." The words were matter of fact and his voice was toneless. "I told them what to do with their damn patch."

"What happened?"

"That dumb shit, Lewis, got himself arrested with a bloody gun."

Lewis was one of the prospects. According to Micky, he'd been transporting the shooter at the behest of a full patch. Micky wouldn't name names but it didn't matter. The end result had been the same. Lewis, having done the dirty work for a 'brother', was left to do the laundry too. In silence.

"Five years minimum," I said.

Micky nodded and stood up. He paced, as best he could, in the confines of the room.

"He was planning on getting married, in the new year."

"That's the least of his worries now."

Mick shook he his head, irritated. "He was desperate to get his full patch. Wanted it in time for the wedding."

"Carry this for the club, it'll show you're a stand-up member, etcetera etcetera?"

"Exactly."

Micky began windmilling his arms. He was just easing the aches from his muscles, but the suddenness of the movements made me jump. He didn't seem to notice that the orbit of his fists meant I had to press myself into my seat.

"What's the club going to do?"

"Fuck all. Someone's going to take the can and better a prospect than a full member."

The warming down exercises suddenly weren't enough and he slotted himself back into the multi-gym. He began rattling off sit-ups at an alarming rate.

"Couple of months ago, Lewis was just one of the guys. Now, he's a prospect, so it's okay to leave him up to his neck in shit." The sentence came out in short bursts, timed to the motions of his workout. "This isn't what I signed up for. Going to three patches was meant to be about everyone looking out for each other."

He stopped speaking and upped the pace of the trunk curls. I don't think he noticed when I left.

I caught up with Smudge, at work, on the door at The House of Ice. There was less of a crowd than the last time I'd dropped by. The average age was up as well and the noise, seeping out into entrance, was recognisable as music. The bulk of the crowd were women, clustered together in groups of five or six. Spirits were high, and everyone seemed to be off the leash for the night. The women nearest age were the loudest.

Smudge was on the lookout for trouble. Another doorman was checking bags and occasionally turning someone away. I guessed for trying to sneak their own booze in, rather than packing weapons.

While he was looking up and down the road and scanning what crowd there was, I managed to creep up on Smudge. There was a mean satisfaction in seeing him jump.

"Edgy, aren't we?" I commented, after he'd stopped swearing. I gestured to the group nearest the door, who were giggling and pretending to flirt with the Handsome Boy checking their bags. "I wouldn't have thought tonight's crowd would be causing much trouble."

The remark was overheard, and someone shouted, "We will do if the prosecco runs out."

Smudge scowled as the chorus of laughter went up. "What do you want, Doc?"

"Quick chat, if you can put riot control on hold for a moment."

Smudge pointedly asked the other doorman if he was okay for a minute. There was another round of laughter when someone called out,

"I'll look after him."

Smudge led me back to the room where I'd spoken with Black Micky, the one where the fire had caught hold. The repairs had been hasty but effective. The smell of new paint was drowning out any smell of smoke.

"I heard about Lewis."

"That's club business."

"Christ all mighty, Smudge, change the record, eh? I don't give a shit about the club, or about Lewis for that matter. I just want to know about the gun."

Smudge glanced at the door. He'd left it ajar, music and noise from the dance floor drifted in. Pulling it shut did little to dampen the sound.

"What about it?"

"Was it Frenchy asking him to carry it?"

The question caught him by surprise and he shook his head, as if the idea was stupid. I didn't bother asking him directly who had made the request. I didn't think he'd answer and I didn't want to risk setting a president for refusal.

"What type of gun was it?"

"An old Browning." I told him to speak civilian. "Service pistol. They were standard issue for donkey's years. They've been replaced with Glocks."

"Does that mean Brownings are coming onto the market?"

Smudge shook his head. "There's always been a few guns drifting out to civvy street. The army used Brownings for forty odd years so they're what's easiest to find. Why does this matter, Doc?"

"Did you know Dago had a shotgun?"

"Legal?"

"Not so you'd notice, it was buried under the insulation in his loft. You didn't know about it, then?"

"No. I take it, it's gone missing."

"Exactly. Sue wanted me to get rid of it for her, and when she went to get it, it had already gone. I'm pretty sure Dago took it. I'd like to know where it ended up."

"And you thought it'd found its way to someone in the club?" I nodded. "But, you don't think he'd have *given* it to anyone in the club?"

"A couple of weeks before he died, Dago went to Sue's ex-husband. He reminded him Mary's birthday was coming up and told him he had to clean his act up, and to be ready to look after Sue and Mary."

Smudge's gaze wasn't on me, but it had stopped roaming the room. To be sure we were both singing from the same sheet, I spelled it out for him.

"Dago knew trouble was on its way. He wanted to leave things in place, for his family, and tie up any loose ends. That's what getting his old tattoo covered up was all about, wrapping things up. He was insured to the hilt, so money's not a worry, but he wanted Sue to have someone looking out for her. Only, he didn't go to the guys in the club."

"And one of these *loose ends* he wanted tied up involved a shotgun."

"And someone in the club is asking prospects to carry firearms for them."

"The Browning came from a guy I knew, left the army at the same time I did. He's a fuck up, nothing but trouble, but useful. I don't think there's any connection to Dago, there."

"Are a lot of the club guys tooling up?" Smudge didn't say anything, not even bothering to tell me it was club business. "You going to tell Lewis' old lady it's club business when she asks why her fiancé's doing a five stretch for someone else?"

Smudge sighed. I took it as a sign that his patience was wearing thin rather than any indication of sympathy.

"What Lewis has done has earned him a full patch, he made a sacrifice. It's for the good of the club."

Which was what Johnny had told Christine the night he died.

25.
Job Done

Gavin's flat had been trashed. The keepsake champagne bottles, from his brief spells in the winner's circle, crunched underfoot as I walked to the end of his sofa. The photographs of him in his high-roller's morning suit had been thrown into a corner, along with his TV set.

"What do you want?"

The question was flat and toneless. He'd opened the door to me without bothering to check the peephole. Left it open and walked back into the flat, not caring whether I followed him or not.

If you live in fear long enough you run out of adrenaline. Then you live in despair instead.

Both Gavin's eyes were black and there was a crusted scab along his left cheek. He'd slumped onto his sofa, indifferent to my presence.

"You've not paid off your debts, then?" I commented.

"Fuck you."

"They charging interest?" He cast me a dirty look that told me yes. "You still gambling?"

"What the fuck's it got to do with you?"

I ignored the question.

"You all excited about becoming a granddad?"

For the first time since I'd knocked on his door, Gavin looked at me properly. He wasn't surprised and didn't ask me what I was talking about. I asked him if Sue had told him.

He turned away from me again and shook his head.

"Mary rang me up. She's thrilled about it. She hasn't got a bloody clue."

"Did she say who the father is?"

"No."

"Did you ask?"

"It's nothing to do with me."

"Your daughter's pregnant and it's nothing to do with you who the father is? You really are a worthless piece of shit, you know that?"

"I've got problems of my own, you know?"

He gestured towards his face.

I leaned in and gave him my finest Cheshire Cat smile. "Well, I can help with that."

For a few seconds, he looked attentive. He was probably imagining a massive cash injection. The mindless optimism of hopeless gamblers and romantics alike. Then he remembered who he was talking to and reality came crashing down around him. He slumped back into the knackered sofa.

"What the fuck can you do?"

"I can get the people you owe money, to back off. They're small fry."

Gavin gestured to his battered face again. "Yeah, right. Like you know anything about it."

"The big boys don't punch you in the face and take a part payment, now and then. They cut off a couple of your toes and make you sign over the deeds to your house. That don't work with losers like you, renting out a council bug-hutch and driving a car worth less than a bus pass. I know *they're* small fry, because *you* are. The big boys aren't going to waste their time on the little bits of action you put their way. They want people with something they can take. Not wankers like you."

"Fuck you."

"You already said that. Now, do you want out this situation or not?"

"How?"

"I know some bigger fish. They'll buy your debt. You'll still have to pay it back, but I can get them to fix a sum and, as long as you make the payments, that'll be it. Think of it as a Get-Out-Of-Goal-Free card. Well, almost free."

Nothing's really free.

Or certain.

Particularly if you're dealing with me.

The deal was simple: Gavin, AKA father of the year, would talk to Mary and do what he could to find out who'd got her pregnant. Then he'd report back to me. In return, I'd do all I could to put his debt into the hands of someone who'd at least play fair.

I didn't have a great deal of faith that Gavin would get Mary to talk. Less faith still that I could make good on my side of the bargain if he did.

I can be fairly persuasive when the occasion demands, though I think it was more in desperation that he agreed.

Strangely, we shook on it.

When Gavin got back to me, a lot of pieces fell into place. But I needed to check if they were in the right places.

Friday 27 October

I didn't get to check until late in the day. Gavin had called me, at the crack of eleven o'clock, and when I rang Sue, her phone went to voicemail. The question I wanted to ask wasn't something to leave as a message. I decided it was probably for the best, calming down is nearly always a good idea. So, I got on with being a tattooist and waited for Sue to get home.

When I called again, it had gone six. The line wasn't very good, but even so, I head the slight hitch in her voice when she confirmed, that yes, Dago's Harley was still in her garage.

Sue wasn't particularly sentimental, but the Glide had been almost as much a part of her late husband as his own skin. I decided asking her to search what was left of it would be bordering on the cruel. When I made the offer to go over and do it myself, I realised it wasn't something I'd relish either. Yakky, who'd been listening to my half of the call, picked up on that.

"I'll do it."

"You don't have to, Yak."

He shrugged. "I barely knew the guy, Doc. It's just a bent-up bike to me."

Something, maybe a sense of duty, made me turn the offer down, though I accepted his offer to ride over with me. That meant I had to wait for him finish working. On his normal mission to work himself to death – it was half eight before we left the shop. I questioned whether my subconscious was procrastinating.

When we got to Sue's house it had gone nine and the cul-de-sac was in darkness. I registered the empty driveway where Sue's BMW should have been.

Mary pulled the front door open the second I knocked. I think she'd been pacing the hallway. She wasn't hysterical, but she was distressed, and desperate for someone else to take over the worry.

When I asked her what was wrong, she babbled out a huge amount of information. The gist of it was Sue had got really upset and left the house, like a whirlwind. Part of the reason was to do with Mary seeing Gavin. I could tell there was more to it. When I saw the internal door to the garage was ajar, I felt my stomach sink.

"Mary? Did you tell your mum what you spoke about with Gavin? What you told him, about Frenchy and Johnny?"

She burst into tears. I left her with Yakky and ducked through the door to the garage.

Dago's Glide was to one side. There had been a Day-Glo yellow cover over it, but it had been pulled away and was rucked up around the twisted handlebars. The side of the machine facing me had been the side that landed on the grass verge. When I'd seen it in Frenchy's yard, the pannier that had been crashed under the bike had been split and jammed shut on itself. Now, its lid was laying on the floor.

Along a ragged edge of broken fibreglass, I could see a smear of blood. It looked as if it had taken a bite out of Sue when she wrenched it free. A couple of rags were laying on the otherwise cleanly swept floor. I picked one of them up. It smelt of gun oil.

Yakky managed to calm Mary down a little, and I asked her

where Sue had headed to. She didn't know. Sue's mobile went straight to voice mail, as did Frenchy's. I managed to get hold of Smudge and asked him if he'd seen either of them. He told me no but said Frenchy might still be at work. I hung up as he started asking questions, then I dialled Gavin's number. Thankfully he answered, and I told him to get round to Sue's, and be with his daughter.

We left Mary, with assurances that her father was on the way. Before pulling my crash helmet back on, I asked her how long since Sue had left. She said we'd just missed her.

In the best tradition of idiots in movies, Yakky and me split up. I headed straight to Staples Corner and the scrapyard, Yakky went in the direction of Frenchy's house. They seemed the most likely places Sue would head to if she was looking for him.

The crosstown ride, in the dark, full pelt through the evening traffic, was hair raising, but every gap I squeezed the Sportster through was a point Sue wouldn't have been able to get her car past. So, I kept the throttle set to loud and trusted Ezulie Dantor to keep me safe.

I damn near beat her to it.

The BMW was sitting outside Frenchy's unit, the driver's door hanging open and the lights still on.

The door of Frenchy's office was open too. I could hear him talking to Sue. He was trying to sound calm; she, clearly, was trying to psych herself up.

I called out her name and walked slowly into the room, with my hands up.

Sue was in front of Frenchy's desk. She had the sawn-off in both hands, held out in front of her. Her posture was awkward, and it was obvious that she wasn't practiced with guns. Not that it would matter. Frenchy was sitting less than three foot away. The situation didn't require marksmanship.

It went very quiet as I stepped into the office. I could hear Sue's breathing, and smell sweat. Frenchy looked away from the gun, across to me. I couldn't see the details of his face.

The office was lit by a freestanding lamp that was positioned behind his desk. Whatever his expression, it was lost in shadow. He didn't have his hands above his head, but they were both raised, maybe in the beginnings of a pacifying gesture.

I'd arrived practically on Sue's heels. Frenchy was still holding the handset to one of the desk phones. Into the hush I'd brought to the room, a voice could be heard, shouting from the other end of the line. Panic and confusion was all I could make out; the speaker's French was beyond my skill.

"Go away, Doc," Sue said, she hadn't taken her eyes off Frenchy.

I took another step into the room. Frenchy began to say something and Sue screamed at him to *shut up*. Another step.

"Sue. You can't do this."

She glanced at me when I spoke, and Frenchy flinched. The movement snagged Sue's attention and her focus snapped back to him.

"Do you know what this bastard did?"

"I've got a fair idea."

There was another stream of French from the handset. I reached across the desk, trying to keep out of the line of fire, and cut the call off.

"He's told Mary he's going to marry her." Combined with her tobacco habit, the anger had turned her voice into something feral. "It's not enough he gets her pregnant, he breaks her heart as well."

"I know, I know. Sue, listen to me, Mary's going to need you. You'll be no use to her inside, you can't trust things to Gavin."

Gavin had told me the story that morning. I didn't know how he'd persuaded Mary to open up. I hoped she'd just held the secret long enough and had needed someone to tell it to. Beyond that I didn't wonder. She'd told him the identity of the father to be. It wasn't Johnny.

I'd suspected Frenchy was the father. The night I'd turned up at his crocked poker game and seen Harri, stoned and relegated to the kitchen. The lack of guile she'd shown when Karla had picked her brains. Frenchy's tastes in women weren't geared up to the mature and sophisticated. Mary's list of French baby names had put another question mark over El Presidente.

Fear sharpens the senses. I could hear the collective muttering of traffic from the Edgeware Road – and I heard a piece of it break away and become the lone voice of a motorcycle engine. It resolved into the double beat pulse of a Harley engine. I filed it under *future events.*

"Sue, Dago wouldn't have wanted you to kill him."

I kept my voice low, trying for calm. I put a hand towards the pared-down barrels of the shotgun.

"Yes, he would." The words were a scream and I jumped. My mind had turned the burst of sound into a blast of gun fire. There was brief flare of elation, as I realised I was still alive. "Yes, he would," Sue repeated.

Quieter this time but no less assured.

"Sue, I know what you think happened but you're wrong. Dago wasn't heading over here to shoot Frenchy, he was coming here to find Johnny."

A moment of doubt creased her face, and the barrels of the gun wavered. I put my fingertips on them and carefully pushed them down and away from Frenchy. At which point he moved.

On the edge of my vision I saw his hands drop. I turned in time to see him push out of the chair and haul himself across the desk. We both grabbed the gun at the same moment. I tried to wrest it away and threw myself against Sue. Frenchy, floundering on the desk, was trying for possession. Before the gun went off, I had time to wonder why he hadn't just stood up.

The gun went off.

Ever been shot? I wouldn't recommend it. It's nothing like the TV, no gritted teeth and heroic posturing. There was a feeling, down the side of my leg, like a hammer hitting home, then a flood of heat.

I think I fell first, but all three of us went down. Sue took the brunt of the impact when I fell into her. Frenchy, still clutching Sue's wrist, thudded against my back, then rolled onto the floor. My adrenaline-hyped brain registered his empty trouser leg; he wasn't wearing his prosthetic.

It evened the fight out.

Sue was winded and lying under the weight of Frenchy. I was grappling for the gun, not wanting either of them to have it. Frenchy's strength and military training were shining through. Only his lack of a limb stopped him swatting the pair of us away.

He got the upper hand on Sue, twisted the gun from her. I grabbed the barrels again trying to force them up, towards the ceiling. Frenchy would have pulled it from my grasp but Sue, now with both hands free, raked her nails down his face and across his eyes.

I made a desperate wrench on the gun and it suddenly came free. I threw it across the room and tried to pull myself from the tangle of limbs.

"What the fuck's going on?"

Smudge was in the doorway. He picked the gun up and held it, one handed, like a flintlock.

I heard the dull smack of a fist and Sue cried out. Then Frenchy pushed himself up onto his good knee and used the desk to haul himself up right. I tried to follow suit and couldn't. Blood was soaking through my jeans; my left leg wouldn't move. I managed to sit, canted over onto my right, and used my hands to 'walk' me away from the gun.

"This crazy bitch ran in here, waving a bloody gun at me. She thinks Dago wanted me dead."

"Dago wanted Johnny dead," I told Smudge.

"That's why Dago killed him," Frenchy shouted, he made it sound like I was backing up his story.

Sue's nails had drawn three furrows on his forehead and cheek. His right eye was already beginning to swell shut.

Smudge was keeping the shotgun firmly pointed in the direction of me and Sue. She was barely conscious, and her nose was broken.

Frenchy, using the desk for support, worked his way back to his chair. I saw him fumbling with something and guessed he was retrieving his plastic foot.

"The night you went to Enfield," I said to Smudge, "the night you burnt all the evidence away, for the good of the club." I emphasized the phrase *for the good of the club* and saw Frenchy start. He had his own tank full of adrenaline fuelling his mind, and he could see where I was going. "Who gave you the address?"

Smudge's gaze, which for once had been rock steady, flickered to the desk and the man wearing the president's patch.

"How did you know the address, Frenchy? All I said was I'd found him in a squat in Enfield. Then Jason went for Yakky, and we all had to deal with that. I never got round to giving you the full address. But, somehow, you knew *exactly* where to send Smudge so he could burn his brother away."

The ends of the shotgun didn't swing around to point at him, but they weren't pointing at me and Sue anymore. Smudge's eyes were fixed on Frenchy now. He was waiting for an answer.

Frenchy hands didn't come to half-mast the way they had when Sue had him in her sights. He was relaxed, a business man about to make his pitch.

"Smudge, listen to me. I knew where Johnny was because I'd asked Dago to find the boy some work. He told me he'd set him up doing live-in security. I knew he was there, but I didn't kill him. Dago did, he came back to me afterward and told me, told me about Mary. I didn't know what to do. I wasn't going to take it to the police, and I was scared of what it'd do to the club if it got out. Then Dago got killed, so I just kept schtum. It was for the good of the club."

"You saw Johnny," I told Smudge, "on his way over to Enfield. Dago was already dead by then."

Smudge looked at me and nodded. "I know."

Then he took a step to the desk and braced himself. With

the gun tucked tight into his body, he pulled the trigger.

And there was a hollow click.

For a moment neither Smudge nor Frenchy moved. Then Smudge cursed, threw the gun across the room and lunged over the desk. Whatever had kicked in – fear, desperation or pure bravado – Frenchy moved fast on it. His arm came up from behind the desk, swinging in a wide arc and there was a flash of something black, trailing laces behind it. For a confused second, I thought he was wearing a boxing glove. Then it connected with Smudge's temple and sent him reeling.

As Smudge staggered, Frenchy made to launch himself over the desk again, the way he had at Sue. This time, the movements were clumsy because he was holding his prosthetic. The steel-toed boot on the end had lifted a flap of skin from Smudge's eyebrow.

It might have been shock setting in, but it struck me as funny. Smudge had been kicked in the head by a man with one leg.

Frenchy grabbed him around the waist and, unbalanced, Smudge went down. He'd shaken off the blow to his head, but now Frenchy was on his chest, using his good knee to pin one of the bigger man's shoulders. He swung the heavy boot down again, but Smudge twisted enough to take the impact with his forearm.

I managed to haul myself into a lopsided squat and when Frenchy reared up for his next strike, I grabbed his arm and let myself fall again.

I underestimated Frenchy's strength; he didn't crash to the floor as I'd intended. I managed to keep his arm down, but I was also adding to the weight, keeping Smudge pinned. With me and Frenchy on top of him, he could do little more than swear. Frenchy's free hand snatched at me and found purchase on one of my ears. The jolt of pain eclipsed the heat in my leg. Twisting to get free, my face came up against the wrist of his other hand.

I put my teeth into the base of his thumb and clenched my jaw.

Frenchy screeched, dropped his prosthetic and rolled away from Smudge to get at me. The back of my head bounced off the floor and met his fist as he brought it down. When his own arm absorbed most of the impact, he took hold of my throat. There was another bolt of pain that went right through my neck. I ground my teeth a notch closer together and suddenly, his weight shifted and vanished. Both his hands were pulled away from me.

Smudge was back on his feet. He'd wound his arms around Frenchy's head and neck, holding him up and clear of the ground. Blood was splashing from Frenchy's hand as he thrashed to get free. I realised I had something soft and warm in my mouth.

The trashing slowed and stopped. Smudge stood, impassively, gripping the limp figure, as if he'd forgotten he was holding him. I remembered Yakky at Frenchy's table, just before Jason went for him, explaining that Johnny wouldn't have suffered. Pinch off the blood supply for thirty seconds and the brain begins to shut down.

Smudge waited a lot longer than thirty seconds before letting the body drop.

None of us moved for a couple of beats. I had the feeling of sitting, somewhere distant, in a capsule of silence. Smudge broke the spell by spitting on Frenchy's body.

"Bastard," he said evenly.

From somewhere outside, there was the scrap-metal shriek of a knackered engine. I'd never been so glad to hear Yakky's bike.

As I turned my head, and spat out the piece of Frenchy's hand, I saw Sue was sitting up. The lower half of her face was covered in blood. She wasn't paying it any attention. She was looking at the body, slumped in a heap on the oil-stained carpet. She nodded, just once, in that way you mostly see men doing: Job done.

26.
Rule 1

I wouldn't have thought Yakky's face could have got any less expressive. He stood in the doorway, took in the scene and a shutter seemed to come down, the way it had with Karla on night of the poker game.

I'd never thought to ask him why he'd decided against nursing as a career. Whatever the reason, it wasn't lack of ability. He looked round all the players on the stage. Took Frenchy's pulse and dismissed the lost cause, without batting an eye. He nodded at Sue and Smudge after cursory glances and started on me.

"What happened?" he said, as he produced a Stanley knife and finished ruining my second-best jeans. I started explaining the events in the office and he shook his head. "Your leg, what happened?"

"Shotgun," Smudge told him.

Yakky pulled away a swatch of bloodied denim and peered at the damage.

"Going to need a compress," Yakky said. Sue moved over to the kitchen area the unit. She came back with a wad of cloth. Probably a tea towel. "We have to get you to A&E."

"No," I said. "Too many questions."

"Well, this is going to hurt," he said by way of reply.

He wasn't lying. I passed out.

Between Yakky's knowledge of nursing and Smudge's knowledge of wounding, they established that most of the pellets in the shell had missed. Smudge had more or less dismissed it. Once he was happy I wasn't about to bleed out, he'd counted perforations. Six tightly packed holes on the side of my thigh, high and to the rear, practically in my backside.

I'd come to, stretched out along the back seat of Sue's car. I was vaguely aware she was sobbing as she drove. Blood-soaked revenge works fine in the movies. In reality, it changes very little. History doesn't get reset and the grief doesn't vanish.

Things began to drift out of focus again, until my shoulder seemed to catch fire. Yakky was leaning through the back door, digging his thumb behind my collarbone. He saw me focus on him and slapped my face a couple of times.

"Wakey, wakey, stay with us you skinny bastard. Pretend you're pissed."

We'd pulled up outside his house and, after he'd all but lifted me from the car, we staggered to his front door. For the benefit of curtain twitching neighbours, drunken survivors of a rough night out.

Yakky and I performed a weird, three-leg hobble along his hallway and I was deposited at his kitchen table. I came close to passing out again when Yakky lifted my leg onto a chair.

"I need your bike keys," he told me. I might have looked even more bloodless than I already did, because he laughed. "We can't leave it outside a murder scene. Don't worry, I'll take care of it."

He told Sue to keep an eye on me, but as he left, he pointed at her then looked at me, pulling at the corner of his eye. I nodded.

"I called Karla. She'll be here soon as she can," he said.

I thought I could hear Yakky's starter motor failing to catch, but it was probably my ears playing tricks. The noise of the TV, from the front room, filled the bottom floor of the house.

I drank tea, fifty percent sugar. And waited for Sue to ask me why Frenchy had murdered Johnny.

She didn't.

Maybe she'd filed it under *club business*. The club, in this case, being men and their pointless lives. Maybe she'd just drawn a line under everything now Frenchy was dead and didn't care *why* he'd murdered Johnny.

For me, *the why of it* is always the point.

Sue asked me where the bathroom was and went to clean up. There was a commotion from the front room when Karla knocked on the front door and Yakky's old man decided he was due some attention. He answered the door and Karla's rage rolled in before her, like a weather front. She swept him aside with an annoyed wave and stormed past him into the hall.

When she got to the kitchen, she dropped a carrier bag on the table, then looked at me for a long time without speaking. Finally, she began pulling boxes from the bag.

"These are for pain. These are antibiotics, you take two three times a day, take the whole box or they won't work."

She filled a mixing bowl with water and collected a pair of scissors from a drawer. She knew where everything was, and I guessed she'd spent a lot of time in the house. After she'd opened a dozen packets of sterile gauze, she examined the lashed-up dressing Yakky had applied. She pulled on a pair of latex gloves and started picking at the duct tape.

"This is going to hurt."

She wasn't lying either.

The fire at the scrapyard had made the second page in one of the local newssheets. It appeared the blaze had been started by a cigarette end.

The remains of local businessman, Jerry 'Frenchy' Morris, 54, had been found in the ashes of an ancient settee that he may have been sleeping on. Friends and acquaintances of the dead man confirmed he often worked alone in the evenings and was a heavy smoker. The fire brigade suspected that he had dozed off with a lit cigarette in his hand. There was the usual advice about fitting smoke alarms.

The settee had been old enough to predate current fire safety regs, and the flames had spread quickly. Helped by the accumulation of oil and other solvents.

The office/staffroom comprised of three prefabricated

units. Oil and petrol cans had been stored, against on of their outside walls.

If Karla had noticed the smell coming off Yakky when he got back home on the night in question, she'd not mentioned it. She'd also not returned his calls since the story had broken.

I wasn't going to lose much sleep over that. I was more worried that she might have some bizarre attack of principles and unload herself to the police. Yakky assured me she wouldn't. Still, paranoia is a rich source of creativity.

After Karla patched me up with her pilfered supplies, and fed me antibiotics to forestall the infection, shed pumped Sue full of painkillers and made more tea. Then she'd told me if the police came around her, or Yakky, she'd point them in my direction without hesitation. Then we'd sat in silence until Yakky reappeared.

While Karla had been dressing my wounds, and stoking her anger, Yakky had been parking his bike half a mile from the industrial estate. He walked the rest of the way and rescued my Sportster. Before riding back, he'd helped Smudge with an arrangement of oil cans and dogends.

Once he was safely home, Karla stood up without a word and left. Yakky tried to hug her or possibly just take her arm. She'd brushed him off.

Yakky took over the shop and told everyone I'd been laid low by the flu. We'd agreed I'd keep out of sight until I could walk without drama. I caught up on my reading and dealt a lot of tarot.

Five days into my convalescence, I had a call from Smudge asking if he could see me. He came round mid-morning, yawning hugely.

"How's life at the top?" I asked, eyeing the president's patch on his cut-off.

He pulled a face.

"Once everything's on an even keel again, I'll step down."

He dropped onto one of the chairs at my kitchen table and yawned again.

I didn't doubt the sentiment, but I didn't think he'd be

giving up office. Smudge wanted to be a part of something and, like any true believer, he thought he was the only one with the purity of vision to build it. He'd keep the president's patch – unable to find anyone else to do it justice – for as long as there was a club to preside over.

He didn't ask after my health. He'd already shrugged my leg off as a flesh wound and, I didn't doubt, he'd have done the same had it been his own. Good luck to him. He was welcome to buff up his machismo all he liked. Me, I sucked down painkillers like Smarties and whimpered every time I moved.

"You haven't brought a get-well card, should I assume this is business?"

"No, well not really. I just want to know what people are going to hear from you."

I sat down opposite him, very carefully. Standing wasn't a problem, sitting down involved gritting my teeth.

"About what?"

"What went down at Frenchy's, what do you think?"

I made a zipping motion across my lips. "I'm not in any hurry to tell anyone about it."

"That's all very well, Doc, but if you do get talkative I'm the one with my head in a noose."

He looked at me for a long moment. I think it was meant to be a reminder of what he was capable of.

After Yakky had duct taped my arse back together, he'd pulled a similar trick with Smudge's face. Frenchy's swing with the booted prosthetic had lifted a four-inch apron of tissue from his skull. Yakky's impromptu repair had since been replaced with a line of neat stitching. Even so, Smudge had lost some of his baby-blonde freshness. The beginnings of the scar were already pulling his eye into a shrewd-looking half wink. It suited him.

"Smudge, as far as I'm concerned, what went on between you and Frenchy comes under club business. Not mine. I'll say this though, if I was in the habit of giving out medals, putting that bastard in the ground would have got you one."

Smudge nodded and sighed. It wasn't ideal. Each of us was

a witness to the other's involvement. Plus Sue, plus Yakky. Secrets tend to be best kept when only one person knows them.

I asked how he was explaining it to the club.

"Going with the official version. Tragic accident. Most of the guys who worked for Frenchy don't buy it, but they're not pointing fingers at anyone. Vic seems to think it had something to do Algiers. Frenchy had some sort of dealings out there, I'm not getting the full story but…" He did an eerily convincing impression of Frenchy's Gallic shrug.

"What happens with the scrapyard now?"

"Nothing. No one's going near it. The place is knee-deep in police, the buggers are all over it."

I wondered if anyone else had taken on board how well Frenchy's crew had been doing, all from the proceeds of a fairly small scrapyard. Another piece slotted gently into place. On a mental tick list, I filled in the box marked *WHY?*

Smudge sighed. "I'm expected to organise a big send off for the bastard."

"You going to?"

"No choice, have I? The president's dead, I can't do otherwise."

I imagined a photo of Frenchy on Smudge's memorial wall, joining the ones of Dago and Johnny. It didn't sit well with me either.

"I don't get why he killed Johnny. Setting him up to take the heat of Dago…gutless, yeah, but there was a reason for it at least. Once Dago was dead, what did he gain killing John?"

"Rule number one: Kill the assassins."

"What's that meant to mean?"

"I heard, off Frenchy, you didn't want to put Johnny on the doors." Smudge opened his mouth to say something, but I held up a hand. "You had your reasons, that's your business. But I spoke to Micky about it, in the hospital the night he was stabbed. I repeated what *Frenchy* had told me: that you didn't want to give Johnny a try on the doors, because he was too close to Dago. Micky laughed in my face, according to him,

Dago flat out told you not to use Johnny."

"Yeah, he did. He told me Johnny was going to get himself in trouble doing that kind of work. Told me, he'd throw us both out the club if he had to."

"Meanwhile, his good friend Frenchy keeps putting work his way. And feeding him stories about his days in the legion, feeding his obsession with the whole brothers-in-arms bit." I stepped carefully around what I said next. Smudge had gone very still, I suspected his self-image wasn't letting him grieve properly. "From everything I've heard about Johnny, he sounds like an innocent. Gullible."

The way Frenchy liked them.

Smudge didn't give me any feedback, but, since he didn't hit me, I assumed he knew it was right.

"He was the same as you, Smudge, a true believer, all the way. Frenchy used that to get inside his head. When the HLB started talking about going to three patches and Dago was against it, Frenchy wound Johnny up and let him go."

Some of it I'd never know – the only people who did, weren't in a position to tell – but finding out that Mary had been instructed to tell Dago she was expecting Johnny's blow-by, made enough of it snap into place.

It was easy enough to construct a plausible scenario. Dago calls Frenchy wanting to know where 'that little bastard Johnny is'. Mary's honour has been taken and Dago has a twelve-gauge repayment plan. Frenchy listens to his old friend and tells him he'll get Johnny to face him. Maybe he tells Dago he doesn't want blood all over his office: 'meet me up the road a way, behind that big car dealership'. Maybe he waited by the side of the road and flagged him down.

Dago pulls up and, while he's listening to Frenchy…bang. Cars, vehicles, were Frenchy's business, it would have been easy enough to sit Johnny in a parked van or four-by-four. Something big. Big enough to punch a quarter ton of Electra Glide ten foot across a grass verge.

Perfect alibi in a lot of ways. Frenchy works up the road and has every reason to be there. *He found his friend and did what he could to comfort him, until the meat truck arrived, too late.*

"While he's waiting with Dago, making sure he doesn't dial nine-nine-nine until it's pointless, Johnny drives over to the scrapyard and fires up the compactor. One more metal cube in the back of a container waiting to be smelted."

"You can't know that, Doc," Smudge told me.

"Let's say it's the most likely series of events, given what I do know. Johnny's girlfriend? Dressed like a jumble sale and talked down to everyone?" Smudge nodded. "She knew Johnny was going to be at that squat in Enfield. He'd told her the day before. It was all pre-planned, the murder, the hide away, then his own murder. He was upset and scared and talking big about doing something for the *good of the club*. When she read about the fire and the body, she put two and two together. She didn't go to the police 'cos she was scared of being next. I think, in the end, she made an anonymous call and gave the police his ID."

The squat would have been Frenchy's idea. Tell Johnny to lie low after the killing's done. Then go round and ensure the secret stays secret.

Rule number one: Kill the assassins.

Setting it up so Johnny was on Dago's books as a live-in security guard was smart. Though I hated to admit it. If the body was found, which it was, it was tied to Dago, not Frenchy. Victim, becomes murderer, becomes alibi.

Neat, if it hadn't been for the shotgun.

Dago, outraged and out for blood grabs his shotgun, goes to find Johnny and then…strangles him? Didn't ring true.

"Then you told me you'd seen Johnny after Dago was already dead. Then it all fell apart."

"But you knew Frenchy was involved before that. He knew where Johnny's body was."

"I didn't think at the time he'd actually killed him. I thought Dago had done it, it was possible Frenchy was just in on the plan. Once he knew I suspected Dago's death wasn't an accident, he switched from keeping a lid on the tension, between the Eight-Six and the Handsome Boys to claiming the Eight-Six had topped Johnny and Dago. Moving everything away from him, while keeping everyone close."

"All so he could be president," Smudge muttered.

I didn't bother correcting his delusion about Frenchy's motives. Given the way of life he seemed intent on pursuing, I didn't think a streak of paranoia would do Smudge any harm.

"Why did you go looking for the gun?" he asked.

"For me it was a kind of proof. Dago wasn't in the habit of riding around with a gun. If he was all tooled-up, then he had somewhere to go. Where he went put him directly in the path of a vanishing motor less than a quarter of a mile from Frenchy's yard."

Smudge gave me a cold smile. His remodelled eyebrow did nothing to warm it up.

"I get that. I mean why did *you* want the gun?"

I could tell he knew the answer, so I shrugged and told him anyway.

"I was planning on settling the score. Maybe not that night but I figured he had it coming. Then I saw Sue had beaten me to it. I didn't want her ending up in prison, didn't want her to have to live with pulling the trigger."

"You think you'd have lived with it?"

"I don't honestly know. I'm glad it didn't come to it. You told me once, I was a friend of the club."

Smudge gave me another cold smile. "Go on."

I handed him a mini cassette tape. "Call this a friendly gesture. Or a life lesson."

"What is this?"

"It's a recording, of the meeting between you and Ramsey. Talks about your business on the doors of the club, the payback on the fella who shivved Black Micky. Next time you talk about sensitive stuff like that, check who's listening."

"You'd taped us?"

There was no use denying it. "And, as a friend, I'm handing the tape over to you. Gesture of trust."

"How kind," he said evenly. And he waited for the next bit.

"Tiny favour to ask."

"As a *friend*, like?"

"Play it right and it could be a nice little earner for someone. Sue's ex-husband, Gavin, he's getting a hard time off a loan shark. I owe him one. I said I'd find someone to buy the debt, then take regular payments form him, rather than an arm and a leg. If a couple of your boys have a *word* with sharky, they'll probably get the debt for next to nothing. Then they get the full amount from Gavin. Pure profit and easy to collect – he's already had the frighteners put on him. Who knows, maybe being a grandfather will sort him out."

Smudge nodded and began pulling ribbons of tape from the cassette. I took the silent treatment to mean he'd taken my life lesson to heart.

I thought about the young gangsta in the back of the van and Smudge's efficient choke hold on Frenchy.

"They say killing gets easier."

The roving gaze scanned some point of interest in my kitchen as he continued to unspool the tape. Maybe he was looking for recording devices.

"There might be something in that."

"Don't let it get too easy, eh?"

I said it out of concern for Smudge as much for anybody likely to cross his path. The baby blue eyes focused briefly on my face and drifted away again.

"You know something, Doc? I never did like the army, I couldn't wait to get out. I didn't like the people. Then when I got out, I found I didn't like civilians. There's so many fuckers like you, acting all superior 'cos they get to keep their hands clean. Not being able to pull the trigger doesn't put you on the moral high ground. It only puts you in the debt of people who can. You might want to bear that in mind." He stuffed the threads of tape into his cut-off and dropped the gutted cassette on the table. He tapped it with a nail-bitten finger. "Thanks."

When he'd gone, I untaped my mobile phone from the underside of the table. The recording I'd made of our chat I downloaded to a USB stick. I put the stick in a drawer, alongside the copy I'd made of the cassette tape.

Before the sound of Smudge's Harley had died away, Yakky rang, making sure I was in one piece. I told him I was and put in an order for a pizza from the local take away.

When he came up at lunch time with a family-sized box of grease, I'd just finished cleaning up the wall.

All the notes and sketches had been reduced to a damp grey smear. The tarot cards had been slotted back into their various packs.

"Job done?" Yakky asked, looking over the empty grey.

I told him about everyone abandoning the scrapyard now the police were there.

"It just came down to money."

"I've got thirty minutes to eat, Doc. Stop playing hard to get, okay?"

"Frenchy told me he was stationed in Algiers when he was in the legion. I'm guessing he made a lot of contacts out there. I've heard him having conversations in French from his office. Algiers is nice and close to Europe, there's a good market in northern Africa for luxury cars and a healthy trade in drugs.

"I think Frenchy may have been shipping both ways. He employed a lot of people and paid them a lot of money. He was dealing in something other than scrap iron."

At a guess I'd say the police, currently swarming the scrapyard, were digging through a ringing operation of dodgy high-end cars.

"What did he gain by killing Dago, though?"

"I think he was probably going to up the ante, with the importing. Smudge was busy, taking control of a big chunk of the local drugs trade. If Frenchy could start suppling…"

"Christmas."

"Pretty much. With the Handsome Boys running the venues, and Frenchy bringing in the merchandise, it would have been a pretty sweet deal."

Dago's negotiations with Eight-Six put it at risk. The Eight-Six didn't want a drugs trade on their patch. If the HLB became a support club, or Dago's deal meant they were simply absorbed, then Frenchy stood to lose a lucrative income source. With Dago out of the way, the deal appeared to die. Until it was revamped by Smudge and Black Micky. So, El Presidente started the rumours that the Eight-Six snuffed Dago and Johnny. Seemed Frenchy was willing to risk an all-out club war, before giving up the money.

In some ways the saddest part was the futility of the whole thing. According to Spooky – who was rapidly running out of clear skin for Yakky to apply ink to – any dealer known to sell within sight of a Handsome Boys-controlled venue was beaten senseless by the Eight-Six. The drop in revenue made controlling the doors largely pointless. The individual members would soon begin to feel the loss.

I suspected that, rather than beat the Handsome Boys into submission, the Eight-Six would start to recruit its disgruntled members.

If carefully manged, it would be a largely bloodless war of attrition, weakening the upstart club, even as the ranks of its rival swelled.

If Tweedle Dum refused to answer any questions in court – and was sent down for possession of a gun – then, in all probability, the club he'd sacrifice his liberty for wouldn't exist by the time he got out.

If Dago had just walked away from the HLB and left them to it, he'd have lived to see his granddaughter. But he couldn't. He'd had to do his best, as he saw it, by the men in his club.

Yakky chewed on his pizza and looked at the only piece of decoration I'd left on the wall. The Justice card, pinned up high, and now overseeing a field of meaningless, grey smears.

"You leaving that there?"

"I think so. Gives things a bit of focus."

THE END

About the author

Russell Day was born in 1966 and grew up in Harlesden, NW10 - a geographic region searching for an alibi. From an early age it was clear the only things he cared about were motorcycles, tattoos and writing. At a later stage he added family life to his list of interests and now lives with his wife and two children. He's still in London, but has moved south of the river for the milder climate. Although he predominantly writes crime fiction Russ doesn't consider his work restricted. 'As long as there have been people there has been crime, as long as there are people there will be crime.' That attitude leaves a lot of scope for settings and characters. One of the first short stories he had published, The Second Rat and the Automatic Nun, was a double-cross story set in a world where the church had taken over policing. In his first novel, Needle Song, an amateur detective employs logic, psychology and a loaded pack of tarot cards to investigate a death.
His fiction has appeared in Writer's Forum magazine and been included in the crime anthology, Noirville: Tales from the Dark Side. In 2018, his short story, The Value of Vermin Control, won the CWA Margery Allingham Short Story Competition.

Acknowledgements

My wife, Liz, for proof-reading my barely literate first drafts and generally putting up with my shit.

Suzi Ring, ink-slinger par excellence, for answering my weird questions about tattooing and for turning my half-arsed drawings into works of art that I'm proud to wear in my skin.

Also a long overdue thank you to Perminder Hunjan, who was kind/brave/reckless enough to read through my first attempt at writing a novel. All 160,000 misspelled words of it.

More books from Fahrenheit Press

Black Moss by David Nolan

In April 1990, as rioters took over Strangeways prison in Manchester, someone killed a little boy at Black Moss.

And no one cared.

No one except Danny Johnston, an inexperienced radio reporter trying to make a name for himself.

More than a quarter of a century later, Danny returns to his home city to revisit the murder that's always haunted him.

If Danny can find out what really happened to the boy, maybe he can cure the emptiness he's felt inside since he too was a child.

But finding out the truth might just be the worst idea Danny Johnston has ever had.

"As one would expect from a writer with the skill and experience of David Nolan, this haunting book deals with very difficult issues in an incredibly sympathetic manner while at the same time throwing a light onto one of the most complicated and shaming areas of our society - the failure to protect those who are the most vulnerable."

Hidden Depths by Ally Rose

In East Germany in the spring of 1989, 14-year-old Felix Waltz escapes from a life of abuse at the notorious Stasi youth prison, Torgau.

On New Year's Eve 2004, a woman awakens from a coma. She's been unconscious for 12 years since being viciously attacked by a lake. As her case is re-opened it soon transpires the events of that night are linked to events that happened before the fall of the Berlin Wall.

Hanne Drais, a criminal psychologist working with a Berlin police team, is one of those involved in reopening the case. As Hanne discovers the truth she's shocked to find both her past and her destiny are indelibly interwoven with the man at the heart of her investigation.

"A real page turner. Gripping and full of suspense with surprising twists and turns throughout, it had me hooked from the start…"

Printed in Great Britain
by Amazon